CW00456507

ROSE

ROBIN P FLETCHER

MAPLE
PUBLISHERS

ROSE

Author: Robin P Fletcher

Copyright © Robin P Fletcher (2021)

The right of Robin P Fletcher to be identified as author of this work has been asserted by the author in accordance with section 77 and 78 of the Copyright, Designs and Patents Act 1988.

First Published in 2021

ISBN 978-1-915164-04-9 (Paperback)
     978-1-915164-41-4 (Hardcover)
     978-1-915164-29-2 (Ebook)

Book cover design and Book layout by:
     White Magic Studios
     www.whitemagicstudios.co.uk

Published by:
     Maple Publishers
     1 Brunel Way,
     Slough,
     SL1 1FQ, UK
     www.maplepublishers.com

A CIP catalogue record for this title is available from the British Library.

All rights reserved. No part of this book may be reproduced or translated by any form or by any means, electronic or mechanical, including photocopying, recording or by any information storage and retrieval system without written permission from the author.

The book is a work of fiction. Unless otherwise indicated, all the names, characters, places and incidents are either the product of the author's imagination or used in a fictitious manner. Any resemblance to actual people living or dead, events or locales is entirely coincidental, and the Publisher hereby disclaims any responsibility for them.

PART 1

Chapter One
Goa, 19th December 2008

Rose was lounging, crayon in hand, beneath a majestic mango tree. When in season the tree bore the sweetest fruit imaginable. It stood in the middle of the front lawn of her grandparents' house in Loutolim, a small and picturesque village nestled on the west bank of the Zuari river.

The Portuguese-style house that the spreading branches of the tree shaded was one of the most beautiful and imposing in the area and had been in the family for over two hundred and fifty years. It was burnt orange in colour to match the setting sun. Upkeep on the property was a labour of love for the couple and kept Victor busy in his retirement.

As she drew, a cloud suddenly appeared, seemingly from nowhere, making her squint upwards at the otherwise clear sky. Rose felt a shiver raise the hairs on her neck.

Young Rose did not have many friends around. It wasn't that she was unsociable, she just preferred animals, especially dogs, to people. She was angelically beautiful, slight of build and surprisingly tall for a girl on the cusp of her ninth birthday.

Rose spent as much time outside as she could. She was a girl born to nature, as her mother would always say. After every meal she gave the family's leftover food to the stray dogs in the area and the chickens that were kept in the compound would flock around her in a frenzy of flapping wings, to feed from her hand.

Carmen Alvares was standing on the spacious veranda watching over her granddaughter as she drew pictures of the garden.

'Here you are, darling,' Victor said as he walked outside carrying two cups of tea for them to enjoy while they surveyed the fruits of Carmen's many years of labour, planting, grafting and pruning in her rose garden. It was her pride and joy, and most of her neighbours were extremely jealous (though none of them would ever admit it).

'Oh Vic, do you see what beauty graces our garden? One day we will see her face on billboards and in the movies, I am sure of it.' After a fleeting self-satisfied grin, she sipped her tea, which was just the right temperature for her.

'I feel sorry for Peter,' replied Victor, chewing on one of the biscuits that he had brought out earlier. 'In ten years' time he'll have his work cut out, with all the boys that will be vying for Rose's attention.' He chuckled to himself as he dunked another biscuit into his over-sweet tea. Carmen gazed lovingly at her husband of forty-two years as he carelessly brushed the crumbs from his lap onto the floor. They had been teenage sweethearts and she adored him.

Victor was a faithful, proud and hardworking man who had retired only the year before after selling the five grocery stores that, like a demanding mistress, had kept him away from Carmen for as long as she could remember. Now she had him all to herself and was the happiest she had ever been.

'Rose, aren't you hungry?' Carmen called to her granddaughter, 'you hardly touched your breakfast. Would you like some puris and tea? I'm sure your grandfather will make it for you.' Rose's ears immediately pricked up at the word 'puri.'

'Yes please, grandma.'

One of Rose's favourite things was to roll up a hot and crispy puri and dip it carefully into her tea. Rose loved staying at her grandparents' house, and there was no better place for her than the garden where she would spend most of the day. Victor finished his tea with a slurp and shuffled off to the kitchen to prepare Rose's food. He would do anything he could to make the little girl happy.

'I'm going into town later to pick up a new dress for church,' Carmen called to Victor, 'I hope the car has fuel.'

'Yes dear, and please no more scratches, ok?' he called back smiling to himself.

'The cheek!' Carmen laughed and Victor smiled again. He loved the sound of Carmen's high-pitched giggle; it had not changed since the first time he had heard it and he felt a tingle run up his spine. Since passing her test only a few years ago, Victor had always joked about her slow and overly careful manner of driving their old blue Maruti Alto. The truth was it worried him to death when she was out in the car alone.

***

Peter Rosario waited patiently outside the cycle shop while his thrifty wife stubbornly held her ground as she haggled over the price of Rose's first bicycle that was to be the major surprise for their daughter's ninth birthday. It was Barbie pink with training wheels and a bell. There was also a basket fitted to the handlebars so that she could carry her essentials around on exciting adventures. The job of teaching her to ride the bike was delegated to her father, who was worried that he would be too busy over the coming month to spend enough time with her.

'Don't worry, Peter, you'll be fine. She's a smart kid and a fast learner; it'll be easy for you and so much fun too!' Maria had insisted on the journey there. She left the shop with a satisfied smile, the price negotiations for the bicycle having gone in her favour.

Outside, Maria saw her husband leaning against a truck with an expression on his face that she found so endearing. He always seemed to be deep in thought. Peter was an inventor by nature and always thinking about his next project.

'Come on my dear, snap out of it, we need to get this hidden before we pick Rose up from mom's.'

'How much did you pay in the end?' he asked.

'Twelve thousand rupees. Good deal, eh?' Maria tried not to look too smug.

Inside the store, Anthony was still stunned. How on earth had that lady managed to beat him down by thirty per cent? He shook his head and gave a low whistle. 'It seems you can't beat an Indian mother at a game of haggle,' he said out loud.

Peter and Maria Rosario did not have much; they owned the family home, which had been gifted to them by Peter's parents after they had died. Maria hadn't worked since Rose had been born, giving up her part-time teaching job to look after the family. Peter was a notary and earned enough money for them to live on, with the occasional treat or two. His passion lay in his workshop, which was his sanctuary away from day-to-day life.

His love for inventing started when Peter's father, Joseph, helped him with a science project at school when he was fifteen years old; it had brought the pair closer than they had been for years. Father and son had a whale of a time engineering a real-life exploding volcano. Peter kept up his interest in science and was often missing for days on end working avidly on one idea or another, barely surfacing for meals. He was always looking for ways to improve on household items in the hope he would find the one thing that would give him his big break, the thing that would make him millions of rupees so he could provide his wife and daughter with a better lifestyle.

If only he knew that all they really wanted was to see him more often. On many occasions, Maria had considered burning down that hideaway of his.

'This is it,' he would say, 'this is the one, I can feel it in my bones!' Only for the whole project to come to nothing, yet again. Although Maria's parents were well off, Peter was too proud to accept any financial help from them, no matter how many times they offered. Buying something like the bicycle was a big deal for him and he was happy that he had been able to earn a bit of extra money over the past month working as a supply teacher at the local boys' school. The Rosarios did not own a family car, they had to make do with a beaten-up old Royal Enfield 350 Bullet motorcycle. A neighbour had loaned them their Gypsy jeep to pick up the bicycle and Maria was clearly happy that she didn't have to sit on the back of that embarrassing machine as it spluttered down the road, for a change.

Rose was licking the remains of her lunch from her fingers.

'Baby,' Victor said, 'it's your birthday next week, nine years old, eh? Do you know what mommy and daddy are getting you?' He was probing to see if she had any idea of what was to come on the big day.

'Daddy says it's top-secret.' Rose fixed him with the bright-eyed stare that always floored him. 'Do you know, grandfather? Please tell me, please,' she begged.

Victor shrugged. 'I have no idea darling, although I will try to find out for you.' He gave her a quick wink; he would never tell, but then she favoured him with her sweet smile and for a moment he was not so sure!

Rose's birthday was on Christmas Eve. Victor and Carmen spoiled her rotten, not only for those two precious days, of course – Rose also had what they called a birthday month! They would start by getting her small gifts from the first of December and would take her shopping for cool stuff that she didn't really need. They would do this until she was too old for it, just because they could.

This year was different, however. A bicycle was the thing she wanted most in the world and it was agreed that her parents would be the ones to give it to her. The doting grandparents had bought various smaller gifts like a Barbie watch and new sneakers, but nothing would give Rose the happiness and freedom of adventure that her first bicycle would. Carmen sat at the kitchen table, drying her hands after washing the dishes.

'Rose, mommy and daddy will be along soon to take you home. You'd better get your things together.'

They were the words that Carmen hated saying; she wished that she could spend every day with this little angel of hers.

The white Gypsy jeep pulled up outside and honked. Victor jumped to his feet; he was still quite nimble for his age.

'That'll be them; I'll go and open the gates.'

Carmen took Rose by the hand and headed to her room to gather her things.

'Young man, how are you?' asked Victor, offering his hand to Peter.

'Hi Vic, not feeling so young any more, to be honest, but I'm good, thanks. How is that diet of yours going?' he replied, gently patting Victor's paunch.

'What diet?'

Peter watched as Victor sucked in his gut and puffed out his chest as much as he could. They burst out laughing as he started to turn blue, finally exhaling so he wouldn't pass out.

'Did you get it?' whispered Victor.

'All sorted, wrapped and hidden,' Peter said proudly, with a thumbs up.

While the men were enjoying their bit of banter, Maria had walked round to the side of the house where her second favourite 'rose' in the world was planted.

The majestic Louis de Funès was a wondrous orange-red, double-flower rose, and what a sight it was. There were several blooms on the bush, which looked as healthy as ever. This was Carmen's pièce de résistance. She had several more rose bushes in the back garden too. When in bloom the rose gave off the most wonderful scent, which always transported Maria back to times when *she* was the little girl playing in the garden. She lowered her head and inhaled until her lungs filled with the sweet-smelling perfumed air. If it could be bottled, Maria would wear the scent every day. She jumped slightly when she felt her mother's hand on her waist.

'Beautiful, isn't it?' Carmen pulled out a pair of scissors from her apron pocket and snipped the flower at just the right spot, quickly trimmed the excess leaves and clipped off the thorns. She slid the rose into Maria's thick jet-black hair, fitting it snugly behind her ear.

'Oh mom, you didn't have to do that.'

'You are more beautiful than any flower, my dear,' Carmen said, brushing the back of her elegant fingers over her daughter's slightly flushed cheek. Maria gave her mother a kiss.

'Thanks for having Rose, was she ok?'

'Of course. She is the sweetest thing, just like you when you were young.' Carmen raised her eyebrows and pulled a silly face with her reply.

Maria laughed, 'yeah right,' she said as they walked, arm in arm, into the house.

Peter was airing his concerns to Victor about his brother Jack, when Rose came stampeding out of her bedroom.

'Daddy, you're back, where have you been all this time?' she cried out joyously as Peter scooped her up into his arms for a hug.

'Just taking care of some business baby, nothing to worry yourself about,' he said, as he brushed her bright bouncy hair away from her eyes and planted a huge kiss on her cheek.

'Have you enjoyed yourself?'

'Yes,' Rose assured them and explained in minute detail everything that had happened in the few hours since she had last seen them.

'Tell me, Maria, has that genius husband of yours got himself a proper job yet?'

Carmen's comment was half tongue in cheek and half-serious. Maria knew that her mother was always worried about them. She could see a hint of sadness, maybe even pity in her eyes. Maria was used to it, but from the day that Peter had asked for her hand in marriage, she knew that she would always stand by him, no matter what.

'He's working on something now, a game-changer, that's what he calls it.' Maria's stubborn chin tilted up slightly as she spoke.

Carmen looked to the heavens for help. Maria ignored her mother's despairing gesture.

'He's spent more time than ever in his workshop over the past few months; it's something to do with energy. I trust him, mom. This time it feels different. He's even fixed a meeting with some foreign investors; they're coming over in February, so fingers crossed.'

Carmen glanced down at her daughter's hands. Maria's fingers were firmly crossed, the knuckles white. 'I hope so darling, I really do.'

Carmen believed in hard work, something that you could do and reap the benefits from, just like the shops that they had once owned. You sold products and you made money, simple. She could not see the idea that was in Peter's head, so to her, it was not real.

'Rose!' cried Maria, 'come on, let's get a move on. Your father has to return the Gypsy and grandma wants to go shopping.'

'Chillax mom, I'm coming.' Rose sneaked up behind her mother and poked her gently in the back. Maria, pretending to be shocked, jumped, crying out, 'you got me.' She bent down and gave her daughter the kind of hug that only a mother could give. Rose meant everything to her, and for a moment her breath caught in her throat – she only hoped that she would be around long enough to see her grow up.

In the living room, Peter was taking the chance to continue the conversation about his brother. Jack was the black sheep of the family – a gambler, a womaniser and an alcoholic. Last week he was at a poker game with some people that turned out to be types you do not want to owe money to. He lost big time and did not have the means to pay his debts. Things got ugly when some goondas came to his house to collect. After an hour of begging, a black eye and some badly bruised ribs, they gave him two weeks to find the money or, 'disappear'.

Peter was Jack's only family; and did not have the six hundred thousand rupees to get his brother out of trouble either. Victor could see where this conversation was leading.

'Well, I'm not giving him any more money, Peter; last time was *the* last time.'

Peter shook his head emphatically.

'I'm not asking you for money, I wouldn't do that. Last year he made you look like a fool after losing what you gave him, and I will always be in your debt for paying his hospital bill. The thing is, Victor, you *know* people, please just see what you can do, some more time or maybe he can work off what he owes? Something like that, please Vic?'

Peter held both of Victor's hands as he spoke. Victor could see the worry in his eyes.

'OK, OK, I'll see what I can do my friend. I will tell you one thing though, I will not put my neck on the line for that fucking drunken fool, so help me God.' His voice was lowered to a whisper. Victor did not swear around his family, he was old-school. He did what he needed to do without a song and dance to go along with it.

Victor was a good guy, a pillar of the community and well known to everybody. He also knew most of the local gangsters. They may not have been his friends as such but to get on in business, sadly, you needed to know these kinds of people.

'I'll see if I can call in a few favours, but Peter, I'm not promising you anything, ok?'

Victor's expression matched the sternness of his words. Peter breathed out a low, ragged breath.

'Thanks, Vic, I appreciate it, I'll see you in a couple of days.'

Peter gave Victor a hug; he hated asking for help, especially for someone like Jack. Victor knew that Jack was screwed; what he had coming to him was not going to be pretty.

Carmen walked her daughter, Peter and Rose to the jeep, Rose in the middle holding a hand of each parent.

'Swing me, swing me,' she cried out.

'OK,' Maria relented. 'One, two, three, go.'

Rose swung and squealed with delight as she got her wish.

Victor looked on from the veranda. Poor Peter, he thought. That useless shit of a brother did not deserve him.

'See you on Wednesday,' he shouted, with a wave.

As Peter helped Rose strap into her seat, Carmen pulled her daughter over and whispered into her ear.

'Don't forget your appointment at the hospital is on the twenty-ninth, I'll pick you up at eight forty-five.'

Something was wrong with Maria. Only Carmen knew, and it was going to stay that way, at least until next month. Nothing was going to ruin Christmas this year.

Waving until the Gypsy had disappeared, Carmen lowered her arm and walked slowly back to the house, admiring the garden on the way.

'Everything ok, darling?' Victor asked.

'Yes my dear, and you?'

'Of course, cup of tea?'

'You always know what I need, don't you Vic?'

Carmen gave her husband a hug.

'I love you, always have and always will, now go and put your feet up for a while,' Vic said, holding her tight.

Carmen made a beeline for her favourite chair in the living room while Victor walked into the kitchen and turned the radio on. From a large tin on the sideboard that had a pattern of elephants around it, worn away on the two points where his fingers always grasped it, Victor spooned some tea leaves into the pot that sat on the stove and turned on the gas. Neither of them had any idea why the other was worried or how their entire world would soon crumble around them.

Chapter Two
Mumbai, 21st December

'Elijah, madam is getting angry. You need to hurry up and finish with that game, otherwise you will lose it for another week,' Preeti announced calmly, as she walked into Eli's bedroom.

The room was every boy's dream, a fifty-inch TV, four games consoles, all the unused and ignored toys that you could possibly imagine, most of them still unopened and stacked neatly in the walk-in wardrobe, which was as large as most adults' bedrooms. He even had his own en-suite bathroom.

Eli, as he was known, was twelve years old, extremely smart, overweight and very rude.

'Go away! Huh! I'd like to see them try!' He did not even look at the maid.

Eli was a gamer. He wasn't interested in anything else, though God knows his parents had tried everything they could to change that. The fact that *they* were the ones who had bought the TV, PlayStation, Xbox, etc., meant that they probably hadn't tried as hard as they thought. Although, in their defence, an Eli staring at a screen for hours was better than an Eli stomping around the house with a face like thunder, slamming doors and constantly complaining.

A few months earlier Jonathan had confiscated all of Eli's electrical equipment because he cursed at his mother for changing his diet. Eli was putting on weight almost daily, because of his binge-eating habits. He could eat packet after packet of wafers and biscuits while he shouted through his headset at some random person in Germany playing Call of Duty online, spraying crumbs everywhere.

Preeti walked out shaking her head and proceeded to the laundry room where she had a mountain of ironing to get through, before changing all the bed covers.

Elizabeth Naik was sitting at the breakfast table waiting for Elijah to join her. These days it was mostly oats and fruit for the Naik family, which Elijah detested; he simply would not accept that eating ten pancakes in one sitting was bad for his health.

'Darling, which one do you prefer?' asked Jonathan holding a selection of silk ties as he walked down the steel and glass staircase of their eight-thousand-square-foot duplex. They had purchased two apartments on the twenty-second and twenty-third floors of Park Tower before it was completed. Jonathan, a well-known architect, had the builders turn the two into one gigantic family home.

Without turning around, Elizabeth said, 'the blue one, why do you bother to ask my opinion when you've already made up your mind?'

Jonathan gave a little chuckle. 'How did you know I would wear the blue tie?'

'Because it's your favourite tie for church, no? Now come and eat, I don't want to be late for mass again this morning.'

Last week they were thirty minutes late because of the police checkpoints that covered the city. It had only been a few weeks since the terror attacks in their home town, which included the Taj Hotel, the location of Elizabeth's favourite restaurant, Wasabi by Morimoto.

The sound of Eli stamping down the stairs, seemingly trying to break every one of the toughened glass steps on the way, caused Elizabeth's shoulders to tighten, almost imperceptibly.

'Elijah, tuck in your shirt and sort your hair out, I'm not walking into the house of God with you looking like that,' Elizabeth said.

'Oh, not this garbage again,' Eli snarled as he spotted the bowl of steaming oats set on the table, ready for him.

'Yes,' Elizabeth's shoulders tensed up another notch, 'now sit and eat because we are out of here in ten minutes.'

Jonathan came down to sit with the rest of them.

'Looking good, Jon,' Elizabeth remarked, raising her eyebrows in a rapid succession of little movements.

'Don't I always?'

By the time the family had finished their breakfast it was seven forty-one. Mass was starting in nineteen minutes.

'Does everybody have everything they need?' queried Jonathan, not wanting to have to waste time on a journey back up in the elevator to fetch a forgotten phone.

'Yes,' replied Elizabeth and Eli. Eli's voice was laced with his usual disdain.

'Then let's go,' he said.

'Car keys?' Elizabeth called out.

'Yes honey,' he replied, swinging the Range Rover fob around his forefinger.

Preeti was walking across the landing of the mezzanine, clothes in hand. Elizabeth spotted her. 'Preeti,' she called.

'Yes madam?'

'Take the smoked salmon out of the freezer, will you? We'll have it when we get back.'

'YUCK,' Eli shouted over his shoulder.

'Certainly madam.' Preeti shot a look at the portly boy's retreating back, his shirt pulled taut across him, sweat marks already appearing under his arms.

Preeti had started out as Eli's live-in babysitter, and it pained her to see what her sweet little fellow of yesteryear had become.

Elizabeth strode down the hallway, after Eli, her Louboutin heels click-clacking on the tiled floor as she went.

The journey down to the underground car park in their private elevator was mostly silent. Jonathan had insisted on installing this extravagance; it had cost him a fortune, but he just couldn't stand being stuck in confined spaces with strangers.

Elizabeth broke the silence as she nudged him and motioned with her eyes to his groin area.

'So how am I going to get my daughter, now we have confirmation that this little fellow isn't working any more?' she whispered into his ear.

Jonathan glanced at Eli but the boy was slouched against the far wall of the lift, earphones in, humming tunelessly to something, a film of sweat on his brow and top lip.

Jonathan did not want to have this conversation. The tests, conducted at two different fertility clinics, just to be sure, had concluded that his sperm count was now close to zero, with no possibility of being able to impregnate his wife, who was yearning for a daughter.

It was true that Elizabeth desperately wanted someone to dress up in pretty clothes, someone to shop with, a best friend. She loved Eli dearly, but he was stuck to a screen every waking hour and besides, he was a boy, and she needed the kind of female companionship that only a daughter could provide.

'I'll deal with it, don't worry,' replied Jonathan, his voice full of resentment. His manly pride had been hurt – being told you are infertile at his age was a massive blow, and he knew that his wife would not give up on the idea.

Jonathan knew what to do and had already set the wheels in motion. The problem was, he had no idea how Elizabeth would react. Whatever happened, dealing with the situation was not going to be a walk in the park.

Eli glared at his father. 'Are you talking about me?' he asked loudly, headphones wedged firmly in his ears.

'No son...'

There was a ding as the polished steel elevator doors opened into the car park. Jonathan was relieved that the conversation had been cut short.

'We'll talk about this later,' Elizabeth said as she reached into her Gucci bag to pull out her phone that was ringing.

Jonathan swallowed hard. Fuck, he thought, as he unlocked the family's brand-new Range Rover.

'Hi, Zeenia. Yes, we are on our way,' Elizabeth chuckled as she was told a titbit of gossip. 'See you soon,' she said, ending the call. Oh, how she loved Sundays. The fifteen-minute journey to St Anne's church was uneventful, apart from stopping at two of the police checkpoints that were now standard in the city. Jonathan stared at his phone as they waited at one of them. He had received a message from an unknown number, which simply read, *'I have it.'*

***

A little later that day, just a few kilometres across town, in a busy and extremely noisy Parsi café, two men sat on either side of a table. They were watched over by pictures of Queen Elizabeth II and Mahatma Gandhi hanging side by side.

This café was part of a dying breed and had been chosen for its anonymity. Once inside, you were lost, incognito. Nobody stood out in the dimly lit interior.

The men's conversation required just such an anonymous and gloomy setting.

'Fifty thousand dollars! You're shitting me?' said a man who looked like he had been breaking rocks in prison for most of his life.

'This is a big score, Avinash – do not mess it up!' the man sitting opposite, whose name was Vikram, insisted. He had sharp, darting, feral eyes and was as hard as nails. He was rising through the ranks of Mumbai's mafia underworld and, having been given the responsibility of this 'job', needed to show his bosses just why he was perfect to enter their upper echelons.

The brief was simple. Someone had placed an order, not for something, but for somebody – a girl. She had to be between six and ten years old, tall and pretty, and definitely from an upper-caste family. It would be an extremely challenging task, hence the colossal price tag.

'Not from this state, obviously, it's too close to home for this kind of thing – do you hear me, you moron? Try Kerala and Goa.' Vikram's eyes darted this way and that.

'Yes, boss,' replied Avinash, 'I have a few contacts in Goa and I know some guys in Kerala too.'

Vikram gulped down the rest of the tea that was going cold in front of him and leaned over as close to Avinash's ear as he could get.

'You have ten days,' he hissed, 'don't let me down. The client is extremely nervous about this situation and doesn't want anything to go wrong. Call me when you have a picture of her.'

He pushed his chair back with such force that for a moment it teetered on its rear legs before tilting forward and settling on the floor. Vikram exited the café, disappearing into the crowds on the street outside.

Avinash waited a few minutes before leaving. 'I'd better call Rasheed, I can't manage this one alone,' he muttered to himself.

As he left the building, he felt the sun burning his clean-shaven head. He pulled on a battered grey helmet and sped off.

Chapter Three
Bangalore, 22nd December

Derek Jacoby was sweating profusely as he strode out of lab number eight, which didn't officially exist. He knew that what he had in his pocket could get him into serious trouble, not only with GreenBay Pharmaceuticals, the company he had spent the last two and a half years working for, but also with the authorities.

Based in the Whitefield neighbourhood, East Bangalore, GreenBay was the second-largest pharma company in India. Derek, a specialist bioengineer, worked in the research and development department that was off-limits to most employees. He was from the US and came highly recommended by his former employers there. Three years previously, while he was on sabbatical, he had fallen in love with a woman called Sita. They married shortly after, to the disapproval of his parents.

The whirlwind romance had grown stale after just a few months, however, and Derek had come crashing down to earth when he realised that he was now expected to support Sita's parents and grandmother in their cramped two-bedroom apartment.

At thirty-one, he looked every inch a fit and handsome all-American guy, but Derek had a very addictive nature and cocaine was his downfall; he absolutely loved it and spent most nights out with a group of close friends that worked for various tech companies in the area.

The issue Derek had was that he could not afford to support his newly extended family as well as his habit. He needed a way out, enough money to disappear, to another part of Asia to continue the hedonistic lifestyle that he loved so much. Inside the locker room, he took off his white coat, grabbed his things and headed for the door. All he had to do was get out before anyone noticed what was missing.

'Where are you off to?' a voice boomed from behind him.

The adrenalin of stealing something so important and the huge line of coke he had shoved up his nose just minutes before revved his already racing heart to warp speed.

Derek turned to see a man with a towel wrapped around his waist. It was Aditya, emerging from one of the changing rooms. He was a short, muscular man who was well respected by his team on the seventeenth floor and was Derek's immediate superior.

Derek was shitting bricks, his face shiny with sweat. 'Erm, it's my wife, she's been in a car accident, I need to leave straight away.' Not the nicest thing to say, but it was all he could think of.

'Of course, just let me know next time. Derek, are you sick? You don't look at all well.'

'Sorry sir, I tried to find you and, no, I'm fine, just hot and stressed is all.'

'OK, you'd better go quickly then. Let me know how she is when you get there. If you need a couple of days off then tell me ASAP, but don't forget, top brass wants NR112 ready for human trials by next week.'

Derek grabbed some paper towels and mopped at his face, threw them in the garbage and hurried for the door, almost tripping himself up. Aditya watched him suspiciously as he went.

'Come on, *come on*,' Derek muttered, repeatedly pressing the call button for the elevator. The doors opened; it was empty. Derek stepped in, hit the button marked G and let a faltering breath escape; he was nearly out. Staring at himself in the mirror, which covered the back wall of the car, he realised that he looked like absolute shit! 'Fifteen, fourteen, thirteen,' he counted out loud as he descended.

Upstairs, Aditya walked into the toilet cubicle, to take the leak he'd been holding in for the last ten minutes.

As he looked down, he saw a white substance on the ledge above the toilet, in between the fake flowers and random decorative dish containing blue sparkly stones.

'What the fuck?'

Aditya was a practising Hindu and had never taken any illegal substances, but he wasn't stupid – he knew what he was looking at. Jacoby, he thought, the man had looked too shifty. Now a rising sense of foreboding and instinct told him to check the lab. It was probably nothing but there was no harm in looking; drug users were an unpredictable bunch.

Aditya pulled on his shorts and a T-shirt and raced back to the lab. As soon as he opened the door to lab zero-eight, he spotted a tray askew in the normally locked refrigerator that stood on the pristine stainless-steel worktop. There was a vacant spot in the vial holder.

At ground level in the building, the elevator doors opened, and Derek walked briskly towards the main entrance, past five or six armed guards. His heart beat painfully in his chest – he wondered if he was going to have a heart attack. Outside was a main road where the traffic was as noisy and busy as usual.

'Get security!' Aditya yelled down the phone, 'stop Derek Jacoby, employee ID six-four-seven, DO NOT let him leave the building.'

Derek glanced at the receptionist on the telephone, who looked back at him. Ten more steps and he was out of there.

'Derek who?' replied the receptionist politely, her eyes following Derek.

'Argh!' Aditya could not hide his exasperation, 'six feet tall, American, shoulder-length curly hair. Stop him before he leaves, get everyone you have to the front door and do not let him out,' he screamed into the handset.

'American, curly hair? I think he's...'

Derek slammed the door of the taxi, which by luck had been waiting outside.

'Where to?'

'Just drive.'

Derek slumped in his seat to avoid being spotted through the window. He had made it out with the vial that was going to net him one hundred thousand good old Yankee dollars, enough for him to get out of this place forever.

The vial that nestled snugly in Derek's inside jacket pocket contained twenty ml of NR112, a very potent but unproven memory suppressant. One dose of this and, in theory, you would permanently forget your entire past. It wasn't fully tested, but Derek had been working on it for over a year and was certain enough that it would work. He had a customer waiting in Mumbai who didn't need to know the finer details; besides, Derek didn't give a damn. He would deliver what he had offered for sale on the dark web only two weeks ago – all he wanted was his money.

As Aditya raced towards the reception, the six confused security guards and the very apologetic receptionist, Derek's taxi was already out of sight.

'Did anyone see where he went after leaving the building, you bunch of idiots?'

'No sir,' they chorused.

'Bastard!' Aditya screamed, kicking over a water dispenser, hurting his toes in the process.

It was too late: Derek and the vial were gone!

Chapter Four
Goa, 23rd December

Danny Lobo meandered along the frangipani-lined pathway that led from the black steel double gates to the Rosario household, grumbling to himself that he had to carry the three pots of food his mother had made for the feast being held the next day in honour of Rose's ninth birthday.

Danny was the youngest of three sons and lived two houses away. His older brothers had moved overseas for work, one to Dubai and the other to the UK. He opened the security grille and knocked on the front door. It was four in the afternoon and the house was hectic. Maria was cooking several things at once and Peter was trying to get through the mountain of dishes that needed washing before he could get back to his workshop. Maria stole a quick look at Peter. 'Darling?'

'Yes, my dear?' Peter dropped a plate in the sink, nearly breaking it.

'Love you,' Maria said in her sing-song voice.

'Rose, get the front door please,' Peter called out. Only he had heard the incessant knocking that had gone on for the last fifteen seconds.

Rose opened the door to find her best friend standing there, struggling under the weight of the large containers that were filled to the brim with pulao, sorpotel and roast tongue, three Goan favourites.

'Hi Danny, come in,' Rose said sweetly. She grabbed the topmost container and led him into the kitchen. Rose inhaled deeply. 'Mmm,' she sighed, 'I'm so hungry now.'

Peter spotted Danny as he entered the kitchen. 'Good afternoon, Mister Lobo.' Peter always called him that for some reason. He liked the kid and if he had a son, he would want him to be like Danny, who was extremely polite and well mannered.

'Hello auntie, uncle,' Danny replied, puffing out his chest. He enjoyed being called 'Mr Lobo'; it made him feel older than his eleven years.

'Ah Danny, tell mommy thank you, I'll be over later to see her, OK?'

'Yes, auntie,' Danny smiled as he and Rose went into the living room to discuss the big day ahead.

'He's a lovely boy, don't you think?' Peter said, his bushy eyebrows jumping up and down rapidly, 'make someone a good husband one day, eh?'

Maria burst out laughing. 'Will you stop trying to marry our daughter off already?'

'It's nice to hear you laugh,' Peter said softly.

Maria hadn't been her usual bubbly self lately and Peter wanted to find out why. He wasn't too good at those kinds of conversations and besides, he had the feeling that in this case his ignorance, at least for the time being, was bliss.

He finished the washing-up, walked over to his wife and kissed her gently on the back of her neck where her hair coiled in a perfect kiss curl, just like Rose's did. 'I love you too,' he whispered, then disappeared out of the back door, leaving Maria alone with her thoughts.

There were only six days left until the hospital appointment. She sought the little solace she could from the fact that there was enough going on over the next few days to keep her mind from her imminent test results.

***

A man stood watching the sun rise through the floor-to-ceiling windows of gate B1 in the departure lounge at Kempogowda International Airport. It was an incredibly nervous Derek Jacoby. He hadn't slept a wink on the rock-hard mattress of the cheap hotel room just a few kilometres away, neither had he been back to see his wife; he couldn't bring himself to tell her that he was leaving. He had destroyed his cell phone on the way to the hotel and was still wearing the same clothes as the day before. The vial containing NR112 was extremely well hidden in the only place he thought safe. Yes, it was uncomfortable, but it would only be a few hours before he got to the relative safety of Mumbai, where he could retrieve it. He only wished that he had spent longer on the toilet before 'insertion'.

Boarding had just started when two armed soldiers came into the lounge and walked towards the boarding gate. Shit, Derek thought to himself, as he tried to sidle off inconspicuously towards the bathroom, just in case. Derek kept a watchful eye on the interaction between the soldiers and the young lady. Ten excruciatingly long seconds passed, then he heard laughter coming from the direction of the gate; the two soldiers were walking off smiling at each other.

'Rows twenty-two to thirty-six board now please, ladies and gentlemen,' a voice crackled over the loudspeaker. Derek retrieved his boarding pass from his jeans back pocket and changed direction.

'Good morning, Mr Jacoby, have a nice flight,' the uniformed young lady said. The name on the badge pinned to her tight white blouse was too long for Derek to pronounce.

'Thank you, miss,' he said, as he walked past her, entering the long, cool tunnel that led to the aircraft.

Sitting uncomfortably in seat 28B, Derek gazed through the window as flight AI003 taxied towards the runway. He was relieved that the aircraft was only half full and that the seats on either side of him were free. He closed his eyes and tried to relax; Mumbai was only an hour away. Jonathan had instructed him to check into the Hyatt Regency on arrival, where a room was booked for him. There would be a package containing a cell phone at reception and he was to stay there and await further instructions. Derek was looking forward to enjoying a touch of luxury over the next few days. He really wanted a hot shower and soft bed all to himself but more importantly, he needed to remove the vial that was very uncomfortably an inch or so inside him.

Chapter Five
Goa, 24th December

Just after seven a.m., Maria and Peter woke to the excited calls for them to *'get up'* by a wide-eyed Rose who had wedged herself between them on top of the sheets and was playfully bashing the pair. Both knew that she would not relent until they had left the comfort of their bed.

'Are you quite sure it's your birthday today?' Peter joked.

'Mom, tell daddy to stop playing games!'

'Happy birthday, my darling,' her mother said as she hugged her. Maria's eyes were still half shut; it had been a terribly busy day yesterday, and she was finding it difficult to hide the pain she had suffered for the past six months. Like a creeping, slithering, malign entity, it was worsening by the day.

'How about some breakfast for my beautiful birthday girl?' Peter said as he kissed Rose on top of her head. She had already been up for an hour; she had bathed, dressed and combed her hair, putting it up into a tight ponytail, the exact same kiss curl as her mother's resting on the nape of her neck.

'Yes please,' Rose replied, leaping off the bed.

Even though Peter had investors coming to see his latest invention in several weeks and the prototype was not yet finished, he would not be in his workshop today. Rose would be the centre of attention, and he could not wait to see her reaction to the gift that was hidden at the Lobo house, away from her prying eyes.

Half an hour later, a still drowsy Maria opened the door to Victor and Carmen, who were weighed down with birthday gifts for Rose. The whole family sat down to breakfast together. After finishing his tea, Victor said 'time for presents?' A resounding 'yes!' was the answer.

Rose sat cross-legged on the floor of the living room; a cursory glance around the gifts had revealed no sign of the present that she longed for. Although she was too young to cycle in the village alone, the family compound was large enough for her to ride all the way around the house and Rose was confident that her mother would let her out into the village with Danny and his cousin Candice, who was fourteen. They both had bicycles already. The family lived on the outskirts of a town called Bambolim. It was a peaceful place, devoid of trucks and fast-moving traffic because there was no through road.

One by one Victor, Carmen, Peter and Maria passed Rose present after present; there was wrapping paper everywhere. Rose was truly having the best day of her life but she still saw no present large enough to be a bicycle, so although happy, she was getting slightly disheartened. Surely they were not going to let her down?

'Rooooose,' a call came from the hallway.

The front door and gate had been left open for visitors and well-wishers. Danny strode into the living room to join the family, the huge smile on his face showing off his white teeth. Danny gave an exaggerated wink and thumbs up to Peter as he sat down on the floor next to his best friend.

'Happy birthday, Rose. Today is going to be so wonderful, I can just feel it.'

Rose looked at him sideways as she accepted the gift Danny held out to her. What's this all about, she thought to herself. Peter jumped to his feet, looked at Maria and gave her a cheeky grin.

'I just have to pop out for a couple of minutes,' he said.

'Daddy, no, you promised you wouldn't work today,' Rose said plaintively.

'My darling, I will be back before you can miss me.'

'OK.'

Rose opened Danny's gift. It was the block game Jenga. She knew it would get plenty of use during the monsoon season, when it would rain for days on end.

'Rose,' Peter called out from the front garden, 'Rose.'

Fast as lightning she was up and out of the door with everybody following, causing a jam in the doorway. This was something not to be missed. Rose was standing on the veranda when her grandparents, Maria and Danny caught up to join them, laughing at the human stampede they had created.

'Where's Daddy?' Rose asked when Victor arrived next to her.

'Peter, we are all waiting for you,' Victor hollered.

Rose's heart was pounding in anticipation. Suddenly, to the right of them, Peter strode around the corner of the house.

'Aaargh, Daddy!' was all that Rose could manage, for even though what Peter was carrying in his arms was wrapped, it was very obviously …

'*A bicycle*!' Rose screamed, as she jumped down the three stairs all at once, tumbling onto the grass. She shot straight up and raced to her father and the bicycle that had just made her dreams come true.

Maria walked over to join them. Carmen and the rest stayed on the veranda, watching the delightful scene. Rose's eyes were streaming with tears of joy as she frantically clawed at the wrapping paper.

After the struggle of revealing it, Rose took a step back to admire what was now her most prized possession. The bicycle was three shades of pink with bright stickers, for added colour. The wheels had steel spokes with big knobbly tyres; at the back were carefully fixed training wheels. The red basket on the front was just waiting to be filled with her things and there were reflectors on the front, back and wheels. She rang the bell on the handlebars, it was the loudest she had ever heard.

Rose turned to her parents, put one arm around each of them as best she could and through her happy tears, she managed to catch her breath and splutter. 'Mommy, Daddy, I love it so much, thank you!' Carmen smiled at her husband; grandparents lived for days like this.

'Get on, Rose, let's see you ride it, come on,' Danny called out excitedly as he rushed over to join her.

***

Jonathan Naik was on an important call. He listened as the voice with a hint of a New York twang said breathlessly, 'I assure you, Jonathan, it will work, you have my word. I have been developing this serum for a long time now, it has not been tested on humans because *somebody* was too impatient to wait another year or so; nevertheless, I am one hundred per cent certain that whoever you use this on, will not remember their past. If you administer the dose correctly, the subject will fall asleep and when they wake up, will not remember a thing.'

Derek Jacoby mopped at his sweaty forehead. He was worried that the buyer was getting cold feet. He was in too deep now and desperate for the money so that he could disappear.

'And you are sure that this effect will last a lifetime? I can't have the girl snapping out of it a year down the line, that would leave me in a world of shit!' Jonathan said nervously.

He was standing in the walk-in closet of their master suite. Elizabeth could not know what was going on until the girl had arrived. Jonathan had already fabricated a story to tell his wife. She would never agree to what he was actually doing.

'A lifetime, no memory return, no problems,' Derek tried to add a reassuring confidence to his tone, knowing full well that he was lying. There was no time to worry about the details now, the only thing on his mind was money.

'I will meet you at lunchtime on Friday; there is a small coffee shop around the corner from the hotel that is suitable. Be ready, I will call you when I get there.' Jonathan hung up before Derek could reply.

'Honey, what are you up to?' Elizabeth had walked silently into the room just as the call ended.

'Ah Liz, there you are,' Jonathan glanced down at his phone to ensure the call had been cut, 'what do you think of this shirt?' he asked, quickly tugging on the first hanger he could get his hands on.

'Yes, that'll do fine, who was that on the phone?'

'Just work, darling.'

'Seriously? On Christmas Eve?'

'There you are!' Elijah shouted, slamming the door open, hitting his mother's back in the process.

'Come on, let's go, I've been waiting for ten minutes now.' He was annoyed at having to leave his room, but the promise of a shopping spree had tempted him out.

'Eli! Apologise to your mother this instant!' Jonathan demanded, feeling guilty at his relief that Elizabeth had been distracted.

'Sorry mom,' Eli said with a long, exaggerated sigh that cancelled any genuine sentiment in his apology. 'I'll be waiting downstairs,' he called over his shoulder as he ran off. Jonathan rubbed his wife's back. 'Are you OK?' he asked.

'I'll live, but that boy won't, the day I give him one tight slap, I tell you,' Elizabeth motioned with her right hand.

'Come on then, we shouldn't keep the little prince waiting, eh?' Jonathan said, looking to the heavens sarcastically.

***

Across town, Derek Jacoby said, 'OK, I will see you then,' to nobody. Jonathan had already hung up. He flipped the phone shut and threw it on the bed. Another two days stuck in this room, he thought to himself. Derek ran his fingers through his hair; he needed a fix.

There was a knock on the door. Derek's heart jumped but then he relaxed, realising he had ordered room service earlier.

'Where would you like me to put it, sir?' asked the young man wheeling a trolley into the spacious room.

'On the desk is fine, thanks.'

Derek had ordered sushi; it was one of his favourites. It was expensive but Derek didn't care, he wasn't paying the bill. The room and everything he could eat and drink was included in the deal, which made up for being alone with only the hotel staff for company. He wouldn't be contacting anybody until he was out of the country, especially not poor Sita, whom he had abandoned the day before.

'Shall I open the champagne, sir?'

'No thanks, I like to pop my own corks,' Derek joked.

'Very good, sir, will there be anything else?' the young man replied, straight-faced.

Derek grabbed his wallet, pulled out a one-hundred-rupee note and handed it to him.

'You are most generous, thank you. Enjoy your meal, sir.'

Derek lifted the cover from his plate to reveal an array of salmon nigiri and tuna sashimi. 'Mmm,' he sighed, as he sat down to eat before polishing off yet another glass of champagne. He was getting used to this, and spending Christmas alone wasn't looking all that bad now. He grabbed the remote and switched on the TV.

***

It was eight in the evening in the Rosario household. Friends and relatives had come and gone, and a feast had been eaten. Rose, the star of the day, was sound asleep on the sofa with her head on her father's lap and Maria was in the kitchen, packing away what was left of the food. Victor and Carmen had said their goodbyes and were just on their way out when a scooter pulled up with Rose's Uncle Jack as a passenger; neither of them recognised the other person.

'Look who's here,' said Carmen to her husband.

She didn't like the man, never had. She could smell bad news from miles away, and *he* was bad news. Jack walked up the pathway to the house, bag in hand.

'Victor, Carmen, good evening, where's the birthday girl?'

'Rose is inside. You're a bit late though, she's already sleeping,' replied Victor.

'Hello Jack, they are in the living room, I'm sure your brother will be pleased to see you,' said Carmen, her tone sarcastic.

Jack lowered his gaze; he knew they didn't like him. Carmen gave the scooter rider a long stare as they walked past him to their car.

'Jack, we were expecting you earlier,' said Peter softly, as his brother appeared in the doorway.

'I'm sorry brother, I got caught up, I know it's late but I couldn't miss my favourite niece's birthday, could I?'

'She's your only niece, Jack,' Peter said evenly. Jack laughed nervously; he obviously had something on his mind.

'How are you, Jack?' Maria called from the kitchen.

'I'm good, thanks.'

Jack removed a badly wrapped gift from the bag and placed it on the table.

'Tea?' Peter offered.

'No, I can't stay, I have to sort some things out.'

Jack glanced towards the kitchen and, with no sign of Maria he moved closer to Peter and asked, 'did you manage to talk to Vic about my, um, situation?'

'Yes, I did but I wouldn't hold my breath if I were you, I think you're on your own with this one.'

'Great,' replied Jack. 'Give this to Rose for me, I have to get going now, brother. I won't be around tomorrow, so I'll say Merry Christmas now.'

He got up and offered his hand to Peter, who shook it briefly over the head of his sleeping daughter.

'Sort your mess out, Jack; I don't want anything to do with it, OK?'

'What do you think I'm trying to do?' Jack snapped.

'Merry Christmas, Maria,' he called out as he left the house.

Ever since childhood, Jack had been one of those people who thought the world owed him everything. From getting into trouble at school to his most recent gambling debts, he always expected somebody to bail him out. This time, however, he owed the wrong people money, and he would not be able to wriggle out of this predicament easily, especially now that everyone had washed their hands of him.

Maria came into the living room, kicked off her slippers and slumped onto the sofa next to Peter.

'You ok?' he asked, as he put his free arm around her.

'Tired, but it was worth it, wasn't it darling?'

Rose had run out of energy an hour ago, having spent half of the day on her new bicycle, which she absolutely adored. She must have done a hundred circuits of the house. Danny had brought his bike over to join her in the adventures.

'She loved it, didn't she?' Peter smiled.

'Yes darling, she really did, we will have to do it all again tomorrow. I'm so glad that mom and dad are taking care of the festivities though.' Christmas Day was to be spent at the Alvares household; Carmen had insisted on it.

'Oh, I bet you are. Tea?' offered Peter, as he substituted two cushions for his lap to support Rose's head so that he could get up. His leg was starting to go numb, and he needed to stretch it out.

'Do we have any rum?' Maria asked through a yawn.

'Rum it is then, for my tired girl; you stay right there and unwind.' Peter gave Maria a big kiss.

'I love you,' he said and went off to find the bottle of local Old Monk rum that was kept for moments like this.

'Love you too babe,' replied Maria, as she pulled Rose's hair from her face and stroked her shoulder. A tear came to her eye as she wondered what they would do without her.

Peter delivered Maria's drink, carefully lifted Rose from the sofa and tucked her into bed.

'Are you ready to call it a night?' a yawning Peter asked as he returned to the living room.

Maria was already asleep. Smiling, Peter took the glass from her grip and finished what was left. He closed the doors to the house, grabbed a blanket and sat next to his wife on the sofa, covering them both up. He fell asleep instantly.

Chapter Six
Mumbai, 25th December

The Christmas tree in the Naik household was twelve feet tall and, as always, lavishly decorated. Elizabeth prided herself on her Christmas decorations. This year the colour scheme was white and duck egg blue to match the freshly painted interior of the apartment. Under the tree, it was rather bare. Eli had been shopping with his parents to buy whatever he wanted so there really was no need to wrap his gifts. There were a couple of expensive items of jewellery for Elizabeth, and she had bought Jonathan a new squash racquet, some ties from her favourite designer and a top-of-the-range telescope. They had an amazing view from their apartment, and she thought it would be fun for them to spy on people; in reality, the gift was as much for her as it was for him.

Preeti was to have Christmas Day off, as there would not be much for her to do. The family were going to their friends' house in Worli for dinner and would not be back until late. She had already prepared breakfast and was waiting for them to wake up. The maid was twenty-five years old, close to six feet tall, with waist-length jet-black hair. Slim but not skinny, and stunningly beautiful.

She was the only daughter of a poor family from a small village in Madhya Pradesh, near the border of Maharashtra. For her, working for the Naiks was a dream job. She had somewhere to live, received a fair salary and was treated well, all things considered.

Preeti sipped her coffee and contemplated life. All in all, she would have to say it was good, but she longed to meet the right man to marry. Preeti sighed. There wasn't much chance of meeting any man, let alone the right man, when she was stuck in the apartment most of the time. She had decided she would go out for a few hours after everyone had left. Preeti had made a friend who worked for a family two floors down in the block and it turned out that they would both be free today.

'Good morning, Preeti. Merry Christmas,' Jonathan said as he made his way down the stairs to the spacious open-plan kitchen/living area.

'Merry Christmas, sir. Coffee?' Preeti jumped up and smoothed down her apron.

'Yes, bring it to my office please.'

Jonathan had a soft spot for Preeti. He loved the way she floated around the place serenely; nothing was ever too much trouble for her. He needed her calmness in his life, and he took care of her like she was part of the family. Elizabeth was always curious as to why he felt that way about their maid and was often unkind to Preeti when the little horned demon of jealousy pricked her with its pitchfork.

Jonathan had a financially rewarding career; he could buy almost anything he wanted, but calm and peace of mind had too high a price tag even for him it seemed. Preeti was the embodiment of what he craved, for his troubled soul.

'Of course, sir,' Preeti replied softly.

Eli was stamping downstairs now, famished as usual. 'Is breakfast ready?'

Eli had little respect for anybody and only showed it when threatened by his parents. He liked Preeti but being a spoiled rich kid, he thought he could do whatever he wanted.

'Merry Christmas everyone,' called Elizabeth from the mezzanine.

'Merry Christmas, mom,' said Eli, spinning on the stool at the breakfast bar, impatiently waiting for his pancakes to be handed to him. Today he would get a break from his diet.

Preeti emerged from the hallway that led to her employer's offices and cinema room.

'Merry Christmas, madam,' she said as she walked to the six-burner stove to make Elizabeth the extra-strong coffee she could tell was needed. She and Jonathan had drunk two bottles of wine last night and Preeti had cleared up after them.

'Merry Christmas, Preeti, where is Jon?'

'Sir is in his office; he will not be long.'

Sometimes Liz really hated the girl and her shiny hair.

***

In the Hyatt Regency, there was a knock at Derek's room door. His heart skipped the usual beat; he tutted. He should be used to it by now, considering the amount of room service that he had ordered over the past couple of days. He had just stepped out of the shower and had only a towel around his slim waist.

'Just give me a minute,' he called out. He pulled the white towelling robe from behind the bathroom door, slid into his hotel-issue slippers and strode over to find out who it was. If only he could get some 'company' he thought, looking through the peephole at a member of the hotel staff holding some hangers.

'Your clothes, sir,' said the middle-aged man as Derek opened the door.

'Thank you,' he said. 'Can you send the concierge to see me?'

'Certainly, sir.' Derek slipped him a tip.

'Thank you, sir. Will there be anything else, sir?'

'No.'

'I will send him straight up.'

Derek shut the door and hung the clothes in the wardrobe. Apart from an extra T-shirt that was in his bag, they were all he had to wear for the moment, so he would stay in boxers and a robe, which suited him fine anyway.

In front of him in the wardrobe, on the middle shelf, was the complimentary safe. He hesitated, his finger over the keypad, then, unable to help himself, he punched in the four-digit code and opened the door. Of course, it was still there, wrapped in a small hand towel from the bathroom for safety. There was another knock.

'Jesus, this is going to kill me,' Derek muttered, as he slammed the safe shut. Outside was a tall bespectacled man, who looked around twenty-five to thirty. He had a trendy spiky haircut and a thin moustache that curled up at the ends. His suit was of better quality than the rest of the staff and by the look of the fit, definitely bespoke. Derek opened the door.

'You wanted to see me, sir?' the man exclaimed confidently, with nothing like the fawning smiles of the staff he had encountered so far.

'Come in, please,' said Derek.

With the door closed behind them, Derek thought about how he could explain what he wanted without getting himself into trouble; both the things he craved were very much illegal.

The envelope that was left at the front desk for Derek also contained one hundred thousand rupees. He had asked the buyer for some spending money as he didn't want to use his ATM card.

'I erm, need, erm...,' stammered Derek.

'Mr Jacoby, my name is Sanjay, and I am the concierge here at the Hyatt. During your stay I will be the person you need to contact for the things you require that are not on the room service menu, if you understand me, sir?'

Sanjay had seated himself on the couch, crossed his legs and was twirling his moustache with one hand and holding his cell phone in the other.

Derek chuckled, 'I do.'

'So, Mr Jacoby, what do you require?'

'Coke, I need some cocaine.'

'No problem, there is some exceptionally good stuff around at the moment, sir. Anything else?'

'Yes. A hot girl. Tall, blonde, big breasts but not fake. Oh, and a Viagra, if you can.'

The concierge's face remained expressionless as he listened to Derek's shopping list.

'Consider it done.'

Sanjay rose to his feet. 'Russian?' he asked.

'Doesn't matter, as long as she speaks English.'

'OK, what time would you prefer?'

'Eight o'clock.' Derek fished the envelope with the cash out of his robe pocket.

'No problem, sir, that will be eighty-five thousand rupees.' Sanjay held out a hand with perfectly manicured nails. The girl will come at eight and I will drop off the other things at around seven, if that works for you?'

'Perfect,' replied Derek, as he handed over the cash. Sanjay swiftly slipped the notes into his inside jacket pocket, opened the door and exited the room.

Derek launched himself onto the enormous bed. 'Yes!' he laughed, 'fucking ace!' He was going to have fun tonight, that was for sure.

***

At the Alvares household, the only guests were the Rosario family. Victor had set the carrom board up earlier and was giving Peter a good beating, as he usually did. Peter enjoyed playing and even though he lost most of the time, he liked that it made the old man happy.

They finished their last game of the session just before lunch. With beer in hand, Victor said, 'Peter, I am sorry, but I can't help Jack. I asked around but the people he has a problem with are a young lot. This guy, the one he owes the money to, is a particularly nasty piece of work. He has connections with the mafia in Mumbai. He has a reputation to uphold and will not want to lose face over a debt.'

'It's OK, Vic. Besides, it's about time Jack stood on his own two feet,' Peter sighed. Victor fixed his son-in-law with a stare.

'I must warn you, Peter, these people are not to be messed with. You need to tell your brother to get the money any way he can, or disappear, because it won't just be a few slaps he gets, it's going to be a hell of a lot worse.' Victor stared at Peter long enough to emphasise the gravity of what he had said, then he patted the younger man on the arm.

Peter sighed. 'Well, let's see what scheme he has come up with. He said he was involved in something yesterday, so who knows?'

The reality was that Jack had run out of options. There was no plan to get the money; he had nowhere left to turn.

'The pain is getting worse, it truly is almost unbearable,' Maria whispered to Carmen, not wanting Rose to hear. The pair were dishing up plates of food for everyone while Rose was busy laying out the cutlery on the dining table. Carmen put her arms around Maria and held her tight for a moment.

'I wish I could make it all go away, my dear, be strong. If you need me, I am here for you, always.' Carmen's voice was hoarse with unshed tears.

'Mom? I'm finished!' Rose called, her voice a sing-song replica of her mother's.

Rose was still on cloud nine from the day before, having only left her bicycle at home because it wouldn't fit in Victor's car along with all of them.

40

'Tell your father and grandfather to come and eat please, baby,' said Maria, holding back her tears as best she could. After Rose left the kitchen, Carmen said, 'Maria, darling, when we come back on Monday we need to sit down and tell Peter and your father, OK? We can't keep this a secret any longer.'

Although she didn't look it yet, Maria was extremely unwell and living on painkillers to try and quell the constant throbbing in her head. She knew she had a brain tumour but would not know the extent of it until her next hospital visit. She'd had an MRI scan and was awaiting the biopsy results. Carmen footed the bill, which had been quite sizeable. She would, of course, do anything for Maria, even sell her house if need be. With a combination of painkillers and a couple of stiff drinks, Maria managed to get through the day. The adults played doubles at carrom while Rose tried her best to officiate, although the more alcohol that was consumed, the more difficult it got, and Rose had given up before the end of the evening.

Chapter Seven
Mumbai, 26th December

It was nearly noon. Derek Jacoby had not slept and was still buzzing from his drug binge. Svetlana, his blonde Russian from the previous night, had left a couple of hours ago. He lay on the bed staring at the ceiling fan spinning around, unable to breathe through his blocked nose. Feeling hungry, he turned over to reach for the telephone. As he did, an acrid smell from his armpit alerted him that he needed a shower. It had been a hot, sweaty and extremely athletic night with the pretty six-footer whom he had, thanks to the Viagra, finally worn out by around six a.m.

Pressing nine for room service, he ordered two smoked salmon and cream cheese bagels, a side order of fries and an espresso. Naked, Derek half-slid, half-rolled off the bed. As he stood up, he felt the full force of a banging headache start up like percussion in his skull. He called down to room service again asking them to add some paracetamol to his order, then made for the bathroom and the shower he so desperately needed.

Derek had just finished drying when his breakfast arrived. He grabbed the two painkillers from a small silver dish and downed them with the espresso.

As he ate the first of the two bagels, Thailand popped into his head.

Hmm, yes, he thought to himself, that's where I'll go. He could indulge his hedonistic ways there until he decided what to do in the long term.

Derek booted up the hotel laptop to check for flights. He should have enough money in his US account now to cover the cost, otherwise he would need to wait until the bank transfer had gone through from Jonathan. He could no longer use his Indian bank account or cards.

Derek had just identified a flight to Bangkok via Kuala Lumpur, leaving Mumbai at around midnight, when the phone rang.

'Hello,' he said cautiously, hoping that it was Jonathan. He was getting nervous now and wanted nothing more than to get the hell out of the country.

'Be downstairs in fifteen minutes.' It was the voice he wanted to hear. 'A car will be outside and bring you to where I am.' The line went dead.

Derek threw the phone onto the desk, sat on the chair, put his head in his hands and breathed a huge sigh of relief. At last, it was really going to happen.

Dressed and walking through the lobby, Derek caught sight of Sanjay, who favoured him with a slight nod of his head. Derek saw the Mercedes outside. The driver signalled to him, so he crossed the road and got in the back. Five minutes later he arrived at his destination, a quaint family-owned coffee shop that was not busy, as it was the holiday season. This kind of place would usually be full of businesspeople staring at open laptops, or tourists folding and unfolding maps and sifting through the assorted information leaflets.

Derek opened the door and as the smell of coffee hit him, he instantly felt better. He saw Jonathan sitting at a table in the corner, alone. The man wasn't hard to find; there was only one other patron inside – an elderly lady.

'Please sit,' Jonathan gestured to the seat next to him.

Derek sat and called over to the counter to order a white Americano in Hindi, putting a smile on the assistant's face.

Jonathan was staring at him intently. 'You have it?' he asked quietly.

'Yes, I'll hand it over when you've made the transfer.'

Jonathan opened his laptop, and after a few clicks on the trackpad, he passed it to Derek. 'Enter your account information and it shall be done.'

'What kind of stunt are you trying to pull?' Derek said angrily when he saw the amount to be transferred. 'The deal is for one hundred thousand dollars, not fifty thousand.'

Derek looked around nervously, half expecting either police or some heavies to come rushing through the door or out of the kitchen.

'Calm down, you're attracting attention to us.' Jonathan leaned in close and put his hand on Derek's shoulder. Jonathan wasn't a tough guy by any means, but he thought in this situation if he acted like it, he might gain the upper hand.

'I'm giving you fifty now and the other fifty when I know for sure that it has worked.'

'The hell you are! I'm out of here.' Derek slid his chair back and stood up.

'Wait! OK.' Jonathan could not afford for the deal to go wrong. He grabbed the laptop, changed the transfer amount and passed it back to Derek.

'Happy now?'

'That's better,' replied Derek sitting back down and typing in his account information.

'*Transfer complete*' flashed on the screen, and Jonathan held out his hand. Derek had a quick look around, reached into his inside jacket pocket and pulled out the vial.

'You need to give the whole dose in one go. The subject will fall asleep for an hour or two and when they wake up, voilà, memory gone.'

Jonathan examined the label on the glass vial, which only read 'NR112-sp-op-08'. He tucked it into his pocket, got up and made for the door and, without a background glance, Jonathan was gone.

'Pleasure doing business with you too, asshole!' Derek muttered under his breath.

The American, now one hundred thousand dollars richer, leaned back in his chair and stretched his arms out. Right on cue, his coffee was put in front of him.

Ten minutes later Derek was outside trying to find a taxi when he saw a car containing four burly men, driving slower than they should have been. Normally he wouldn't have paid too much attention, but the fact that they were all staring at him was worrying.

A tuk-tuk honked from behind and, his nerves jangling, Derek spun round, ran over to it and hopped in.

'The Hyatt, and make it quick,' he said.

Safely back at the hotel, he couldn't help thinking about the men in the car. Was he being targeted because he was a foreigner? Surely GreenBay couldn't have caught up with him so quickly? He often caught people staring at him, that was just the way it was. Derek tried but failed to dismiss the idea that there was something more to it.

He logged into his account to check the money was there and let out a sigh of relief when he saw the balance. The whole thing was nearly over. He would book his flight and call Sita from a payphone at the airport, she deserved that at least.

***

The next day in Goa, Jack was called in to see Rasheed. He was on his way to a village on the outskirts of Panjim. The guy that had been driving him around on the scooter for the last couple of days was one of Rasheed's henchmen, there to make sure that Jack didn't do anything stupid like run away or contact the police. Rasheed, who was from Mumbai, had been sent to Goa a few years ago to try and wrestle control of the drugs trade from the Russians and Nigerians, which he was slowly managing to do.

Jack was terrified. He felt that begging was his only option, but he knew it wouldn't help with this guy. They pulled up outside a set of gates to a compound that housed an industrial unit and Jack got off the scooter. The gates opened and he was ushered in by a hefty-looking guy with a pistol sticking out of the waistband of his jeans. Jack stepped into the building, an electric equipment supplies company being used as a cover for Rasheed's network of drug dealers.

'Wait there.' The guard with the pistol pointed to a chair. Jack did as he was told and sat. The building had lofty ceilings and was virtually empty apart from several pallets with large boxes stacked on them. They looked like televisions. Two guys were sitting at a table not far away, playing cards. Jack could overhear their conversation; it was about somebody wanting a girl for a family in Mumbai. He didn't take much notice; he was too busy worrying about his own predicament. A few minutes passed, then he heard a door slam and some choice swear words shouted. From behind one of the pallets of boxes, Rasheed emerged.

'Aah, there you are Jack; a little bird tells me that you don't have my money.'

Jack was staring at the floor. His heart racing, he looked up at Rasheed. 'No, I don't, I've tried everything.'

While he was waiting for Rasheed, Jack had been thinking about his family and how he wished he had spent Christmas Day with them. Regret and guilt made his eyes fill with tears. Now he watched Rasheed put on a brass knuckleduster, knowing that very soon it would be slammed into the side of his face. Just then, one of the guys playing cards got up, walked over to Rasheed and whispered something in his ear.

'I've given you this job, Sunil. If you can't come up with the girl then what use are you to me?' raged Rasheed.

Something in Jack's mind clicked; a girl, he thought – Rose? No, even *he* couldn't do that to his family.

Rasheed turned his attention back to Jack.

'I need to make an example of you, Jack. Too many people are running up debts and giving bullshit excuses because they don't want to pay.'

Jack was shaking as Rasheed held up his hand ready to deliver the first of many blows to Jack's face.

'Wait,' he screamed, 'you need a girl, I'll give you one, my niece, she is nine years old.'

'What are you talking about?' Rasheed hissed.

'I overheard your men.' Jack pointed in their direction. Rasheed turned to Sunil. 'Fucking bigmouth fool,' he growled.

He turned back to Jack. 'You're willing to give up one of your own family to save yourself? You are even more of a dog than I thought!'

Jack's head dropped. 'What else can I do?' he replied.

'Fine, you have two days. If you deliver the girl your debt is paid – if not, you're a dead man. I'll be watching you.' Rasheed removed the knuckleduster and returned to his office.

Sunil followed Jack out to the gates. 'Don't mess this up Jack, or the boss is going to fuck all of us, you understand?'

'Yes,' was all Jack could manage, already regretting what he had offered to do. He was not a clever man, but to do this, to do this to his brother, there really was no lower he could go!

Jack jumped onto the back of the scooter. 'Take me home,' he said. He needed to work out how he was going to manage this in such a short time.

Chapter Eight
Mumbai International Airport, 28th December

Derek had just hung up on a call to his wife, who was heartbroken. He, on the other hand, felt only the hugest relief; he just couldn't stand living with her or her family any longer.

Sita had told him of a visit the previous day from some shady-looking government types who had roughed her up a bit to make sure she was telling them the truth when she said that she didn't know where he was. Derek was annoyed. Sita didn't deserve to be caught up in his mess. Removing his wedding ring, he attempted to forget about his wife. That part of his life was over now, and he had a future in Thailand to look forward to.

Derek decided he would travel to Koh Samui from Bangkok and stay there for a couple of months. Beer, drugs and cheap women were on his mind, and he knew that soon, Sita would be a distant memory. He finished the tea that he purchased from the small kiosk in the terminal, got up and threw the cup in the bin. An announcement informed him that his plane had started to board; he needed to use the bathroom. Derek was nervous when he had first arrived at the airport, but after a couple of hours, with nothing to arouse his suspicions, he had calmed down.

He opened the cubicle door, unzipped his fly and started to urinate when a sudden wave of drowsiness fogged his mind. Damn. Derek shook his head; it must be the stress, drugs, booze and lack of sleep. He finished, turned around and walked to the washbasin. As he held his hands under the tap he heard the bathroom door open. Looking in the mirror he realised that he couldn't focus properly, and his legs felt weak. Derek thought it strange that he still hadn't seen anyone enter the room and there had been nobody in there when he arrived. He looked down at his hands and as his eyes returned to the mirror he could just make out three figures behind him. That was the last thing that Derek Jacoby ever saw as he slumped, lifeless, to the floor.

'How was the chai?' came Aditya's voice from behind him.

Chapter Nine
Goa, 29th December

It was a beautiful morning. Christmas Day had come and gone, and everybody was looking forward to New Year's Eve. The whole family had tickets to the local dinner and dance, which usually ended at around eight the next morning.

Rose and Danny were zooming around the compound at lightning speed; they were either racing each other or being chased by some imaginary monster. There was pop music playing from across the road, loud enough for the whole village to hear.

Peter was in his workshop, desperately trying to finish his latest invention, which was a self-sufficient energy supply, running in perpetual motion or at least as close to that as the universe would allow. It was a simple system using super-strong neodymium magnets, which could produce upwards of one kilowatt of power. Peter knew that this was a big idea. It still didn't work but he was certain it would; he just needed more time.

Rose was still waiting for her first cycling training session without stabilisers, but that would have to wait for a while, as

Peter's potential investors were coming in less than two weeks and were expecting to view a working prototype.

Maria was standing on the veranda, watching her daughter and Danny fly past on their bicycles, the multi-coloured ribbons on the back of Rose's bike streaming out behind her.

'Slow down you two!' Maria called every time they went past, but of course, they never did.

Even though she was worried about her appointment, Maria still managed a smile. She looked around her at the joys of her life in the village that she loved dearly. The children's happy laughter, the music, the birds, the perfectly clear blue sky, her garden, in superb condition, and the rose bush her mother had given her a few months before, which had finally begun to bloom.

Life for Maria was wonderful, if only... A car horn brought her back down to earth. She looked over to the road and saw her mother pulling up. On the next pass of the racing bicycle duo, Rose screeched to a halt, jumped off and ran over to Carmen.

'Grandma!' she cried out as she reached Carmen and hugged her tight. Carmen reciprocated and kissed Rose on top of her head. 'How are you my sweet?'

'I'm fine thanks, grandma,' replied Rose, still out of breath. The pair walked up the garden path, narrowly missed by Danny, who was still doing circuits of the house. 'Hello Aunty,' he cried out as he rode past, but before Carmen could reply, he was already gone, his strong legs pumping the pedals.

Carmen looked at her daughter as she climbed the stairs to the house. 'How are you feeling, darling?' Maria didn't look well, however much she tried to hide it.

'I'm fine, mom. You're early.'

'Well, I suppose we can have a cup of tea before we get going. The AC in the car has made my throat parched.'

'Don't worry, I'll make it.' Carmen held her daughter by the shoulders and steered her towards an easy chair. 'You sit yourself down.'

'OK.'

Maria had always coped with everything that life had thrown at her, but this... This was something else, and for the past few days she had struggled with the simplest of tasks.

'Where's dad?'

'I dropped him off at the Fernandez house next to the church, he'll be here in a few minutes. He thinks we're going for a girls' day out. Peter?'

'Where do you think?' replied Maria, with a roll of her eyes.

'I hope all of this is worth it in the end, my darling,' said Carmen, stirring the pot of tea on the stove.

'Well, we shall find out very soon, that's if he ever finishes it.' They both laughed.

'I trust him, mom, he'll surprise you this time,' Maria said and tilted her chin. They laughed again, louder this time, although Carmen noticed her daughter wince and put her hand to her head.

'Hello baby,' Victor said as he spotted his daughter. 'Are you ok?' he asked, 'you look a bit pale.'

'I'm OK, just a bit tired.' Maria changed the subject. 'Thanks for looking after Rose, we shouldn't be too long.'

'My wife and daughter out shopping together, not too long? Yeah right!' he chuckled.

'Where's Peter?' he asked. Carmen and Maria both gave him a look and they all burst out laughing.

'I won't bother him. You two go and enjoy yourselves.'

They said their goodbyes and the ladies walked down the stairs.

'Bye mom, I love you, you too grandma,' Rose sang out. 'Watch us go round just once, OK?' she shouted, as she turned the corner in front of Danny.

The kids whizzed past, and Maria and Carmen headed off to the car. Carmen turned to see her daughter craning her neck to catch sight of Rose before they left. 'It's bad today, isn't it, Maria?'

'Mom, it hurts so much, I can't take it much longer.' Maria choked back tears.

Carmen held her daughter's hand.

'We will see what they can do about the pain when we get there. Darling, I don't care what you say, we are telling Peter and your father later when we find out what the situation is. Your father has been asking questions and I can't lie any more, he knows something is wrong.'

'Peter too.' Maria dabbed at her eyes.

Carmen started the engine and they left for the hospital. Neither of them saw Jack lurking behind a tree across the street, holding a digital camera. He needed a photo of Rose for confirmation, so as nonchalantly as he could, he crossed the road and entered the compound. He spotted Rose and Danny at the side of the house. They had finally tired themselves out and were washing their cycles down.

'Hello Rose, how's my favourite niece?' he said.

'Hi Uncle Jack, dad's working but grandad is in the kitchen making lunch.'

Jack was standing right in front of the children.

I forgot to take a picture of you on your birthday, pumpkin, so smile,' he said, holding up the camera. Danny and Rose posed flashing toothy grins but in the viewfinder, Jack could only see Rose.

'This will look nice in the family album,' he said. Danny and Rose looked at each other, shrugged and continued with what they were doing.

Jack sent a text message to Rasheed, which was swiftly followed by a visit from Sunil to pick up the camera.

'We will let you know what's happening later, OK? Don't disappear.'

***

In Mumbai, Jonathan was in his home office reworking some plans when he received a message from an unknown number on the spare phone that he had bought. He opened it and the image of a young girl standing next to half an image of a boy appeared. The message below read, 'What do you think?' Before he could reply the phone rang.

'Hello.'

'Well?' Asked the voice. It was Vikram, the man he had charged with finding the daughter his wife longed for.

'Yes, I want her, can you take her today?'

'Consider it done. We will need to bring her by road, of course, so you can expect her some time tomorrow, if all goes well.'

'Don't hurt her – nobody is to lay a hand on her, do you hear me?' Jonathan warned.

'I want cash on delivery, and by the way, the price has doubled. It has taken a lot of effort to find this girl, there are people that need to be paid, neither of us wants any comebacks from this. Kidnap is a serious offence, I'm sure you understand that Jonathan.'

'Doubled? Fine, whatever, I'll have the cash with me, I will send you the address tomorrow morning. In the meantime, head for Mumbai and don't, I repeat *don't* let her come to any harm or the deal's off.'

That one phone call sealed the fates of the Alvarez, Rosario and Naik families, for ever.

Jonathan walked into the master bedroom to find his wife sitting on the bed with towels wrapped around her body and hair.

'You look, happy darling,' she said, as she turned to see his grinning face.

'You'll be receiving your biggest Christmas present tomorrow, the one thing that you have always wanted,' Jonathan said coquettishly.

Elizabeth looked at him speculatively. 'Well, I can't wait...' She tried guessing. 'A Lamborghini? Hermès Birkin bag? Five-carat diamond earrings?'

'No, no and no,' Jonathan chuckled as he left the room to get a glass of wine.

'Tell me!' Elizabeth called after him.

'You'll find out tomorrow, darling,' he replied, still smiling

***

Maria and Carmen had been in the hospital for four hours, and after several extra tests they were still waiting for the results of the MRI scan. Maria was sitting upright on the bed staring into space in the private room that her mother had insisted on.

Carmen, with two more cups of coffee for them, breezed in, a forced bright smile on her face in the hope that she would not give away how worried she was. She sat down next to Maria on the bed and squeezed her hand.

'Is there anything you need, are you hungry?'

'No mom, the only thing I want is for this pain to go away,' replied Maria through gritted teeth, massaging her temples. The pain was worse today because of the stress of being at the hospital and the fact that she would need to come clean to Peter, Rose and Victor when she returned home.

Peter had seen Maria save herself from collapsing a couple of times by hanging onto something in the house. She had brushed it off, blaming it on tiredness when he asked what was wrong. Peter didn't press her further for answers, but he knew there was something wrong and Maria was sure that he had been hiding himself away even more, just to avoid the conversation. Her husband and father would be upset with her for suffering alone, and God only knows what she would say to Rose.

There was a knock on the door.

'Come in,' Carmen said brightly.

Doctor Vaidya entered with a solemn look on his face, carrying a handful of papers and x-rays. Arun Vaidya was one of the top cancer specialists in the country and had been at the hospital for the last fifteen years, and he didn't come cheap.

'Ladies,' he said.

'Hello doctor,' replied Carmen, her bright tone sounding strange, even to her.

Maria had her eyes shut, trying to block out what was going to be said.

'I have asked Doctor Gordon, a neurologist from th` e UK, to join us,' the doctor said, softly. 'He has been in India for the past year and we are lucky that he is in Goa at present. He is a good man, one of the best.'

Carmen smiled. 'Thanks, doctor.'

Dr Thomas Gordon arrived as Dr Vaidya was slipping the x-rays into the lightbox that was fixed to the wall opposite Maria's bed.

'Doctor Gordon, thank you so much for helping us,' said Carmen with a half-smile. She knew it was probably bad news but was trying desperately to keep her spirits up; it was either that or dissolve in tears.

'Maria, the doctors are here,' Carmen announced. Maria opened her eyes. 'Hi,' was all she managed to say.

'Hello Maria, I'm Thomas Gordon, but please call me Tom.'

Maria reached out her hand and he took it. She squeezed hard enough to show her appreciation. Doctor Gordon was on a year's sabbatical from University College Hospital in Central London and was touring hospitals in India, to get a feel of how things worked in a different part of the world.

'Arun, if you'd like to start us off, please?' Doctor Gordon smiled. Doctor Vaidya gave him a nod.

'Maria, how are you feeling today?'

'I don't think it could get much worse, to be honest.' Maria held her forefingers to her temples again.

'OK, we will deal with that after this meeting, there is something we can do to help alleviate the pain somewhat.'

Maria managed a smile, tapped her mother on the hand and pointed to the bed control to sit her up.

Dr Vaidya let her adjust herself then continued.

'Maria, you have a brain tumour. This you already know; the issue is not only the position of it but also the rate at which it is growing. Tom, if you don't mind.'

Dr Gordon walked to the lightbox and pointed to the middle of the three x-rays.

'Maria, you have a tumour that is literally in the most difficult place to operate.' He pointed to a large, shaded shape at the bottom of her skull.

'It's between the cerebellum and the spinal cord. Six months ago, maybe we could have operated with a decent chance of getting you up and running again, but this tumour has grown exponentially and, to be honest, neither I nor Doctor Vaidya has ever seen anything like it before.'

Maria turned to face Carmen, who was sitting on the edge of the bed. Her brow was furrowed, tears spilled from her eyes and her hands were held together as she mouthed a prayer.

Maria squeezed her eyes shut as hard as she could; perhaps when she opened them, none of this would be happening.

'Maria, this is not good news, I'm afraid.'

Doctor Vaidya had taken over now. He pointed to the MRI scan to the left, which was a view from the top of her head.

'You can see the shape of the tumour. It looks like a doggy bone, meaning that it's being squashed and putting pressure on your spinal column and your brain and is tucked in so tight that we, well, we cannot operate as there would be zero chance of success.'

He paused for a moment.

'I am so sorry, Maria.'

Doctor Gordon took over. 'The tumour is malignant, growing at an extraordinary rate and if you look at this image here.' He was pointing to the X-ray on the right now, which showed shading in Maria's neck and shoulders. 'It's spreading fast.'

'What's going to happen, doctor? Please tell me there is something that you can do, please, please,' begged Carmen, through her tears.

Maria was still silent, staring at the images on the wall.

Doctor Gordon cleared his throat.

'I'm sorry, there is nothing we can do to help, except ease the pain during the time you have left.'

Maria patted her mother's shoulder.

'It's OK, mom, it's OK, we will get through this. Doctor, how long do I have?'

With a low, animal-like moan of pain, Carmen clutched Maria to her.

'Four, maybe five weeks.'

'Please give us a moment alone,' Maria asked. Her voice was calm and her smile warm.

'Of course,' the doctors chorused, and Doctor Gordon left the room.

'I will be back with the medication in a short while,' said Doctor Vaidya, 'until then ring the bell if you need anything. A nurse will come.'

As the door closed behind him, Maria looked at her mother. They hugged and the tears finally came.

Chapter Ten
Goa, 4:43 p.m., 29th December

Victor had dozed off in the living room after eating too much for lunch, leaving Danny and Rose to amuse themselves.

A stolen car with Sunil at the wheel accompanied by one of his associates pulled up outside the house next door.

'There she is,' Sunil said, pointing to the garden of the Rosario house. Maalik, the man in the back, stared at the children.

'What about the boy? He will be a problem, no?' he said.

Just then the boy, Danny, shouted, 'I need to pee.' He ran up the stairs two at a time and into the house. Sunil was watching closely, his leg shaking nervously.

'Let's go, now!' Maalik hissed. Sunil glanced around. He couldn't see anyone else about.

'Fuck it,' he said, starting the engine.

They stopped outside the house and Sunil called out of the car window, 'Rose, can you give this to your father?' He was holding up a package that contained nothing but an empty box. Rose looked at him with suspicion. 'Daddy is out the back,' she replied.

'Please take it for me, I'm in a hurry, there's a good girl,' said Sunil.

'OK.' Rose hopped onto her bicycle for the short ride to the front gates. Maalik got out of the car, took the package from Sunil's hand, and waited for her.

Danny had finished in the bathroom and was walking to the front door when he felt his stomach rumbling. He could see Victor asleep on the sofa, so he turned and made for the kitchen. Finding a plate full of parathas, he picked one up and gazed out of the back window where he could see Peter through the open door of his workshop.

As Rose arrived at the now open front gates, Maalik dropped the package which he had clumsily been rubbing against his shirt, and before she knew what was happening he grabbed her in a vice-like grip, his tobacco-stained hand over her mouth. Maalik slipped in through the open door of the car like an acrobat, clutching the girl, her legs flailing. As the door closed Sunil put his foot down and they sped off.

Danny trotted back into the garden, happy that he had cured his hunger pangs. 'Rose?' he called out. He could see her bike by the front gates on its side with the wheels still spinning. She would never throw her bike over like that. Where had she gone?

He ran down the path and into the street. 'Rose, Rose?' he called at the top of his voice. Looking up and down, he couldn't see anybody, let alone his best friend. He ran to the house at full speed, flew up the stairs and into the living room, tripping over his own feet and coming close to smashing his head on a table as he tumbled onto the floor. As he was getting up, Victor stirred.

'Uncle, uncle,' cried the boy, frantically shoving Victor's leg, 'wake up uncle, Rose is missing!'

Victor was just coming to his senses, and as he opened his eyes, he saw Danny's anxious face in front of him babbling incoherently.

'Calm down, Danny, what's going on?'

Danny took a couple of deep breaths and wiped his eyes on his T-shirt. 'I went to the bathroom and when I got back outside, Rose was gone. The gates were open and her bike was lying there like she had thrown it over and, and, and uncle I can't find her.' Danny started bawling.

'Right,' said Victor, 'go to your house and see if she is there. If not, bang on every neighbour's door and get them all outside looking for her. I'll fetch her father.'

Danny got up and bolted out of the door. 'Rose?' he called, all the way to his house.

'Shit, shit, what have I done?' Victor shouted as he got up. He was wide awake now and it had started to sink in that it was *he* who should have been looking after the kids. Moving as quickly as he could these days, he slipped out the back door and headed to the end of the garden.

'Peter!' he cried out.

Peter emerged from inside, looking confused as to why his father-in-law was shouting so loudly.

'Vic, what's going on?'

'Rose has disappeared.'

'Come on, Vic, don't mess around like that; you know I'm busy,' said Peter smiling, confident that the old man was playing a pretty tasteless prank on him.

'I'm fucking serious, Peter, she's gone, we need to get out to the front of the house, Danny is knocking all the neighbours up.' Victor was almost shouting.

Peter's expression changed in an instant.

'Let's go, I'll tell you what I know on the way.'

***

Doctor Vaidya had prescribed two weeks' worth of oxycodone, seven-milligram tablets for Maria, two of which she had taken straight away. The pair were standing just outside the hospital lobby while Carmen was bringing the car round.

'I do strongly advise that you stay here, Maria,' the doctor said.

'I want to go home to my family,' Maria said in a tone that indicated she would not be moved.

The doctor shrugged slightly and relented, admiring Maria's strength and courage; he knew there would be no changing her mind.

'Doctor, you have been such a friend to me, and I appreciate your concern but I'm going home, I hope you understand.' Maria's tone had lost a little of its sharp edge. She was starting to feel drowsy as the drugs kicked in, but at last the pain was subsiding; finally, she had some respite.

Maria looked out at the hustle and bustle of the frenetic life on the street.

'I'm going to miss all of this – the busy people, the noise, the energy,' Maria said, squinting at the descending sun.

'How are you feeling now?' the doctor looked at her, smiling. He could see that the oxycodone was working, as Maria's expression had changed from one of pain to quiet contemplation.

'I don't actually feel anything now,' she replied with a thumbs up.

'No more than four per day, Maria,' said the doctor, holding up four fingers to emphasise his point.

'OK.'

Just then Carmen pulled up.

'Take care of yourself and please spend your time wisely, and don't do anything but relax. If you need me, you have my number, OK?' The doctor smiled.

Maria gave him a hug. She knew that was unorthodox, but she didn't care.

'Thank you,' she whispered in his ear.

Maria released the doctor, who straightened his pristine white coat and gave her a wink.

'Thank you for everything, doctor,' said Carmen, shaking his hand.

'No problem at all, I only wish there was more that I could do. You keep an eye on her Carmen, and if you need my advice or anything, no matter how trivial, you must call me.'

'I will.'

Carmen helped Maria into the car, took her seat and waved the doctor goodbye as they drove off to break the news to the family.

As Doctor Arun Vaidya walked back into the hospital, he couldn't help questioning whether there was something more that he could have done, but if truth be told it was Maria's courage and strength that was her downfall. She had chosen to bear the pain instead of visiting the hospital when she first started getting the headaches. There may have been a chance of saving her life if she had come sooner.

He shook his head as he pressed the elevator call button. A few moments later the doors opened, and he walked in. He was alone. As the elevator started to move, he screamed at the top of his voice, punching the wall. At work, he was a control freak. One of the things he hated most was losing, and he knew that Maria was going to be chalked up as a loss.

The doors opened on the third floor. Arun shut his eyes and took a deep breath. 'Let's hope the next one's a win,' he muttered, as he exited the elevator, disappearing back into his world of trying to save lives.

***

It was now confirmed that Rose had disappeared. Danny had told his mother Juanita, who had searched their house and garden thoroughly. There was no sign of the child. Outside, there was already a large gathering of neighbours, and the police were on their way. Peter and Victor were standing at the centre of the crowd, they had no idea what to do now. The sun would be setting in an hour or so and without daylight, their task would be much harder.

Everybody seemed to be talking at once; many of them were on their phones calling family and friends to come and join them. Rose was well loved by everyone, and they all wanted to see her back home safely. The immediate area had already been searched and the neighbours had double-checked every home, shed, outbuilding and storm drain on the street. The shouts of 'Rose' had not stopped since Peter and Victor appeared outside the house.

'Please, everybody, can you all quiet down,' Victor called out.

After a few seconds he had the attention of everyone that wasn't on the phone calling for help.

'Somebody must have seen something,' Peter shouted. The people in the crowd turned to each other; all of them seemed to be shaking their heads. A few women were crying, and the rest of the kids in the street were huddled in a small group near the centre of the adults surrounding them.

Peter was about to say something else when two police jeeps came flying down the street and screeched to a halt ten metres from the group. There were three policemen in the lead car and three policewomen in the other. The officer in charge was Sub-Lieutenant Roger Moreas, who would not normally have come to an incident like this but Victor had been the one to call the police and he was well respected by most of them.

When Moreas heard, he had pulled his best officers off of what they were doing and made this their priority. He would be overseeing the investigation and search personally. He and Victor had been friends for many years.

The crowd parted as Moreas and his team approached. Victor and Peter joined Sub-Lieutenant Moreas.

'Roger, thank you for getting here so fast,' said Victor. Peter was still trying to take it all in and could only manage 'hello' as he surveyed the area, still in the hope that Rose would pop out from behind a bush or run out of somebody's front door. The other five officers already had their notebooks out and were speaking to people in the crowd.

'No problem, Vic, you are family; we will find her, don't worry!' Moreas put his hand on his friend's arm.

'I have another twenty or so officers coming from other stations as we speak. I have also ordered roadblocks and checkpoints to be set up on the main roads, they won't be getting far.' Peter's face went grey at the thought of his little girl being kidnapped. 'Peter, it's just a precaution, but we need to be quick and cover all bases.'

'OK.'

Roger Moreas took charge of the situation straight away. Peter and Vic were relieved at the response from the police; in Goa, things could be slow sometimes.

Moreas was a tough-looking guy, six feet tall with a slight paunch but still quite fit for his sixty-two years. He had twenty years in the army under his belt and had joined the police force straight after. Moreas quickly rose through the ranks due to his intelligence, firm-handedness and most of all, his dislike of bribe-taking. With his thick moustache, crisply starched uniform, gun on his hip and the well-worn lathi stick that he always carried, even at his age he was clearly not a man to be messed with.

'Right, what do we know? asked Roger. Victor called Danny over to join them.

'Danny, our neighbour's boy, was the last to see her – they were playing in the front garden.'

Danny arrived and eyed the man up. Roger Moreas was a formidable figure to a boy of his age. Danny had never been in trouble before and was clearly a little nervous.

'I, I, ...,' he started. Moreas lifted his hand.

'Slowly son, Rose is your friend, no?'

'Best friend,' Danny corrected, trying hard to hold back the tears in front of this group of grown men. Roger continued.

'We are all here to help, you understand that don't you?' Danny nodded.

'You were the last person to see her, so, without rushing, tell us exactly what happened before she disappeared.' He fixed Danny with a firm but benevolent stare, 'and I mean everything, because something that you think may not be important could be a big clue for us.' Moreas bent down to Danny's level. He had a rather soothing deep voice for such a big man, which put Danny at ease.

The boy gave a half-smile. 'OK, uncle,' he replied.

Moreas put both hands on his shoulders and gave him a wink. 'Good boy. Now, in your own time,' he said, rising to his full height. Danny took several deep breaths and the sub-lieutenant called over a female officer to take notes.

'Well,' Danny started, squinting up to the sky and frowning as he concentrated hard trying to recollect the events in question. 'We were by the steps, taking a break from riding and I was trying to fix Rose's basket – it had shifted down and was loose. Rose wasn't happy because it's new, so I found a tool and was trying to put it straight, but then I really needed to pee, so I went into the house to use the bathroom.'

'Do you remember anything strange before you entered the house, any cars that you didn't recognise, any people that you don't know?' asked Moreas, studying the boy's face intently.

'Erm, I don't know, uncle, I wasn't paying attention, but I don't think so.'

'And then what?'

'I went inside and peed, and after, when I was on the way out, I felt hungry so I looked for food in the kitchen. I knew there was lots left from lunch, and I took a paratha but only one, I promise,' said Danny, worried that he may get in trouble for stealing food.

'The food is not important, son,' the sub-lieutenant said. 'Did you hear anything when you were in the kitchen?'

'No,' said Danny with his eyes tightly shut, trying with all his might to remember. They lived in what was considered a safe neighbourhood and, being children, they were totally carefree. Worrying wasn't something they needed to do.

'There was music playing from someone's house.'

'Did you hear anybody talking, or cars going past? Anything Danny, think hard please,' Peter begged.

Victor had been calling both his wife and daughter for the last twenty minutes or so, but neither of them was answering. He had to break the news to Maria that her beloved Rose was missing, and it was his fault. The whole reason that he was at the house that day was to look after her, but he had fallen asleep. Victor had become too complacent with village life and never in his wildest dreams imagined anything like this could happen.

Danny was finishing his version of events when a male sergeant approached them holding a package wrapped in brown paper, about the size of a small house brick.

'We found this just inside the gates under a bush, does anyone know anything about it?'

The group looked at the package, then at each other. Next, they all turned to Danny, who shrugged.

'I've never seen that before,' he said, his voice a half-wail.

'Any information, address or label of any kind on it?' Roger asked.

'No.' The sergeant gave it a shake. 'It seems it is empty too.'

Peter looked at Moreas. 'That's strange, why would there be an empty parcel in my garden?'

'This is what we need to find out,' the sub-lieutenant said. 'Get it bagged please, sergeant, this needs to go to the lab ASAP, it's too much of a coincidence for this to just appear after what has happened.'

Peter looked down the street. A car was approaching; it was Maria and Carmen. He turned to Victor and motioned with his head in the direction of the oncoming vehicle.

'They're back,' Victor said, and with a heavy heart he made his way to greet them, wondering how to deliver the dreadful news about Rose.

Chapter Eleven
Somewhere in north Goa, 5:27 p.m.

Sunil pulled off the highway. In the back, Rose was still struggling, but by now she was running out of energy and short of breath with the huge disgusting hand still clamped across her face.

Rose was scared out of her wits; she wanted her dad. She saw a small knife in the footwell on the opposite side of the car and tried to focus on that so she wouldn't be consumed by the stench oozing from the man that was holding her so tightly. The car came to a halt on a dead-end road next to a coconut farm. There was not a house in sight.

'This will do,' Sunil said. He looked in the rear-view mirror at Maalik, who seemed to be enjoying his current task a little too much. Sunil could see the girl's eyes, wide and terrified, over the man's hand. He reached into the glovebox and retrieved one of the syringes that Rasheed had given him. 'This will give you a break,' he said to his colleague.

Maalik gave a chuckle, 'I'm happy like this.'

Sunil pointed the needle towards the sky, tapped it a few times and squeezed until the first drop of liquid spilled out.

'Are you ready? Hold her as still as you can, we don't need any complications now.'

Rose spotted the needle and emitted a muffled scream. As Sunil was opening the rear door of the car, she held her breath and bit down hard on one of the fat dirty fingers.

Maalik yelped, let go and Rose made a lunge for the knife. She had no idea what she was going to do with it but that didn't matter, because before she could touch it, she felt herself being yanked back into the grip of the larger of her abductors.

Now, with Maalik's firm hold on the girl, Sunil grabbed the top of her arm and thrust the needle into her. As the contents emptied into her arm, Rose's eyes flickered then closed and her head flopped back onto Maalik's chest. She was out for the count and would stay that way for the rest of the journey, Sunil hoped.

He had another dose, just in case; it was going to be a long drive and they needed Rose to be as quiet as possible if they were going to pass the many police checkpoints that lay ahead of them. Sunil opened the boot and picked up the sleeping girl, laid her head on a dirty old cushion that was inside and slammed it shut.

'Night night, baby,' he said as he got back into the driver's seat, started the car and headed for the NH66 towards Mumbai.

***

The journey back to the house had been a quiet one. Maria's eyes were shut; she was half asleep now. Carmen's attention focused on navigating around the many potholes in the road so as not to disturb her daughter. They had both turned their phones to silent before they entered the hospital, which is why Victor's attempts to contact them had been ignored.

Neither of them had even thought of checking, otherwise they would have seen the dozens of missed calls that he had made. The sun was setting, and as the car pulled round the corner on the final stretch of their journey, Carmen noticed a large crowd near Maria's house that included several police cars, so she slowed down.

'Maria, look, something is going on.'

Maria opened her eyes; she was still drowsy, her vision blurred. 'What's happening, mom?' She muttered, wearily. Carmen edged closer to the group of people and cars to see Victor walking towards them.

'I don't know, dear.'

The car pulled to a stop; Carmen felt panic rise when she realised that most of the crowd was outside Maria's house. Victor arrived at the car, closely followed by Peter, and as he opened Carmen's door, 'I am so sorry' was all he could manage.

When Peter reached the passenger side of the car, Maria, now fully aware of the commotion, was halfway out of the door.

'What is it, Vic?' Carmen asked.

She had already scanned the throng of people and not seen Rose, who ordinarily would have been by her father's or grandfather's side.

'Can one of you please tell us what is going on right now?' Carmen shouted.

Maria, a cold fist closing around her heart, could tell by the look on Peter's face and the absence of Rose that it was to do with her daughter.

'She's gone,' Victor croaked. It was the hardest thing he had ever had to tell his wife in all their years of marriage.

'Where is Rose?' Maria demanded of her father, her voice low, almost menacing.

'She disappeared about an hour ago. It's my fault, I fell asleep.' Victor covered his face with his hands.

Maria and Peter had moved around the car to join her parents. 'Daddy, don't joke with me please, where is my baby girl?'

Peter put his arm around her shoulder, but she shrugged it off. Maria's face was like thunder, and she was staring at her father as though she was going to kill him.

'Rose was out front with Danny; he went to the bathroom and by the time he came back she was gone, and nobody has seen her since.' Peter's voice tailed off.

'Where the hell were you, Vic?' shouted Carmen.

'I fell asleep on the couch,' he wailed.

'You idiot,' Maria screamed and ran towards the house. 'Rose!' she called out as she went. 'Come on darling, mommy's home!'

Her eyes were streaming, and she was running on adrenalin. Peter chased after her, but he had no idea what to do or say. Carmen was left staring at Victor, shaking her head. 'One job Vic, you had one job!' she said harshly as her voice broke.

'Who is in charge here?' Carmen shouted. She was on autopilot, wanting to take control of the situation.

'Roger Moreas is here.' Victor tried to redeem something of her respect for him. 'Come with me.'

Victor grabbed Carmen's hand and started off to find the sub-lieutenant. On the way, Carmen asked, 'why didn't you call us?' As she spoke, she realised she knew the answer to her question.

'I tried many times, my love, but you didn't answer.'

The closer they got to the house the louder Maria's cries for her daughter got. She was standing on the veranda, her eyes full of tears. Her hair was a mess, and she was leaning with both hands on the railings, shouting her daughter's name with all her might.

'Rose, that is enough, naughty girl! Come to mommy NOW!'

'How could you let this happen?' Carmen said to her husband.

'I don't know...,' he started but Carmen rounded on him, hissing.

'You have no fucking idea what we have been through today! Maria is dying…'

At that moment Roger Moreas greeted her.

'Carmen, let me fill you in on what has happened and what we are doing.'

Carmen noticed her daughter was now prone on the veranda. Peter was on his knees beside her shouting for someone to call for an ambulance. Moreas and Carmen ran to join them, Victor following. Moreas was first there.

'Get an ambulance here, right now!' he shouted. His voice was so loud that he got the attention of everybody in the vicinity. Immediately one or two officers reached for their radios. Moreas let out a high-pitched whistle.

'Get over here guys,' he shouted, and some officers rushed to the bottom of the stairs.

'You two, get everybody who is not family out of the garden and onto the street.'

He pointed at two female officers, who immediately started ushering the ever-growing crowd out through the gates.

'You two,' Roger pointed at two male officers this time, 'block the street at both ends, don't let any vehicles in or out, and for God's sake make sure the ambulance has a clear run through to the house.'

The sergeant, a trained paramedic, had arrived and was assessing Maria, who was lying on her back, her head resting on Peter's folded suit jacket.

Roger watched as the situation unfolded, hoping for no more terrible news that day. He could already hear the ambulance's siren.

'Can you tell me if Maria has any underlying medical conditions, or if is she on any medication?' The sergeant asked. 'She has a very weak pulse, which is worrying.'

Victor looked at Carmen for an answer. Carmen stood up straight and took a deep breath.

'She has a brain tumour and is taking oxycodone for the pain.' Carmen pulled the bottle from her trouser pocket. The sergeant read the label.

'That would explain it then,' he said. 'I think that she has just fainted from the stress, but she will need to go straight to the hospital, she is extremely weak.'

The ambulance arrived and the medics quickly pulled the trolley out of the back. Peter and Victor were staring at Carmen open-mouthed.

'What do you mean, she has a *brain tumour*?' Peter asked. It was just too much to take in.

'Victor,' Roger called, as the two medics climbed the stairs to the veranda. Victor, who was on his knees, got up and turned to his old friend.

'You, Carmen and Peter, follow Maria to the hospital, one of my men will take you. I'll deal with everything here, there is nothing more you can do now anyway. It seems like you all have a lot to discuss. If I hear anything, I will call you straight away, I promise.'

The ambulance doors were closed, with a now-stabilised Maria inside; the trio got into the police jeep. They sat in silence, none of them able to speak. Peter had his head in his hands and Victor was in a state of shock, his eyes red and his skin grey.

Carmen, who was sitting next to Victor, took his hand and patted it. 'They will find her,' was all she said to him as the jeep sped off towards the hospital.

Back at the house, Moreas and his team were busy organising what their next move was to be. The crowd was still growing as more police arrived. They hadn't heard anything from the roadblocks.

'What do you think, boss?' the sergeant asked Moreas.

'Doesn't look good, I can't believe that nobody saw anything, it must have happened so fast,' Moreas said.

'Almost like it was planned,' the sergeant replied. Roger stared at his colleague for a few seconds, deep in his own thoughts.

'This package that was found by the gates. The fact that the gates were open, and Rose's bicycle was lying on its side definitely suggests foul play, and if this was an organised operation then we have a very brief period of time in which to find her before she disappears forever.'

The sergeant nodded in agreement.

'That package could be the key to all of this,' said Roger confidently. He had been in this game for a long time and his hunches were usually right.

'I'll get it over to the lab right away, we need to get Fernandez to look at it,' the sergeant said.

'Yes,' Roger agreed. 'Fingerprints, DNA, the full works, and tell him that I said to drop whatever he is doing. I promised I would get this girl back to her family and that's what I am going to do.'

The sergeant ran to his jeep, leaving Moreas alone on the veranda. 'Where are you Rose?' he asked, staring into the street. In his experience, these situations rarely ended well. If he found the people involved – he was quite certain now that they were dealing with a kidnapping – every one of them would feel the full force of his lathi, and then some. He made his way downstairs to organise the officers that had just arrived. It was no use them all being here, they needed to get out searching for her.

'Everybody over here,' he bellowed, 'let's find this little girl and bring her home.'

***

Maalik and Sunil pulled off Highway 66 to pick up cigarettes and a snack. They had made good time. It was the holiday season so there wasn't much traffic. Had it been a normal working day, they wouldn't have got anywhere near as far as they had. Maalik got out of the car.

'You want anything else, boss?'

'No,' Sunil said, 'just get on with it.'

Maalik walked quickly to the store.

Sunil waited with the engine running and the AC on full. He had started to feel bad about what he had done, but to hell with that, he thought. He was going to get a nice payout for this, if it all went to plan.

Sunil's phone rang, making him jump. He grabbed it from the dashboard and flipped it open. It was Rasheed.

'Well?'

'It's done, we are on our way.'

Maalik returned to the car with water, cigarettes and samosas. There was a bottle wedged in his jeans pocket. Seeing Sunil was on the phone, he looked concerned.

'Where are you?' Rasheed barked.

'We just crossed the Colvale-Dhargal bridge,' Sunil offered.

'Perfect. The police have set up a checkpoint by Mapusa.'

'We are well past it then,' Sunil reassured his boss.

Maalik pulled a samosa from the bag, leaned back in his seat, and started to eat.

'Don't be too complacent, Sunil,' Rasheed warned. 'You may encounter one or two more on the way, so stay alert. I don't know who the girl's family is, we didn't have time to check them out, but they have friends in the right places. The police are throwing everything at this. I will call every couple of hours for updates.' The line went dead.

Sunil put the car into gear and rejoined the highway.

'All good?' asked Maalik, with a mouthful of samosa.

'Yes, we were too quick for them,' Sunil boasted, 'now pass me one of those before you eat them all, you greedy pig.'

Moreas's men had missed them by around five minutes. Rose's chances of being found were decreasing by the hour as she slept in the boot of the car, which, with every revolution of its wheels, took her further and further from home.

Chapter Twelve
Manipal Hospital, 6:30 p.m., 29th December

Maria felt as though she was looking through a fog. She realised that she was back in the same bed less than two hours after leaving the hospital. Through her half-opened eyes, she could see Carmen, Peter and Victor in the room with her. Maria had been hooked up to machines monitoring her blood pressure and heart rate, along with a saline drip. She hadn't eaten all day and, although she had come round, her eyes were still closed.

The atmosphere in the room was tense. There were so many questions her husband and father wanted to ask, but Carmen had told them to wait for Doctor Vaidya, who was busy with another patient.

Peter was pacing up and down the room, constantly checking his phone. Carmen sat in a chair next to Maria's bed, holding her hand and talking softly to her. Victor was on a call trying desperately to find out if anyone in the criminal underworld had any information on a kidnapping. Rose had disappeared on his watch and the guilt was eating him up.

Doctor Vaidya opened the door and walked over to Maria's bed; all eyes were on him. He checked Maria's notes and the monitors and, raising his hands, asked, 'what the bloody hell is going on here?'

He glared at the trio, waiting for answers.

Carmen decided that she should be the one to do the talking.

'Rose, Maria's eight-,' Carmen corrected herself, 'nine-year-old daughter is missing. It happened before we got home. It may be an abduction, but we aren't sure yet.'

The news clearly knocked the doctor for six; that this had happened at all to Maria was too awful, let alone today.

'The police are out in full force looking for her and everyone that we know is helping,' added Victor. Carmen gave her husband a cool stare, forcing him to swivel his gaze to the floor. He knew she held him to blame. Arun Vaidya filled the men in on what Carmen already knew.

They were both utterly devastated. Peter was on the other side of Maria's bed, holding her hand. He started to pray.

'She is not to leave this hospital, not for any reason,' the doctor said sternly. 'I have no idea how this is going to affect her, she was low enough as it was but with this tragic turn of events ...' He shook his head, 'Maria will need to be looked after by my team 24/7 until she passes.'

As the family heard the word 'passes', which sounded so final, the inescapable reality hit home. They were going to lose Maria, and none of them was prepared for that.

'You can all visit at any time of the day or night, OK?' the doctor softened his tone, looking at each of them until they nodded silently, indicating that they had understood. 'I am going home soon but will be back in the morning. Anything you need just pop out to the nurse's station. Maria is stable now, I'm quite sure that she just fainted from fatigue, and the stress of what happened today.'

Victor's phone rang and he pounced on it, but it was only somebody returning his call.

'This is going to be a long night for you,' the doctor turned to Peter and then Victor, who nodded. 'You don't all need to be here now, Maria will sleep until the morning, I've told the nurse to give her a sedative. What she needs most now is rest.'

'You two,' Carmen barked, 'get out there and find my granddaughter.' She was mad, so damn mad at them. Two grown men in the house and Rose disappears from the front garden. How could they be so stupid? She was barely holding herself back from losing it completely. But the time to dish out the telling off that they had coming to them was not now, not today.

Peter kissed Maria on the head, thanked the doctor and left the room. Victor went to kiss Carmen but stopped, lips puckered, when he saw the look in her eyes.

'Call me straight away if you hear anything,' she said to her husband, not waiting for an answer, she turned back to her daughter. Victor nodded to the doctor and joined Peter. They didn't talk on the journey back to the house.

They found Roger Moreas shouting into his phone at someone. The police had set up a temporary base in the garden; most of them had left to search further afield. A few neighbours were milling around wanting to do anything they could to help. Danny Lobo was sitting on his bicycle at the side of the house. He had moved Rose's bike there too after the police had finished with it, not wanting it to get damaged.

The boy had been in a daze since it happened; if only he hadn't stopped to eat, would his best friend be sitting next to him right now? He felt the full weight of blame on his young shoulders.

Victor and Peter joined Sub-Lieutenant Moreas, as he finished his call.

'Anything?' Victor asked.

'Not yet, my friend, we have checkpoints on all major roads, and nothing is getting through without being searched. Some of our officers are scouring the surrounding area just in case she wandered off and fell over or into something, somewhere; it's a long shot, but you never know. I've got every man and woman that I can spare out tonight; if Rose is in Goa, we will find her.' Roger was clearly approaching the task with military precision.

'How is your wife, Peter?' he asked.

'She's stable. The doctor is keeping her at the hospital, thank you.'

Peter felt as though he was in some sort of nightmare.

'Best place for her at the moment,' said Roger.

'Right,' said Victor, 'what can we do?' He couldn't just stand around waiting for something to happen.

***

In Panjim, Jack was sitting alone outside a small bar. His chaperone, whose name he still didn't know, had abruptly ridden off ten minutes previously, without a word. That could only mean one thing, Jack thought, as he swigged from his bottle of Kingfisher beer.

The bar was situated on the main road, opposite the Mandovi river. Jack loved the view and would often come here to think. His phone, which was on the table, started vibrating. He grabbed it and flipped it open.

'Hello.'

'We have her.' It was Rasheed.

'So that's it then, this is over?' Jack asked.

'Yes, we are even now, Jack. But you know what will happen if you tell anybody, don't you?'

'Yes,' Jack replied, reaching for the beer and draining it.

'And don't come to my place any more, you are not welcome there.' Rasheed was referring to his illegal gambling den, which was situated less than a mile from where Jack was sitting.

'No,' he replied, 'don't worry, you won't be seeing me again.'

Rasheed hung up. He had written off six hundred thousand rupees worth of debt, which, given the circumstances, was a shrewd move. He knew that Jack wasn't about to lay his hands on what he owed any time soon, and what he was being paid would more than cover the loss.

Rasheed leaned back in his chair, stretched his arms above his head and smiled. He enjoyed making money and didn't care where it came from. He was a heartless bastard and didn't give a shit about anyone or anything except himself.

Jack called for another beer. He was far from celebrating but would be able to sleep with both eyes shut tonight. What he had done was about as low as any man could stoop, although the enormity of it hadn't really hit him yet. The only emotion he felt as his fresh beer arrived, was relief.

He needed to go to his brother's house. There he would play the outraged and devastated uncle. Jack knew that the moment he saw their faces, the repercussions of his actions would hit home. If he didn't make an appearance, however, it would look suspicious. It was clear that by now he would have heard what had happened, and he would be expected to offer his help, whether it was needed or not. Jack decided to go tomorrow – for now, he just wanted to enjoy the moment.

***

The hospital room was quiet, except for the beeping of the heart monitor and occasional staff member checking up on them. Carmen had not left the chair beside Maria's bed, not even to stretch her legs. The cup of tea that the nurse brought her an hour earlier had been left to go cold.

Maria was still, not making even the slightest noise, her breathing so shallow that her chest barely moved. Carmen was grateful for the machines surrounding the bed. They were the only indication that her daughter was still alive. She felt helpless, her heart was broken but her mind, unlike her still exterior, was whirring. How could she cope with this all at once? She needed to be strong, she had a daughter to take care of and a granddaughter to find. Carmen jumped as a ringing started up in her handbag. It was her phone; she had finally turned the volume up when her husband left the hospital and knew she would be the first to hear if there was any news. Anxiously she scrabbled around in her bag not wanting to miss the call.

'Carmen, it's me Juanita, Danny's mom,' came the voice on the other end of the line.

Carmen's heart sank, not because she didn't like Juanita – the Lobo family were close friends and good neighbours who would do anything to help – but she had really hoped it was Vic with news on Rose.

'Hi Juanita,' Carmen replied softly. She was feeling completely drained by now and finding it hard to stay awake.

'Oh God, we are all praying for Maria and Rose,' Juanita gushed. 'I can't believe this is happening. How is Maria?'

'She's ok, sleeping now. I just don't know what to do.' Carmen's voice broke.

'OK,' Juanita said authoritatively. 'Don't you worry about a thing. Victor and Peter are out searching – there are so many people involved, I tell you. The whole neighbourhood is lit up with torches and by the grace of our Lord Jesus Christ, Rose will be found. I will look after Maria's place, and I assume that you will not leave her side, so I'll be there in the morning with a hot meal for you both.'

'Thanks, Juanita. Can you make sure the boys eat something too, there is food in the house, I think,' replied Carmen. 'How is Danny?'

'Ah, the poor boy,' Juanita said. 'He has been in his room since you left and hasn't stopped crying. He is in so much pain, he keeps saying it's his fault. I tell him no it's not, but he won't listen to me. Oh, Carmen, there is so much pain in this village right now.'

Juanita broke off, trying to compose herself. Carmen's eyes were filling with tears, and her throat ached from holding them back. Juanita was right, there was far too much pain to cope with.

Just then, Maria stirred. Carmen spun her head round quickly, but her daughter was still sound asleep and the constant reassuring beep from her heart monitor continued.

'Give Danny a kiss from me will you and tell him that I said it has nothing to do with him, OK? Nothing at all! I'll see you in the morning. Oh, and Juanita,' Carmen added.

'Yes?'

'Thanks for everything. I can't do this on my own, I really can't.'

'No problem, if there is anything you need just let me know.'

Carmen cut the call. Her aching throat was dry, and she desperately needed the bathroom. She decided it would be OK to leave her daughter's side, just for five minutes. She would stretch her legs, get a drink, use the bathroom and be back before Maria could miss her. She raised herself from the chair with a groan and glanced at Maria, who looked peaceful. Carmen laid her hands on the hospital blanket over her daughter's leg, said a prayer and left the room.

***

At the Lobo household, Juanita knocked gently on Danny's bedroom door; the boy was still sobbing, although not as loudly as earlier.

'Baby, it's mommy,' she said, letting herself in. Danny was laying on his stomach with his head buried in the pillow. He raised himself up and manoeuvred into a sitting position with his legs hanging over the edge of the bed. His mother joined him, putting her arm around his shoulders.

'Where is she, mom?' Danny asked as he wiped the tears from his face. He had been crying so much that his pillow was soaked, and his eyes were red and puffy.

'I don't know, son,' his mother replied. There was no news from outside, which was still buzzing with activity. Juanita had stepped out for a minute to see if she could find Michael, her husband; he was scouring the neighbourhood with Victor and Peter.

There were a couple of police officers manning the operations control, which was just a desk that they had set up in the Rosarios' front garden. It wasn't much but it was serving as a central point for people who had any information. There were also five or six neighbours standing at the small family chapel on the left side of the garden. They had lit candles and were praying for Rose's safe return.

'I spoke to Aunty Carmen, and she said to tell you that this isn't your fault,' Juanita assured Danny, as she kissed him on the forehead. Danny just looked at her blankly; he didn't believe it, of course.

'What happened to Aunty Maria, is she sick?' he asked. His voice was thick and his nose blocked, making him sound strangely muffled.

'She had to go to hospital and is feeling better, but she will stay there for a while.'

Juanita would not tell her son any more for the moment, he'd had enough bad news already.

'Everybody in the village is out looking for her, Danny, I'm sure it won't be long before Rose turns up with some crazy story of an adventure that she has been on.' Juanita gave a forced laugh. She knew it sounded stupid, but she would say or do anything to keep Danny from such misery.

Danny and Rose had been friends since before they could walk. They had grown up together and were virtually inseparable. At weekends and during the holidays, if you came across one of them you could guarantee that the other was not far away.

'I hope so,' said Danny, staring at the wall that had a montage of photographs of the pair. The one hanging in Rose's bedroom was identical; they had made them together, earlier in the year.

'Try to get some sleep, son,' said Juanita. Every now and again his chest would rise with a sob. She stood up, ruffled his hair and went out to the kitchen to make some coffee. This was going to be a long night and she needed the caffeine.

Chapter Thirteen
Bambolim Village, 29th December

Peter and Victor were joined by Juanita's husband Michael and were searching a dimly lit street close to the house. There were nearly seventy men, women and teenagers out that night, all searching for the missing girl. Roger Moreas had organised them into groups of threes or fours and sent them on different routes so that they could cover the area quickly and efficiently. Everybody had torches, some even had two – blackouts were frequent in Goa and people were always prepared.

As he walked, Peter was parting bushes with the long stick he carried; each time he did so he held his breath until he saw that the undergrowth did not contain the broken body of his daughter.

On the other side of the road Victor and Michael were doing the same and every few seconds a cry of 'Rose!' would emanate from one or other of them.

The girl was nowhere to be seen. Peter had just found out that his beloved wife had only weeks to live, but for now, he was focused on looking for his only child whom he loved more than life itself.

Suddenly, a stray dog ran across his path, obviously spooked by all the noise; on any other night, this part of town would have been almost eerily quiet. Peter jumped, shone the torch at the offending dog, swore under his breath and continued.

On the other side of the road there were cars and a few houses. Michael dropped to his knees to look under each and every vehicle while Victor shone his torch into gardens. He was desperate. If only he could find her then maybe, just maybe, he could forgive himself.

'Why didn't you tell us about Maria?' Michael asked Victor as he jumped up from checking underneath the last vehicle on the street. It was an old food delivery truck. He had also tried the vehicle's back doors, but they were locked.

'We didn't know, Michael. Peter and I only found out today ourselves. Apparently Carmen knew, and they were going to tell us after they returned from the hospital today. Oh God …,' Victor's voice was tortured. 'Maria doesn't have long, and I can't spend what precious little time that we have left with her because I'm out here looking for the granddaughter that *I* lost.'

Victor had worked himself into a frenzy thinking about what had happened and with a strangled sob, kicked a pile of garbage.

'Stupid old bastard,' he shouted. 'It's all my fault,' he added, as he lowered himself onto the wall that was just behind him.

Victor dropped his head into his hands, repeating the word 'stupid' over and over again.

Peter, hearing the commotion, came over to join them. He knew it wasn't Vic's fault; their village was a safe one and nothing like this had ever happened there before. This was one of the few places left where you could still leave your kids outside and not worry about them. Until today.

'Vic,' said Peter as he sat next to him. 'Stop torturing yourself and get your shit together. Maria needs us to be strong and we have a lot of searching to do so come on, snap out of it. Whoever would have imagined that a man couldn't take a nap without his granddaughter being abducted? Nobody! All of us have done just the same. You are not to blame!'

Victor had always been a tower of strength and Peter admired him. But he looked old and frail all of a sudden and his father-in-law's decline, before Peter's very eyes, added another notch to the panic he felt.

***

It was nearly eleven p.m. and the car containing Rose was now well on its way to Mumbai. Sunil received a text message with the location of a truck that had been left for them; it was in a car park just off the highway, the keys hidden on the rear tyre. Vikram was quite adamant that the child should arrive in one piece, so he had organised this changeover vehicle. It was safer too, just in case someone was trailing them from Goa. Driving slowly through the car park, Maalik spotted the vehicle and they pulled over beside it. After a minute or two, to make sure they were not being watched, Sunil got out and grabbed the keys. He unlocked the driver's door, hopped in and started it up. Good, he thought, as he noticed the tank was full. He jumped out and met Maalik at the back of the truck. They grabbed the handle of one door each and opened them to reveal a couple of old mattresses and some cushions on the floor.

'At least you'll be comfortable,' Sunil announced.

'What the fuck?' replied a shocked Maalik.

'Well, one of us needs to look after her and I'm driving, so...'

'Bastard!'

Sunil laughed – he was glad to get some peace and quiet, away from his colleague's noisy eating.

'Get her out then,' he barked, 'we don't have time to hang around.'

Maalik popped the trunk and tucked both hands underneath the girl. 'Motherfucker,' he shouted and leapt back.

'What is it?'

'She's pissed herself,' said Maalik, who was now strongly regretting being involved in this.

'It's not her fault, she's out of it! Stop complaining and hurry up, we need to leave.'

Maalik sneered at Sunil, reached into the car again and picked Rose out of the trunk, holding his breath. Turning his face to the side, he climbed the two steps into the back of the van and laid the sleeping girl on one of the mattresses.

'You ready?' asked Sunil as he threw one full and one empty water bottle into the back.

'What's this for?' asked Maalik holding up the empty bottle.

'Well, we don't want both of you pissing yourselves in there do we?' chuckled Sunil, 'and don't you fucking touch her, the big boss in Mumbai's orders, so keep your dirty hands to yourself. If you need me or she wakes up call my cell phone.'

Sunil secured the doors and climbed back into the cab. They had around ten to twelve hours of driving ahead, depending on the traffic. Maalik slumped onto the free mattress and pulled out the half bottle of whisky he had stashed in his pocket. At least he could get some rest, he thought.

***

It was still dark in the village; the first glimmers of daylight would not illuminate the sky for at least another hour. Juanita and a couple of neighbours worked tirelessly through the night, making the search parties and police officers refreshments to keep them going. It had been a long twelve hours since the little girl disappeared and apart from a few false alarms, the search had been fruitless. Peter, Michael and Victor had walked miles together. They decided to return to the house and see what their next move should be.

The trio were standing in the front garden waiting for Sub-Lieutenant Moreas to return from the police station. Juanita approached them with a tray full of hot, sweet tea. They all gladly took a cup; tiredness had set in, and they needed the caffeine and sugar. Taking a seat on the front steps, Victor took a sip and let out a sigh. 'What are we going to do now?' he asked.

Peter sat next to him. 'We keep looking until we find her, Vic, that's what we do.'

Michael joined them, tea in hand, taking a seat one step below them.

Ten minutes later, a patrol jeep containing Roger Moreas arrived, and the weary men walked over to join him by the front gates.

'Anything?' asked Peter.

'No, I'm afraid not, my forensics guy lifted a couple of partial fingerprints from the parcel that was found but it may not be enough to find a match. The roadblocks haven't turned up anything yet and I can't keep them for much longer because of the disruption they are starting to cause.'

'What?' exclaimed the trio in unison.

'I know, I'd keep them there for another week if it was up to me, but my superiors have given me a deadline of lunchtime. Rose is my number one priority; the sad fact is she isn't theirs, I'm afraid. Anyway, where was I? Oh yes, my officers have searched every abandoned building in the local and surrounding areas, we have questioned all the neighbours, and nobody has seen a thing. It's like she vanished into thin air. The only lead we have is the package, and we don't even know if it has any connection to this ... case.'

Victor and Peter looked shocked to hear Rose being referred to as a 'case', but truth be told, that's what she was. With the emotion taken out, Rose was just another missing person case.

'I'm going to be straight here.' Moreas glanced from Peter to Victor and then back again to Peter, 'it's not looking good. If she had wandered off, we would have found her by now – at the last count, there were seventy-two civilians and officers out looking in every direction. The later it gets the more likely it is to have been an abduction and that's how I'm going to be treating it from now on. The thing is, if she was taken and they had headed for the state border straight away, we probably would have missed them. And if that is the case, she will be long gone by now. Our only hope is that we get something from forensics or, dare I say it, Rose gets a chance to escape somehow.'

Peter looked at Victor. The older man had his head bowed and his eyes closed.

'What's our next move?' Victor asked, his eyes still tight shut as a solitary tear squeezed out from under his eyelid and tracked down his cheek.

'I have as many officers as I can spare working on this. We will pursue every lead, no matter how small, but I think that we can wrap it up here, for now. I have my feelers out in the underworld, which I am sure you do too, Vic. If any criminal has heard a whisper of this I *WILL* find out.'

Victor nodded in agreement, swiping the tear from his cheek and looking at Moreas.

'You should go to the hospital and then get some rest,' the sub-lieutenant suggested. 'The moment I hear of anything I will be straight on the phone to you. Give Maria my best wishes.'

Moreas gave a small nod, almost a bow, and marched over to the two officers hovering around the table that they had set up in the garden.

'Right, let's get this back to the station and resume our enquiries from there.'

Peter had followed the sub-lieutenant.

'Roger, what do you think our chances are of finding her? And please tell me the truth.' Peter looked terrible. The bags under his eyes had almost doubled since yesterday, he was dirty from searching every place that he could crawl in or under and his shirt was hanging outside of his pants.

'Honestly,' Moreas put his hand on Peter's arm and shook his head slowly, 'not good, these things are very time-sensitive, and the more time goes by, the less chance we have of finding her – I'm sorry, Peter. But we must remain positive. I promised I will find her, and I will do everything in my power to do just that. Don't give up hope, never give up hope – now, please, get yourself to the hospital.'

Peter took both of the sub-lieutenant's hands in his and looked him in the eyes. 'Thanks, Roger, you're a good friend.'

'I'll speak to you soon Peter; if not tomorrow, then Friday. You and Vic can come to the station to see what we have on this mysterious package.'

Peter rejoined his father-in-law, Michael and Juanita, who herself was having a well-earned rest.

Chapter Fourteen
Nariman Point, Mumbai 7:20 a.m., 30th December

Detectives Tendulkar and Chandekar had just started their shift when they were told by their superior officer that the body of a foreigner had been found in the water. They were to get over to Marine Drive straight away. It was only a few minutes' walk, and they were there before they had finished their coffee. Six uniformed officers were already on the scene, joined by a growing crowd of people. The pair pushed their way through the onlookers and stepped onto the sea wall. Chandekar jumped down onto the wave breaker stones while Detective Tendulkar stayed put. He wasn't a great swimmer and that was close enough to the sea for him. The officers first on scene were waiting for forensics to arrive before they could remove the body.

'Anything to go on?' asked Chandekar, pulling out a dog-eared notebook.

'Not much, only a wallet and what looks like a wedding ring in his pocket,' replied one of the officers that had dragged the corpse out of the water. Detective Chandekar carefully negotiated the stones to take a closer look. Tendulkar was now sitting on the wall, paying close attention to a couple of pretty girls in the crowd. Chandekar looked the body over and scribbled: *White male, mid to late thirties, Western clothes, shoulder-length curly blonde hair, obvious wounds -ve. In the water 24? 48?* He put on gloves and took the wallet from the officer then climbed back up to join his partner.

'What you got?' asked Tendulkar.

'Same old shit, brother, just another hippie tourist, got drunk or high, thought he could walk on water and drowned.'

'Open and shut case then?'

'Probably, there's no ID in the wallet, just a few thousand rupees; let's see what the post-mortem shows up. Other than that, yes, just another stupid foreigner,' detective Chandekar said.

He had seen a few of these kinds of deaths in his ten years as a detective, a body with no way to trace the family.

'Come on then, I need some breakfast, man, I'm starving' Tendulkar said.

They left the scene and the body of Derek Jacoby behind them.

Chapter Fifteen
Patansai, Maharashtra, 6:45 a.m.,
31st December

Sunil was aching from being stuck behind the steering wheel for over thirteen hours. He was tired and desperately needed a pick-me-up. They had stopped only once to fill the truck with fuel, grabbing the last two lukewarm cans of energy drinks from a nearby store.

He was trying hard to not fall asleep; he'd already had a couple of close calls but had woken just in time, yanking the wheel back in line. Suddenly, just above the roar of the engine, Sunil heard banging. At first, he put it down to the bad roads, but after a minute it grew louder, more insistent.

He dialled Maalik's number on speaker. He hadn't heard from him in a few hours.

'I hope that fool hasn't fallen asleep,' he muttered. The phone went to voicemail. Sunil glanced towards the back of the van. The banging had not stopped, and he realised that it must be one of them in the back hitting the truck's side wall.

Again, he dialled Maalik's number, again no answer. 'Wake up, you useless fuck!' he shouted.

In the distance, as he approached the Amba river bridge, he could see some floodlights; the sun had just started to rise, but he could still make out the unusual brightness up ahead. Cursing, he redialled Maalik's number. Events not so long ago in Mumbai meant that there were now checkpoints set up on the main routes in and out of the city. 'Fuck!' he screamed as his call was forwarded to voicemail once again.

It was too late to stop and check what was going on in the back. That would surely arouse suspicion and the officers would be all over them in less than a minute. Sunil clenched his teeth and decided that his only option was to carry on and hope for the best.

In the rear, Rose was awake. It was dark but not pitch black; Maalik had switched on a dim light that was attached to the roof of the truck.

Rose was disoriented – tired, hungry and scared out of her mind, her jeans still damp from wetting herself earlier. Confused, she had got up and fallen straight over. Her hands were bound in front so she couldn't break her fall; luckily she was beside the dirty mattress and landed face down on it.

Her head hurt and she had no idea where she was. She remembered being grabbed and dragged into a car but after that, nothing. Rose, knowing that she needed to escape, got up and toppled over again. Realising that she must be in a moving vehicle she shuffled her way to what seemed to be the side wall.

Resting herself against it, Rose started banging with her hands as best she could. It hurt but she didn't care; she missed her parents and just wanted to get back home.

Her mouth was gagged so no matter how hard she tried to scream, all she could manage was a muffled gargle. Just yesterday she was with her best friend in the garden playing, and now... At the thought of Danny and home, she started to cry, still banging with her fists and even her head now with all her might. Rose heard a phone ringing but didn't want to move to find it for fear of falling and hurting herself further.

She remembered the dirty stinking hands over her face. The thought of that, and the bandana that was tied tightly around her mouth, biting into her cheeks, made her want to vomit. 'Mom,' she tried to cry out; she was losing strength and the only thing that propelled her was the thought of getting home.

Bored, Maalik had finished the whisky and with the alcohol and the motion of the journey, had quickly fallen asleep. In the cab, Sunil, who by now was panicking, had noticed that the banging had become weaker, although it hadn't stopped.

That buffoon Maalik still hadn't answered his phone. Which meant his worst nightmare must have come true – the kid must have woken up while that fat, useless pig had dozed off. The truck was less than two hundred metres from the checkpoint. Sunil redialled Maalik's number constantly, with no answer. He wracked his brain and decided there was only one thing he could do. Straightening his back and cricking his neck, Sunil braced himself for trouble.

Rose was running out of energy. She was weak from the sedative and the tears streaming down her face were the only thing keeping her mouth from completely drying out.

Sunil, playing the only card he had left, slammed the brakes on hard. The truck screeched to a halt five metres from the police officer that was standing in the middle of the road with his hand up motioning for him to pull over. In the rear, Rose was flung onto her side, again saved by the mattress.

Maalik, on the other hand, had rolled off his mattress and crashed face-first into the front wall of the truck, just as Sunil had hoped. Maalik woke up. He was dazed but awake, at last.

The officer held his finger in the air and spun it around; Sunil wound down the cab window.

'ID,' said the officer.

'Hang on,' replied Sunil, as he scrambled to open the glove compartment. He found his fake ID and vehicle documents and handed them to the policeman who, as he started to examine them, heard a faint banging sound.

Rose was lying on the mattress with her back against the side wall. She heard voices and knew that it was now or never. She was becoming drowsy again; her will to carry on was ebbing away but she managed to raise her arms and attack the side of the truck with her elbow, hitting it as hard as she could. The noise was barely audible, but anything would do now. There must be somebody outside that may just hear her.

Turning his attention to Sunil again, the officer's ears had pricked up to the three or four bangs that seemed to be coming from the back.

'You hear that?' he asked.

'Hear what?' Sunil felt his mouth go dry.

'What's in the back?'

'Says food on my sheet here.' Sunil tried to sound nonchalant but his heart was racing. He hoped his stunt had paid off and that idiot in the back would finally stop the girl.

The officer studied Sunil as he heard one fainter knock. 'Is there anyone in the back of the truck, sir?'

'Of course not, you know the way they stack the goods in these vehicles nowadays, it's probably all tipped over, still falling down as we speak. Not my business though, I'm just the driver.'

In the back of the truck, Maalik had come to his senses and could just make out Rose, a metre or so away from him. He heard voices and immediately deduced that they were at a checkpoint.

'Fuck,' he whispered and got up as quietly as he could. Rose managed one more bang on the side before Maalik grabbed her, threw her down on the mattress and lay on top of her, Rose's face was pushed into the mattress and her arms pinned under her. There were no more chances left.

'Get out and open the back up,' the officer ordered.

'Come on, boss, you're going to make me late, it's just all the shit falling over in there, you see the way I stopped, the brakes are playing up and I wanted to make sure I didn't hit you – here, take this and let me get on my way.' Sunil pulled a five-hundred-rupee note from his shirt top pocket. 'My boss always makes me carry something to avoid any hold-ups.'

The policeman looked at the money, looked at Sunil and then back at the money again.

'Open up,' he repeated.

Maalik could not make out what was being said but he knew that the longer they were stationary the more likely it was that something was wrong. He was crushing the girl but didn't dare move, just in case it allowed her to make any more noise.

'Listen, officer, I'm late as it is and I'm going to get my ass fired if you make me open the back and all that shit falls out. Besides, who's going to put it back in? Not you, I'm sure!' The officer looked at the money again, then Sunil and deciding that he just couldn't be bothered with the hassle, snatched it from the driver's hand and waved to his colleague to let the truck through.

Sunil grabbed his documents, gave the policeman a salute and put his foot down.

Damn, that was close, he thought, sweat running down his back. Feeling the truck begin to move, Maalik let out a sigh of relief and rolled off the girl, hoping that she was still alive. He was a heavy guy and had been on top of her for several minutes. He shook her by the shoulder and Rose sucked in a lungful of air.

She had been so close, her energy depleted, all she could think of was her family. She heard the phone ringing again and after twenty or so seconds, the man in the back with her said, 'you need to pull over and bring the other needle, that was far too close for comfort.'

Sunil found a secluded side road a couple of miles from the checkpoint, pulled to a slow stop this time and got out to check the situation in the back.

He opened the doors and Maalik jumped out. 'Bastard,' he screamed and shoved Sunil. 'You could have killed me.' Maalik was just as angry with himself as he was with the driver.

'Well, if you weren't asleep and had actually answered your fucking phone, none of this would have happened. Besides, if it weren't for me, we would be on our way to a long prison sentence by now.'

Maalik stormed off to take a piss behind a tree, leaving Sunil to retrieve the other sedative injection.

The doors were wide open, and the kidnappers were busy. Rose had her opportunity to escape at last, but now she didn't even have the energy to get up and if she did, she would not get more than a few feet.

Defeated, she rolled onto her side and shut her eyes. Even her tears had dried up now.

Sunil, syringe in hand, hopped into the back and jabbed the needle through her shirt into her arm. This time she didn't struggle.

Rose felt the needle enter her skin. She just let it happen; in fact, she was glad to fall back to sleep.

With the girl out cold and everything back on track, Sunil rejoined the highway. He was to find somewhere inconspicuous in the city to wait until he received details of the location for the handover.

Rose's heart sank as she felt herself drift off, but the pain had gone. As she lay there she mouthed the words 'I love you mom,' then she passed out.

Chapter Sixteen
Manipal Hospital, Goa, 9:12 a.m., 31st December

Victor made the journey to the hospital alone. Peter was at home, still in a state of shock, sitting silently on the sofa and staring at the wall, rocking slightly, his hands clasped in front of him.

Victor would stay with his daughter and relieve his wife so she could get some rest. As he approached Maria's room, Juanita was just leaving with some empty bowls in her hands.

'How is she?' Victor asked.

'She's awake and managed to eat something. She's tired but seems to be holding her own, all things considered.' The woman smiled kindly at Victor.

'Thanks for looking after her,' Victor smiled in appreciation, 'you have been a true friend to us.'

'My pleasure, any news on Rose?' Juanita asked hopefully, her bloodshot eyes barely open.

'No, nothing yet. You should get some rest, you look worn out,' said Victor, squeezing his eyes shut to hold back his tears.

'I'm going home now; I need to make sure Danny is OK.'

Victor nodded. He took in a deep breath, letting it out as he opened the door to Maria's room.

He saw that Maria was sitting upright on the bed, with Carmen standing over her. As he entered, they both looked at him with naked hope in their eyes.

Victor shook his head woefully.

'No sign of her yet,' he said as he leant over Maria and kissed her shallow cheek; she was losing weight fast.

He hesitantly approached his wife. What kind of reception would he get? Carmen looked at him and, seeing the sadness in his eyes, wrapped her arms tightly around him.

'I'm sorry,' Victor said, close to tears.

'Pull yourself together,' replied his wife.

He sat down and spent the next half an hour filling Maria and Carmen in on what had happened since he had been away.

Maria looked bereft and it broke Victor's heart to know that there was nothing that he could do for his girl.

He had exhausted all his contacts and come up with nothing. 'Why don't you go home darling and get some rest?' Victor suggested to Carmen.

Carmen looked at her daughter, not wanting to leave but desperately needing to freshen up and get a change of clothes.

'It's OK, mom, you go,' Maria smiled weakly.

'I'll stay here until you come back,' said Vic.

Carmen rose from the chair; she ached and couldn't wait to feel the comfort of her bed.

'I'll pick you up of a bag of clothes and check in on Peter on the way back, I'll only be a few hours.'

'Thanks,' Maria said.

Victor handed Carmen the car keys and kissed her gently. She whispered in his ear, 'try not to fall asleep,' gave Maria a smile and left the room.

Victor took his wife's seat next to Maria's bedside and held her hand. 'How are you feeling?' he asked.

'Numb, daddy, I know that my poor Rose is out there, scared and in danger and I'm laying here useless. I can't even get up to use the bathroom,' Maria said, sobs wracking her body.

'Hey, hey, hey, come now baby.' Victor gathered his daughter into his arms. 'Everybody is doing their best to find her. You just concentrate on getting better.'

'Don't you get it, daddy?' Maria wailed, 'I'm not going to get better; I'm going to die in a few weeks and my daughter is missing!' she shouted.

Victor held his daughter closer. He was in denial about Maria's condition, hoping that it had all been a big mistake.

'I will find her, my darling girl, I swear to you. If it's the last thing I do, I *will* find our Rose.'

After a few minutes, Maria's tears stopped and she drifted off to sleep. Victor slumped back into the chair, his wife's last words to him repeating over and over in his head, *try not to fall asleep.*

He knew that Carmen was a wonderful, forgiving and compassionate lady, but this, this she would never forget. He stood up and decided to get himself a strong coffee, he **would not** make the same mistake again.

***

In Mumbai, Jonathan was on a tight schedule; the girl would be arriving in less than two hours, and he needed to empty the apartment before that happened. Elizabeth only agreed to leave the house for the day when Jonathan handed over his Amex Black card.

She had arranged to meet two friends at a local spa for a morning of pampering, then they would hit the shops for some serious spending.

Elizabeth's NYE parties were one of the highlights of the social calendar in her circle, and she would have some explaining to do to her friends as to why it was cancelled this year. She did have a good excuse to use, plus after just having had the apartment painstakingly repainted, she was happy that it would be kept in pristine condition.

At Jonathan's request, Elizabeth had organised for Elijah to sleep over at his friend Oliver's home. His parents were close friends of the Naiks and agreed without fuss. Elijah was happy with the arrangement because he could stay up all night playing video games without getting moaned at.

Preeti remained in the duplex with Jonathan; he would need her help to get the girl presentable for his wife.

'Are you sure you will be OK without me, darling?' Elizabeth asked sarcastically.

'Yes,' Jonathan laughed, 'you go and enjoy yourself and please, don't come back before six o'clock, I wouldn't want your surprise to be ruined.'

What the hell was he up to? Liz thought. She had absolutely no idea what was going on; even Preeti didn't know why she was needed yet.

'Mom, Oliver's downstairs with his father,' Elijah shouted from his room.

'Let him in then,' said Jonathan.

The boy lumbered over to the intercom and buzzed them into the car park then went back to his room to grab his two backpacks.

'What on earth have you got in there boy?' asked his mother.

'Just clothes and stuff,' Eli said defensively.

'What's *wrong* with this family?' Elizabeth joked.

Elijah avoided the attempts to kiss him by both parents and headed for the door, dragging his bags behind him.

'Behave yourself and don't give your uncle and auntie a headache, OK?' Liz called after him.

'Bye mom,' was all he said, as he screwed up his face. 'Always ordering me around,' he muttered to himself as the elevator doors closed.

Elizabeth left not long after, leaving Jonathan and Preeti alone.

'Make us some coffee, we need to talk,' said Jonathan as he sat on a stool next to the kitchen island. Preeti obeyed; she had many thoughts running through her head as to what was going on. When she was finished, Preeti placed Jonathan's cup of coffee on the marble counter and stood holding hers.

'So, Elizabeth's major surprise that I have made so much fuss about, is arriving today,' Jonathan smiled; he was clearly very pleased with himself.

'That's nice,' said Preeti, glad to be a part of it.

'It's a slightly different present than usual, so please don't freak out when I tell you what it is.'

'OK?'

'Well,' Jonathan said, 'Elizabeth has always wanted a daughter, and for reasons that you don't need to know, this has not been possible.'

Preeti had heard the two of them arguing about the subject on several occasions. She already knew the situation but said nothing. Like most employers of household staff, Jonathan and Elizabeth were under the mistaken impression that their conversations, especially the heated ones, were never overheard.

'I see,' replied Preeti, feigning ignorance, 'so, what is this all about?'

'Well, I have fast-tracked an adoption for us. Let's just say, right time, right place.'

The maid looked startled.

'Don't panic, Preeti, I haven't done anything wrong, just cut a few corners. I have a contact in the child services department. They had a nine- or ten-year-old girl come in, a few days ago. She was in a car accident in which her parents tragically died. It turns out that the child was the only one wearing a seatbelt, which is why she survived.'

'Oh no, poor girl!' Preeti put her hands to her face.

'Yes, poor girl indeed, both parents died instantly, and she suffered a concussion. She has been unable to remember anything about her life before the accident. Other than that, just a few bruises,' Jonathan said.

'So, she's lost her memory?' Preeti gasped.

'That is what I've been told, yes.'

'When will she arrive?

'I'm going to pick her up shortly. She may be asleep. I have been informed that because of the trauma, she has been sleeping quite a bit. Now, here is what I want you to do,' Jonathan said.

Preeti was over the moon with this news. She loved Eli because she had known him since birth, but he was a rude, pompous, spoiled brat, and Elizabeth didn't have much time for her. Oh, how she would enjoy the company of another female in the house.

'This is wonderful news for you and madam.' Preeti could not help letting out a little squeal. Beaming from ear to ear, she clapped her hands.

'Preeti, focus please, we need to get her bedroom ready before Elizabeth comes home. The guest room down here will be better for the moment, we don't want her waking up confused, wandering around and falling down the stairs. This is a list of things that I think you should buy and here is thirty thousand rupees.'

Jonathan handed Preeti an envelope.

'Buy posters, teddy bears, toys, clothes, toiletries, anything to make her feel at home – you know what I mean, don't you?' You could almost hear the cogs whirring in Preeti's head; she was a very smart girl, and this kind of thing would be easy for her.

'Don't worry, sir, I know exactly what to do.'

'I'll call you a taxi now, you had better get ready to go.'

Preeti virtually danced off to her quarters.

As Jonathan sipped the last of his coffee, he thought, well that went well. He unlocked his phone.

***

Back at the Rosario household, Peter had just finished talking to Danny, who'd popped in hoping to hear some good news but left feeling like his world had collapsed.

There was a knock at the door. Peter left the kitchen where he was preparing a flask of tea to take to the hospital. He opened the door to find Jack standing there.

'Brother,' Jack said, as he crossed the threshold to embrace Peter. 'I am so sorry – please, if there is anything I can do, I am here for you.'

Peter held Jack for a moment. 'Thanks for coming,' he said as they separated. 'I'm making tea, you want a cup?'

'Yes please,'

Jack followed his brother into the kitchen and took a seat at the dining table.

'Do the police have any leads on Rose?' Jack asked.

'No.'

'What about Maria, how is she?'

'Not good,' Peter replied. He joined Jack at the table with the tea.

'What madness, I can't believe this is happening,' Jack shook his head.

'Yes,' replied Peter, then, fixing his brother with a direct stare, said, 'Jack, do you know anything about Rose's disappearance?'

'Why would I know anything?' Jack spluttered on a mouthful of tea. He sounded stunned.

'I mean, have you heard anything? You mix with the wrong kind of people, don't you? Someone must have said something by now, surely?'

'Well, as you know, I am no longer popular in those circles. I've turned over a new leaf, and no, I haven't heard anything.'

'I don't understand how my daughter could have been abducted, because that's what the police are calling it, Jack. Someone has *taken* my little girl, and nobody has a fucking clue why, who is involved or where she is! Rose is nine years old, she is all alone, and God only knows what's happening to her or who she is with.'

Peter's voice had become louder with every word and ended with him shouting as his fingernails dug so deep into his palms that they drew blood.

Jack had never seen his brother this angry.

'I'm sorry,' exclaimed Peter, 'I'm not blaming you, I just can't believe this is happening to us.'

'Peter, I will do whatever I can to help – you know that, don't you?' Jack put a hand on his brother's shoulder.

'Then get out there, Jack – you do *me* a favour for once in your life. Yes, it's your turn to help *me.* Go and find your niece, Jack, I'm begging you. Find Rose for me.' Peter slammed his fist on the table, nearly sending the cups flying.

Jack decided that it was time to leave. He felt terrible for what he had done. 'OK, I'm going,' said Jack, gulping his tea down as he got up from the chair. He paused before leaving and placed his hand on Peter's shoulder again.

'Give Maria my love, will you,' he said.

Peter sat there for several minutes after his brother had left; he was angry, sad and full of hate for the people that had taken his daughter. He also had no idea how he would cope after losing Maria, the love of his life.

Aimlessly looking around the kitchen trying to work up the courage to face the world outside, he spotted a picture stuck to the fridge, drawn with crayon. It depicted Maria and himself with Rose in between them, holding their hands. It was a couple of years old and although, like most kids' artwork, it was no masterpiece, you could easily make out who the happy family were.

He rubbed his face, feeling two days' worth of stubble, finished his tea, washed the pinpricks of blood off his palms and with everything packed for the hospital, left the house. Walking the path towards the gate, Peter's heart skipped a beat when he noticed the riderless pink bicycle next to the house.

Carmen couldn't sleep, and the long shower that she had taken only revived her slightly. To distract herself from the events of the previous day, she started cooking at six a.m., but it hadn't helped. Picking up her phone from the kitchen table, she called her husband.

'Hi Victor,' she said.

'Darling, how are you?'

'I didn't sleep much but I'm OK. How is our girl?'

'She's been out for most of the night, but she's awake now.' Victor passed the phone to Maria.

'Hey, mom.' Maria sounded stronger than the day before.

'Baby,' was all Carmen could manage, fighting hard to hold back tears. Clearing her throat she said, 'I'm leaving now, I'll be with you soon, OK? I love you.'

'Love you too,' Maria replied.

'Hello?' Victor said as Maria passed the phone back to him, but Carmen had already ended the call.

Collecting the tubs of food, Carmen left the house for the journey to the hospital, where she would take over from Victor.

'Carmen, how are you?' Doctor Vaidya startled the lady; she hadn't noticed him standing in the corridor as she walked to Maria's room

'I'm fine,' she replied bravely, 'more importantly, how is my daughter?'

'Maria is stable now, but she is fading. It seems that the events of yesterday have affected her rather badly.'

'What does that mean?'

'Carmen, I am doing the best I can for Maria, you do know that right?'

'Yes, of course.'

'The pressure of the whole Rose situation is only speeding up what was inevitable, I'm afraid.'

'How long, just tell me how long she has left,' Carmen whispered.

'One, maybe two weeks. I would advise you to make the most of the time you have left together and if there is anything you need to say to her, say it in the next day or two. I do not know how much longer Maria will remain conscious. Her body will start shutting down soon and unfortunately, once that happens, she will stay that way until she passes. The only thing I can do now is to make sure that she is pain free.'

Carmen thanked the doctor for his honesty.

In Maria's room, Carmen saw that Peter had already arrived.

'Mom,' Maria said smiling. She was jacked up on painkillers and her eyes were glassy.

Victor got up to offer Carmen his chair. He was aching and very tired but surprisingly, had been able to stay awake all night.

'Tea, food, all brought to me in bed, maybe I should die more often,' Maria teased, watching her family for their reactions.

All three visitors shook their heads.

'Mom, do you have any paper?'

'What for, darling?'

'I would like to write a letter to Rose,' Maria replied, 'I need to do it today before it's too late.'

Carmen glanced at her husband.

'The doctor has already filled us in on the situation. Maria knows that she is on borrowed time,' said Victor.

'I don't have any with me,' replied Carmen, patting her handbag.

'Your father can go to the store and get what you need. Victor, get some writing paper, a pen and an envelope, will you?'

Carmen shot her husband a look that he knew meant, *go right away.*

'Yes, dear.' He held out his hand for the car keys.

Before Victor's return, not much was said apart from a few anecdotes and recollections of happier times that even in themselves were torture.

'There you go, my love,' said Victor as he presented Maria with far too much writing material.

'Give me half an hour alone, please,' Maria asked. She needed some peace to gather her thoughts and emotions and put them down on paper.

Maria instinctively felt that she would never see her precious daughter again, so the best she could do was write her a letter and pray to God that one day she would read it.

'But…' Peter started.

'You heard the lady,' barked Carmen, 'we will go outside for some fresh air; we won't be far away, baby.' Carmen kissed Maria on the cheek.

'Thanks, mom.'

After the door closed behind the trio, Maria pulled the top off one of the five pens that her father had brought and began to write.

Chapter Seventeen
Panjim, 10:49 a.m., 31st December

Jack had gone to the only place he felt at ease. Even for him, it was too early for beer, so he ordered a coffee. He was distraught. Seeing his brother had broken his heart and after finding out about Maria, he felt sick that he had sacrificed his niece for his own safety, but it was done now and there was no turning back. Jack knew there would be a heavy price to pay, and karma would catch up with him one day, of that he was sure.

He couldn't forget Rasheed's words – 'you sick bastard.' Coming from him, a man with absolutely no morals, it was condemnation indeed. What the hell have I done, Jack thought, as his coffee arrived.

Before he could finish his drink, Rasheed appeared, sitting down on the free chair opposite. Jack felt panic rise in him – had something gone wrong? He had assumed he was in the clear and was not expecting to hear from the gangster again.

'What's up? Please don't tell me there's been a problem?'

'No, no problem, not yet anyway.' Rasheed did not disguise his contempt as he looked at Jack, 'but there is an awful lot of heat surrounding your niece. This Roger Moreas is turning over every stone in Goa in the search for her.'

Jack had crossed paths with Moreas in the past. He was a real terrier, and once he got a hold of something he was like the proverbial dog with a bone.

'I'm just checking that you will be keeping your mouth shut. I'd hate for you to have a change of heart and blab to the police, because you know what will happen, don't you? Your niece's ordeal will be a walk in the park compared to what you can look forward to if you breathe a word of this to anyone.'

Rasheed raised his hand to his throat and drew his thumb slowly across it.

'No, of course not,' replied Jack, wincing at Rasheed's reference to Rose.

'I'm watching you,' repeated Rasheed as he pointed two fingers at his eyes, then at Jack. And just as quickly as he had appeared, Rasheed was gone.

Jack sat, staring at his cup. 'I can't live like this; I need to get out of here!' he muttered.

He left money for the coffee on the table and crossed the road to walk along the river. He needed to come up with a plan to escape this hell that he had created for himself before he lost his mind, or worse…

***

It was nearly noon and Jonathan had been assured that the girl was asleep and would be for some time. He had been waiting in the car park for twenty minutes before the truck pulled up outside. The security guard had opened the gates just as Jonathan had directed him to after greasing his palm with a couple of thousand rupees to buy his silence.

The truck slowly made its way to where Jonathan was parked, closely followed by a blacked-out Audi A8. With both newly arrived vehicles now stationary and hidden from the

CCTV at the entrance, the Audi passenger door opened and Vikram emerged, in what Jonathan noticed was an expensive suit, not anything close to what he wore himself, but expensive nonetheless. The driver trailed behind him; he was a large man, the kind of guy you would not like to be on the wrong side of. Jonathan felt a twinge of fear. He had a lot of cash on him and knew these guys would have no problem overpowering him and taking everything he had, including his watch and car.

'The money?' demanded Vikram. Although the car park was dimly lit, he hadn't removed his shades.

'I have it, one hundred thousand dollars cash, and the girl?'

Vikram signalled to the driver of the truck, who jumped out and walked round to the back of the vehicle. Jonathan retrieved a small black holdall from the Range Rover. He eyed the two men in front of him, unsure of what to do next.

'Jonathan, if I wanted to rob you, you would be dead already, no?' Vikram said reasonably.

Avinash relieved Jonathan of the holdall and unzipped it, reaching inside and pulling out a bundle of one-hundred-dollar bills bound with a rubber band. He flicked through it to check whether the genuine top notes were hiding dummy notes underneath. He repeated this with the other four bundles and, satisfied that the notes were complete, zipped the bag shut.

'It's all there, you can trust me,' said Jonathan reassuringly.

'I don't need to trust you; I know where you live,' Vikram replied menacingly.

Jonathan looked startled.

'You're a well-known man, Jonathan. Don't panic – if it's all there, as you say, then we will never meet again.'

He nodded to Sunil and returned to his car, closely followed by Avinash carrying the bag of cash.

Sunil opened the rear doors of the truck and Maalik jumped out. Jonathan joined the pair, who were peering inside, to see the girl lying on a mattress.

'As promised, in one piece and untouched boss,' Maalik said.

'Although she could definitely do with a shower,' Sunil added, remembering what had happened on the journey. 'She's all yours.'

'Aren't you going to help me with her?' Jonathan asked.

Vikram was already on the way to the opening entrance gates. Maalik spotted an opportunity and held out his hand.

'Seriously?' Jonathan asked.

Maalik smiled as Jonathan reached into his back pocket and pulled out a wad of one-thousand-rupee notes, flicked off a couple and slapped them into Maalik's grubby hand. The obese man swiftly tucked them in his shirt pocket and struggled back into the truck. He picked up the girl, holding his breath as the acrid smell of stale piss hit him.

Maalik placed Rose inside the Range Rover with exaggerated concern, just for show. 'Goodbye kid, I won't miss you,' he said, as he climbed into the passenger seat of the truck.

Jonathan watched the truck leave – it was just him and the girl now. He looked down at her sleeping face; there was no doubt that she was beautiful, and he knew that Liz would be over the moon. He stood there for a few minutes as the enormity of what he had done sunk in; that, and what money could buy.

Jonathan covered the child with a blanket and carefully closed the door. He had a lot to do before his wife came home and was relying on Preeti to play her part.

'I've done it,' he said to himself in disbelief as he pulled out of the car park and headed home.

***

It had been two days since Rose's disappearance and Roger Moreas was sitting at his desk, waiting for his lunch to arrive. He had hardly been home, let alone slept. He could not believe a girl could vanish in the middle of the day without anyone seeing anything. There had been several calls that led to nothing. The roadblocks had now been dismantled and there was mounting pressure on him to reduce the manpower on the case. His superiors were ready to chalk this up as just another missing person, but Roger would not give up without a fight.

He was reviewing the witness statements for the umpteenth time when the duty sergeant approached. 'Boss, you look like shit,' he said.

Moreas rubbed his stubble, lifted his arm, gave a sniff and grunted in disgust.

'I smell like shit too,' he replied.

'Why don't you go home and get some rest? I've got this place covered. If anything turns up, I'll call you.'

'Yes, I suppose you're right,' said the sub-lieutenant, accepting that there was nothing more he could do for now.

'Boss?'

'Yes.'

'That package is all we have to go on now, I hope it turns up something.'

'Me too, because if it is a dead end then this case is as good as closed,' Moreas said.

'You go home for a while – have a shower at least!'

Roger smiled and nodded in defeat.

'I'll take an officer and start talking to the neighbours again,' the sergeant said. 'Now that the residents have had a couple of days to settle, someone might just recall something they'd forgotten about in all the excitement on the evening in question.'

'Good idea,' Moreas smiled gratefully. 'There's no harm in trying, plus the police presence will reassure the folks in the area.' Roger pushed his chair out from under his desk and stood up, stretching himself. He picked up his hat and keys and headed for the door. 'I'll see you soon.'

Outside, sitting in his police vehicle, Roger Moreas could not ignore the pressure he felt. He had promised Carmen that they would find Rose but, as things stood, if forensics did not get a match on the prints or DNA from the package found at the scene, the chances of them finding the girl were slim to none. And he would have to be the one to tell them that.

***

Back in Mumbai, Jonathan pulled into his parking space next to the private elevator leading to the apartment.

He opened the door. Looking around he couldn't see anyone else, and the public elevator that stopped at the lobby and all thirty-two floors of the building was around the corner, out of sight. He was alone.

Jonathan entered his code and held his thumb to the scanner on the wall. The brushed steel doors opened smoothly and silently. He retrieved the girl from the car and pressed the button marked twenty-two that was embossed in gold, contrasting against the steel.

Staring at himself holding the girl, his new daughter, in the mirrored wall at the back of the elevator car, he smiled to himself. 'I'm a father again,' he said.

The doors opened into the apartment, and he walked straight to the sumptuous sofa that faced the main balcony, which was already covered with a blanket. He laid his new daughter down carefully and stepped back. He noticed that Preeti had not yet returned.

He rushed upstairs to his walk-in wardrobe, finding the vial of serum in the safe, right where he had left it. Vial in hand, he headed for the medicine cabinet located in the pantry, just off the kitchen. Inside he found two sealed hypodermic needles. They had come with the cabinet, which was a complete kit containing everything that you could possibly need in a household emergency. He pulled one out and shut the door.

Nobody was to know about this part of the plan, and he needed to do it before Preeti came back. Where should he stick the needle? He decided on the top of the arm, just like a vaccination.

He was working up the courage to administer the drug when he heard a commotion at the main entrance. Preeti had arrived, bags in hand, with one of the security guys from the lobby helping her.

Jonathan quickly slipped the vial and needle into his jacket pocket. He heard the door close and the faint sound of Preeti's bare footsteps approaching. She had left all the bags in the hallway that led to the new family addition's bedroom.

Walking towards Jonathan, she raised her eyebrows questioningly; her employer merely gestured towards the sofa. Preeti looked down at the girl, her hands to her face. The child's long hair was a mess, her clothes were dirty, and her jeans had a dark stain at the crotch. She was also missing a shoe.

'She looks like an angel, sir,' said a smiling Preeti, staring at the girl on the sofa.

'An angel, yes,' he agreed.

'Madam will be incredibly happy, I am sure.'

'I hope so,' Jonathan replied.

'Did you get everything?'

'Yes, sir, we have everything we need for the next few days. When do you think she will wake up?'

Preeti could not wait to get started; she almost felt like the sleeping girl was her own.

'They told me that she should wake up sometime this evening.'

'OK, well she needs to bathe for a start,' Preeti said, sounding very business-like. 'I have underwear, PJs, slippers, a comfortable sweatsuit and I even found a set of Powerpuff Girls bedclothes,' she finished proudly.

'Powerpuff who?' quizzed Jonathan. He held up his hand – 'OK, I don't want to know!' he laughed.

'Sir, will you bring her into the bathroom, please? If you can put her in the empty tub, I will have her cleaned up in no time.'

Jonathan nodded. He lifted the girl off the couch and headed towards her new room. With the bathroom door shut, Preeti undressed the girl cautiously and placed her filthy clothes into a plastic bag, tying a knot in it.

Armed with bottles of shower gel, shampoo and conditioner, she set to work filling the tub with warm water, and gently washed the girl like she was a newborn baby.

After rinsing her off, Preeti admired the girl for a moment. Her body was still, except for the rising and falling of her chest. Her hair was no longer matted, and her clean light brown skin now smelled of lemons instead of urine.

'You are beautiful indeed, aren't you little madam?' Preeti whispered. She lifted the girl out of the bath, noticing that she wasn't very heavy.

Preeti was amazed at how she was able to do all of this without waking the child. After drying she slipped on her PJs and covered her up with the duvet.

'That's better,' Preeti said, smiling proudly.

Jonathan was on the terrace, staring out at the view, although paying no attention to it. He was so close, but time was running out now and soon the girl would wake up and ruin everything.

'All finished, sir,' came Preeti's voice. She was standing behind him, the sleeves of her cardigan still rolled up, looking pleased with herself. 'All I need to do is arrange the finishing touches to her bedroom.'

'Good, can we get rid of all her old clothes and the blanket off the sofa, put them in the garbage? They stink, I don't want them in the house.'

'Yes, sir, I will do that now.'

Preeti picked up the blanket and headed to the girl's room to fetch the bag of soiled clothes. 'Sir?' she said.

'Yes.'

'What's her name?'

'Nobody knows.'

'Oh,' replied Preeti who had started thinking of names for her own children, if she ever got around to having any.

Garbage bag in hand, the maid opened the front door to go to the chute situated halfway down the hall.

Jonathan spotted his chance. He raced to the girl's room, pulled the syringe from his pocket and, copying what he had seen on a YouTube video, inserted it into the vial to suck up the serum. He pointed the tip to the ceiling and flicked his finger on the side to displace the air and squeezed gently until the first drop of clear liquid appeared.

As he pulled back the bed covers, Jonathan fumbled and dropped the syringe. It fell onto his foot then rolled underneath the bed.

'Shit!'

He dropped to his knees just as he heard the front door shut. Reaching with his right hand he managed to grab the syringe and was back on his feet in seconds. He had no time to waste; he could hear footsteps coming his way. Taking a deep breath and crossing himself, he jabbed the needle through the girl's pyjamas, pushed the plunger and slipped the empty syringe back into his pocket. Turning around, he saw Preeti standing in the doorway.

'I've come to finish off the room, if that is ok, sir?' she said, pointing to the bags on the bedroom floor.

'Yes, carry on.' Jonathan made a quick exit. 'I will be in my office – let me know if she wakes up.' He was gone before she could answer.

Preeti frowned; her boss was acting very strangely. When she'd arrived at the door to the girl's room, Jonathan was blocking her view, but she could tell by how startled he was that something was amiss. Emptying the bags onto the free side of the bed, Preeti pinned the two posters she had bought of leading Bollywood actresses to the walls, arranged the small teddy bears on the pillow next to the girl and put away the new clothes. The last thing she unpacked was the pair of fluffy monkey slippers, which she left at the side of the bed.

Preeti looked around, happy at what she had accomplished at such short notice. Suddenly, the girl let out a groan, turned over and then turned back again. She held her upper arm as though she was in pain, then fell silent.

Preeti bent down and was about to pull the duvet back over the girl when she noticed a small red dot at the top of her arm, contrasting against the light pink of the pyjamas. Taking a closer look, the maid realised that it may be blood. Preeti frowned. 'I did not see any cut on her arms, and she was not bleeding from anywhere when I bathed her,' she murmured. Just what had Jonathan done?

Jonathan hid the syringe and vial in the top drawer of his desk and locked it. He could dispose of them another time. He poured himself a large whisky and sat down, trying to regain his composure.

Preeti pulled the bedroom door, so it was nearly closed; she wanted to keep an eye and ear out for any sight or sound of the girl waking. In the meantime, she decided to check something before she forgot. She headed to the medicine cabinet. Preeti knew everything that was in the apartment and exactly where it all should be.

Her suspicions were right – one of the two hypodermic needles was missing! Was Jonathan telling her the truth about the girl? Whatever happened, she would be keeping a close eye on her; the poor thing had obviously been through enough over the last few days or so.

Chapter Eighteen
Manipal Hospital, 2:48 p.m., 31st December

Peter was at Maria's bedside. She had finished writing the letter and given it to her husband to look after.

'Whatever you do, make sure that Rose gets this when you find her – promise me, Peter,' she implored, her hand on his arm, the knuckles white.

'I promise, darling. I will find her, even if it takes me the rest of my life, I will find our beautiful Rose,' he replied, his voice thick with unshed tears.

After a minute or so's silence, Carmen said, 'you two go and see what you can find out, you're of no use hanging around here.' They both did as they were told.

'Peter?' Maria said, her voice hoarse, 'don't forget what I said.' He tapped his jacket pocket and left, behind Victor.

'How are you feeling?' Carmen asked. She could tell by her daughter's drawn and gaunt face that she was in agony.

'I asked the nurse to give me a break from the painkillers, I wanted to be awake while I was writing that letter.' She pressed the button by the side of the bed and a nurse responded instantly.

'Are you ready now?' The nurse asked.

Maria nodded.

The pain in her neck was so bad, she thought her head was going to explode. Carmen watched her daughter wincing as she tried to get comfortable. She shut her eyes and, clasping her hands in front of her face, said a prayer for Maria's pain to end soon; she did not want her to die, but knowing it was inevitable, she just wanted the pain to stop. Wanting her daughter to live for as long as possible in this state would just be selfish. No matter how much Carmen loved Maria, she couldn't bear seeing her like this, it was heartbreaking.

***

In Mumbai, Elizabeth's Mini Cooper Sport came to a halt in the parking space next to her husband's Range Rover. She had enjoyed a couple of glasses of Sauvignon Blanc over lunch with her friends. On the back seats were several bags from designer stores, containing things that she didn't really need, but a girl can never have enough lingerie, handbags or shoes!

Getting out of the car, she straightened her dress, picked up her clutch and retrieved her purchases; Elizabeth knew she was still in great shape and enjoyed lots of attention from men. Jonathan, on the other hand, rarely showed any interest in what she looked like these days. He was always too busy working.

In the bags were some things she was sure would change that, and in the mood she was in, maybe even tonight, if he was lucky. She had bought a pair of the latest Louboutin leopard-skin, six-inch spiked heels and an extremely racy white lace underwear set with matching hold-ups. If this doesn't get him going, nothing will, she thought, as she ascended in the elevator.

In the apartment, Jonathan was pacing between the kitchen and living area. He had knocked back another large whisky to take the edge off his anxiety.

The girl was fast asleep, and he still had no idea how he was going to make the introduction.

Preeti was busy preparing their evening meal and had been checking on the young girl every ten minutes, possibly every five.

The front door opened. Jonathan looked at Preeti, who already had her eyes on him. They both turned to Elizabeth, who sauntered into the living area, heels clip-clopping on the tiled floor.

'Everything ok?' she asked.

'Yes,' replied Jonathan, walking over to greet his wife, with a perfunctory kiss on the cheek. 'Good day?'

'Yes, it was,' Liz hiccupped, making them both laugh.

'Preeti, when you have finished, take the rest of the evening off,' Jonathan said, giving her a knowing look. His eyes shifted in the direction of the girl's room.

'Yes, sir,' she replied, with a nod.

She was to stay with the girl until she woke up, and from what he had been told, that was likely to happen within the next hour or so.

'Glass of wine? Jonathan asked.

'Yes, darling, just let me get these shoes off.'

Liz made for the bedroom to put away her purchases and change into something more comfortable. We'll be alone tonight, maybe he has something planned she thought, excitedly.

Jonathan poured his wife a large glass of white wine; he wanted her well-oiled but not for the reasons she hoped. After dinner, Elizabeth and Jonathan were enjoying their second glass of wine, sitting on the terrace.

'If we had a daughter, what would you name her?' Jonathan asked.

'That's a bit out of the blue!' Elizabeth swirled the wine around in her glass for a moment, as she contemplated the question.

'Something heavenly, knowing that she would be beautiful, just like her mother,' Elizabeth said, as she posed, pouting, as though her picture was being taken.

They both laughed.

'Celeste... Eden... Angela... Angelina, wait, ...' She looked up into the clear starry night for inspiration. 'Angelica, Angelica Naik, how about that?'

'Sounds perfect.' Jonathan smiled at his wife.

'Anyway, why ask such a silly question? We both know we are not going to have another child, don't we?'

Elizabeth's mood changed. She put down her glass and picked up the packet of Marlboro Gold and a lighter from the table. She lit a cigarette, and Jonathan shot her a disapproving look.

'Come on, don't be a misery, I've only had one today!'

'You told me you were giving up.'

'I am,' Liz replied, rolling her eyes.

Jonathan knew when to stop and left it at that.

Preeti was sitting on the royal blue wing-backed armchair for what seemed like hours. She had pulled it next to the bed to watch over the sleeping beauty, barely taking her eyes off her since entering the room. The girl had been restless over the past half an hour and Preeti was sure that she would be waking up soon. She still didn't know what to do when that happened as Jonathan had not given her any further instructions. Sitting there in the low light of a lamp in the corner of the room, Preeti had been thinking about the whirlwind of events that day and puzzling over what she may or may not have seen Jonathan doing.

Preeti's instincts were to look after the child, and if she had lost her memory, would need extra care and attention – that was a job she looked forward to doing.

Preeti needed to use the bathroom and was now at the point where she could wait no longer so she got up, arched her back to stretch and headed to the en-suite. At the last minute, force of habit made her decide against it and she turned and made her way to her quarters, just down the corridor. Preeti knew her place, and using any of her employer's bathrooms was not allowed, even in this situation.

Preeti gazed into the mirror above the sink and smiled to herself. She knew she was attractive and would one day find a husband, but being low caste, she could never marry a rich or powerful man like her boss. She would most likely end up with a guy twice her age from the village where she grew up, in a marriage arranged by her mother, who whenever she called home only had that one topic of conversation.

Preeti was an intelligent woman, full of love and compassion; she deserved more than what her future was most likely to bring.

She splashed some cold water on her face and snapped back to the present. Remembering the sleeping girl, she quickly dried her face and made her way back to the bedroom. Opening the door, Preeti nearly jumped out of her skin. The girl had woken up and was sitting on the edge of the bed looking dazed and confused, her eyes half open, hair covering one side of her face. She was holding a teddy in one hand and rubbing the back of her head with the other. Preeti stood in the doorway, not knowing what to do, or what to say. Assuming the girl spoke English, she simply started with, 'Hi, sweetheart, how are you feeling?'

Rose was aching; her arm hurt, her head hurt, she had no idea where she was and more to the point, didn't seem to remember anything at all. She sat there looking at the lady in the red flower-patterned sari. Rose could see that she was talking but could not take in what she was saying. It was like she was in a dream. She looked down and, seeing the monkey slippers beside her, tried to slide her feet into them but they seemed to be too far away, and her coordination was off. Preeti approached the bed and sat down next to her. She could tell that it would be a while until the girl was fully awake. She noticed her fumbling with the slippers and helped her put them on.

Rose didn't recognise this woman. She looked friendly though, so Rose didn't put up a fight when she guided her feet into the fluffy footwear.

The truth was that Rose had been given far too much sedative, and what with being crushed by Maalik in the truck and the serum administered by Jonathan, she was extremely lucky to be alive.

The girl continued to sit in silence. She was very groggy and felt that if she tried to get up, she would surely fall back down again, so she just stared blankly at the empty doorway.

Preeti felt so sad for her, this beautiful child, lost and all alone in the world. The maid tentatively placed her arm around the girl's shoulder.

Rose allowed the lady's arm to rest across her – everything seemed to be happening in slow motion. She felt the warmth of the woman's body next to hers and rested her head on the stranger's chest.

Rose had been pulled about, bounced around and crushed half to death. She was tired and ached, but most of all she had started to get the worst hunger pangs, although what she needed most at this very moment was a hug. Her eyes flickered shut; she was still drowsy.

On the terrace, Elizabeth remembered the gift she was promised.

'So, where is it then?' she asked, raising her eyebrows.

'Oh yes, I'd almost forgotten,' replied Jonathan.

'Stop messing with me, Jon, please,' Elizabeth said, stubbing out her cigarette in the heavy marble ashtray.

'OK, OK, wait here, my darling, I'll be back,' Jonathan replied.

He got up and headed to their new daughter's bedroom. He gasped as he saw Preeti sitting next to the upright girl.

'She's awake?' he whispered.

The girl's eyes were now open again, staring inquisitively at this new figure in the doorway.

'Do you think she's OK? Has she said anything, can she talk?' Jonathan fired off the questions without waiting for answers. He cared about the girl, obviously, but right now the most important thing for him was did she remember anything.

'Bring her to meet Elizabeth in ten minutes,' he said nervously.

'Yes, sir.' Preeti tightened her arm protectively around the girl.

After Jonathan pulled the door closed, the girl turned to Preeti.

'Who is that man?' she asked.

'That's your father,' Preeti replied.

The girl screwed up her face in concentration. She didn't remember the man who had just left, or the lady sitting next to her – come to think of it, she didn't even know who *she* was.

Rose glanced around the room, looking for anything that she could recognise but nothing really stood out. She was clean, the room smelled nice, and she wasn't scared, she definitely wasn't scared.

'Are you my mom?' she asked.

'No, dear, my name is Preeti, I am the maid, but will also be the one looking after you, so anything you need you just let me know.'

'I'm hungry and need to pee,' said Rose abruptly.

'Come on then, madam, let's show you where the bathroom is,' Preeti said, with a small reassuring laugh.

Rose sat on the toilet still clutching the bear; it was comforting her somehow.

'Shall we go and see mom now?' Preeti asked as the girl came back into the bedroom, shuffling along in her new monkey slippers.

'OK,' Rose agreed.

'Good, I will get some food for you, you must be starving, you've been sleeping for quite some time, madam. What would you like?'

Rose thought for a minute. 'I don't know.' It wasn't that she couldn't decide but she had no idea what she liked.

'Don't worry,' said Preeti squatting down to her level. 'I will get you something you will love and listen, trust me, sweetie, everything is going to be OK, I will look after you.'

Rose could see the sincerity in the lady's eyes, 'OK,' she said and gave her a big grin.

'You ready?'

'Yes.'

Preeti straightened up and took the girl by the hand. Elizabeth was sitting with her back to the world; she liked it that way – she enjoyed admiring her home, it was beautiful. Jonathan had been shifting around in his chair nervously for the last ten minutes.

'What are you up to and where is my present?' Elizabeth demanded, tired of this nonsense.

'You'll see,' he replied, and no sooner had he spoken, Elizabeth noticed Preeti walking towards them. She should be in her room, she thought. Then she saw the smaller figure holding the maid's hand.

Elizabeth stood up and walked to the glass door. They were closer now and she could see that Preeti was holding the hand of a young girl.

'Jonathan, what is going on?' she demanded.

He joined his wife and put his hand round her waist. 'That, my love,' he said, pointing at the girl, 'is Angelica.'

'What, wait, what, who, where, what the fu...?'

Elizabeth couldn't string a sentence together and was now physically shaking. Jonathan laughed and briefly explained his version of events. Elizabeth was barely listening, her eyes fixed on the beautiful little girl. She was struggling to comprehend what was going on.

All she knew was that the child staring at her through the glass was hers now.

'Come on, don't you want to meet your daughter?' Jonathan asked gently, as he slid open the heavy glass door, pulling his wife inside.

Preeti had stopped a few metres away and she and the girl stood there waiting silently. Elizabeth rushed over to get a closer look; Preeti squeezed the girl's hand, released it and went to the kitchen. She felt an unexpected twinge of jealousy.

'Oh my God, you are so beautiful,' Elizabeth cried out, as she bent down to gently grasp the girl's face in her hands. 'Mom?' the girl asked.

'Yes, baby, I'm your mommy,' Elizabeth threw her arms around her, barely able to contain herself, she was so happy. Jonathan glanced over at Preeti, caught her eye and smiled. The maid had done an excellent job.

Elizabeth loosened her grip on the girl but was still on her knees holding onto her forearms and staring into her big brown eyes.

'So, Angelica, I hear you're hungry,' said Jonathan.

She nodded and then, Elizabeth, realising what he had said, repeated the name softly, almost in a whisper, 'Angelica.' She turned to her husband and nodded, 'Angelica it is then.' They smiled at each other and then at their daughter.

'Shall we sit down, darling, you can't stand there all day?' Elizabeth asked.

The girl smiled and let her new mother lead her by the hand to the sofa. Angelica flopped down and Elizabeth turned to her husband, who was right behind her. Wrapping her arms around his neck, she took a deep breath. 'This... this is the most wonderful thing you have ever done, darling; I love you so much.'

He held her tight. 'Anything for you, my dear.'

'You said that she has lost her memory, what are we going to do about that?' Elizabeth asked, worried.

'Let her settle in, she needs lots of rest and love. We shouldn't push her to remember anything.'

'Angelica, is that my name?' the young girl asked. She was sitting cross-legged on the sofa, fiddling with the TV remote control.

'Yes, Angelica, it is,' Elizabeth announced proudly. The girl shrugged her shoulders and smiled, then went back to studying the remote.

Preeti brought over a plate of chicken fried rice. She handed it to the girl, along with a fork and tissue. Rose took in the aroma of the food and cautiously lifted a small amount to her mouth.

'Mmm,' she said appreciatively.

'Good?' Preeti asked.

Rose gave an exaggerated nod and started to shovel forkful after forkful into her mouth. Preeti turned to the parents.

'Will there be anything else?' she asked.

'No, thank you, you've been very helpful,' said Jonathan. They said goodnight and Preeti went to her bedroom. She was exhausted now but pleased with herself for what she had done, and for gaining a new friend.

Rose Rosario was now Angelica Naik. Jonathan was happy that his plan had worked, Elizabeth was happy that she now had a daughter. And Angelica was happy filling her belly. She had woken up confused and didn't know much about anything. She had questions but would leave them for another time, she just wanted to enjoy herself for now. Poor Angelica had no idea who Rose was and what and who she had left behind.

***

In Goa, Peter had asked Maria's parents to allow him to be alone with his wife for the day, so they left early in the morning to get some well-deserved sleep. They would return later in the evening with food and fresh clothes. Considering the situation,

Maria had been upbeat, and the pair enjoyed the bittersweet experience of taking a trip down memory lane, chatting about how and when they met, which had been purely by accident.

Maria had disliked Peter at first until he broke down her defences with his infectious charm and wit. They discussed the torturous labour that Maria had endured and which Peter had almost missed because of working on one of his 'crazy ideas', as Maria used to call them.

'I know you think I'm pretty useless,' Peter confessed.

'What? Don't be silly, of course not, darling, I think you are amazing!' Maria gave a weak smile.

'I know you've always thought that I could have made more of my life instead of spending so much time on my inventions.'

Maria took her husband's hand in hers. He flinched as he saw the cannulas inserted in the back of her elegant soft hand and the thin tubes leading from them to the bags of God knows what hung on hooks above the bed.

'You are who you are Peter, and I love you for that – don't ever let anyone try to change you. One day you'll make this world a better place.'

'Well, I hope so, this clean energy solution for homes is nearly finished, I just can't focus on it right now, I want to spend all the time I have left with you, by your side.'

'Aww,' Maria gushed, 'you always were a softy.'

Peter was itching to finish his project; he hoped that it would fetch a sizeable amount of capital, having decided that every penny he made would go towards finding Rose. His wife may be dying but he had a daughter out there somewhere.

'Darling, I'll be gone soon....'

'Don't say that, please,' Peter interrupted.

'Like it or not it's the truth. Now listen to me.'

'Yes, dear.' Peter bowed his head.

'No matter what happens, *do not fall apart.* Yes, I'll be gone, but you have so much to live for. Mom and Dad will help you out with anything you need, and I've told them to check up on you because I know you won't eat and you'll end up staying in that workshop all day, every day. Don't be too hard on yourself – you're a good man, you have always looked after us and never let me down, not even once and I love you so much for that.'

'But Rose, I was there and...'

Maria raised her hand to cut him short.

'It wasn't your fault, don't beat yourself up. Besides, Dad was watching the kids and even if he hadn't fallen asleep, what's to say he would have heard anything? Spend the rest of your life trying to find her. I already know that's what you are going to do, I can see it in your eyes.'

Peter smiled.

'Do not do it full of guilt and self-loathing or I will come back as a ghost and give you one tight slap!'

They both laughed for a few seconds until Maria's laughs turned into a bout of coughing.

'You OK, my love?' Peter asked.

'Yes, yes, stop fussing man.'

Peter admired his wife; she was the strongest person he had ever met, and he always felt lucky to have married her.

'I'm tired,' Maria admitted. She reached out to Peter, and he shifted his body to put his arms around her.

'I love you with all my heart and soul,' Peter declared.

'I know, you big softy, I love you too,' she replied, giving him a wink.

Ten minutes later, Maria fell asleep. Peter sat watching her breathing, cherishing every second that he had left to hold her, feeling her warm, soft skin. He had no idea that would be the last time they would speak, as, within an hour, Maria had slipped into a coma. He sat there with her, holding her until Victor and Carmen arrived.

Chapter Nineteen
Outside the Figueiredo residence, Andheri, 4:21 p.m., 31st December

Elizabeth had called ahead to let Eli know that she was coming to pick him up and would wait outside. She was too nervous to go in and make small talk with Oliver's parents. Gabriel and Zeenia were close friends, close enough to pick up on the fact that she was worried about something. She didn't want anyone quizzing her at the moment; there was enough to deal with, having to inform her son of the new arrival.

Elizabeth had called Zeenia and made her excuses saying that they were in a rush to get some place; she wanted to get this conversation with Eli about his new sister over with and had decided to take him to his favourite BBQ restaurant, to soften the blow. She only hoped that he would accept what was going on; he could be extremely difficult at the best of times.

'Hi mom,' Eli said as he opened the rear door and carelessly threw his bags onto the back seats.

'Did you have fun, darling?' Elizabeth asked as he flopped himself onto the seat next to her.

'Oliver has the new Call of Duty game, it's not even out in the shops yet!' he declared in a tone that suggested she was a dreadful mother for not affording him the same privilege.

Liz glanced at her son. Elijah looked tired; there was no doubt that they had been up all night playing.

'That's great,' she replied, absently.

'No, it's not! It's not good mom, because *I don't have it,*' Eli said petulantly.

'Oh well, we will see what your father can do, I'm sure he can find it for you.' Liz sensed the possibility of a bribe to grease the wheels of her son accepting his new sister.

'OK, well you better make it soon!' Eli said sulkily.

'Hungry?'

'Starving,' Eli replied, buckling up his seatbelt. There was only one restaurant that served American-style BBQ in the area; it was called Sam's and Eli loved the place.

They were seated at a table next to the window. The family were regular patrons and knew the owner, Sam, a larger-than-life, middle-aged man from Goa. Elijah and Elizabeth placed their orders. Eli ordered baby back ribs, fries and a large soda, Elizabeth opting for a healthier grilled chicken salad and sparkling water. They chatted about life in general until Elizabeth plucked up the courage to ask, 'how would you feel about having a sister?'

Eli stared at her, a piece of rib spilling out of his mouth and making a greasy trail down his chin.

'You're having a baby?' he asked, his face contorted with disgust.

'No.' Liz did not like the thunderous look on Eli's face.

'What then?' Eli took another bite of his ribs.

'How would you feel about it?' Liz asked again.

'I don't know, stop talking crap, you're not pregnant so no screaming baby – duh!' he said, spraying barbeque sauce onto the table.

Elijah didn't know whether the addition of a sibling would change things for the better or worse. Would it mean less for him? Or more for him, to compensate? He decided it might be good.

'I'm not bothered, do what you like.' He shrugged.

Liz breathed a sigh of relief. 'Do you know what adoption is, Eli?'

'Kind of.' Eli was looking wary again.

'Well, it's when a child has parents that can no longer look after them, and they find someone else to give that child a new home.' Elizabeth had decided to put it into the simplest terms for her son to understand.

'Whatever.'

Liz pressed on despite the lacklustre response from her son.

'Your father and I have adopted a girl, and she is going to be your new sister.'

'What, already?' Elijah almost shouted. 'And now you're asking me how I feel? Tough if I had said no! Is that it?'

'Eli, shh!' Liz scolded as his voice echoed around the restaurant.

'Yes, it came up fast, this girl has had some really bad luck and was in immediate need of help.'

'Yeah?' Eli sneered.

'Yes, her parents died in an accident.'

'Oh,' Eli looked slightly less annoyed.

Elizabeth felt a glimmer of hope again; he seemed to be a bit more reasonable.

Elijah locked eyes with his mother for a few seconds. Liz held her breath; she had no idea what was going through his mind.

Eventually he shrugged and said, 'what's her name, how old is she, what does she look like, have you given her my things, will she be taking my bedroom?'

'Woah, woah, woah,' Elizabeth replied, holding her hands up. 'Her name is Angelica, she is ...' Oh God, she thought, they didn't actually know how old she was. Elizabeth made a call, based on her size and the way that she had acted last night before she had gone to bed, which was not long after they were introduced.

'Nine, ten maybe,' she said hastily.

'Good, I am the older brother,' Eli said, in a macho voice.

'She will get her own things and is in the guest bedroom downstairs until we sort out a permanent room for her,' Elizabeth finished.

'Come on, let's go, mom.' Eli got up from his chair; he seemed excited now, not at all the reaction that Elizabeth expected but she was relieved beyond measure. She fished the cash from her purse to cover the bill and tip, waved goodbye to Sam and off they went. Halfway home Eli asked, 'does she speak English?'

His mother laughed. 'Of course, son, of course.' In the elevator, Eli looked more animated than Elizabeth had seen her son in a long while and she felt hope burst into life in her heart.

'What do I say to her, mom? Do you think she will like me?'

'Just be nice. She hurt her head in the accident and has lost her memory so go easy on her and be patient. I'm sure you two will get on just fine.'

Elizabeth opened the front door and Eli pushed past her shouting out, 'OK, where is she?' He came to a halt a few feet from where Angelica was sitting on a stool in the kitchen. She had been eating non-stop since waking up and had kept Preeti busy. She was still wearing her pyjamas but had finally relinquished the bear.

Hearing the commotion to her right she glanced around to see the fat boy standing there. He was looking her up and down, scrutinising every part of her.

Angelica jumped from her stool and trotted over to him until they were standing barely a foot apart. They eyed each other for another minute without a word being said, like two wild animals sizing up a rival before a fight, neither wanting to back down.

Elizabeth and Preeti watched nervously, both hoping for a positive outcome. Liz had her fingers crossed behind her back.

Jonathan was out and Elizabeth realised that she had no idea what she would do if Eli rejected the young girl.

Angelica gave Eli the biggest smile ever. Elijah's guard instantly dropped and he beamed back at her, then at his mother. Liz realised she had been holding her breath and let out a long, ragged sigh of relief.

'Want to see my room?' Eli asked, 'I've got loads of toys and games.' He didn't wait for an answer and took off towards the stairs. Angelica looked at Elizabeth, who motioned with her head that she should follow the boy.

'Wait for me,' she called out as she made off after him, finding it difficult to run in her monkey slippers. Preeti watched as Elizabeth smiled after the children, clearly relieved.

'Coffee, madam?'

'Definitely,' she replied, as she took her daughter's place on the stool at the counter. Elizabeth was mightily relieved that the introduction had gone smoothly. She really had expected the worst. If there were no signs of fighting or screaming coming from Eli's room within the next few minutes then things should be OK; she prayed they would be, anyway, as she kicked off her heels.

Later that evening, Jonathan found his wife, relaxing on her favourite armchair reading the latest copy of Vogue.

'How did it go?' he asked.

'You can see for yourself, they're in Eli's room,' Elizabeth said smugly.

Approaching Elijah's bedroom, Jonathan heard the loud screeching of car tyres and excited voices. The door was open, so he stepped inside to find Eli and Angelica sitting on the floor with a huge bowl of popcorn between them, racing each other on Eli's newest car game on Xbox. 'Argh,' he cried out.

'No, no, no,' Angelica squealed, as he overtook her. Jonathan stood there for a moment, not wanting to disturb them; they looked like they were having a lot of fun. Elijah, who was normally selfish and withdrawn around his peers, had shown the girl how to master the joypad controls and she was loving every minute of it. It was a huge weight off his shoulders

He left them to it, walked down the stairs and headed to the wine cooler where he pulled out a bottle of Dom Perignon.

He grabbed two champagne flutes from the cupboard and took them over to where his wife was sitting.

'Well?' she asked, peering over the top of the magazine.

'Happy New Year, my love!'

He popped the cork, beaming from ear to ear. His plan had worked better than he could ever have hoped. Elizabeth had the daughter that she had wanted for so long and now they were a family of four.

'Cheers,' Elizabeth said as she chinked glasses with him.

'Cheers,' he replied with a wink.

⸺⊷◁▷⊶⸺

Chapter Twenty
Manipal Hospital, 8:42 a.m., 1st January 2009

It was approximately eighteen hours since Maria had lost consciousness. Peter hadn't realised how much time had passed since she last moved. Worried, he called the nurse, who in turn called Doctor Vaidya, who was at home. He returned within the hour. Victor and Carmen had raced to the hospital after receiving Peter's call and the three of them had been in the room since last night, alternating between praying and crying, each one trying to comfort the next, only to break down themselves.

The doctor checked Maria, who was now wearing an oxygen mask.

'She is in a coma,' he declared sadly. 'She is slowly slipping away and I'm afraid there is no real hope of her regaining consciousness now, I'm so sorry.'

Carmen let out a wail. She didn't get to say goodbye to her daughter and that cut her to the core; her little girl would be gone soon, and she'd never get the chance to hear her voice again or to tell her that she loved her.

Stepping over to the bed she grabbed her daughter's hand and started shaking it gently. 'Wake up, wake up,' she repeated, tears streaming down her cheeks.

Peter, who was the last to speak to her, was heartbroken but felt at peace and was glad to have enjoyed their conversation yesterday.

They got to profess their undying love for one another, and he thanked God, Jesus and the Holy Spirit for giving him that opportunity.

He would never forget her kind words of encouragement; she truly was selfless until the end.

'Is Maria in pain?' Peter asked the doctor.

'She won't be able to feel anything now.'

'How long?'

'A few days at the most,' the doctor said.

'And you're sure she won't wake up?'

'It's very unlikely.'

'Thank you, doctor,' said Peter, 'you've been ...'

'I wish I could have done more, my friend.'

'You've done enough, I won't forget this.' Peter shook the doctor's hand.

'I had better get going,' suggested Doctor Vaidya, 'if you need anything, well, you know what to do.'

Peter released the doctor's hand and turned to Maria, who was being hugged by her mother. He began to cry.

'Do not fall apart,' he heard Maria repeat to him. He took several deep breaths. 'Keep it together, Peter,' he whispered, 'keep it together.'

Chapter Twenty-One
Naik residence, 10:12 a.m.,
1st January

Preeti heard the children before they reached the top of the staircase. They had bonded at first sight and become inseparable ever since.

'Good morning,' she said.

'What's for breakfast?' Eli asked as he took a seat.

'Pancakes and fruit?' Preeti suggested.

He screwed up his face at the mention of fruit, looked at Angelica and, seeing her smile, said, 'OK.'

They were having the same thing as they did yesterday; Angelica had wolfed it down, closely followed by Elijah, who seemed to mirror everything his new sister did.

Preeti turned to find the ingredients from the pantry and was startled to see the young girl standing there. Angelica flung her arms around her.

'Good morning,' she said, as she released the maid, looking up at her, smiling.

Preeti felt her heart swell with love for the child. Today was a wonderful day, and she was floating on air.

⋯⋯◆◇◆⋯⋯

Chapter Twenty-Two
Bambolim, Goa, 4:19 p.m., 1st January

Victor got a call from Sub-Lieutenant Moreas. He and Peter left Carmen at the hospital and went to meet him at the station. Both men were downcast and tired. Neither of them said a word, not even to discuss the possibility of a breakthrough in the case because when Roger called, he hadn't seemed too confident. All they could do was keep their fingers crossed.

They pulled into the car park next to the police station. As they got out Victor looked at Peter.

'You ready for this?' he asked.

Peter nodded in silence and walked ahead of his father-in-law into the station. Roger Moreas was waiting for them at the front desk. 'Gentlemen, come through to my office, please, I'll be back shortly,' he said.

Victor and Peter sat staring at the comings and goings of the station until Roger returned with another man.

'This is Sergeant Fernandez; we don't have much of a forensics team, but this guy is in charge, and one of the leading forensic investigators in the state,' Roger said.

The sergeant, a tall, thin man with glasses who looked almost boyish, smiled at them.

'Hi,' he said.

Victor guessed the man couldn't have been more than twenty-five years old.

'Don't judge a book by its cover,' said Roger noticing Victor's expression, 'he's the best we have.'

'Shall we get down to it, sergeant?' Moreas suggested.

'Yes, sir,' he replied, looking to the sub-lieutenant's desk, where everything he needed was already arranged. He pointed to the parcel. 'OK, this item was found at the scene and seems to be the only piece of evidence that we have to go on. We have confirmed that it is empty and believe that it was used as a diversion.'

There were nods of agreement all round, but nobody spoke. They didn't want to interrupt, all eager to hear what was coming next.

'My team and I have checked it inside and out.'

'And?' Peter prompted.

'Nothing much,' replied the sergeant, 'all we have are a couple of partial prints which seem to be from two different people but there isn't enough to get a match on our databases. We ran them through several times and came up with nothing. As for DNA, we don't have a match on record. Whoever did this was either incredibly careful or extremely lucky. We found nothing else at the scene to go on, not even a cigarette end.'

'So what does that mean?' asked Victor.

Roger turned to his old friend. 'For the moment, Vic, there really is nothing else we can do but wait.'

'You said you would find my daughter, you promised!' Peter shouted, slamming his fist on the sub-lieutenant's desk.

'Peter, you know that I will do everything in my power to find Rose, but we have nowhere left to look. She hasn't been seen or heard of since she disappeared.'

Peter bowed his head in defeat.

'There is one hope,' Fernandez added. 'Although not available yet, me and a group of tech guys from Bangalore are in the initial stages of developing the software to deal with scenarios like this. Where there is a partial print, the software will be able to recreate the rest of it with a ninety per cent success rate.'

'When will this be ready?' Peter asked, his eyes full of hope.

'I'm sorry, sir, but it's going to be a couple of years at best.'

Peter slumped visibly and handed Fernandez a business card. 'Call me when you've done it,' he said and left the room.

'I'm sorry for Peter's outburst,' Victor offered.

'Hey, we all feel the same, Vic, don't fret. Peter is allowed to be angry.'

'Did you mean what you said?' Victor asked the sergeant.

'Oh yes, absolutely, this kind of situation is exactly why we are developing our software, it's just not ready yet, but you can rest assured that this will be one of the first cases we put through the system when we do get it up and running.'

'Then don't you dare lose Peter's number,' said Victor.

'What next, Roger?'

'Not much else but pray and hope that someone somewhere spots her. If she turns up, we will bring her home, I'll keep in touch.'

Victor left to join Peter, who was sitting on the bonnet of his car.

'Hospital?' he asked.

'Take me to church, please.'

'Get in then son, let's see what the Big Man can do for us.'

***

At the Naik apartment, it had been five days since the innocent young girl arrived, dirty, bedraggled and fast asleep. She was settling in well, all things considered, and was totally oblivious to what was happening in Goa with her real family.

She had no recollection whatsoever of her former life. Jonathan had been on tenterhooks for the first couple of days, watching her every move and listening intently to everything she said, just in case there was any sign of her remembering her past. But Angelica seemed to be no more than a kid who had lost her memory and her parents.

She didn't talk too much but seemed to have enjoyed her first few days with them. She ate an awful lot and had a penchant for puris. Her face was brightening by the day, and everything looked like it was going to plan for Jonathan.

That was until this morning when Angelica woke up crying in pain. Preeti informed Elizabeth, who in turn called their family doctor, who arrived within the hour.

After thoroughly examining the girl, 'I can't find anything wrong with her,' the doctor informed Angelica's anxious new parents.

'Are you sure? She doesn't look well to me,' Elizabeth snapped. Jonathan shot her a look.

'I'm sorry, doctor,' she continued, 'Angelica has had a stressful time, I just don't want her to suffer any more.' Jonathan had filled the doctor in on the circumstances of the child's sudden arrival a couple of days ago. He had also set the wheels in motion for them to officially adopt her.

Angelica was holding her stomach, letting out intermittent groans.

'It's more than likely just a tummy bug. As you said, we don't know where she has been or what she has eaten or the quality of the water she was drinking before you took her in.' Jonathan looked at his wife and they both nodded in agreement.

The doctor wrote something and handed the piece of paper to Jonathan. 'Get these for her, it's a course of antibiotics, best to be on the safe side. Give her an aspirin every four hours until the pain has gone. If she is not feeling better by tomorrow evening give me a call.'

Jonathan showed the doctor to the door, 'thanks for coming at such short notice.'

'No problem,' replied the doctor as he accepted the envelope that Jonathan was holding.

Angelica had not slept well that night and felt terrible; there was an aching in her stomach and her heart. She had no appetite but did not feel nauseous. Upon being told to stay in bed and after a lot of tossing and turning, she had finally fallen back to sleep.

'She will be ok, won't she?' asked Elizabeth, as she stood in the kitchen with Jonathan.

Although Jonathan looked calm, inside he was extremely worried. Had the serum affected the girl adversely?

'You heard the doctor, she'll be fine,' he said to his wife, slipping his arms around her waist.

Comforted by his words, Elizabeth nuzzled her face against her husband's chest.

***

Maria had lain in the same position for the last four days; her only movements were involuntary, when the nurses bathed her every morning. On the last day that they spoke, Peter had gone to the nearest church and sat for hours. Praying, crying and begging any and every God there might be to help him find Rose and to send Maria off peacefully. That was the only time that Peter had left Maria's side since she lost consciousness and while he could still see his wife's beautiful face, he would cherish every moment until he had no choice but to let go.

During the night, Maria's heart rate had slowed. The faint beep, beep, beep from the monitor was the only sound inside the room. After checking her vitals, Doctor Vaidya had informed them that there was not much time left. All three had been trying to squeeze in every last moment with their beloved Maria. Seconds seemed like minutes, minutes like hours and hours like days until it felt like they had been in the twelve-by-fifteen-foot, fluorescently lit hospital room for a lifetime.

'She truly was amazing,' Carmen stated, after the doctor left, breaking the eerie silence. Peter gave a half-smile and Victor nodded. Maria's breathing had slowed and only the closest inspection could detect her chest rising and falling.

The family were all standing now, with Peter on her left and her mother and father to the right. Both of her hands were held tight, one by her husband and the other by Carmen. Victor completed the connection through his wife. Victor started mumbling the Lord's prayer as best he could and halfway through, Peter and Carmen joined in, repeating the prayer slowly, and in unison, over and over. Peter stared intently at Maria's face and, just for a moment, thought that she had opened her eyes. Maria made a sound, which made all three of them jump, almost like a short, nasal laugh and then the heart monitor's beep, beep changed to a continuous tone. There was no rushing into the room of nurses and doctors, no crash team, no alarms going off. With one final laugh at life, Maria had passed, and they all knew that there was nothing to be done but accept it.

Peter swallowed the lump in his throat, leant over his wife and kissed her gently on the forehead.

'I will always love you, my queen,' he promised her and, looking up as if to the heavens, begged. 'Please Lord, take care of her until we meet again.' He left the room with tears streaming down his face.

Head spinning, he made his way along the corridor, ignoring the looks of people as he passed. Peter flung open the exit door and walked out into the stifling air. He couldn't breathe.

He reached for his tie and yanked it from his neck, took off his suit jacket and threw them to the ground. He walked aimlessly towards the other side of the car park, where the only thing that stopped him was a concrete wall.

Peter stood there staring at nothing. Now crying uncontrollably, he let out an almighty roar, the kind of sound that could have been heard a mile away. It was pure anger; all this time he had muddled through life letting things happen to him without putting up a fight, but now, something inside had snapped.

In the minute or so since Maria's peaceful death, Peter had changed. He roared again and was now slamming his fists into the wall. A couple of passers-by stopped but then carried on walking, deciding that he was better left alone in that state.

It took Peter a full ten minutes to calm himself. He had roared, shouted, sworn and cursed. Maria was dead and there was nothing he could do about it. His mind was now totally focused on Rose; he may have lost his wife, but he was not going to lose his daughter too. He turned from the wall, composed himself, took a deep breath and whispered, 'I'm coming to get you, Rose.' And with a steely determination, he wiped his face on his shirt sleeves and headed back into the hospital.

During Peter's absence, Carmen and Victor held their heads silently in prayer, neither wanting to acknowledge their daughter's lifeless body. Doctor Vaidya had seen Peter storm out of Maria's room and knew that the inevitable had finally happened. Seeing him return, the doctor decided that he would give the family a while alone to say their goodbyes before making the necessary arrangements for the body.

'Come here,' Carmen said to Peter, as she stepped over to hug him.

She held him tight and was joined by her husband. The three of them stood at Maria's side holding onto each other, crying until Victor finally broke off. 'We had better let the doctor in,' he said.

Peter went to find Doctor Vaidya, who was standing at the nurse's station. Noticing Peter, he motioned him to come over. 'She's gone,' Peter said.

The pair made their way to join the grieving parents. This must have been one special lady, the doctor thought.

Amid all the heartache, crying and praying, nobody had seen the light rise from Maria's body and hover at the ceiling. Maria's spirit watched them for a few seconds before she could no longer resist the pull. She was going to a better place now, a place where pain did not exist. She turned towards the light and let herself drift off into the ether.

Chapter Twenty-Three
Our Lady of Merces Church,
12:45 p.m., 8th January

Seven days had passed since Maria's death and, being well loved not only by her family but by the whole community, the church was full to bursting for her funeral.

Peter, Carmen and Victor were sat in the front row with the Lobo family. Maria was an only child so there were no siblings, nieces or nephews. Roger Moreas and his family were also there, along with a plethora of police officers, neighbours, and doctors and nurses from the hospital who had all taken Maria to their hearts. Jack sat a couple of rows back from his brother. He had needed a peg of rum just to face the family. The next day he planned to travel to Mumbai and stay with a friend who had some work for him; he couldn't get away from this place fast enough.

The priest concluded his sermon and asked Peter to step up to say something. Peter had barely uttered a word to anyone since leaving the hospital. Making his way to where the priest was standing, he remembered what Maria had said; it had been playing over and over in his mind, *'do not fall apart'* – he could still hear her voice.

He shook hands with the priest and took to the pulpit. 'Thank you everybody for coming today,' Peter began. He took a moment to look down at the faces of the people sitting in the pews, most of whom he recognised but some he didn't; however, all present were totally focused on him.

'Maria, my wife...' He took a deep breath to suppress his tears. 'Those of you who were close to her would know just how wonderful a person she was. Her smile was intoxicating and her laughter contagious. She never had a bad word to say about anybody and was always optimistic, even when she knew she had only days to live. I am sure you all know that our daughter was abducted just before her mother died.'

There was a murmur across the church, as people turned to one another in acknowledgement. Most already knew but you could tell who didn't from the gasps and looks of shock on their faces.

'Yes, that's right, our Rose never got to say goodbye to her mother.' There was a collective murmur of sympathy

'I promised Maria that I would find our daughter Rose and with the help of our Lord, Jesus Christ, I will fulfil that promise.'

There were cries of 'Amen' from the pews and everybody crossed themselves at least twice, for good measure. Peter turned to the polished teak coffin containing his wife's body and then back to the congregation.

'Maria, the love of my life, my beautiful wife, my best friend, one day we will be together again, but until then I will look after myself and I will try not to fall apart.' Peter shut his eyes tight to stem the flow of tears that were welling up.

The priest stepped in and took over. As Peter returned to his seat, Carmen got up to speak; she squeezed his arm supportively as she passed him. A few other people followed Carmen and after, a few hymns were sung. With some final words from the priest, the ceremony ended. Peter, Victor and Michael carried the coffin with two neighbours and Sub-Lieutenant Moreas. The sombre walk out of the church was slow and controlled. All six men marched in unison, like an army detail. The expressions on the faces of the congregation as they passed were a mixture of sorrow and pity.

Outside the church, the band was waiting and started up, as the coffin was carried out. The traffic had stopped, and cars were waiting respectfully on both sides of the road for the coffin to pass, followed by the band and the congregation. The procession snaked out of the churchyard and along the middle of the road for thirty metres, before it crossed into the graveyard and Maria's final resting place.

It was a lengthy line with over one hundred and fifty people, women in black dresses, some with veils, men in black or brown suits. Peter was at the front of the coffin; he looked down to his right to see Danny matching his stride, chest puffed out and head held high.

When he noticed Peter looking down at him, Danny met his gaze and with tears in his eyes, said, 'It's OK, uncle, I'll help you find Rose.'

The boy was only eleven, had lost his best friend but look at him, what a tower of strength he was. In that moment, for the first time in what seemed like an eternity, Peter felt a tiny spark of optimism flicker to life in him.

He gave Danny a smile and placed his free hand on the boy's shoulder.

Chapter Twenty-Four
Naik residence, Mumbai, 12:08 p.m., 9th January

Jonathan was working on site at his new development, Elizabeth was at a client's house playing interior designer and Elijah was at school. Angelica had awoken in the early hours to the feeling of a presence in her room but after looking around she had shrugged it off and fallen back to sleep.

She slid her feet into her slippers, which still made everyone laugh at the way the monkey heads wobbled around when she walked. Angelica was, as usual, in search of food.

'Hey, sleepy head,' Preeti called out from the mezzanine. She was polishing the glass panels in between the steel handrail and the tiled floor. 'Hungry?' she asked.

Angelica smiled up at her and nodded. The child sat on the sofa to watch TV. Preeti retrieved the bowl of fruit from the refrigerator that she had prepared earlier and set it down on the counter. Angelica frowned.

'No more eating like a slouch, madam,' Preeti insisted, as she beckoned Angelica over to sit with her.

'OK,' Angelica smiled and turned the TV volume up so she could hear it from the kitchen. She did enjoy watching the satellite music channels.

'How are you feeling?' Preeti asked as Angelica pulled herself onto the stool.

'Better,' the girl replied.

'Good, you know that you will have to start school soon. I heard sir and madam talking about it yesterday.'

Angelica screwed up her nose. She enjoyed spending all day in the apartment, and although she liked her new parents, Preeti was her favourite; she didn't know why, maybe it was because she always looked so happy, plus she got away with more when they were alone, or at least she used to.

'Preeti?' Angelica said, with a mouthful of banana.

'Yes.'

'Can I tell you something?'

'Of course.'

'Promise you won't laugh?'

'Come on, what is it?' the maid prompted with a chuckle.

'See, you're laughing already,' Angelica said.

'OK, OK, sorry!' Preeti straightened her face, 'what is it?'

'Well, something was in my room when I woke up this morning, when it was still dark.'

Preeti looked shocked.

'What was it? Not a rat, we don't have rats here! I keep this place spotless!'

'No, not an animal, it was ...' Angelica paused. 'Are angels real?' she enquired, with a studious look.

'Well, I am Hindu, and you are Catholic – in both of our religions angels are said to exist, although we think of them in different ways. I have never really thought about it, to be honest – why, did you see an angel?' asked Preeti, genuinely interested.

'I think so, maybe. I don't know,' Angelica said.

'Did it speak to you?'

'No, I just had this strange feeling that somebody was watching me, I wasn't scared though,' Angelica smiled.

'Wow,' exclaimed the maid.

'It was like a glowing light, but it disappeared before I could see it properly,' the girl continued.

Preeti gave a low whistle.

'And now you feel good, no more pain in the tummy?'

'No, I'm fine.' Angelica patted her middle.

'Maybe you *were* visited by an angel.'

'Maybe,' Angelica said, 'but I won't tell Eli, he will definitely laugh at me.'

'Yes,' Preeti agreed, 'we should keep this to ourselves.'

'Our secret?' the girl said as she resumed her breakfast.

'Yes, our secret' Preeti confirmed, smiling.

'*You* are an angel, don't forget,' Preeti said as she walked to the staircase – 'Angelica!'

The girl looked bemused for a second or two.

'Angel-ica,' Preeti called out.

'Oh yeah!' Angelica giggled with delight.

***

Two days later Peter was in his workshop, which had always been a haven away from the real world. Now, bizarrely, he hated it.

It was the place that had kept him from his wife and daughter and his only reason for being in there now was to finish this invention. After that, he had sworn he would never step foot in there again.

After the funeral, Peter had gone straight home, changed into his overalls and started work. Focusing on this project was the only thing that kept him from breaking down. He had barely slept and only eaten because Juanita was leaving bowls of food in the kitchen for him. Victor and Carmen had not yet visited, and he was glad of that; the last thing he wanted was to talk about the past week or so.

He had called Mr Smith, one of the investors, and put them off until the twenty-third of the month. The guy wasn't happy; they were taking a huge risk investing money in something that didn't even exist yet, but if it worked it would pay off big time. There were less than two weeks to finish what Peter referred to as 'the box', and it was literally a box, made of plywood measuring two feet by two feet by three feet. It contained one central steel shaft, which was set through the middle of ten moulded plastic wheels. Each wheel had powerful neodymium magnets set at an angle, spaced around their edge.

Inside the box there was the same number of magnets set at opposing angles. The goal of this project was to get the central shaft to rotate using the force of the opposing magnets so that it spun indefinitely. It would, he hoped, produce enough electricity to power the essentials in a small home, including a refrigerator. His invention was aimed at people living in remote villages where there was no electricity supply. Regular servicing should give a working life of at least twenty-five years. The units could be manufactured at low cost, using better materials than Peter's prototype and possibly even subsidised by governments.

Peter also had plans for a larger, slightly more expensive version, which would produce enough power for the average family home, including all appliances.

None of that mattered, however, if this prototype did not work, and until now the arrangement of the magnets had been stubbornly wrong. For his third attempt that day Peter released the brake, full of hope – but still to no avail.

'Damn,' Peter shouted. He picked up a wrench and threw it against the workshop wall.

'OK, let's try again,' he said in an attempt to calm himself.

'Cup of tea?' he heard a voice call from outside.

It was Juanita – she had already made one and was holding it out to him.

'Thanks,' Peter said, grateful for the break.

'How are you feeling?' she asked.

'Just the same.'

'How's it going in there?' Juanita questioned. She had no idea what he was working on but was trying to get him to talk.

'It's going, not where I want it to, but it's going,' Peter said with a grimace.

Juanita gave him a smile.

'There's chicken and rice in the fridge for you – don't forget to eat it, ok?

'Thanks,' Peter replied, managing a smile.

Juanita left him to it. This was the one thing that would give him the resources to find his little girl and he needed it to work, it HAD to work.

The next evening, at the Alvares' household, Carmen was already in bed reading a book, or rather staring at the words on the page. Maria's death had hit her hard. For any parent to lose a child was disastrous, but to lose a daughter and granddaughter within a few days was unimaginable. Carmen had spent a lot of time wondering what she had done to deserve this.

Victor left the bathroom wearing his favourite blue striped pyjamas. He slipped into bed holding his own book. He wasn't an avid reader like his wife but reading helped him fall asleep. They hadn't spoken much; they'd made small talk but neither of them was ready to discuss their daughter's death. They both knew it was not the way to move forward with their lives, but for now it was all they could do.

The search for Rose had effectively come to a halt. It was almost like everyone had given up looking for her. Victor felt useless. All his enquiries had been fruitless, and he still couldn't help blaming himself.

'Why don't you go and see Peter tomorrow? It's been a few days, he may need to talk to someone,' Carmen suggested.

'He hasn't even called, what if he is busy, what if he doesn't want to talk to me because…?'

'Don't start that shit again, Vic,' Carmen snapped. 'It wasn't your fault, now drop it or you're going to drive yourself, and me, crazy! Put your energy into something positive and see if your son-in-law needs any help, take a bottle of rum or some beers, it may do the pair of you some good to get drunk.'

Victor laid his book on his lap and his head dropped as though he was going to cry.

'Stop it,' Carmen shouted at him, 'pull yourself together.'

Victor nodded, 'I'll go round tomorrow evening.'

'That's better,' Carmen said approvingly.

Victor decided against the book, closed it, put it on his bedside table and pulled the sheet up to his neck. 'Goodnight darling,' he said.

The reason Victor didn't want to see Peter was because, for the first time since Rose's disappearance, they would be alone, and it was inevitable they would end up discussing the events of that fateful day.

***

Victor didn't tell Peter he was coming and, knowing it was highly unlikely that he would be anywhere else, he made his way to the house where his daughter had once lived, stopping off to pick up two bottles of Old Monk rum. Carmen held him as tight as she ever had before he left and let him know he needn't worry about rushing back, especially after drinking. 'Sleep on the sofa,' she had told him.

Pulling up outside, Victor noticed that there was a light on. He walked up the pathway towards the house, which had been a hive of activity on the day Rose went missing. Now it was deserted.

Victor's breath caught in his throat as the echo of the cry 'grandfather is here' rang in his ears. How often had he heard that little girl's voice raised excitedly as Rose saw him coming?

The front door was unlocked, so Victor let himself in, with one of the bottles in hand. He made his way through the house. The place was a mess; there were clothes on the floor in the living room and the kitchen sink was full. The bin was overflowing, with a line of ants that led all the way to the garden. Surprisingly, Victor managed to find two clean tumblers and walked over to the open back door. He could hear noise coming from the workshop and the lights were on. Victor paused for a moment, putting the glasses and bottle down on the kitchen counter. He needed some Dutch courage, so he poured himself a good slug and gulped it down. He felt the warmth of the alcohol as it travelled down his throat and a few seconds after, felt the effect as it hit his brain.

Victor grabbed the glasses and bottle and started purposefully towards the workshop, at the bottom of the garden.

Peter had slept for only two hours the previous night. No matter how tired he was he just couldn't seem to manage a full night's sleep. He was exhausted, drained and stressed. Things in the workshop weren't going his way and he was making silly mistakes with his calculations.

Peter heard a knock and turned round to see his father-in-law standing in the open doorway.

'Drink?' Victor asked, as he held up the rum bottle. Peter smiled. 'Oh Vic, how glad am I to see you?' he said, as he dropped the screwdriver he was holding onto the bench.

'You look like shit, son, it's time you took a break. Let's go and sit down,' Victor said. Without waiting for an answer, he turned and headed for the wooden table in the middle of the garden.

Peter followed. Both men sat, with Victor doing the pouring – a good three-finger measure for each of them.

'Thanks for coming, I could do with some company,' Peter said, as they clinked their glasses.

'Have you eaten?' Victor asked

'Yes, there is plenty of food in the fridge if you want some. Juanita keeps bringing more than I can manage to get down.'

'I may need to, after a few of these,' Victor chuckled.

'How's Carmen?' Peter asked.

'She looks like she's coping, but I don't think she is. She invited a couple of friends over for the evening, so I'll be staying here the night, if that's OK?'

Peter nodded and emptied his glass in one, 'will this be enough?' he asked, picking up the bottle.

'Don't worry, there's another in the car,' Victor replied with a smile.

'I hear you're working on something special in there; would you like to tell me about it?'

Peter explained his latest project as they drank. The night was humid but there was a cool breeze blowing, which both men were glad of. The first bottle only lasted an hour, and the relaxing effects of the alcohol provided a welcome break from the stress of their current situation.

Victor had fetched the other bottle from his car while Peter dished out a plateful of food for them to share. They ate, drank and talked into the early hours of the morning.

'I'm sorry, Peter,' Victor blurted out; he had finally worked up the courage to broach the topic pressing on both of their minds but that neither of them had wanted to bring up first.

'Look, Vic, I have thought non-stop about what happened that day and what you did or didn't do doesn't matter. We are all so complacent about life here, thinking that nothing bad could ever happen. You weren't the only one present; don't forget, I was in the workshop.' Peter motioned to the open doorway.

'But I was supposed to be watching them, and I fell asleep.' Victor was now slurring his words.

'Vic, I don't want to hear about this ever again, OK? The only person blaming you for what happened is you!' Peter poured his father-in-law another drink.

'I think this should be my last,' Victor insisted, with a hiccup.

'Me too,' replied Peter, 'besides, I *am* going to find her, I will find my Rose.'

'I hope so, Peter, I really do.'

Peter changed the subject and soon after, they decided to call it a night. It was past three a.m.

'I love you like my own son, you know that don't you, Peter?' Victor declared as he lay down on the sofa.

'I love you too, Vic, goodnight!'

Carmen was right, they needed that night and the rum, because it wasn't until just before noon when Peter came downstairs to find a very hungover Victor, head in hands, sitting on the sofa.

'Coffee?' he asked.

'You read my mind, got any painkillers?' Victor groaned.

'First cupboard on the left,' Peter laughed, as he made his way to the kitchen. He was hungover himself, but the sleep had done him the world of good; he felt like today could be a turning point.

Peter opened the back door to the sound of birds chirping and music playing. He felt a renewed sense of purpose and was going to seize the day, that was for sure.

Chapter Twenty-Five
Naik residence, 5.24 p.m., 14th January

Preeti was preparing the evening meal for the family, Jonathan was still at work and Angelica was laying in her room reading a book when Elizabeth had called out to join her downstairs.

The girl was recuperating well and had put on a couple of kilos since her arrival. She looked healthier and the colour was returning to her cheeks.

'You really are beautiful, my girl,' said Elizabeth proudly. The pair had bonded well. Elizabeth was happy to have a daughter and even happier at the effect that Angelica's arrival had had on Elijah. He was no longer the rude, obnoxious son he once was; it seemed that some of Angelica's charm had rubbed off on him.

'Are you excited to be starting school on Monday?' Elizabeth asked.

'I suppose so,' Angelica said unconvincingly.

'Don't worry, sweetie pie, Eli is in the year above and the teachers will be looking out for you too,' Elizabeth reassured her. They had fast-tracked her enrolment in the same school as her brother to keep them close.

'Mom?'

'Yes, dear?'

'Why can't I remember things?'

Elizabeth found herself unable to speak.

'I mean, I know what that is,' she said pointing at the TV, 'but I can't remember anybody and when I lay in bed, I try really hard to think of things that I have done but there is nothing there!' Angelica slapped her head in annoyance.

Elizabeth was not ready for this conversation; she hadn't thought it would come so soon. There was no way she was going to tell her poor daughter the truth or what she herself had been led to believe was the truth. If anybody was going to tell Angelica that her real parents had died then it would be Jonathan.

'Oh baby, you were sick, and the doctor says that you lost your memory because something happened to your brain while you were sleeping. Hopefully you will remember things soon, just be patient. All you need to know is that we love you, OK?' Elizabeth said. She knew it sounded just as ridiculous as her explanation to Elijah, but she hoped it would postpone any further questioning for now.

Angelica shrugged her shoulders and stared out at the city through the wall of glass that she was pressing her nose against, making it fog as she exhaled.

'Anyway, we're going shopping tomorrow,' her mother said brightly, trying to change the subject.

'What for?' Angelica asked.

'Clothes and shoes and more clothes.'

The girl needed a complete wardrobe and that included school wear.

Elijah jumped down the stairs two at a time to join them on the sofa.

'Have you finished your homework, Eli?' his mother asked.

'Of course! Angelica, are you ready to die?'

'What?' Elizabeth said, 'really Eli!'

The two kids laughed at their mother.

'Not if I kill you first,' shouted Angelica, and took off, running for her brother's bedroom.

'The games, always the games,' Elizabeth said to herself, shaking her head.

Chapter Twenty-Six
Peter's workshop, 12:10 p.m., 23rd January

Two days after the drinking session, having slept a lot better, Peter had finally got the correct angle and arrangements of the magnets, so that when he released the brake the cylinder had started to rotate; it was a crude machine, but it finally worked! Peter connected the power meter and got a reading of one point seven kilowatts.

Peter Rosario, a part-time inventor, had managed to accomplish what many people through history had attempted but failed. From Aristotle to Da Vinci to Johann Bessler, Peter was the first person to make it work. He stood there staring at the meter reading. It remained constant.

He started to laugh. Peter laughed and laughed and laughed until he cried.

'This is for you, my darling,' he proclaimed, looking to the sky. He was sure that Maria was watching his every move and he would have loved her to have seen this for herself.

Peter spent the next day tinkering and fine-tuning 'the box' until the power output measured two point one kilowatts. After that, he had left it running and it hadn't stopped since.

Now Peter, wearing his best brown suit, was standing in his workshop with the two American investors, who had brought their own engineer with them.

They spent a while studying the device, making sure there was no power input secretly rigged up to it. The previous day, Peter had changed the top cover from plywood to clear Perspex so that the inner workings could be seen.

'Well?' asked the larger of the two investors, peering at the engineer.

'Well?' the engineer asked. His name was Hank, and he was a typical Texan – large, loud and friendly. 'Well?' he asked again.

'Hank, can you please give us your opinion on this.' Klaus, the investor who had a German accent, was getting impatient now.

'OK guys, I will put it simply for you,' Hank started, his hand resting on the top of 'the box'. He enjoyed the feel of the movement coming from within.

'This guy is a goddamn genius,' he shouted, pointing at Peter.

Klaus looked at his partner and then back at Hank. 'So what does that mean?'

'It works. I have never seen or heard of one of these working, actually working, producing power with no input, and to be honest, it shouldn't be possible.'

Klaus turned to Peter. 'We will need a moment alone, if you don't mind?'

'I'm a genius,' Peter said to himself quietly; he liked the sound of that! He chuckled as the men left the workshop.

'This is big, guys, this is fucking huge!' Hank said. Klaus looked at his partner, Benjamin Smith.

'Looks like we were lucky to have found this guy before anyone else,' Benjamin said.

'We are all going to be extremely rich men,' Klaus stated. They slapped each other on the back and rejoined Peter in the workshop.

'We want it,' Klaus confirmed.

'It's yours at the right price, of course,' replied Peter.

The two men shook hands. Benjamin held out his hand too.

'Mr Rosario, you are going to be a very rich man. We will get the contracts drawn up and sent over to you within the week. You'll need to come to the United States and spend some time with Hank here until our first prototype is working, is that OK with you?'

They clearly were not going to hand over anything until they had a fully working prototype in their state-of-the-art premises.

'Whatever it takes,' Peter agreed.

Later that evening, with the Americans having already left for home, Peter was sat in the living room of the Alvares house with Victor and Carmen. He wanted to tell them the good news in person.

'She would have been so proud,' Carmen said, a tear in her eye. 'She always believed in you!'

'I know,' Peter said softly.

'How much?' asked Victor, getting straight to the point.

Carmen rolled her eyes at him, 'Vic, honestly!'

'It's OK,' Peter said, 'it all depends on us being able to complete a working prototype in America.'

'You're going to America?' Carmen asked.

'Yes, for three or four months maybe.'

'And then?' Victor asked.

'Well, they didn't say too much about the numbers, but if all goes to plan it's going to be a lot. Millions. Yes, definitely millions. Millions of US dollars,' Peter exclaimed proudly.

Victor looked at Carmen; they were both in shock.

Peter laughed. 'You all thought I was crazy, didn't you?' He was over the moon; he didn't care about his invention; he didn't care about the money as long as it was enough to cover the cost of his search for Rose.

'To Peter,' announced Victor as he held up his glass.

'No, to Maria,' Peter corrected.

'To Maria,' they chorused.

PART 2

Chapter Twenty-Seven
West-side Heights, Bandra, Mumbai,
8:46 a.m., 17th October 2016

Peter was standing on the terrace of his newly constructed penthouse apartment. He had aged well and was now sporting a greying beard with matching hair, making him look older than he was. In the years he had spent away from India, Peter had become a different man. He was stronger and no longer felt the need to hide himself away from the world. Finally, he was ready to face life head on.

It felt like a lifetime since Maria's death and Rose's disappearance, but whenever Peter shut his eyes the images of their faces were all he ever saw.

Staring out across the city he whispered, 'where are you, Rose?'

Rain-heavy clouds had finally made way for a clear cerulean sky, the sun now in full force, drying out the streets and buildings. The haze of steam hovering over the landscape was a beautiful sight to see. Peter loved monsoon season; the soothing sound, the smell of vegetation, fields turned into lakes and areas that were dry and dusty the rest of the year now covered in a hundred shades of green. He was always sad to see it come to an end.

Peter had returned from the US a couple of years ago. Initially, there had been complications with the design of the prototype that they were building, but with the help of Hank and his team they had finished it.

Klaus and Benjamin got the company up and running and the orders were coming in by the thousand. Peter enjoyed his stay there and had spent a lot of time with the men.

They got on well together but after Peter was no longer needed, he left that part of his life behind and had only spoken to Benjamin on two occasions since.

The workshop and his inventions had kept him away from his family and wanting no part of the company, he had opted for a settlement of fifteen million dollars and eight per cent of all profits. He had money in the bank and was investing it wisely in property, including the apartment that he was standing in, which cost just over one million US dollars.

On his return, Peter had travelled across India to all the major cities, making the most of the Royal Enfield Bullet 500 motorbike that he had bought for himself. At every stop he made, no matter how remote, he handed out flyers with Rose's picture, his contact number and reward details.

After doing everything possible on the road, he decided to base himself in Mumbai. The truth was that he couldn't bear to stay in Goa, not in that house, there were too many memories.

He didn't know why he chose Mumbai but for some reason, he felt drawn to the city.

As he walked back into the spacious apartment, he heard his phone ringing.

'Hello?' he answered.

'Peter, it's Vic ... he's gone.'

'What do you mean?' Peter asked, recognising Carmen's voice.

'He passed last night. It was a heart attack, there was nothing I could do,' Carmen sobbed.

'I'm coming, I'll catch the next flight there,' he said.

'Thank you, Peter.'

'I'll see you later,' he said and hung up.

Shit, he thought, he had only been in Goa a couple of months ago and the old guy had seemed fine.

He made a quick call.

'Hello boss?' a voice answered on the first ring.

'Get me on the first flight to Goa,' Peter said, 'I'm heading to the airport now.'

'No problem, consider it done.'

The young man on the other end of the line was Peter's new assistant, Mackben, or Mack for short. Mack was well educated, smart, loyal and despite his young age knew a hell of a lot about everything. Peter had hired him to deal with his day-to-day business; now that he was a very wealthy man, Peter didn't need to do everything himself. He slipped off his robe and pyjamas and stepped into the oversized shower. Twenty minutes later he was wearing a slick bespoke Armani three-piece. Gone were the days of the ill-fitting brown mismatched suits that he used to wear in Goa. It was nothing but the best for him now.

Peter exited the lobby to find his white Jaguar XF waiting outside. 'Airport, sir?' the driver asked.

'Yes.'

If only Maria could see him now – he had made it, but it all meant nothing without her. His phone rang again.

'Mack?' he said.

'Sir, I've found a jet that can leave at noon.'

'Thank you.'

Peter slipped his phone into his jacket pocket, his thoughts on his family. He was sorry for Carmen; Victor was a great man and had been like a father to him since he and Maria married.

There would be another car waiting for Peter in Goa; he no longer used taxis, with their reckless drivers and dirty seats. Peter was not a snob with his new-found wealth but there was no doubt that he had started enjoying the finer things in life. He was getting older and could now afford to do the things he wanted to, so he did. Things were going to get hectic soon – he and Mack had put together a plan to find Rose, and Peter would have the team of people he needed at his disposal, within a month.

***

Walking the pathway that led to the Alvares house, Peter could smell the perfume of the roses that were in full bloom. Behind him, the ambulance doors slammed shut, ready for the trip to the morgue.

'Carmen,' he said as he approached his mother-in-law with outstretched arms.

'Oh Peter, I couldn't save him. When I woke up, he was cold.' Carmen sobbed as she threw her arms around him.

'It's OK, it's OK now, I'll take care of everything,' Peter reassured her.

***

Victor was a popular man, and his funeral was a huge affair; police and gangsters alike attended, even the chief minister was there, whom Victor had known for years.

After the service, they gathered at the Alvares house where Carmen was accompanied by Peter, Roger Moreas and his wife, the Lobo family, and a few neighbours. Roger had been trying to get Peter's attention for the last couple of hours and now that most people had left, he seized his chance. Having exchanged words of condolence earlier in the day, it hadn't been the time to talk about what he wanted to discuss with Peter.

'Looking good, Peter,' Roger said, noticing his expensive suit.

'You too, Roger.' The sub-lieutenant had retired from the police force a year earlier and was enjoying life to the full, especially the eating part!

'Do you remember the forensics guy from a few years ago, Fernandez?'

'Yes, just about.'

'Well, he called me last week, regarding the package we found outside your house. He has been trying to get in touch with you, but it seems you have changed your phone number.'

'What is it, Roger?' Peter had virtually forgotten about what the guy had told him seven years ago. As he recalled snippets of the conversation, his heart began to beat faster.

Roger handed Peter a piece of paper, which he unfolded. Written on it were two names: Maalik Aggarwal and Sunil Patel.

'The kid's finally done it,' Roger said, 'took him a lot longer than expected but there you are, two partial prints now confirmed as these guys, and they have records as long as your arm! Petty theft, drugs, extortion, etc. The last time they were seen was close to two years ago; they were picked up in Calangute trying to rob a jewellery store. To say they're not the sharpest tools in the box would be an understatement. After grabbing a bagful of items, they couldn't get out of the door. They were pushing it, shoulder-barging it and even fly-kicking it until the local force arrived and walked straight in to arrest them. All the idiots had to do was pull instead of push! You should have seen the CCTV footage, it was hilarious.'

Peter gave a courteous chuckle but his mind was poised, ready to hear more on the first useful thing he had heard in years.

'Where are they now?' he asked.

'They served eighteen months and have not been seen since their release. I had their last known addresses raided, but it seems like they have gone to ground.'

'Thank you, Roger, you have no idea how much this means to me.'

'It seems like you have more resources than the police now from what I hear,' Roger smiled. 'Good luck with this, and anything you need from me, or the locals, just let me know.' Roger had heard a rumour that Peter was going to conduct his own investigation and was pleased that he could finally be of some help after all this time. The case had stalled and been shelved as just another missing kid, and he hated retiring with unfinished business.

Roger took his old friend by the hand. 'It was good seeing you, Peter, take care of yourself and don't forget what I said.'

'I won't. And Roger, thanks again.'

Peter popped the note into his inside jacket pocket. This was the break he had been hoping for. He was going to find Rose! Even if he had to turn the whole of India upside down to do it.

'Uncle,' he heard a voice behind him.

'Danny? Look at the size of you!' Peter exclaimed as he got his first proper look at the young man. They hadn't seen each other for seven years.

'You live in Mumbai now, so I hear.' Peter took in Danny's muscular figure; he had clearly been hitting the gym.

'I do, yes, we're neighbours again,' Danny smiled; he had missed the man a lot since he disappeared to America.

'Take my number,' Peter insisted. 'I have a job for you if you're interested.' He knew Danny was a smart boy and he would also enjoy the connection that he made to the past.

'A job, uncle, what kind of job?' Danny said eagerly.

'Does it matter?' asked Peter. 'Call me in a couple of days, we can discuss it at a more appropriate time.'

'Sounds good!' replied the young man.

The next day Peter was packing to leave when Carmen handed him an envelope with his name written on it. He looked at her enquiringly.

'Victor wrote this about a year after, you know...'

'What's inside?'

'No idea, he just said that you were to have it if anything happened to him.'

Peter placed the envelope in his overnight bag and zipped it shut. They shared a cup of tea on the veranda. His car pulled up outside and Peter hugged his mother-in-law goodbye.

Carmen looked into his eyes. 'What are you up to?' she asked, having not seen that look before.

Peter didn't answer, just gave her a wink.

'I'll see you soon,' he said as he walked to the car.

Peter directed the driver to the cemetery with a stop at the local florist first. He had made sure there was time to see Maria before he left; he wanted to tell her what was going on.

Chapter Twenty-Eight
Naik residence, 6:18 p.m., 22nd October

Angelica Naik stood in her bedroom in front of the full-length mirror, wearing skinny jeans and a baggy Ralph Lauren knitted jumper. Angelica was sixteen years old and five feet six. She had convinced her mother to let her have her almost waist-length hair cut into a trendy bob for a high-paying photoshoot.

Angelica was constantly being told that she was beautiful but like most beautiful people, she still found fault with her looks.

A few months after her arrival at the Naiks', she had moved from the guest room to a bedroom upstairs, opposite her brother's. It was much larger and had walk-in wardrobes and a very spacious bathroom.

Elizabeth had entered Angelica into beauty pageants from the age of thirteen and the beautiful child had been crowned queen in nearly all that she entered. Her seventeenth birthday was approaching, and she was on the verge of signing her first modelling contract with an agency.

At school, Angelica was a straight-A student across all subjects. She excelled in sport, which was her passion and was now attending a top all-girls school in the Cumballa Hill district of Mumbai. She was the captain of her soccer team, basketball team and an avid long-distance runner and to top it all, she was probably the most popular girl in the school. Angelica was kind-hearted and stood up to bullies, which had made her many friends over the years. The only negative thing on her school record was a couple of fights, which of course she had won! Angelica had been defending younger girls on both occasions.

Elizabeth and Jonathan wanted their daughter to one day become a doctor or business guru. Angelica, on the other hand, was quite happy with her modelling career. She had already earned a substantial sum for a girl of her age and securing this latest contract would see her financially independent by the time she was twenty.

'You will always be beautiful, but will get old one day. You can't rely on your looks for your income for the rest of your life,' her mother had warned her.

Angelica studied her nose, wondering whether the bump in the middle needed attention when she heard Elizabeth walk past her open door.

'Mom, do you think my...'

'Ah, don't even go there young lady,' Elizabeth said as she saw her daughter studying her face, 'nobody is getting a nose job this week!'

Angelica rolled her eyes.

'You know what, sweetheart? I've got used to seeing your hair that short now and I quite like it,' Elizabeth said.

'Can I dye it pink after this shoot?' Angelica said hopefully.

Her mother shut her eyes and took a deep breath; Angelica was a wonderful child, but she could be rather testing at times. 'Nope,' she said over her shoulder, as she walked off.

Angelica had not recalled any memories from her previous life as Rose. It wasn't until around a year after joining the Naik family that her new parents had sat down with her and told her

Jonathan's fabricated story of the car crash. Angelica cried and sulked for a day or two but had found it hard mourning those that she didn't remember. After that, not another word was spoken on the subject.

She had a passport in the name of Angelica Naik, and to anyone on the outside, she was undeniably one of the family.

Bored, Angelica walked the few paces to her brother's room.

'Fuck, bro, what's your *problem*?' Elijah shouted at her as she opened the door without knocking. He was on the phone, probably to one of his many girlfriends. 'Can't you knock? I could have been doing … anything.'

'Like what?' Angelica probed.

Eli picked up a cushion from his bed and threw it at her. 'I'll call you back,' he said into the phone and dropped it on the bed.

'Busy?'

'Always busy,' he answered, raising his eyebrows. Angelica laid down next to him and sighed.

'What's up?' Eli asked, his tone softer.

'I am sooooo bored!'

It was a Saturday evening and Angelica's two closest friends were at family gatherings, leaving her in limbo.

'Want to watch a movie or something?' she asked.

'No, I'm going to Ollie's house, I told you earlier, don't you remember?'

'Whatever, so you're just going to leave me here alone?' Angelica pouted.

'That's the idea, yes,' Eli laughed.

Angelica meant the world to Elijah, and he was the perfect big brother, although he did love to play tricks on her. His phone beeped.

'Ollie just messaged me and said you can come if you like,' Eli said, looking at his phone.

'Really? Yes!' she said excitedly.

'No, just kidding,' Eli laughed as he covered his face with a pillow ready for the onslaught of slaps from his sister.

'Bastard,' she shouted.

'Play something?' Eli said to his sister as he handed her the games console control.

'Naah,' she replied, 'you mind if I hang in here for a while?'

'Stay here as long as you like. Is there something bothering you?' Eli shot a glance at his sister.

Angelica was normally full of energy and didn't seem herself.

'I'm good, it's just, oh I don't know...'

Eli's phone rang. 'They're downstairs, got to go, I'll be back before midnight, mom's new curfew time, we can watch a movie and eat as much ice cream as we like when I come home, OK?

'OK,' Angelica said smiling; he always knew how to cheer her up. As he ran out of the room Angelica thought that her brother, now that he had lost weight, was really rather good-looking. She slipped under the duvet and closed her eyes.

Preeti was in her room. She was thirty-two years old now and still single. Her position in the household had been fortified with a raise and one day off per week. Her mother had finally stopped pestering her about marriage; she knew that this job was her life now and that she wouldn't give it up for a husband. Preeti loved living in the apartment. Her employers were kind and the kids were her best friends, especially Angelica, who was always helping when her parents weren't around.

Jonathan was still married to his work and was looking for investors for his new project but was having a difficult time – there was so much construction going on in the city. He was out entertaining a couple of potential clients and had annoyed his wife by cancelling the dinner date she had arranged the previous week.

Chapter Twenty-Nine
West-side Heights, Bandra, 9:45 a.m., 1st November

After calling Danny Lobo the previous day, Peter had arranged for his driver to pick the young man up and bring him to his apartment. Peter was in the process of turning a sizeable chunk of the double-height living area into an office for the team that he had hired in conjunction with his new head of staff, the tech genius and hacker extraordinaire who went by the name of Kush. The epitome of a geek, Kush was twenty years old and overweight from spending far too much time sitting in front of a computer screen. He was from a small village fifty kilometres north of Ahmedabad. His talent had shown from an early age and got him into trouble far too many times to remember.

Kush was wanted by several large companies in India and the US for hacking their systems and releasing valuable information. Kush wasn't a thief, but he was always out for justice and would take any chance he got to stick it to the Man. Mack had found him in a dark web chat room and Kush made

Peter jump through exacting hoops to prove that he wasn't a cop. Having finally met in person three months ago, Peter had taken to the young man instantly, hiring him on the spot after a brief display of his computing capability.

Kush wore round bifocal glasses, had a big mess of jet-black hair and was trying his hardest to grow a moustache, but it wasn't working, with just a few wispy hairs hanging on manfully to his upper lip.

Together they had hired two private investigators and two data analysts. With the arrival of Danny, Peter was satisfied that his team was complete.

'There you are,' Peter's voice welcomed his new recruit as he watched him stride through the front door. 'Thanks for coming.'

Danny looked around the vast area in awe. There were desks being set up and data cables were being laid. To his right, Danny saw a multitude of boxes stacked up and, with just a glance, could tell they contained computer equipment.

'What's going on uncle, what is all this?' Danny asked looking around him.

'You want the long or the short story? And stop calling me uncle, you're a grown man now – my name is Peter.'

Danny nodded. 'OK, Peter, short story please.'

'All this is what I've been working on for a year now. This is our new office and here there is only one job, one goal that we will all be focused on, for however long it takes.'

'And the goal?'

'Finding Rose, of course,' Peter replied as he squared his shoulders.

'What?' Danny stared at Peter, open-mouthed.

'Yes, Danny, we are going to find my daughter.'

'Uncle..., er..., Peter, it's been seven years!' The doubt was obvious in his tone.

'Kush, come over here.' Peter beckoned the hacker.

Kush had been busy kitting out the office; he wouldn't let anyone else get involved. He didn't need any help and besides, he had trust issues and wanted his network fully secure. With his know-how and Peter's money, the set-up that he was creating was on a par with any government or multinational company's arrangements.

'Danny, meet Kush,' Peter said, introducing the two young men. 'A lot has changed since Rose disappeared and Danny, now we have a lead, names. Do you remember the package left in our garden that day? I now have the names of two men that held that package.' Peter pointed to a board near the seven desks. Pinned to the board were two mugshots.

'These two had something to do with what went on that day. We also have Kush here, who is a genius with computer technology, and alongside him, we have four more staff and the computer power to get into anywhere we want to.'

'Anywhere,' Kush reiterated smugly.

'I also have a never-ending pot of money at my disposal, so what do you say? Will you be the final member of our team? Money, as I have said, is not an issue and ...'

'Peter,' Danny interrupted, cutting him off, 'I don't care about the money. Count me in, I want to find Rose.'

'Welcome to the team,' said a smiling Kush, as he slapped Danny on the arm.

'Perfect,' said Peter, handing the young man an envelope. 'This should last you at least a month,' he added. Danny looked inside to see it was full of cash. 'Peter, I said...'

'Be back here on Friday at nine a.m. sharp, we start then, OK?' Peter said, holding his hand palm out at a ninety-degree angle to his wrist as Danny tried to return the envelope.

'See you Friday,' Danny replied. He pocketed the cash and headed for the door.

Peter smiled to himself; the plan was coming together, and nothing was going to stop him from achieving his goal. He knew his little girl was out there somewhere, he could feel it in his bones.

Chapter Thirty
West-side Heights, Bandra, 9:00 a.m., 4th November

Peter was up before sunrise in anticipation of the day ahead; the day that he had been waiting far too long for was finally here.

The guys arrived early that morning and were left to get to know each other over coffee for the first half-hour before getting down to serious business.

The team consisted of Kush at the helm, then there was Vijay and Saira, independent private investigators who came highly recommended. Vijay had recently been involved in the widely publicised recovery of a kidnapped child in New Delhi whose parents were millionaires.

Saira was well known for her dogged determination and had many contacts in the city's government departments. Next came Vanya and Rahul, who were officially data analysts; one of their roles would be sifting through the thousands of hours of CCTV footage from all over the city, looking for the two kidnappers.

Kush had run a photograph of Rose through the computer ageing simulation that he created especially for this search; there were others out there, but they were nowhere near as efficient as his version.

Vanya had terrible OCD and was on the autistic spectrum. She wasn't good with groups, crowds or noise so, at her request, her desk was set apart from the others. She always wore over-the-ear headphones to drown out the world and communicated mostly by text.

Her outstanding skill was that she had a photographic memory and Peter had been assured that she could fly through pictures at a rate of five per second looking for a face. Rahul was there for his expertise with numbers; he could find a discrepancy in anyone's accounts, no matter how clean they tried to look. One of his jobs would be to find Rose through records – medical, school, anything that he could think of. Rose wouldn't be known by her real name, so they didn't have much to work with, but they had access to data, and lots of it.

With their separate skills and areas of expertise, this group of people made a team, a perfectly balanced team with every member having an IQ of no less than one hundred and forty. Peter had bought all the computer hardware that Kush requested. They had the latest tech available and some that wasn't, including the highest-speed broadband in the country.

Peter gathered up the completed employment contracts and non-disclosure agreements that his lawyer had drawn up. They were to receive a substantial salary on an indefinite basis, which would see them all employed until Rose was found. Upon finding Rose alive and well, they would also receive a lump sum as a thank-you.

The NDAs were to ensure that they kept their mouths shut. Peter didn't want any of this leaked; it was a clandestine operation and nobody else was to find out unless informed by Peter himself.

Using his foot, Kush slid a cardboard box containing a Faraday bag across the floor to the centre of the group. They looked at him quizzically, except Vanya, who walked over and placed her cell phone into it. Kush smiled and placed his in too, followed by the rest of the team.

'For everyone's safety, your phones will be kept in this bag and locked in my room. You will get them back when this is over,' Peter said, 'you all have new phones sitting on your desks.' Peter nodded at Kush – he would let the kid explain, seeing as it had been his idea.

'Guys, your new phones are chipped and tracked, the only numbers programmed into them are for the people that you see here now. All calls and messages will be recorded and saved to this baby.' He pointed to the PC he had custom-built over the last few days. Next to it sat two thirty-two-inch screens. 'This is for the boss's peace of mind and everybody's protection.'

They all nodded in agreement.

'There are files on each of your desks containing all the information that we have so far,' Kush said, pushing his glasses up his nose. 'Guys, you are the best in the business so as a group we should be unstoppable. We are going to find this young lady.'

The team took to their seats, opened the files and fired up the hardware.

Danny was left standing with Peter.

'I don't understand, where do I fit into all of this?' he asked.

'Don't worry, son, your time will come,' Peter said.

Danny frowned. 'Hang on, I'm not just here to make coffee for these guys, am I?'

Danny had done OK in school, but this team were head and shoulders above him, and he knew it.

'Danny, you have your own desk,' Peter said, pointing it out, 'your time will come, and when it does, your role will be a vital one.'

Peter did not yet know what Danny was going to do but he wanted him around, he was his only connection to Rose in the city.

'Fine,' Danny said smiling, 'who wants a coffee?' Peter laughed, 'hey, I have a meeting at twelve o'clock, but I won't be too long, OK?'

Mack walked in. He wasn't part of the team, Peter had decided to keep him separate from the group. Mack knew what was going on and was subject to the same rules as the others, it was just that Peter wanted Mack focused on him.

'You ready, sir?' he asked.

'Give me one minute,' Peter replied, 'you can wait for me in the car.'

'Yes, boss.'

Mack gave Danny a nod as he walked off.

Peter looked back to survey what had taken him so long to accomplish. With the help of Mack and Kush he had put together a perfect team, and Danny, well Danny would get his chance soon enough.

Chapter Thirty-One
Construction site, Bandra East, 10:38 a.m.

Peter and Mack were a little late to the meeting with the architect, but considering that Peter was the money-man, he had that privilege. Besides, he had heard that investors were hard to come by and that meant he would be in the driving seat with this deal, *if* it was what he was looking for.

The payment that Peter had been given initially for his invention had turned out to be a drop in the ocean. GreenCorp were mass-producing their products and had orders up to five years in advance. The company had made a profit from its second year of trading and Peter had seen over one hundred million US dollars land in his bank account.

In twenty years or so, GreenCorp would be the biggest energy supplier in the world. People were loving the chance to become self-sufficient with, after their initial purchase, only a small yearly service fee. They had an army of newly trained engineers on the payroll and every customer was tied into a contract with them. There was no profit margin in servicing costs, it was purely so the units were maintained by their engineers only. It was still a fraction of the price of regular electricity suppliers.

Peter had money to burn, but, having always been frugal, had decided to invest it wisely. Having started with buying pre-constructed properties, he had now progressed to investing in development, which would yield far greater returns in the long run.

'Mr Rosario, it's good to see you.'

'Please, call me Peter,' he said, shaking Jonathan Naik's hand. Peter could tell the man was on edge and judging by his dark eyes, he hadn't been getting much sleep – he knew exactly how that felt.

'Mr Naik,' Mack said with a nod. He was standing behind Peter holding a bundle of files.

Jonathan Naik talked them through the plans for the two thirty-storey apartment blocks. Peter was impressed with the buildings and the figures, but he would not make any decisions until his trusted lawyer and accountant had been over everything, and that included the man running the company, 'Naik and Associates'. Peter would have his team check him out, it wouldn't hurt. He had them, he thought, so why not use them?

'Jonathan, it looks good, give me a couple of days and I will get back to you.'

'Certainly, Peter, I look forward to hearing from you.'

They left Jonathan. On the way back to the Jaguar, Mack said, 'that is one worried man.'

'Isn't he just?' Peter agreed.

'He's in trouble; there's nobody else around with your kind of money who's interested in investing at the moment and if he doesn't get a cash injection soon, he'll be paying out of his own pocket, and he doesn't have it,' Mack said with confidence.

Mack knew everything – the markets, the housing sector, he could even read people; heck, he could tell what you'd had for breakfast from the smell of your breath. These were just a few of the reasons why he was Peter's right-hand man.

'I will get the guys to check him out,' Peter said.

***

After a few days of researching the project, Peter had been advised that it was a sound investment and he instructed his people to offer the funds, but he wanted an extra eight per cent. He was pretty confident that he could squeeze the architect; there were two other investors in place already, the third having pulled out because he was under investigation by the government for financial irregularities.

Rahul had pulled all of Jonathan's personal info and he was as clean as they come – trophy wife, two kids, no criminal record, etc.

'Boss,' Kush called out; he was standing at Vanya's desk staring at her computer screen.

Peter joined the pair, 'you've found them?' he asked, as he zoomed in on the grainy CCTV capture on the screen.

It was a picture of Maalik Aggarwal.

'No, not both, just this one, he's been spotted on a few occasions, but nothing for the last month,' Kush said. 'Vijay, Saira, you know what to do!'

The pair were already gathering the necessary equipment for the visit.

'Well done, Vanya,' Peter said, giving her a thumbs up because he knew she wouldn't hear him. He received a nod in return as she got back to work.

Peter looked at Kush, 'this is good news.'

'It's a start, boss, it's the first sighting we've had. Hopefully he's still in Mumbai because if he is, we'll find him.'

Chapter Thirty-Two
Juhu Beach, Mumbai, 5:47 p.m.,
24th December

Although Peter could afford a fleet of luxury cars, he really enjoyed walking. His favourite route was north to the Holy Cross Catholic Church, which took him around twenty minutes each way with a ten-minute rest inside. It was a welcome break from being in the apartment. Today he was feeling down; it was Rose's seventeenth birthday, and the team had made no further progress finding her or the kidnappers.

Mack had told him time and time again that he should not walk alone in the area; Peter was a very wealthy man now and would be an easy target for muggers. Peter mostly shrugged off Mack's incessant worrying about everything, even though he knew the young man was probably right.

He did his best thinking while he walked, the distractions helped him focus.

After leaving the church he decided to head towards the beach. Being from Goa, he missed the sea that had been a big part of his life growing up. Swimming was advised against in

Mumbai because of the very poor water quality, but just being next to it made Peter feel better.

Continuing north, Peter spotted a rough-looking man, probably a beggar. There were not many people about as, being Christmas Eve, most were at home or enjoying meals with friends. Anyone hanging around on the streets probably had no home to go to.

Peter gave the man a wide berth; he had seen the guy eyeing him up. He decided to cut his walk short and had just crossed the road when he felt someone grab his shoulder from behind. There was something sharp pressing into the small of his back and just as he was trying to work out how he would deal with the situation, another man appeared in front of him.

'Money and your watch,' the man snarled. His teeth were dirty and stained from chewing paan, his clothes were filthy and he was barefoot. He did, however, have a knife, which he was waving far too close to Peter's face for comfort.

Peter had treated himself to a Rolex when he moved to Mumbai. It was expensive but not worth losing his life over. With a knife at his face and one to his back, he didn't struggle; he didn't need to, he would give them what they wanted. Hell, if they had just asked him for some money, he would have given it to them. He always carried enough to help somebody out and would regularly make donations to worthy causes.

'OK, OK,' Peter said slowly, raising his hands, 'calm down, nobody needs to get hurt here.'

He reached for his watch to take it off as he felt the guy behind him fish the wallet from his back pocket.

Peter had barely undone the clasp when the attacker at his rear seemed to fly away from him as if he had been sucked down into a black hole. He heard a scream and a cracking sound. The second attacker was staring over Peter's shoulder with a look of shock on his face. The next thing Peter saw was a foot come from behind him to strike, with deadly accuracy, at his attacker's temple. The man went down like a sack of rice, out cold before he hit the ground.

Peter turned around; he had dropped his watch in the melee and his wallet was the last thing on his mind. Standing before him was the rough-looking man he had passed. He was a Sikh, judging by the turban on his head, although it wasn't fixed properly, and the man's long hair was half hanging out of it. 'You OK?' the stranger enquired, as he bent to retrieve Peter's wallet and watch.

'Ye... yes,' Peter managed, as he accepted his belongings.

'Good, I would be careful walking around the city alone wearing that.' The man pointed to the watch that Peter was now returning to his wrist. 'You're making yourself a target,' the stranger laughed and shook his head as he turned to walk off.

Peter was speechless. Only minutes ago, he had dismissed the man as a beggar and now the same man had just saved his skin with some lightning moves, the like of which Peter had never seen before, even in a movie.

'Woah, woah, woah, where are you going?' he called after the man. 'You can't just do that and walk off!'

'Yes I can,' replied the man coldly, without stopping.

Peter had caught up now and grabbed his good Samaritan by the arm. He was rewarded with a cold, menacing stare that made him withdraw his hand immediately.

'Let me buy you dinner, tea, whatever. I owe you something, surely!'

The man stopped, looking intently at Peter.

'Please,' Peter implored.

'OK,' the stranger shrugged, 'I am hungry.'

'Then let's go, I know just the place,' Peter replied happily.

It was a short walk to the restaurant. He often took the team there and, despite arriving this time with someone of a pretty shambolic appearance, they were seated straight away.

'What's your name?' Peter asked.

'Does it matter?'

'To me it does.'

'Harpreet, Harpreet Singh.'

'I'm Peter Rosario, and thank you for what you did back there.' Peter held out his hand, which clearly surprised Harpreet. He knew he looked dirty – hell, he was very dirty – yet here was a man who was not afraid of touching him.

After months of being spurned, ignored, told to move on, shouted at and spat on, this man was willing to shake his hand. Harpreet extended a grubby mitt and held Peter's hand tight for a few seconds, his gaze never wavering.

'Call me Harps,' he said, and Peter detected a slight lowering of his companion's guard.

The waiter arrived, doing his best to hide his astonishment at this pair of mismatched diners. They ordered food and tea.

'So, what's your story?' Peter asked, 'I mean, if you don't mind, I'd like to know.'

They spent the next two hours in the restaurant, with Peter doing most of the listening. Mack had called him three times, concerned as to why he had not returned. Peter ended up shouting at the young man to reassure him that he was OK.

As the minutes ticked past, Peter began to realise that he had met the final member of his team, one that until then, he didn't even know was missing. Harpreet Singh was a thirty-one-year-old Sikh from Amritsar, near the Pakistan border. His parents had been killed by Pakistani insurgents when he was young and, Harpreet told Peter, he had signed up to the Indian army as soon as he was old enough.

He was a natural and became a captain in the marine commandos by the age of twenty-five. Next, Harpreet had joined a back-ops counter-terrorism team and had served all over India. He'd also undertaken missions in Pakistan and the Middle East.

Harpreet was a top marksman and excelled in close-quarters combat, having been trained in ju-jitsu, Pencak Silat and Sqay. The man was so highly trained that he could kill you with one hand while disarming a bomb with the other.

Peter was impressed with his story. 'What changed? How the hell did you end up on the streets?' he asked.

'My wife,' replied Harps, looking down at the table. 'She, … she was killed by a mugger, just like the ones who held you up earlier. She was stabbed in her spleen and kidney and died within an hour – and all for five hundred rupees.'

Peter could see the pain in the poor man's eyes.

'After that, I was making mistakes at work. I couldn't cope and they branded me a liability and ultimately I was released. I only knew the military and there is not a lot of call for my skills in civilian life,' Harpreet gave a wry smile. 'I was destitute, I ended up here around a month ago and have been looking for work ever since.'

'Will you work for me?' Peter asked immediately.

'I don't want your pity,' Harpreet said.

'Oh, this isn't charity – I'm offering you a job, somewhere to live, a fresh start in life because I need a man like you.'

'Doing what?' Harpreet sounded far from convinced.

'I need you to find someone,' Peter said.

'That's what I do, I can do it with my eyes closed.' Peter saw a glimmer of hope spark into life in the man opposite him.

'And when the person is found you will need to protect them, make sure that nothing bad ever happens to them again.'

'I can do that too, no problem.' Harpreet could tell that Peter meant what he was saying from the passion with which he spoke and the look in his eyes.

Harpreet took inventory of his potential employer and Peter felt a little unnerved by the man's unblinking scrutiny.

'OK,' he said, 'why not? I'm not exactly fighting off offers at the moment.' He didn't know what he was getting into, but the man opposite him seemed genuine enough.

Harpreet was like a human polygraph machine and could detect subtle changes in breathing and movement and interpret what a subject's intentions were. They were well-honed skills that he had used for interrogating people on many occasions.

Peter stood up and held out his hand once again. Harpreet stood too and shook on the proposal.

'What now, when do I start?'

'Let's get you somewhere to stay first, there are a few places near here that will suffice until I find you an apartment. You will need a damn good shower and a solid night's sleep.'

'It's been a long time since I had both of those in the same day,' Harpreet said.

'I owe you, brother,' insisted Peter, 'let's get you settled tonight and tomorrow I will send my assistant over with some clean clothes and cash. You can start the day after, how does that sound?'

'Sounds perfect.' Harpreet followed Peter out of the restaurant.

After checking his new employee into a hotel, Peter was about to walk away when he felt a hand on his arm. He turned to look into the eyes of a man that was tired but relieved; he maybe even had a hint of a tear in his eye.

'Thank you, Peter, thank you,' Harpreet said.

'No, thank you, you saved my ass today, God knows what those guys would have done to me. Get some rest, I'll see you in a couple of days.'

Harpreet nodded and made for his room; he couldn't wait to get into the shower.

***

Two days later, after Christmas, the team had all turned up on time, although some may have been a little hungover. They were exchanging stories about the previous day's goings-on, over coffee. Kush was holding court as usual, when the room fell silent and everyone who wasn't facing the door turned to see what the rest were staring at. They saw a six-foot-two guy dressed in a slim-fit black suit, his hair done up inside a perfectly wrapped turban. He had a neatly trimmed beard.

He was immaculately groomed and very handsome, but not in a pretty boy way; he was rugged and looked like he'd led exactly the kind of life that he had indeed led. There was a scar above his right eye, cutting his eyebrow in half. His muscular physique could be seen through his suit jacket.

'Erm, can I help you; how did you get in here?' Kush demanded.

Harpreet said nothing.

Peter himself hardly recognised Harpreet from two days ago.

'Wow,' he said, shaking the man's hand, 'you brush up well!'

'Thanks,' Harpreet replied.

'Everybody, meet Harpreet Singh, or Harps as he likes to be called. He is the last member of our team, please make him feel welcome.'

They all took turns to greet the stranger, the guys with suspicion and the girls trying hard to conceal their obvious appreciation of his superb looks. Kush was the last to shake the man's hand.

'Fuck, bro, I don't know whether you've come to take me out or literally *take me out*?'

They all laughed, and the ice was broken.

'Don't worry, I won't hurt you, little man,' Harpreet assured him.

'So, where does our new friend fit into our ever-expanding team?' asked Vijay with just a hint of sarcasm.

'Where shall I start?' Peter said. 'Our man Harpreet here has spent many years in the army, several of those in black-ops. He is an expert in three different martial arts, a crack shot with a gun, a specialist in counterintelligence, interrogation, torture and a general bad-ass. Have I missed anything?' Peter asked.

'I'm not a bad singer,' Harps informed them, which made everyone laugh, so incongruous was it, coming from this hard man.

'Oh yes, one more thing,' Peter added. 'I have first-hand experience of Harpreet's fighting skills.'

Peter paused to see the response on the faces of the team, a mixture of confusion and shock.

'What happened, boss?' asked Rahul.

'I was in the process of being robbed a couple of days ago and our new friend here saved me by knocking the hell out of the two guys who wanted to relieve me of my belongings.'

'I told you about wandering around alone, boss, didn't I?' Mack wailed, rushing to Peter's side. 'Are you OK, did they hurt you?' he asked, physically trying to check his employer for damage.

'I'm fine, Mack, stop fussing man,' Peter said, swatting him away. After straightening his suit, Peter held out his hands towards his team, 'so now we have the magnificent seven,' he announced.

'Harps is going to be our muscle, our man on the street, our ghost if you wish. He has been briefed on what we are doing, and he will be here for not only our protection but to help in finding our targets, including Rose, so please, give him whatever he needs. I trust him with my life and so should all of you, OK?'

Everybody nodded. They already felt safer with this guy around.

'Has anybody got any leads on this Maalik character yet?' Peter asked. A collective shaking of heads was his reply. 'Then what are you waiting for?'

The team all made for their desks, leaving Danny, Peter and Harpreet alone.

'You look fantastic,' Peter informed Harps, grasping the man's broad shoulders.

'I feel great, Peter, thank you. Who picked the suit? It fits perfectly.'

Mack gave him a salute; Peter had described Harpreet to him, and Mack had made the appropriate choice in clothing, even down to the correct size of shoe.

'How does he do it?' Peter asked.

'If I told you I'd have to kill you,' Mack called out from the coffee station.

'Harpreet, Danny here was Rose's best friend before she was taken. You two should spend the day together, get to know one another, maybe you can get something out of him that's been locked away all these years.'

'As long as he doesn't waterboard me,' Danny joked. He needed a change in any case; he was getting bored spending all day feeling of very little use.

'Shall we go out for a drive?' Harpreet suggested. 'I'd like to get to know the layout of the area.'

'Sure,' Danny agreed, picking up the keys to the silver sedan car that they had been using. It was old and discreet; Peter had bought the car for tailing someone if need be, but until now it had only been used to pick up food orders. Peter walked over to Mack to make himself a drink.

'Why didn't you tell me, boss?'

'I didn't want to trouble you, Mack.'

'Can you trust him? You hardly know the guy,' Mack insisted.

'Believe me, if you had seen him when I met him, seen the pain in his eyes and then the hope, such feelings do not come from someone with bad intentions. This guy is a trained killer, yes, but he was at rock bottom two days ago – he lost his wife, his job and he was homeless.'

'I understand, boss,' said Mack sadly.

'We've already discussed firearms and agreed that Harps should carry one. When we catch up with these guys, who knows what we are going to face?'

'A gun?' Mack looked at Peter with wide eyes.

'Yes, something top of the line, and don't tell me you don't know where to get one,' Peter replied, giving him a look that said, *just get on with it.*

In the car, Danny and Harps were cruising the area, going nowhere in particular.

'So, she was your best friend?' Harpreet asked the younger man.

'Yes.'

'And she was taken from outside the house?'

'From the front garden, yes.'

'And nobody saw anything?'

'Nope.'

'That's very unlikely,' Harps announced.

'Well, if anyone did see anything, they didn't tell the police and everybody loved Rose, why wouldn't the neighbours help?' Danny asked.

'In my experience, a lot of kidnappings have someone close to the family involved, especially where money is involved. Humans are horrible creatures; some even sell their own children for a few hundred rupees. As no one has confirmed it is a kidnapping, she could be anywhere.'

Danny slammed on the brakes. 'Wait, you don't think that Peter had anything to do with Rose going missing, surely?'

'No, Danny, that's the only thing I am certain of in this case. Peter would never knowingly let any harm come to his little girl.'

'Good,' said Danny, pulling out into the traffic again.

'What was she like?' Harpreet asked.

'She was the best,' said Danny. He tried to imagine what Rose would look like now and how great it would be to see her again.

The pair drove and talked for hours; they got on well and the time flew by before Harpreet suggested they should return to the office. He was aching from being cooped up in the small vehicle.

'How did you guys get along?' Peter asked when they got back.

'No problem, he's good company,' Harps replied, smiling at Danny.

Chapter Thirty-Three
Naik residence, 6:23 p.m., 1st January 2017

Christmas had come and gone; it had been a subdued affair. Elijah would be going to the US to study law at an Ivy League university and although Elizabeth and Jonathan were proud parents, they would miss him terribly. They boasted to their friends at every given opportunity about their son's achievement.

Angelica had been sad ever since her brother told her that he was leaving at the end of the month. She had grown so attached to him that she used every trick in the book to convince him to stay, including emotional blackmail, which hadn't worked as no matter how much he loved his sister, nothing was going to stop Elijah from fulfilling his dream of becoming a lawyer.

Jonathan and Elizabeth had decided that as they did not know when Angelica had been born, the day after she arrived should be her official date of birth. The first of January was agreed on – new year, fresh start – but Angelica just wasn't in the mood this year and was sulking as she contemplated her brother's imminent departure.

'Come on, darling, I've booked a table for eight o'clock, are you going to get yourself ready?' her mother asked, stepping into Angelica's bedroom.

Angelica had her earphones in with the volume on full.

Elizabeth waved her hands to get her attention. The girl pulled out one of her earbuds and looked enquiringly at her mother.

'We're going out for dinner, it's time to get ready,' Elizabeth said.

'I don't feel like it, I'm not hungry,' Angelica replied. Elizabeth sat beside her in an attempt to cheer the girl up. 'I can't bear to see you like this, baby,' she said.

'Then tell Eli not to go, mom,' Angelica begged.

'You love your brother, don't you?' Elizabeth said.

'Yes.'

'Would you really want to hold him back from pursuing his dream?'

'No,' Angelica replied. She knew she was being selfish but just couldn't help it.

'Come on,' Liz said, with a smile. 'Let's see that happy girl face!'

'OK, whatever.' Angelica gave a weak smile.

'Good girl. Hey, it's a big day for you on Wednesday, are you excited?' Elizabeth tried to change the subject.

'I suppose so.' Angelica dragged a brush through her thick hair. Having been scouted by one of the top modelling agencies in Mumbai she had already been chosen to be the face of a new fashion label aimed at the younger generation. This was a huge deal, and she would soon be seeing herself on billboards and social media all over the country.

'We are so proud of you too – you know that don't you?' Elizabeth said.

Angelica shrugged. 'I don't have to do much, most of the time I just stand around.'

'I mean, we are proud of you in everything that you do, my darling. You are a wonderful, caring person, you are outstanding at school, you're not just a pretty face.'

Angelica gave a cheeky smile; she did like a compliment.

'I'm going for a shower, I love you – now keep that smile on your dial,' her mother joked, as she left the room.

***

A few days later, Angelica, accompanied by the whole family, went to the meeting at the model agency. They were all excited, even Elijah tagged along but that was mostly so that he could gawk at the models. The meeting had gone as expected. Angelica was to start shooting in two days and within a couple of weeks, her pictures would be everywhere. Jonathan was very uneasy. He didn't want Angelica's face plastered all over the place but could not tell his wife the real reason. Elizabeth would not back down, she was determined that if her daughter wanted to be a model; she was going to be a famous one. Jonathan had been worried since hearing of the assignment but had no option other than to accept that it was going to happen. Besides, Angelica was eight years older now and with her short hair, and the way that her face had changed as she blossomed from a girl into a woman, surely no one would ever recognise her now? Jonathan felt a cold wave of fear engulf him. Or would they?

Chapter Thirty-Four
Peter's apartment, 1:39 p.m., 17th January

Rahul had already done a deep dive into his boss's new business partner, Jonathan Naik, and found nothing much of interest. The investigation into Rose and the kidnappers was at a standstill, and since the CCTV footage, Maalik hadn't been seen again. It was like he had disappeared off the face of the earth.

Frustrated with the way things were going he decided to have another look at Naik – nobody could be that clean, not in Mumbai. He trawled every known associate of his, which drew a blank.

Rahul turned his attention to the family; Elizabeth Naik was a lady about town and earned her own money through redesigning her friends' homes. She'd had a brief affair with her masseuse a couple of years ago.

The son, Elijah, seemed a good kid and hadn't even been booked for smoking pot.

Moving on to Angelica Naik, the daughter, flicking through the pages of her records, suddenly something hit Rahul like a truck. 'How the hell did I miss this?' he muttered.

He looked at the board, where Rose's details were pinned next to the mugshots of the kidnappers.

'Kush!' he called out.

'Wait a minute, bro.' Kush was busy typing.

'I think you'll want to see this.'

Kush looked up to see that Rahul had been joined by Vanya, who, for once, had removed her headphones.

'What is it?' she asked, staring at the board.

She had only got up to make a coffee, but the look on Rahul's face had caught her attention.

'How could I have missed this?' Rahul repeated.

'Missed what?' demanded Vanya.

Rahul ripped the sheet from the board and rushed back to his desk, followed by Vanya and Kush.

'Rose went missing on the twenty-ninth of December 2008,' Rahul said.

'Yes, so what?' they replied in unison.

'Look at this!'

Rahul clicked on a folder that opened a scan of an adoption certificate. Kush read it aloud, 'Angelica Naik, adopted on the twenty-third of January 2009.'

'It states here that her age was ten at the time,' Rahul continued, 'but on her birth certificate here,' he clicked on another file and up popped Angelica's birth certificate. 'This is a strange one, the date of birth is blank. We have the parents' names and the child's name but no date, just the date of registration, which is the same day as adoption.'

Jonathan had made the terrible mistake of not updating Angelica's birth certificate.

'What does that mean?' asked Kush.

'It means that when she was adopted, they didn't know how old she was,' Vanya said softly. 'Hang on,' she continued, 'This isn't Angelica Naik the model, is it?'

No one except Vanya had heard of her. Vanya knew the name because she had bought a couple of items from the new clothing range, before twenty-foot-high full-length pictures of her had been posted outside the apartment block.

Vanya pushed Kush out of the way to get to the keyboard on Rahul's desk and googled the girl's name.

'Are you fucking kidding me?' Kush shouted as he rushed over to grab the picture that his simulation had produced of what Rose would look like as an older girl.

Kush laid the picture on the desk underneath the photograph of Angelica Naik. Vijay and Saira were now standing behind them trying to get a look-in when Rahul said, 'it's her, we have found Rose! Fuck man, it *has* to be her!'

Vijay pushed his way to the front of the desk; he was the oldest and wisest of the bunch and didn't want them jumping to any conclusions. He studied all the information while everybody else held their breath.

'Kush, can you run both pics through your program and see what comes up? I mean the pic of young Rose and the pic on the screen here?' Vijay asked, 'this is far too good to be true.'

'It will take two minutes!' Kush declared.

Vijay screen-shared his monitor and let Kush sit down to work his magic.

'Well?' Rahul asked Vijay, who was still studying the information on the screen and Rose's photograph.

'Ninety-eight per cent match,' Kush shouted and turning to Vijay said, 'this girl is Rose, she has to be, it can't be a coincidence.'

A stunned Vijay agreed; he didn't want to accept it but it seemed like the girl that they had all been looking for was right under their noses and was now displayed on fifty per cent of the advertising space in the city.

'Where is Peter? Can somebody get hold of the boss, for fuck's sake?' Kush shouted.

Saira had already dialled his number and was waiting for someone to pick up. Mack answered the phone. Peter had been out with Danny, Harpreet and Mack, and they were waiting for a takeaway lunch to bring back to the office.

'What's up, sis?' he asked.

She hated him calling her that, but this wasn't the time for a telling off.

'Get Peter back here now, and hurry up!' she shouted. Mack jerked the phone away from his ear.

'Oh my God!' he shouted.

As he reached for the door handle, he saw the three men leaving the restaurant.

Peter always liked to order his own food, Harps had been at Peter's side whenever he wasn't in the apartment and Danny just wanted to stretch his legs. Peter sat in the back of the car next to Mack.

'You're wanted back at the apartment.'

'What for?'

'Don't know, boss, but they seem pretty excited about something, the way that Saira just screamed at me,' said Mack, holding a hand to his left ear for effect.

'Danny, let's get home,' Peter demanded.

Danny obliged, and they were inside the apartment within ten minutes. Peter was first through the door to the sound of everyone clamouring to tell the story at the same time. He held up his hands.

'Can just one of you please tell me what is going on?' he asked.

The team looked at Rahul since he was the one who had made the connection.

'Erm,' he started, 'Peter, boss, we've found Rose.'

Peter sat down on a chair. 'Where, where is she?' he said softly.

Kush pulled up the best full-face picture that he could find on his screen. It was one of the advertisements that were all over social media and which he had been totally ignoring since the campaign had started a few days ago.

Peter leaned in closer, 'that's her,' he confirmed, his voice breaking, 'that's my Rose.'

'We've checked the simulation three times and it's a ninety-nine per cent match,' said Kush.

'It's a one hundred per cent match,' Peter informed the group.

'How can you be so sure, boss?' asked Saira.

'Do you see the tiny nick at the top of her right ear?' Peter asked, pointing to the screen, as they all jostled to see.

'There's your other one per cent.'

'I remember when she did it, falling off the swings. It was my fault,' Danny admitted, 'an accident of course.'

'She is so beautiful,' Peter said, smiling. He couldn't take his eyes off the screen.

Peter finally tore himself away and hugged his employee. There were high-fives, handshakes and kisses all round, and when Danny suggested that he go and pick up a couple of cases of beer, Rahul held his hand up.

'Boss, you need to hear this,' he called out.

Peter, who was in the process of handing some notes to Danny, stopped in his tracks.

'You've not heard the whole story yet; this you are not going to believe,' Rahul said.

Peter looked at all the evidence, and as he read the adoptive parents' names he jerked his head from the screen to Rahul and back several times in disbelief.

'Wait, THE Jonathan Naik, from Naik and Associates?' Peter asked incredulously.

'The very same, boss, it's all here in black and white.'

'OK,' Peter replied.

There was a long silence before Rahul spoke.

'What's next then, do you have a plan?'

'Rahul, you've done well, you've done extremely well today, you found my Rose alive and by the looks of these photographs, she is healthy. Tonight we celebrate, tomorrow we plan. I've got this guy by the balls already. I fucking own him and now I am going to ruin the bastard.'

Rahul noticed Peter's sadistic smile, a smile that he had never seen before.

'Cool, let's party,' he shouted, as he ran off to join the gang who were fishing in the bags for their lunch.

Harpreet approached Peter, worried that his new-found job had ended almost as soon as it had begun.

'I'm incredibly happy for you, Peter, I guess you won't be needing me any longer?' he asked.

'Harpreet, you are going nowhere, this has only just begun, I'm going to need your skills now more than ever,' Peter assured him.

Chapter Thirty-Five
Peter's apartment, 8:45 a.m.,
18th January

Peter was sitting at the head of the meeting table that had been delivered just a couple of days earlier. This was its first time in use, as the team were glued to the screens at their desks for most of the day. Kush had left the celebrations early the night before so he could rig up the two seventy-inch screens and finally put them to use. He was now standing at his laptop, which was linked to his PC, ready to begin.

Vijay, Vanya, Saira and Rahul were sitting on one side, with Danny, Harpreet and Mack on the other.

Everyone was slightly hungover, except for Harpreet and Vanya as usual.

On screen were various pictures of Angelica Naik, from the uploaded photograph of her as a nine-year-old to the earliest that Vijay could find on Elizabeth's Twitter account, to her latest photoshoot. And now it was plain to see that Angelica Naik actually and undoubtedly was Rose Angel Rosario.

'Yesterday came as a shock to all of us and although we are triumphant in finding my daughter,' Peter started, 'we still have a long way to go to find out what happened, where the kidnappers are and who orchestrated the whole thing. Let's go round the table and start with everyone's thoughts on the situation. Who would like to go first?'

Saira got up and stood behind Rahul, who was seated to her right. Placing her hands on his shoulders, she said, 'For a start, we should give this guy a hand.'

Rahul cringed – he'd been thanked enough and didn't like being made a fuss over.

'So, the facts we have,' Saira continued, 'we now know that Rose is safe, and she is doing well, so the one thing we need not do is rush at this.'

Everybody agreed.

'Good point,' Peter said, 'but what we don't know is whether her "parents" are aware that she had been kidnapped.'

'If I may say so,' said Harpreet, 'people don't generally kidnap a child for no reason, and if it were a random kidnapping then it would be highly unlikely that she would end up with such a wealthy family by accident.'

'Where are you going with this?' asked Peter.

'Children from poor families are taken all the time to be sold into child labour or as sex slaves.'

Vanya gasped. She was quite a sheltered person and stayed away from TV news. Peter blinked several times and a muscle in his face tensed, but he said nothing.

'That's true,' added Vijay.

'Now, when a child is taken from a good family, a high caste family, and appears again in a wealthy family of similar caste then my opinion is that she was taken to order,' Harpreet said authoritatively.

'You mean, someone ordered her like a fucking takeaway?' an angry Danny asked, a little too loudly.

'Yes, Danny,' Harpreet said sadly.

Kush looked up from his laptop, 'so assuming that she was taken to order, then one or both of the parents must have been involved.'

'Correct,' replied Harpreet.

'Let's get these bastards,' Mack shouted emotionally. He had become awfully close to his boss and felt his pain.

'Calm down, Mack, it's upsetting I know, but we have the upper hand here. You already know that Jonathan Naik has been having some cash flow problems and I bailed him out of the shit. He owes me, and we will use that to our advantage,' Peter said.

'Peter, may I suggest something?' Vijay said, rising from his seat and moving to the TV screen.

'The evidence we have seems to confirm that this is your daughter.' Vijay was pointing to Peter's photograph of Rose. 'This is all well and good but even with Kush's face ageing simulation we don't have any concrete evidence, it's still only circumstantial.'

Kush looked put out but agreed with the older, more experienced man.

'What do you suggest?' asked Peter.

'A DNA test would be definitive proof.'

'How do we do that?'

'Hair would be the easiest thing,' Saira announced, taking over, 'we need a sample from this young lady,' she said, nodding at the screen.

'We would also need a sample from Rose. Do you still have the hairbrush that she used at your home?'

'Her bedroom has not been touched since I left Goa,' Peter said sadly.

'So, we would surely find some of Rose's hair at the house then?' said Vijay.

'Mack, book yourself and Saira on a flight to Goa leaving this afternoon, I want this done ASAP. You know the address. I'll give you the keys before you go.'

'What about the other sample?' Vanya asked.

'That's easy,' answered Vijay, 'we know where she lives and within the hour, we will know her daily routine. All I need to do is get close to her, I've done it a hundred times before.'

'I want to do it; I want to see her face to face,' Peter said quietly.

'No Peter, not a good idea,' Harpreet said shaking his head. 'Leave it to a professional – as you said, we are in no hurry, there's no need to risk complicating things. Your time will come to meet her, but that time is not right now, at least not until we confirm that she definitely is Rose.'

'She is Rose.' Peter's voice was still low. 'OK, Vijay, I will leave it in your capable hands, how long will it take?'

'If you guys can get back here by tonight,' Vijay said, looking at Saira, 'I will hopefully obtain the other sample tomorrow. If that all happens we can get the results in a couple of days.'

Mack was already online booking flights for himself and Saira.

'Excellent work, guys, I think we should wait for the test results before we think about our next move. Vanya, you help Vijay with tracking Angelica's movements. Rahul and I will continue searching for these two bastards,' Kush said pointing at their pictures.

'I have another angle I want to try. You two come with me,' Peter said to Danny and Harpreet.

***

'You need to eat something, Angelica,' Elizabeth pleaded. Her daughter had been holed up in her room ever since they returned from the airport the previous day. Elijah had left on an early morning flight, heading for Logan International Airport in Boston with a short stopover in Dubai. The place at Harvard University that Eli had secured for himself was costing his father a small fortune in fees and accommodation.

Angelica looked at her mother, her face puffy and her eyes red from crying so much.

'I miss Eli too, you know, it's not like you'll never see him again,' Elizabeth reassured her.

'I don't care, he was my best friend and I miss him more than you do,' Angelica shouted, getting up from the bed and storming out of the room.

She was dressed in sweatpants with a matching jumper, and her hair was a mess. Elizabeth followed her daughter and found Angelica putting her running shoes on.

'Where are you going?' Elizabeth demanded.

'Out,' Angelica screamed back at her.

Angelica was in no mood to be reasoned with. She slipped out the front door, leaving it open.

'You come back here right *now*,' Elizabeth shouted after her daughter. It was too late. Angelica was already running down the main stairwell heading for the lobby.

Elizabeth let out a scream, a mixture of anger, frustration and sadness. Preeti, having heard the shouting, approached her employer and said, 'Madam, Angelica is a teenager, she is angry and upset. Leave her for a while, she'll come back, you'll see. Just give her some space.'

Elizabeth turned to Preeti, her expression cold.

'When I need parental advice from my *housemaid* I will ask, is that understood? Get back to work,' she shouted.

'Yes, madam.' Preeti was reeling, she had never been spoken to like that before.

Downstairs, Angelica raced across the lobby past the security desk.

The man on duty was surprised to see her in this area, given that the Naiks had their own private elevator.

'Good morning, madam,' he called out, rushing to open the door, but she was gone before he could reach the entrance.

Angelica started running. She wanted to get away from this place and needed somewhere to think, so headed for the coffee shop where she used to hang out with Eli. They had whiled away many an hour there, chatting, planning and making fun of the people walking by. She needed a connection to him and that was the only place outside of the apartment she could think of. Her eyes were full of tears; she didn't notice the white Jaguar heading towards her, containing four men.

'Peter, what are we doing here?' asked Harpreet, having noticed the girl from his front seat position. Danny and Peter were in the back and only Peter knew where they were going; he had handed the driver an address. Having found out where the Naik family lived earlier and, going against the advice of his team, decided he wanted to see his daughter.

Why was she running? 'Is she crying?' Peter asked.

He had spotted his Rose right away and was dismayed to see the state that his daughter was in.

'Turn around,' Harpreet ordered the driver, who immediately did as he was told.

'I just want to make sure she is safe!' Peter protested.

Harpreet looked worried.

'After that, we are going back to your place, we are *not* doing this today, Peter.' Harpreet left no room for doubt.

Peter realised that he should trust his employee's judgement.

'He's right, we don't want to spook her,' said Danny. He was desperate to see his friend but realised that emotion should not be allowed to interfere with what they were planning. As they watched, Angelica stopped running, took a couple of deep breaths and walked into the coffee shop. The driver stopped across the road, far enough away not to be spotted but close enough to see what she was doing.

'Flat white, please,' Angelica asked the girl at the counter, wiping the last tears from her face.

'Are you OK, madam?' the girl asked.

'I'm fine,' Angelica replied.

'Take a seat, I will bring it over to you.' The girl, who was about the same age, gave Angelica a reassuring smile and turned to the espresso machine.

Angelica sat at the window, her chin on her hand. There were only two other customers, a middle-aged couple engrossed in conversation who hadn't even noticed her enter.

'Happy now?' Harpreet asked, 'she's a teenager, she's emotional – situation normal!'

'I'm going in, I want to talk to her.' Peter had his hand on the door handle.

'DRIVE, NOW!' Harpreet shouted to the man next to him; he wanted the car moving before Peter could do something completely stupid.

The driver put his foot down and headed for home. Nobody uttered a word for the next ten minutes until Peter spoke.

'I'm sorry.'

Harpreet turned to look at his employer.

'OK, OK, I won't do that again, I've just missed her so much.' As the car pulled away, Peter had strained to get a last glimpse of her through the window, a tear in his eye.

The team were working late that night while they waited for Mack and Saira to return. Their flight had landed an hour ago.

Peter had been scolded by all his employees for putting their plan in jeopardy, and Vijay and Vanya had confirmed that Angelica visited the café almost daily. The CCTV footage placed Angelica at the premises most days between five and seven p.m., sometimes with Elijah Naik her brother and occasionally alone.

The front door opened and a smiling Mack walked in, followed by Saira. He was delighted to have completed his first 'mission' and was proud that it had gone to plan. Saira placed her handbag on the table; all eyes were on her, waiting for the reveal. With a flourish she pulled out a transparent plastic bag containing Rose's old hairbrush and handed it to Vijay.

'Perfect,' he said, noticing the amount of hair that was entangled in the bristles. 'It's all up to me now. Saira, would you like to go on a date?' he asked cheekily.

'As long as you're paying, old man,' she laughed.

Chapter Thirty-Six
Café Coffee Day coffee shop,
7:15 p.m., 19th January

Vijay sat across the table from Saira. They were on their second cup of coffee. Saira was eating a piece of chocolate cake and Vijay was pretending to be engrossed in something on his phone.

The pair had arrived at just after four p.m., to be on the safe side. They didn't even know whether Rose would turn up today but a stakeout was a numbers game – you wait long enough, and your target will show up eventually. The door opened. Vijay raised his eyes to check; it was a young couple.

'My legs are starting to seize up,' Saira complained. It was now a quarter past seven.

'She's obviously not coming today. Let's go, and try again tomorrow.' She really needed to stretch her legs.

'Patience,' Vijay said, 'just another half-hour.'

'OK, but seven forty-five, we're out of here.'

As Vijay nodded in agreement, a lone, hooded figure approached the entrance. The door opened and in walked a young lady. She unzipped her top and took it off as she walked over to the counter.

'That's her,' Vijay said, motioning with his eyes.

'You sure?' Saira asked.

Vijay nodded. 'Wait five minutes for her to settle in, then follow my lead.'

'OK.'

Vijay quickly hatched a plan after seeing the girl hang the top over her chair. He slipped out a small roll of sticky tape from his pocket and discreetly started to wrap it around his right hand, sticky side out.

Angelica sat at the table behind them with a coffee and a donut. She was distracted by her cell phone, which was beeping continuously

Vijay leant over to Saira. 'I am going to get up and shout at you; you need to push me in the direction of the girl, so I land behind her chair.'

Saira realised what he was up to. The crafty old dog, she thought. Vijay slammed his non-sticky palm onto the table and kicked his chair back, 'you never bloody listen to me!' he shouted. Saira got up and swore at him. He grabbed her arm and mouthed the word, 'now.'

Saira pushed him as directed. Vijay fell, grabbing the back of the young lady's chair and placing his tape-covered hand inside her hood before Angelica could even notice what was going on. Vijay landed on the floor, bracing himself with his left hand, while Saira was already on her way to the door.

'Baby, wait, I'm sorry,' he called after her. She didn't look back.

Vijay got up. 'So sorry, miss,' he said to the girl who he had disturbed.

'Idiot!' she scolded. He had made her spill coffee on her pants.

Vijay followed Saira out of the coffee shop, shouting 'come back!' for good measure.

The young girl serving at the counter went over to Angelica. 'I will fetch you a fresh cup, madam, are you hurt?' she asked.

'No, I'm fine, just a bit wet. Why can't these people keep their domestics behind closed doors?'

As Angelica's second cup of coffee was placed in front of her, the silver sedan was already halfway back to the apartment. Saira was driving and Vijay had placed his right hand into a bag for protection.

'That was slick, old man, I'll give you that,' Saira said.

Vijay laughed. 'Oh, I have a few tricks up my sleeve, don't you worry, and next time try not to push me like you mean it.'

'It had to look real, no?' Saira laughed.

Back at the apartment, Vijay carefully removed the bag from his hand and held it over a large sheet of white paper. He lifted the tape-covered hand for a closer look. 'Oh yes, there are more than enough on here. Saira, bring the tube so we can get these sealed up, please.'

'Did she look ok?' Peter asked.

'She wasn't crying. She looked a bit sad though, but I didn't have the time to take a close look at her as I was too busy beating up Vijay.'

'You really need to be careful with the old man,' laughed Kush, 'you don't want to break him, he's quite useful.'

'Hey, since when did my name change to "old man?"' Vijay protested.

They all laughed and now that the tape was removed, he lifted his arm to threaten them all with a tight backhander. A few minutes later, he left for the lab where his friend worked, which was only a twenty-five-minute drive away. Peter paced nervously; he had no idea how he would cope, waiting a whole two days for the results.

'Peter, I know why Rose is upset,' Rahul stopped his boss in his tracks.

'Why, what happened?'

'It's the son, Elijah, he left for the US yesterday, that must be why she has been so sad.'

Peter breathed a sigh of relief. 'Thanks, Rahul.'

A couple of hours later, Angelica returned home to a worried Elizabeth.

'You're late, you know I don't like you being out after dark on your own,' she fussed.

'Mom, I was only round the corner in the coffee shop, stop harassing me will you?'

'What happened to your pants?' her mother asked, noticing the brown stain on Angelica's leg.

'Oh that. Some bastard ...'

'Angelica, mind your language!' her mother insisted.

Angelica rolled her eyes.

'Some guy was arguing with his girlfriend or wife, and she pushed him. He nearly pulled me off my chair.'

'Are you hurt?' asked Elizabeth, circling her daughter looking for damage.

'No mom, just the stain.'

'Get them off and give them to Preeti before it dries, otherwise it'll be a permanent stain.'

'Yes, mom,' replied Angelica, rolling her eyes again. 'I hate this place,' she muttered to herself, as she walked up the stairs to her bedroom.

Angelica was met by Preeti, who had just come out of Elijah's room with a handful of clothes.

'He didn't sort out his dirty washing before he left,' Preeti told her.

Angelica looked at the pile and pulled out a worn-out baggy sweater; it was Eli's layabout top – he would wear it for weeks on end without washing it.

Angelica held it to her nose and breathed deeply. She could smell cologne – God, she missed him!.

Preeti went to take it back but decided not to. 'How are you feeling?' she asked.

Angelica shrugged her shoulders and screwed her face up just the way she used to when she was young. Preeti gave her a sympathetic smile. She missed the way that Angelica used to hang around her and cuddle her at every opportunity, but it was obvious that the poor girl was going through a rough patch, and all she could do was be there for her.

'If you need to talk, just come and find me.'

Angelica nodded and opened her room door.

'Oh, Preeti. Mom said I was to give these to you,' she said, pointing at her stained pants.

Preeti smiled. 'Leave them outside, I'll pick them up after I've dealt with this lot,' she said.

Chapter Thirty-Seven
Peter's apartment, 3:21 p.m.,
21st January

'I swear it was him,' Danny insisted. He and Harpreet had been out for the past couple of days, visiting the places where labourers hung around looking for work in the mornings and also to the gambling dens at night. They made a good team and Danny was learning fast from his new mentor, whose calm demeanour was rubbing off on him. Vijay was running the number plate of the car that the man had got into, the man that Danny said looked a lot like Maalik Aggarwal.

Harpreet wasn't convinced, but it wouldn't hurt to investigate. There hadn't been a fresh lead on the kidnappers since the sighting at the restaurant, which had frustratingly come to nothing.

'Guys, guys, it's here,' Vijay shouted excitedly. He let the team gather round his desk as his finger was poised on the mouse, ready to open the email. Peter was crouching down next to Vijay. 'Are you ready?'

'As ready as I will ever be.'

Vijay opened the email and clicked on the attached document. Everybody huddled together to hear the results of the DNA test. Vijay proudly made the announcement.

'Peter, the paternity test result for you and Angelica Naik is a ninety-nine-point-nine per cent match. Congratulations, you have officially found your daughter.'

The team let out a collective, 'YES!'

Without saying a word, Peter walked to his living area, entered his bedroom and closed the door behind him.

'Do you think he's OK?' Saira asked.

'Let's give him some time for this to sink in,' Harpreet advised.

'He's right, the boss has had a bit of a shock,' added Kush.

Harpreet turned to Danny, who looked slightly dazed. 'You OK?'

Danny nodded; he had a tear in one eye. 'I can't believe it's really her.'

Harpreet hugged the young man. 'We have a long way to go yet. I don't know what Peter is planning but I'm sure we'll find out soon,' he said quietly.

'Come on, I'll make you a cup of tea,' Harpreet said.

Peter was on his knees in his room, hands together in front of his face. He thanked God that he had finally found his girl, then spoke to Maria, something he usually did last thing at night, but today, the news couldn't wait.

'I've found her, Maria, I've found our girl,' he whispered.

The team sat around the meeting table, taking Peter's absence as an extended break. The mood was upbeat and there was laughter all around. It was a win for them, and the long days and nights were finally paying off.

Peter, having removed his suit jacket and tie, approached the waiting group of people who he now counted as friends. He was smiling, the kind of smile that only a person that was in total control could wear.

'Now you're going to find out what he's been planning,' Harpreet said, turning to Danny who was sitting next to him.

'OK everybody,' Peter said. 'We now know that we are heading down the right path, but we have an awful long way to go. Are you still with me?'

'All the way, boss,' they called out in unison.

Peter took a seat.

'Now, who would like to hear about phase two?'

'Hell yeah,' Kush said.

'Bring it on,' added Rahul.

'I am with you, Peter,' Harpreet said; he would be loyal to the end.

Peter had concocted an ingenious plan of attack. He aimed to get someone inside the Naik residence and had decided that Harpreet was the perfect choice for the role. The first part he would put into motion now and the second, a week later.

'I've found a way to get somebody close to the family without rousing suspicions,' Peter started. 'We need someone that can be in contact with them on a daily basis, befriend them, become part of the family, so to speak.'

The team looked doubtful.

'I understand where you're coming from, Peter, but how in God's name are we going to manage that? They have one full-time member of house staff, and she has been with the family for many years, it will be difficult to...'

Peter cut Vijay off. 'I don't want to change staff, I propose adding a *new* member of staff.'

'Whom, and in what capacity?' asked Saira.

'This is where you come in.' Peter turned to Harpreet.

'What do you have in mind?' Harpreet asked suspiciously.

'You will be the family's new personal security guard,' Peter answered.

'And how do you intend to make that happen?' Rahul questioned.

'They have never had any security because they have never needed it. The family has a private elevator that leads from the manned underground car park straight into their apartment which is accessed via a fingerprint and password combination. The main entrance is also manned by two guards at all times,' Vijay insisted.

'Correct,' said Peter, 'so Jonathan is safe tucked up in his little world. What we need to do is make him feel like he needs to protect his family and then provide a solution.'

'Ah, I understand now,' laughed Harpreet, 'does your plan involve staging some kind of disturbance?'

'Exactly,' replied Peter.

'Don't tell me we're going to rob their home, because I didn't sign up for this boss, I'm sorry.' Kush looked worried.

'No, no nothing like that. Just Jonathan, we need to rob him; somewhere outside, when he is alone. Rough him up a little, just enough to scare him. Once that seed of doubt about their security has entered his mind, then after a couple of days I will give him a friendly call for an update on building progress. I'm sure you guys are smart enough to guess the rest.'

'You offer him my services,' Harpreet added.

'Exactly. Harpreet here will be in and out of the apartment on a daily basis until Jonathan feels safe again. I'm assuming that will take at least a few months and during that time you can use your multitude of skills to locate any information the team needs, and as an added bonus you'll be able to find out about my daughter's life in detail,' Peter concluded and leaned back in his chair, waiting for questions.

'OK, I mean it's a great idea, and having someone on the inside, having access to this guy's office will be invaluable,' Vijay agreed.

'One thing, boss, who will be doing the robbing part of the plan, because he can't?' Kush asked pointing to Harpreet. 'Even with a mask on, well, it's pretty obvious…,' he trailed off.

'I'll do it. Harps has been teaching me a few moves,' Danny announced standing up and throwing a combination of punches, which brought a round of laughter.

Danny motioned a movie-style karate chop. 'Hi-yaaa,' he shouted.

'Sit down, Danny, the grown-ups are talking,' Saira said. An embarrassed Danny took a seat.

'Nobody is going to get hurt, not yet anyway, and Danny is an excellent choice. Now all we need is an accomplice,' said Peter.

'I'm too old, at least that's what you all keep telling me.' Vijay wanted his name out of the hat.

'Rahul?' suggested Peter.

Kush looked relieved; violence was not his cup of tea, unless it involved a computer game. Rahul looked at his boss and then at Harpreet, then back to Peter.

'No violence? I mean I'm sure we would all like to inflict some form of damage on this guy for what he has done but, if it came down to it, I don't think I'm the man for the job,' Rahul stated.

Harpreet stood up, taking control of the situation. 'This guy will spook easily,' he assured them, 'two masked men jump out on him; he will shit his pants and give up exactly what is demanded from him. Our Jonathan is not a fighter, you won't have a problem, I guarantee it.'

'OK,' said Rahul, 'I'll do it.' He leant over the table and fist-bumped Danny.

'Harpreet, you oversee this, get the guys ready, I will leave the planning to you,' Peter declared.

'Very good, you will have your fake robbery within a week.'

***

A couple of days later, with Harpreet distracted by his task, Peter sneaked out of the apartment alone, deciding to take it upon himself to see if his daughter remembered him. He had even removed his beard and looked just like he did when he last saw Rose. After three hours sitting in the café, he was sick of drinking coffee.

The door opened and in walked a trio of young ladies. Peter was facing them and immediately recognised the one that entered last. His heart started to race; he had no plan for what he would do next and definitely didn't expect Rose to arrive with company. They were laughing as they made their way to the counter. Peter could see their reflections in the window; he was now breathing heavily, on the verge of having a panic attack. Noticing the first two girls had placed their orders, he counted to ten and decided that he should forget the whole thing and leave.

Standing up, he reached for his jacket on the back of the chair just as the girls left the counter to find a table. Peter froze, holding onto the shoulders of his jacket. He watched them walk by – the first stared at him, the second sneered and the third, Rose, locked eyes with him. He wanted to reach out and hold her, call out her name. Time seemed to stand still as Angelica Naik looked at him intently but his heart broke as he realised there was no sign of recognition.

'What are *you* staring at, old man?' she asked.

Peter's eyes followed the girls as they took their seats. Angelica whispered something to her friends. Now they were all watching him, suspiciously.

'Pervert,' one of them declared as they all giggled. Dejected and demoralised, Peter took his jacket from the chair and left. His driver was waiting for him just around the corner. The driver opened the rear door and Peter fell onto the seat. 'Are you OK, sir?'

'Just take me home.' Peter put his hands to his face and burst into tears.

As the car took off, he could see the girls sitting in front of the window, still laughing amongst themselves. He was heartbroken. He had found his daughter and she didn't know who he was. Angelica and her friends were busy sharing a joke and didn't see the stranger pass by the window in the white Jaguar.

'Men! Why are they all such fucking perverts?' Angelica asked.

'Bastards,' another of the girls added.

***

Rahul was upstairs with Danny and Harpreet; the rarely used space was large enough for Harpreet to prepare his duo for the scenario that was going to play out. Harpreet and Danny had followed Jonathan for the past two days. The plan was to wait for him by his car, shove him around a little and demand his possessions.

Peter walked in, shoulders hunched, his eyes bloodshot; he had obviously been crying, even though he was trying his best to hide it.

'Peter, what's up?' Saira asked her boss.

He didn't answer. Worried, she got up and walked to his side.

'Peter, look at you, what's happened?' she demanded. Peter still said nothing; instead, he breathed in a lungful of air, wrapped his arms around his employee and let out a howl that sounded more animal than human.

Saira rubbed his back.

'It's OK,' she said.

The rest of the team moved to them. Peter held Saira tight. She did not mind; the guy was clearly in serious need of a hug, she thought, and she'd let him go only when he was good and ready.

Harpreet immediately realised what had happened. Peter was unmarked, his clothes not torn; he obviously hadn't been in a fight.

'He's been to see Rose,' he whispered to Danny, who looked at Harps, surprised.

'You knew?'

'If I'd known he wouldn't have gone!' Harpreet said.

Vijay pulled a bottle of whisky from the cupboard and poured a good measure for his employer. Twenty minutes later, they were all sitting at the table. Peter had calmed down enough to explain what had happened and was scolded by Harpreet. Boss or no boss, he had put their plans in jeopardy with his impulsive lapse.

'It's OK, no harm done, I suppose,' Vijay announced, 'she didn't recognise him.'

Vanya piped up. 'Does anybody else find it strange that she did not recognise her own father? I mean, it's not like Rose was a baby when she was taken. She was nine years old, *surely* she would remember him?'

'There was no spark of recognition in her eyes at all, you say?' asked Saira,

'Nothing,' Peter said sadly.

'No look of shock, no double take, nothing?' Vanya asked.

'No, she was blank. She had no idea who I was apart from some old man who was annoying her by invading her space.'

'And how long did it last?' Saira asked.

'How long did what last?'

'The eye contact – half a second, one second, how long?'

'Oh, I don't know, must have been a couple of seconds.' Peter said.

'Hold on, guys, is nobody else getting this?' Kush asked, holding out his hands like he was illustrating the blindingly obvious.

'Getting what?' asked Vijay.

'I know, I know what it is,' Vanya yelped, running over to the board where the printout of Angelica's birth certificate was. She ran back holding the paper out in front of her.

'Look,' she exclaimed, 'on this birth certificate, there's a date; this was issued a year after the other one. The date of birth is wrong, the first of January 2001, which makes her just turned seventeen. We all know that she is eighteen and was born on Christmas Eve. At first, we thought it was a mistake, but now!' She looked at Kush, not wanting to steal all the thunder.

'With her not recognising you it means that something must have happened to her. She was nine years old and had just celebrated her birthday – how could she forget when her own birthday is?'

'That's right! We bought her first bicycle that year, she was so happy,' Peter added.

'Correct!' continued Kush, 'so now she celebrates her birthday a month later, we've seen her social media accounts, no? Number one, how the hell does she not know when her own birthday is, and two, why doesn't she recognise her own father?' Kush finished.

'So, let me get this straight,' Rahul said, looking at Kush. 'In between being kidnapped and arriving with the Naiks, Rose suddenly lost her memory? Come on, that's a bit far-fetched, even for you.'

'What if it was …?' Vijay started.

'What?' they all shouted.

'It's a stupid idea, forget it.'

'Spit it out, man,' demanded Peter.

'Well,' Vijay continued, looking embarrassed, 'what if there was some sort of drug that could do just that, wipe someone's memory?'

He scanned his colleagues' faces, wishing he had kept the thought to himself.

'Oh, come on, that's a bit James Bond!' Kush scoffed.

'Harpreet, you're quiet, what do you think, does anything like that exist?' Peter asked.

'I heard a rumour a while back but nothing confirmed, and this was a long time ago.' The team fell silent.

All of a sudden Harpreet's eyes lit up. 'Fuck,' he exclaimed. He hardly ever swore, especially in front of his female colleagues.

Eight pairs of eyes swivelled towards him, waiting to hear what he knew. They could all see his fingers moving like he was counting; his eyes were screwed up as he tried hard to remember. They could almost hear the cogs of his brain whirring. Nobody spoke, none of them wanted to interrupt the man, who had already shown that his ability to recall detail was outstanding.

It must have been a full minute before he started to talk. 'I know exactly what happened,' he told them.

The team looked at each other.

'At the start of 2009, I joined a black-ops team working out of Bangalore. There had been a few high-profile kidnappings of company directors and CEOs. Myself and three others had gone there to help deal with a certain situation, but it wasn't anything to do with a kidnapping.' He paused for a moment. 'There was a guy, worked for a large pharma company and apparently, he had stolen something. It must have been important, the company hired us through certain channels the very same day...'

'And?' Kush said impatiently.

'We trailed him here to Mumbai. The client told us to hang back, they didn't say what they were looking for. I remember this guy's face; he was a foreigner, a white guy with blonde hair.'

'So, what happened?' asked Peter. He needed to hear the end of this story.

'We got pulled from the job, no explanation. The next thing you know, blondie is being fished out of the sea not far from here. The cops couldn't ID him but somebody from our company did.'

'So what does that mean?' Danny voiced everyone's confusion.

'Well, he worked for a pharma company, he stole something, he wound up swimming with the fish. Rose loses her memory at the same time. Rose was taken to order, and so was whatever the guy stole. It means our man Jonathan has been a very naughty boy.'

'But you don't know for sure what he took?' asked Peter.

'I think the fact that whatever he took was so secret he wound up dead confirms what it was.'

'It makes sense,' Vanya agreed.

'This is getting heavy,' Saira added.

'So, are we assuming that Rose was given a dose of some kind of secret memory-erasing drug?' Kush asked, looking for confirmation.

'Yes, that's what it seems like,' said Harpreet. The rest of them could not seem to find fault with the explanation, no matter how unlikely it seemed.

'What now then, boss?' asked Kush.

'We have a plan, and we will stick to it. Harpreet, do you have a day in mind for your operation?' Peter said.

'I think tomorrow will be good,' he answered.

'Very well, let's see what happens before we decide our next move,' said Peter. 'Oh, and Danny, you will have a new part to play soon,' he added.

Chapter Thirty-Eight
Naik residence, 9:17 a.m., 25th January

Angelica was sitting in the kitchen eating breakfast. She had deferred going to university for a year and wanted to concentrate on her modelling career, much to the disappointment of her parents.

'Good morning, how are you feeling today?' Jonathan asked, joining her at the counter.

'I'm OK, I have to go to the agency later, they're having a meeting with all the girls for some reason.'

'Oh, OK. Eli messaged me in the early hours, he said he will call later this evening when he gets the chance.'

Angelica smiled. She had shared a few video calls with her brother since he left, but it was difficult with the time difference and Eli being so busy.

Angelica fixed her father with her direct gaze and said, 'Dad, why are men such perverts?'

'What do you mean?' asked Jonathan, almost choking on his coffee, 'what's happened?'

'I was in CCD with my girlfriends...'

'CCD?'

'Café Coffee Day, it's easier to say, like OMG, obvs,' she explained, rolling her eyes. 'Oh, and obvs is obviously, obvs!'

'Oh,' her father replied.

'There was this old guy in the café and he was staring at me.'

'Well dear, you and your friends are pretty girls, I am sure a lot of people notice you. Did this man say anything to you?' A faint warning bell was beginning to ring in Jonathan's mind.

'No, that was the strange thing, he was only looking at *me*, not the others, and then he took off in a big hurry.'

'Maybe he recognised you from the campaign; your face is everywhere, you know – you're going to have to get used to it, I'm afraid.' Jonathan realised he was trying to convince himself as much as he was trying to reassure his daughter.

'You don't get it, dad,' Angelica insisted. 'It wasn't so much that he was looking *at* me, it was more the look in his eyes. I can't explain it; it was as though he knew me.'

The faint warning bells in Jonathan's head were now sounding more like sirens.

'Had you seen him before?'

'No, don't think so,' Angelica replied.

'Well, there isn't much I can do about people staring at you, darling, we Indians are well known for that.'

Angelica laughed it off. 'Yeah, I suppose you're right.'

'Listen, if you see this guy again or if you ever feel threatened, you call me straight away, OK? Just be careful and do not wander down to that place alone,' Jonathan insisted.

'Yes, dad.'

'I'm going to work now, I love you!' Jonathan tried to reassure himself that he was just worrying about nothing.

'Preeti,' Angelica called out.

The maid was on the terrace sweeping up. Getting no answer, Angelica left her stool and went out onto the terrace to find her.

'Preeti?' she called, startling the maid who was deep in thought and didn't see her approach.

'Yes, Angelica, was breakfast OK? D'you want some more?'

'It was nice, thanks, I'm full now. Tell me, are all men perverts?'

Preeti laughed at the strange question.

'Well, yes the answer is that unfortunately, most of them are, I think.'

***

That evening, Danny and Rahul were sitting in the back of the silver sedan, which was parked out of sight of the building entrance of Naik and Associates. Vijay had given them a small remote camera, which Harpreet had set up early that morning, facing the entrance. The pair were dressed in black outfits with rolled-up balaclavas on top of their heads. Harpreet was in the driver's seat and would stay put throughout, as overwatch. He couldn't see there being any problems, but he lived by the six P's – proper planning prevents piss poor performance – and wasn't taking any chances. He could easily have done the job alone. Rahul seemed calm but Danny was expelling his nervous energy by fidgeting. The target's car was situated in the car park across the street. Harpreet had found a blind spot on the fifty-metre route to where it was parked and the plan was that when they saw Jonathan exit the building, Rahul and Danny had two minutes to ambush him at the designated place, scare him enough to be convincing and then get back to the car before anyone noticed what was going on.

'You guys ready?' Harps asked. He had spotted their mark in the lobby heading for the doors.

Both men nodded.

'Do NOT deviate from my instructions,' Harpreet said with emphasis. 'Go!'

On his command Rahul and Danny jumped out of the car, crouched over, running low under the cover of the parked vehicles. They had pulled their face coverings down and were now barely visible. They followed the route planned by Harpreet, to within an inch.

Jonathan ambled along, his mind on his conversation with Angelica that morning, oblivious to what was about to happen. Rahul and Danny stopped behind a blue hardware truck. Harpreet was counting down the seconds in his head; he had already started the car up and was on his way to the rendezvous point that was twenty metres to the left of where the two men now were, well-hidden and sandwiched between two high-sided vehicles.

Rahul looked at Danny, held up three fingers, then two, then one. At that moment, Jonathan came into view and Danny leapt out in front of him brandishing the twelve-inch kitchen knife he had been concealing inside his jacket. Jonathan was just about to cry out for help when Danny hissed in his ear.

'Make one fucking sound and I will stick this in your neck.' Jonathan froze and dropped his briefcase. Rahul came from behind and swept his left leg away from underneath him, making him fall to one knee. Danny's heart was pounding; he could feel the adrenalin pumping through his veins.

'Take what you want, just don't hurt me, please,' cried Jonathan, pulling out his wallet.

'Throw it to me,' Danny demanded.

He had never felt so powerful in his life; this guy had flipped over like a dog and was begging for mercy. As Danny stood there holding the knife, the thought of what this bastard had done to his best friend consumed him and, for a moment, he wanted the helpless man on the floor to scream just so he could stab him, but Danny knew that if he started stabbing the coward, he wouldn't be able to stop.

Realising that their time was running out and seeing that Danny had frozen, Rahul took charge of the situation. He punched the man in the side of the head, not too hard but hopefully enough to daze him.

Jonathan went down, Rahul grabbed his left arm and unclasped his Rolex watch then picked up the wallet that had been dropped. Danny snapped out of his daze. Rahul shoved him in the direction of the car.

'Done?' Harpreet asked, as they bundled into the car.

'Done,' Rahul confirmed.

Danny was amazed at what had just happened. He had made a grown man piss his pants without even touching him. That was a feeling that he would savour for a long time.

'Nice watch,' Rahul declared, holding up the Rolex.

'Put it in this,' Harpreet told him, holding up a small plastic bag.

'Well done you two, Peter will be happy,' Harpreet said with a brief smile.

Danny hadn't said a word since getting in the car; he was still trying to process what had happened. Rahul hadn't noticed the dark stain appearing at the front of the man's pants but Danny had, and, surprisingly, he actually enjoyed the rush.

***

Elizabeth let out a blood-curdling scream when she saw her husband walking towards her and dropped the glass of wine she was holding, smashing it to pieces as it hit the tiled floor.

'Jon, what happened? Preeti, call the police!' she shouted.

Elizabeth could see the blood that had trickled down the side of his head and onto his usually pristine white shirt collar. His trousers were dirty and wet around the groin area. Preeti heard the scream and ran downstairs to join her employers.

'Call the police, NOW!' Liz cried out. Preeti took the phone out of her pocket and dialled 112.

'I'm ok,' Jonathan said holding his hand to his head.

'What happened to you?' his wife demanded; she was shaking uncontrollably.

'I've been robbed,' he said, dropping his briefcase for the second time that evening.

'Oh my God, are you hurt?'

'Just this,' he declared, revealing the cut to his temple.

Preeti had already given their address to the police, who said that they would send a patrol car over straight away. Angelica, having heard the commotion, was looking over the mezzanine balcony at her bedraggled father. 'Daddy,' she cried and ran down the stairs.

'Can everybody stop fussing,' Jonathan said. His pride had been hurt and he couldn't bear the embarrassment of his family seeing him in such a state.

Angelica stood staring at him, noticing that he had wet himself.

'They had a knife and threatened to kill me, I had no chance,' Jonathan announced as he made his way over to the bar and poured himself a large whisky.

'We need to get you to the hospital,' Elizabeth said. Jonathan shook his head and winced.

'Cancel my cards, Liz, they took my wallet, and the watch you gave me. I'm sorry, there were two of them, I was so scared. I'm not a fighter, I didn't know what to do, it all happened so fast.'

'Hey, hey, hey, it doesn't matter, you are here and safe now, that's what counts. Where are the bloody police?' Liz said.

An hour and a half later, the police had left after taking a statement. The doctor arrived just after and gave him the once-over. Jonathan had a bruised knee, sore leg and a small cut on the left side of his head that didn't require stitches.

He hadn't seen their faces and heard no names. 'They knew what they were doing, they were waiting for me,' Jonathan said.

The police didn't seem too hopeful – no evidence, probably no CCTV either. Jonathan could claim on his insurance but that wasn't the point; he had never been attacked before, and this shook him to the core.

'I'm going for a shower,' he said.

Elizabeth pushed herself along the sofa to sit next to Angelica. 'Come here,' she said, pulling her daughter, whose eyes were wide with fear, in for a hug.

Jonathan was leaning against the wall with both arms outstretched, the enormous two-foot-square shower head pouring hot water onto his aching head and back. With eyes shut he stood motionless for the best part of ten minutes, wracking his brain for answers. Was this just a random attack? Was he being watched, and if so, was this the end of it or would he still be a target? What about his family?

He knew of nobody that would want to hurt him, he had no enemies to think of. OK, he had pissed people off in the past, but that was part and parcel of being in business. His wallet meant nothing to him. The watch, a gift from Elizabeth, was special but could easily be replaced. What hurt the most was his wounded pride. Jonathan had never been in a fight, not even in school. He could always talk his way out of a confrontational situation.

Being a control freak he hated that things were going on in his life that he could do nothing about.

The bathroom door opened and Elizabeth came in, wearing only a silk robe. She untied the belt and let it slip to the floor. Even with the events of the day, Jonathan could still appreciate his wife's firm body.

She had curves in all the right places and for her age was still stunning naked. She joined him. He moved aside to share the falling water, the shower full of steam, the air thick with sexual tension. Elizabeth positioned herself in front of him and let him enter her. They made love more passionately than they had done in years. Elizabeth knew that after what had happened to her husband, who had been humiliated by wetting himself, this was the one thing she needed to do to help him feel like a man again.

Chapter Thirty-Nine
Peter's apartment, 9:10 p.m., 25th January

The three men got back to base after taking a detour through the city. The car they were using was left a couple of miles away, just in case. Peter's driver had picked them up. During their detour they stopped at Powai Lake where Harpreet put the watch, wallet and knife inside a bag weighed down with a brick he had ready and, making sure he wasn't seen, had thrown it as far as he could.

He watched as the bag disappeared into the depths of the lake.

The team gathered for the debrief and were all excited to hear how the mission had played out. Pretending to be an innocent couple, Vijay and Saira had gone to the scene of the crime, and without raising suspicions, checked the area for anything that could have been left and retrieved the hidden camera. Peter seemed satisfied with the way things had gone but was confused about something.

'Danny, what happened?'

'What do you mean, what happened?'

'What happened to you? You froze, it was lucky Rahul acted quickly.'

'Nothing happened, Peter, it's OK, we worked as a team,' Rahul answered for Danny, trying to cover for him. He had no idea why Danny had hesitated and didn't really care; he was happy to have done the job and got out of there.

But Peter was staring at Danny; he wasn't going to leave it until he got an answer from the young man that he had put in possible danger. Peter was starting to regret ever getting him involved in the first place. He thought Danny could handle the mission but maybe he was wrong.

'You want to know what happened?' Danny shouted, rising from his seat. His demeanour had changed in an instant. He was now angry and breathing heavily. Surprised, the team waited for Danny to continue. Peter said nothing.

'I wanted to kill him!' Danny shouted, 'I wanted to stick that knife in him a thousand times for taking my best friend away from me and for what he did to you and Maria, God rest her soul, and for making Uncle Victor blame himself until his dying day. I wanted to kill him for all the pain he has caused, Peter. I wanted to cut his fucking head off and shove it up his own ass! *That's* what happened!'

He walked off towards the kitchen area, sadness now replacing his anger. He had shown no real emotion since joining the team and his outburst surprised everyone.

Danny clearly needed to be reined in. Peter did not want to find out that Jonathan had been murdered, not by Danny; he would not let the young man that he loved like a son end up with blood on his hands, no way!

As Peter got up to follow Danny, Kush looked around the team; they were all still sitting there, open-mouthed in shock at the outburst that none of them thought Danny was capable of. 'Fuck,' he exclaimed.

'Well, I wasn't expecting that!' Vanya shook her head.

'Me neither,' said Saira.

'There's a lot of pent-up hate and aggression for what has happened; he just didn't realise it was there, until today,' Vijay added.

'His eyes!' Rahul said, 'you should have seen his eyes, he scared the shit out of me. I swear if I hadn't pushed him away, he would have done it, man, I'm telling you!'

'What did we expect?' asked Harpreet, who until now had been silent, 'did any of you think that he would just be OK? This has affected him more than even he could have known; we need to be here for him now, we are a team.'

Harpreet circled his finger in front of them, 'we all need to look after him, OK? No more situations like this for Danny and definitely no more knives!'

'Amen to that.'

'No more knives is good,' agreed Rahul.

Peter found Danny with his head in his hands and put his arm around the younger man's shoulder.

'I'm sorry, uncle,' he said. 'I don't want to feel so angry but I can't help it; it's eating me up inside.'

'Listen, son,' Peter started, leaning his head against the young man's. 'When Rose disappeared, I wanted to kill everybody that was involved. I hated the police, even Roger, for not being able to find her, but in time I realised that I needed to let go, I needed to find clarity in my thoughts, otherwise if I had let the darkness take over, none of us would be here now, having found Rose. We *have* found her, remember that Danny. Let the hate go. I know what I am doing, we all have a job to do, and yours will start in a few days. I will explain what it is in a while. Right now, you need to think straight. I should never have put you in that situation and I'm sorry.'

Danny lifted his head and pulled away to meet Peter's eyes. 'I so nearly made a huge mistake and Rahul saved me; he was amazing by the way.'

'There was no harm done, you guys executed the plan just as I wanted.' Peter gave Danny one of those sadistic smiles that he was getting better at by the day.

'Do you know how I know it worked?'

'No,' replied Danny.

'You made that man piss his pants; you saw it for yourself.'

Danny chuckled at the thought. 'Yeah, I did.'

'Only a very scared man would do that, and I want him scared Danny. I am going to push this son of a bitch into a living hell. I am slowly going to take away everything that he holds dear to him.'

Danny could tell that Peter meant every word.

'Come join us when you are ready,' Peter said as he left the room. The door shut.

Danny cried for a full hour. Then, after washing his face, he rejoined the team.

'What's the job you have for me?' Danny asked.

'Ah yes,' Peter replied. 'Everybody settle down, I want to tell you all about my latest investment. Mack, come over please.'

Mack had been at his desk beavering away with something; he didn't mind a bit of interaction with the team but preferred to be focused on his own workload, which was getting heavier by the day. Peter had been keeping him extremely busy with his recent acquisitions. Mack picked up a folder and walked over to join the group. He laid a couple of documents on the table for all to see.

'Hold on, you've bought a model agency?' Saira declared, glancing at the important bits. 'Why?'

'Not just any model agency,' Mack stated, 'THE model agency.'

'Aah, you mean Tip Top,' Kush said, the penny dropping.

'Yes, I have purchased the agency that Rose is signed to. It should be a done deal in a day or two. I will keep the current staff for the time being but will be making Danny a company director.'

'I don't have the first clue about what goes on in these places, Peter,' Danny protested.

'Patience, young man, I have done this for two reasons. Firstly, I want you in there so I know that Rose is being looked after and not exploited.'

Danny nodded. 'OK,' he said doubtfully.

'Secondly, when you are ready I will transfer the company into your name. It will be yours, Danny, this is your future. It's the least I could do; this is your stability and will provide for you and your family, if and when you start one.'

'I don't know what to say.' Danny stared at Peter.

'Thanks will do,' Peter laughed.

'Thank you, thank you – of course, a million thank you's,' Danny gabbled.

'That's a smart move, Peter,' Vijay exclaimed. 'All we need is for Jonathan to take the bait when you offer him the services of our friend here,' he said pointing to Harpreet, 'then we will have eyes and ears everywhere.'

'That's the plan,' Peter replied. 'Everything should be ready by Friday, and you will start work on Monday.'

Danny smiled; he liked the sound of running his own business. 'What about Rose?' he asked.

'What about her?' Peter asked.

'If she didn't remember her own father ...' Harpreet started. 'Sorry Peter, just stating a fact here.'

'Carry on, it's OK,' Peter assured him.

'If she didn't remember her father, it's highly unlikely that she will remember you, Danny.'

'I suppose so,' Danny replied.

Saira stood up. 'So, we have found Rose, Danny will be at her workplace and, God willing, Harps will be looking after the family soon, so what's your endgame boss?'

'Good question,' Peter declared, 'what do I want out of all this? Well, I want my daughter back. At this moment in time she isn't "my" daughter, or at least she has no idea that she is, and we can't just kidnap her because... well, that would be stupid and potentially very damaging to her, given that she does not know me from a bar of soap. We have time on our side, as I have said before. Rose will be protected by us from all angles and knowing that she is safe will allow us to continue our search for the men who took her away from us. I want them punished for what they have done to my family.'

'Wait, what does that mean, Peter?' Vanya asked.

'It means that I am going to take down every single person involved.'

'Take down?' she persisted.

'I will put it bluntly, people.' Peter rose to his feet and slowly started to walk around the table. 'I am going to kill every single one of them, with this Jonathan motherfucker last.'

There were a lot of shocked faces in the room. Nobody had seen this coming.

'What about the police? Why can't we just hand them over?' Rahul asked, hopefully.

'There will be criminals involved in this, Rahul, bad people, and who knows how long they would spend in prison? As long as these bastards are alive, I will never consider my Rose safe from harm. I understand that this was not part of the original plan and am now giving each and every one of you the opportunity to leave, with full payment and a bonus on top if what I have planned is too rich for your blood. I will not force you to stay, you are free to go. What my wife went through, lying on her death bed, not knowing whether her daughter was alive, let alone safe.' Peter bowed his head and shook it sadly.

'She died not being able to say goodbye to Rose; what myself and her grandparents had to endure for so many years – the pain, the worry, …' Peter trailed off.

Harpreet stood and took over. 'I will be doing all the dirty work,' he assured the team.

Everyone was clearly calculating what involvement in this would mean for them. What they were being asked to do was illegal, but was it morally wrong? That was up to the individual to decide.

'I have grown close to all of you,' Peter told his team. 'Help me do this, we will only be doing the world a favour, I promise you. And as Harpreet has already mentioned, what he will be doing will be on him, or me, and not on you guys. Stick with me, it may take a year or two but when this is all over…' Peter paused, then, deciding to throw caution to the wind, said, 'when this is over, I will give you all one million dollars on top of the payment already agreed.'

'Fuck,' said Mack.

'Even you, Mack,' Peter added.

There were raised eyebrows all round. The payments that Peter had offered were already substantial and by now the team were emotionally involved.

'Forget the money boss, I'm in,' declared Vijay.

Peter had put forward a convincing case. Getting bad people off the streets was a good thing and knowing how corrupt the judicial system was in the country, Vijay agreed with the idea of a solution more final than a jail term.

'Me too,' said Saira, who was still standing.

'Vanya, what about you?' Saira asked.

Vanya stood up. 'I say we fuck them up big time!' she shouted.

'I take that as a yes,' Peter said.

Rahul, Danny and Kush all rose to join them.

'We stand together,' Kush announced, 'we will all see this through to the end, Peter – for you and for Rose!'

Peter smiled.

'There is one thing I still don't understand,' said Vanya. 'How is Rose supposed to get her memory back, and if she doesn't, isn't all of this pointless? For her, the family she is with *are* her family, wouldn't we be traumatising her just as much as the kidnappers did when she was a child, by taking her away from them?'

'To be honest, I have no idea how she will get her memory back, but we need to try; we will find a way, that I promise you,' Peter replied, despite the fact that this was the only thing he didn't have a plan for.

Chapter Forty
Naik residence, 11:11 a.m., 26th January

Jonathan had fallen asleep as soon as his aching head hit the pillow and, although it was nearly noon, he still hadn't woken up.

Elizabeth and Angelica were drinking coffee at the kitchen counter with Preeti fussing around them. Preeti had been shaken by what happened the day before, not only for herself but for her 'family'. She was worried about them, especially Angelica.

'What do you mean the agency has new owners?' Elizabeth was asking Angelica.

'Just that,' her daughter answered. 'It's no big deal, same staff, new owner – oh, and they are bringing some young guy in to join the management team.'

'Well don't let him mess you about, make sure they don't start taking advantage of you. If the new owner is stingy, they may want to cut corners to save money,' Elizabeth said.

'As long as they still have the free donuts in reception, I don't care,' Angelica laughed.

'Be serious, Angelica!' her mother said, 'just remember what I said, don't take any shit from them.'

'I'm going to check on your father.' Elizabeth went upstairs to see if he had woken up yet.

Jonathan was awake when Elizabeth opened the door. Seeing that his eyes were open, she asked, 'how are you feeling, darling?'

'Not bad, bit of a headache.'

'D'you want a coffee, I'll bring it for you?'

'No, no, I must get up now anyway, I have a few things to do.'

'Don't even think about going to work today, Jon,' Elizabeth said sternly.

'I wasn't planning to, I can work from home,' he said, wincing as he got out of bed, 'besides, I can't face going back to that place yet.'

'You don't need to, that's why you have staff, it's pointless being the organ grinder *and* the monkey,' she said.

'I know, I know.' Jonathan looked her up and down. 'Hey, last night, that was fantastic,' he said.

'Yes it was, maybe we should do it more often,' Elizabeth said dreamily, having lost count of how many times she had been brought to climax.

'I promise I will spend more time here and not work so late, darling,' he said.

'I'll believe that when I see it,' Elizabeth told him, but she kissed him warmly, allowing the tip of her tongue to poke into his mouth to tease him before she left the room.

'I'll come down in a minute, you temptress!' Jonathan called out.

'OK, take your time!'

That afternoon, Jonathan was sitting on the sofa, watching a movie and, although it was early, he'd allowed himself a glass of whisky to relax. His phone started buzzing. He had told the office that he wouldn't be in for the rest of the week. He didn't want anyone to know what had happened, but they'd found out anyway from the police that had arrived earlier in the day to check the CCTV and interview the staff.

'Hello? Jonathan speaking,' he said.

'Jonathan, it's Peter Rosario.'

'Hi, Peter, everything OK?'

'Don't worry about me, your secretary told me what happened, are you OK?'

'Yes, I'm fine, just a little shaken up.'

'Is nowhere safe in this city any more?' Peter asked, tutting.

'You have to wonder,' Jonathan said.

'Did they take anything?'

'Watch and wallet.' Jonathan had been trying not to think about the incident and didn't really want to discuss it. In an attempt to cut Peter off he asked, 'Is there anything you need? All the paperwork is in the office, and I won't be there until Monday. Feel free to call my secretary, she should be able to deal with any questions you have.'

'Listen,' Peter said, 'some guys tried to rob me a while back.'

'Tried?'

'Tried and failed,' Peter added.

'What did you do? How did you stop them?' Peter had Jonathan's attention now.

'Me? I didn't do anything, my man Harpreet was with me. I never walk around alone, Jonathan. This guy is ex-special forces, hard as a rock – he can put a man down with his eyes closed.'

'Really? Maybe I need someone like that,' Jonathan mused.

'It's definitely something worth considering. Hey, just an idea, I'm going to be out of the country for a month or so, if it would make you feel better, you can borrow him while I'm away.'

'No, it's OK, but thanks for the offer.'

Peter had to think fast, he couldn't pressure the man too much, that would arouse suspicion, but he needed to get him to agree now before the opportunity was lost.

'These guys were professional, or so I hear, what if they are not finished with you yet?'

'I don't know, Peter.'

'What harm can it do? Harpreet is a very smart guy; at the very least he can advise you on how to beef up security around the home, etc., make your wife feel secure.'

'Is he trustworthy?'

'Jonathan! I trust him with my life, I have never felt safer. His salary is covered, why don't you meet him and see what you think? He doesn't like flying, and I'm going to London next week so he will be at a loose end anyway.'

Jonathan pondered the proposition for a moment. Having a security guard around would certainly make the girls feel safer and, he thought, he could go out with Angelica, who certainly wouldn't be going anywhere on her own for the foreseeable future, what with the mugging and the creepy guy in the coffee shop.

'OK, that would be great, Peter, but only if you don't mind.'

'Mind?' Peter exclaimed, 'I practically insist man, I can't be having my friends walking around not feeling safe.'

'Thanks, Peter, I appreciate this, you will have to come over for dinner with us when you return, it will be the least I can do.'

'Looking forward to it, Jonathan, send me your address and I will have my driver bring him over tomorrow afternoon, if that suits you. His name is Harpreet Singh.'

'Will do, thanks again, Peter.'

'My pleasure, I'll see you when I get back.'

The whole team had been listening to the call on speakerphone and as Peter hung up they cheered.

'Are you ready?' Peter asked Harpreet.

'Yes, boss, this will be a walk in the park.'

'Peter, how do you propose getting out of having dinner with the family, in your new role as creepy old man?' Saira asked.

Peter laughed and the others joined him. 'Well, we will cross that bridge when we come to it, won't we – maybe I could wear a disguise?' he joked.

Peter's plan was in place, leaving only the kidnappers to find, and now that Rose was covered, the team could focus all of their efforts on doing just that.

'Right, that's enough messing around for the day, it's about time you found these two bastards,' he announced, pointing at the mugshots on the pinboard.

Chapter Forty-One
Peter's apartment, 10:14 a.m., 27th January

'Guys, guys,' Vijay shouted.

'I don't know whether this is good or bad news,' Vijay called out as the team, including Mack, approached his desk.

'I've got contacts in nearly all of the police stations in the city and as you are aware, when we first started out I informed them that when there were any arrests, no matter how petty the crime, I was to be informed and provided with a name and photo, no questions asked.'

'I know, it's costing me a fortune in bribes,' Peter said ruefully.

'Well, it has finally paid off. On top of arrests, I asked to be notified about murder victims too, just in case,' Vijay continued.

'*And?*' asked the ever-impatient Kush, trying to hurry Vijay along.

Vijay clicked on the attachments in the email he had received that morning.

'We've got the fucker!' Kush shouted, his hand raised, looking for someone to high-five.

'We've found one of them, the one called Sunil,' Vijay announced, 'murdered, found face down in a ditch, ten miles north from here, took a knife to the chest! My contact is almost sure it was mob-related. That's all I have for now, but this guy, he's now a dead end.'

'Nice one,' declared Rahul, sniggering at the pun.

'Where does that leave us?' asked Saira.

'It's not all bad news; if we find out who he is connected to, then we may be further along in our search than we think,' added Vijay.

'You're right, this could be a turning point, although I would have liked to have seen his face as his miserable life ebbed away,' added Peter, angry not to be given the chance to end the life of one of his daughter's kidnappers.

'Got what he deserved, the bastard,' Vanya said.

'What now?' Peter asked.

'We wait,' Vijay said, 'it will take a day or two, but we should let the police do their jobs, let them stir the pot and when they have handed us what they know, then we can take over.'

Peter nodded.

'In the meantime, let's focus on finding this other prick, Maalik. I want results people – come on guys, let's start earning our pay cheques,' Kush said.

With all the tech and smart people on the case, the lack of progress in finding anyone connected to the kidnapping was getting embarrassing.

**

The doorbell rang at exactly one p.m. Jonathan had already been informed by the building's reception desk that his visitor had arrived. Harpreet was a stickler for being on time, it was something that the army had drilled into him, especially on a covert mission, where being even a second late could mean losing a life. Jonathan opened the door to find an impeccably dressed Sikh man in front of him; his beard was neatly shaped, his black turban had a subtle white trim to match his black suit and he wore a dazzling white shirt. He was instantly impressive.

Jonathan held the door open for the man, and as he walked past him noticed that he smelled good, almost too good for his role. He could easily pass for the employer and not the employee, he thought.

'Mr Naik, I am Harpreet Singh, my employer Peter Rosario sent me.'

Jonathan accepted the man's outstretched hand, noticing his well-manicured nails. His handshake was firm.

'Come in Harpreet and please, call me Jonathan.'

'Everybody calls me Harps,' the turbaned man replied.

The ladies of the house were waiting for the new arrival; Elizabeth felt her heart begin to race. Wow, she thought to herself, noticing Harps' guns bulging in his suit jacket, this guy is hot.

'This is my wife Elizabeth and my daughter Angelica,' Jonathan announced.

Harpreet greeted them both with a small bow.

'So, Peter says you saved him from being robbed a while ago?' Jonathan quizzed.

Harpreet had been told to lie about their meeting and how long they had known each other. He told his story and his experience to the Naiks, who couldn't help but be impressed.

'What do you require me to do, Jonathan?' Harpreet asked.

'I suppose if we are home then you hang around here and if one of us leaves the house then you go with them.'

OK, what if two of you leave separately?'

'Ah, I hadn't thought about that!'

'Tell me who is your priority?' Harpreet asked.

'Angelica, of course, she goes out for hours with her friends.'

'And then?'

'Well, my wife, and then me. I'm just worried that these guys must have been watching me, and that means they could have been watching my wife and daughter too, they probably know where we live.'

'I understand,' Harpreet said, seeing the fear in Jonathan's eyes. 'OK, here is how it is going to work. The security here is so-so, your private elevator is a nice touch though, I have already seen the entrance downstairs.'

'Wait, how did you get into the car park?' Jonathan asked.

'That's part of my job,' Harpreet smiled.

Angelica smiled too; she liked this guy.

'Your front door would easily take ten to fifteen minutes to break down. You are on the twenty-second and twenty-third floors and walking around the outside of the building I noticed there is no way to climb all the way up to this level.'

Jonathan raised his eyebrows. 'Keep going,' he prompted.

'What I am saying, is that when you are here you are relatively safe. Your problem is when you leave this place.'

Harpreet walked over to Angelica. 'You, miss, will not leave home without me or your father, do you understand?'

Angelica frowned. 'Dad, he can't talk to me like that,' she complained; maybe she didn't like this pushy man after all.

'Darling, it's for the best, I don't want you getting hurt, you'll do what you are told, OK?'

Angelica was truly pissed off now, she loved her freedom.

'You are quite famous, miss, I've seen your face everywhere, which makes you a target for evil, heartless men that take what they want from girls like you, now I assure you, **you really do not want that to happen.**'

He slowly enunciated every word to scare her, and it seemed to have the desired effect. It was the truth, he had seen the mutilated bodies of women that had been taken and abused for days, even weeks. It was real and this little princess would have to face up to it.

'I bet he's all talk anyway; he probably can't even fight,' she said disdainfully.

She got off the stool and flounced past him. Just behind him now, she swung a right hook at his head. Harpreet ducked without even looking and stopped her punch in mid-air, catching her wrist at lightning speed.

'Miss, you will need to try a bit harder than that, but if you like I can teach you how to defend yourself, that's if your parents agree. Knowing some self-defence would serve you well.'

Angelica had tried to embarrass the man but in turn, had only managed to embarrass herself.

'Whatever,' she sneered and walked off up the stairs towards her bedroom.

'I am so sorry about that, Harpreet,' Elizabeth gushed. 'Sometimes that girl has no manners.

'It's OK, how old is she?'

'Eighteen.'

'Youngsters of that age always think they know best – now, where was I? Yes, when you are all home I will be here from nine a.m. to nine p.m., unless you need me at any other time; if so, just let me know. I will shadow Angelica, and you Elizabeth. If both ladies are out separately, we will decide what happens at the time.'

Jonathan agreed.

'Do I have the use of a car?' Harpreet asked.

'Yes, sure, you can use one of ours whenever you need.'

'Very good.'

'Oh, by the way, Harpreet,' Elizabeth smiled, 'this is Preeti,' she said as she saw the maid approaching. 'If you need something to eat just ask her, she also makes an amazing cup of coffee!'

Preeti had seen the man arrive and was trying to hide how attractive she thought he was. She didn't want her employers to see her blush, because although she was dark-skinned, she could still turn bright red.

'Nice to meet you.' Oh God, she thought, he smells divine, I'm going to faint.

'Would you like a cuf of coppee?' she stumbled on her words; this handsome guy had awoken something deep inside her.

'A what?' Elizabeth quizzed.

Preeti realised her mistake and hoped nobody else had; she had been tongue-tied for the first time in an awfully long while. 'Coffee, a cup of coffee?' she corrected, clearly flustered.

'Please – black, no sugar,' Harpreet replied giving the maid a small smile that did nothing to help her confusion.

'Harpreet will be spending a lot of time here over the next month, he is here to look after us.'

'Oh, that's good,' Preeti said as nonchalantly as she could manage. She spun a one-eighty and made off for the kitchen beaming from ear to ear – this was the best news she had heard in ages.

***

A few days later and after spending some time with her newly appointed bodyguard, Angelica had warmed to him and agreed to take up Harpreet's offer of self-defence tuition; her parents had practically insisted that she start right away. They thought that if she could defend herself they would feel better about her being out on her own in the future.

Peter would want his man back at some point and while he was here, they should put his skills to use.

'Are you ready?' Harpreet asked.

Angelica nodded. She was wearing a sweat suit and an old pair of running shoes.

'Good, let's warm up.'

Harpreet took her through a series of stretches which she found easy enough after playing so many sports in school. Angelica was still supple, even if she hadn't done anything energetic for a while.

Harpreet showed her a mixture of blows, holds, kicks, etc. and despite herself, Angelica found she was really enjoying it.

They trained for an hour and a half and agreed to continue the next day if Harpreet wasn't needed by her parents. Angelica felt good, and although it was only her first session, she had taken to it like a fish to water. Harpreet was glad of the exercise too. They had barely left the house; his only outing was to accompany Jonathan to his office and back.

Harpreet left the apartment just after nine p.m. He was meeting Peter for the first time since starting in his new post.

The place was empty except for himself and Peter, who had sent the team home an hour ago. He didn't want his conversation with Harpreet interrupted.

'Well, what's she like, is she OK, is she a nice person, do they treat her well?' Peter was desperate for information.

Harpreet laughed. 'Your daughter is fine, she is a genuinely nice young lady, a bit highly strung, but what teenager isn't these days?'

'Do they take care of her?'

'From what I have seen yes, very well, she's even pretty spoilt I would say. They look like a normal family.'

Harpreet instantly regretted his choice of words when he saw Peter's face. 'I mean, they treat her well, but she isn't their daughter.'

'Have you had a chance to search his office yet?'

'No, he only started back at work today, and his wife is always hanging around, I'm sure she has the hots for me.' Harpreet gave a little laugh. 'Oh, and Rose took up the offer of self-defence classes. We started today, she's a fast learner!'

'Good,' Peter replied, 'there must be something connecting Jonathan to the person who orchestrated the kidnapping. You need to get into his office; if there is anything to find, it will be in there.'

'Peter, I can only do that when I am alone and at the moment that is proving to be difficult. Let's bide our time, the opportunity will come and when it does, I assure you, I will take it.' Harpreet could see the desperation in his employer's eyes but knew he would need to wait for the right moment.

⊷⊶⧫⊷⊶

Chapter Forty-Two
Peter's apartment, 3:32 p.m.,
15th February

Peter was sitting at his desk, having barely moved all day; it was two weeks since their last lead on the kidnappers.

Harpreet had fitted in well with the Naiks. Peter had informed them that he would be away for a few months, and they were happy to keep Harps around.

Danny was settling in at the model agency and proving to be a natural. With his daughter covered in all aspects of her life, Peter was satisfied that no more harm could come to her, but he desperately wanted to find the bastards that had taken his little girl from him; he was growing more and more frustrated as the days went by.

'Peter,' Vijay said for the second time, standing next to his boss trying to get his attention. He laid a hand on Peter's shoulder, snapping him out of his reverie.

'Sorry, Vijay, I was daydreaming, what's up, anything new?'

'Are you OK, boss?'

'Yes,' Peter assured him, 'just thinking, that's all.'

'I received an email yesterday regarding a possible connection to Maalik and Sunil. There's a guy called Vikram, I don't know his last name, there isn't much information out there on him, but I have had confirmation from another source that this guy is quite high up in the Mumbai Mafia, not a top dog but no foot soldier either.'

'Go on,' Peter said.

'He has links to the two men we are after. Now we know that this guy Sunil was definitely murdered, right? Maalik is our target, and my people assure me he has been working for this Vikram character.'

'Do we know what he looks like? Where he operates?' Peter asked hopefully.

'No, he is rather elusive, but there have been a couple of robberies recently that he has organised, and this Maalik guy must be involved...'

A shout from behind the pair cut Vijay short.

'Found him!' It was Rahul.

Peter and Vijay turned round to see Rahul running over towards them.

'What have you got?' Vijay asked.

Rahul laid a printout of a CCTV still and the mugshot of Maalik on the desk. 'That's him,' Rahul insisted, stabbing his finger at the mugshot.

Peter looked at Vijay for his opinion.

'Seems like we have found our man,' he said quietly.

'Right, let's get him before he disappears too, I want this fucker in front of me ASAP!' Peter commanded.

'Fantastic work,' Vijay said, 'tell me, where and when was this taken?'

'Last week, he and three others robbed a safety deposit company in the Bandra Kurla complex. By the time the police arrived they had cleared out nearly a quarter of the boxes in the room. Two cops were shot and injured, one robber was shot dead and the others escaped,' Rahul explained.

'Please tell me it wasn't our man that died.' Peter looked to the heavens. He wanted this man alive; he needed this man alive.

'No, definitely not,' Rahul confirmed.

Peter heaved a sigh of relief.

'OK, let's get trawling through traffic cams, store CCTV and everything else in between,' Vijay said, as he accompanied Rahul back to his desk.

⸻◈⸻

Chapter Forty-Three
Tip Top Model Agency head office, 2nd March

Danny was trying hard not to stare at the young lady in front of him. Angelica Naik had been called in for a meeting to talk about a new offer from a technology company. They wanted her to head up the publicity campaign for their new smartphone release. There were five people in the room: two advertising company representatives, Angelica, Danny and Diane Barbosa. Diane was the previous owner of the modelling agency and had agreed to stay on for six months to help with the transition. She had been in the industry for nearly twenty years and knew everything there was to know about it. She had organised beauty pageants all over India and had picked Angelica out of the crowd, three years ago.

Angelica caught the young man staring at her again, only for him to redirect his attention to the floor; she had heard about him and seen him around the offices, but they had never spoken. The meeting successfully concluded after an hour and a half, and Diane offered to walk the advertising people to the car park, leaving the two youngsters alone.

'What's your problem?' Angelica asked.

An embarrassed Danny didn't know what to say.

'You've been staring at me the whole time, don't think I haven't noticed!' she snapped.

'I'm sorry, it's just that you remind me of an old friend.'

Danny wanted to tell her everything but, just as had been the case with her father, she clearly didn't recognise him at all.

'A former girlfriend?' she asked. Angelica knew what effect she had on men and enjoyed it, although she had never had a boyfriend.

'No,' Danny said, 'just a friend.'

Angelica smiled. At least he wasn't being pervy – in fact, he was quite cute, she thought. Danny's tongue was tied and although he wanted to find out anything he could about her, he had no idea how to carry on the conversation.

Angelica helped him out. She had to wait for her bodyguard to pick her up; he was running late after escorting her mom on a shopping trip.

'So, you're taking over this place, are you? she quizzed.

'Yes,' Danny replied.

'Where are you from?'

'Goa, what about you?'

Angelica paused. 'Here, I'm from here,' she said. The pair drank coffee and made small talk until Harpreet entered the room. Danny looked at his friend, whom he was not supposed to know.

'You must be Angelica's bodyguard?' Danny said as he held out his hand.

'Something like that,' replied Harpreet, winking as he shook Danny's hand.

'Are you ready, young lady?' he asked.

'Yes,' she replied. 'I'll see you around,' she told Danny with a cheeky smile.

'You will,' he replied. 'Take care.'

***

A week later after taking the Naik family to a charity gala evening that would last until late into the night, Harpreet returned to their apartment to find Preeti sitting at the kitchen counter.

'Hey,' she said.

'Hello Preeti,' he replied, 'you look tired.'

'Yes,' she said, as she closed her eyes and dropped her head, pretending to fall asleep.

This was the first time they had been alone, and Harpreet was keen to find out what the maid knew about Rose. He needed to ask questions, but not too many, he knew that Preeti was devoted to the family. He would need to ease into the conversation carefully to avoid her becoming suspicious.

'Do you know that Angelica is adopted?' she asked. Yes, Preeti was loyal but, like all maids, she also loved to gossip.

'No?' replied Harpreet sounding shocked.

'Would you like a cup of tea?' Preeti asked.

'I'll make it,' he insisted, raising his hand, 'you stay there, relax.'

He wanted to let her talk; this was going to be easier than he thought. He put some tea leaves in a saucepan with water and turned on the stove.

'She came here when she was nine or ten years old, we don't know her exact age. She looked like she had been through hell. Her clothes were filthy and she smelled awful, I had to bathe her myself before madam came home,' Preeti started. 'Her parents were killed in a car accident, well that's what sir said anyway.'

'You don't believe that?'

Preeti reigned herself in, 'of course I do!'

'You said she looked like she had been through hell?' Harpreet said, not wanting to push too hard. 'Was she involved in the accident too?'

'Yes.'

'So, if she came from the hospital, surely they would have cleaned her up at least, no?'

Preeti didn't answer straight away, she shouldn't have mentioned it but had not spoken about that day to anybody, until now.

'You have to promise me that you will not tell sir or madam any of what I am saying.' She looked at Harpreet, obviously worried that she was being disloyal.

'I promise,' Harpreet assured her.

'I can't live with this any longer,' Preeti announced.

Harpreet felt his pulse quicken slightly. Here was a lady who was always composed, yet now she looked close to breaking point. He turned to the stove to finish the tea and with his back to the maid, secretly turned on the voice recorder on the smartphone that Peter had given him.

'Here,' he said, as he placed the steaming sweet tea in front of Preeti.

'Talk, if that's what you want. I will listen, it seems like you need to get something off your chest.'

'It was sir who brought her here, he asked me to clean her and dress her. She was asleep when she arrived and didn't wake until a few hours later.'

'Didn't you find that strange at the time?' he asked. 'Jonathan suddenly appears with a young girl and she's in a wretched condition?'

'Well, I was just so overwhelmed at her arrival, all I wanted to do was look after her and keep her safe, that's what I have been doing ever since that day. I treat her as if she were my own child.'

'What about papers, visits from the adoption agency?'

'I wouldn't have seen any documents, I'm only the maid, Harpreet. But there were no visits, not that I can remember.'

'So what do you think happened?' Harpreet said gently.

'I don't know, I wouldn't have been so worried about it all apart from one thing...' Preeti stopped herself again; if she told someone else of her suspicions there would be no going back. But the man opposite was looking at her so kindly that she decided to throw caution to the wind.

'I walked in on him when she was in bed, before madam came home that first day. He was doing something to her.'

The bastard! Harpreet thought, although he said nothing. He would kill Jonathan that very night if he had been molesting Rose. He despised paedophiles. Girls in India and the rest of Asia were constantly being exploited by men they trusted and there was a huge trade in foreigners paying for underage sex.

'He was molesting her?' Harpreet prompted her gently.

'No, no, not that,' Preeti said, waving her hands. 'Sir is not like that, he has never touched her in that way, he loves his children very much, but he, well, I found a spot of blood on the sleeve of her pyjamas, and it looked as though he may have injected her with something. Later I found out that there was a syringe missing from the medicine cabinet that we have. There were two before and one had gone missing; I assumed that she was diabetic or something... oh how could I have been so stupid? I can't lose my job; my family rely on me for the money and...' She started to cry.

'It's OK,' Harpreet said, putting his arm around her. 'Did you find any evidence – the empty syringe, maybe an empty glass vial?'

'No, I didn't see anything, and it wasn't my place to ask him what he was doing, but I am sure that was the only time it happened.'

The pieces were falling into place for Harpreet now. It was obvious to him what had gone on and what the syringe contained. Harpreet had found an ally in Preeti and would leave her in ignorance until she needed to know anything.

'Would you want to find out what happened that night, Preeti?' he asked calmly.

'Can you help me?' she asked. 'I may only be a maid, but I am not stupid. Angelica turns up here suddenly, and on top of that she has lost her memory, it's all too convenient. I know she was kidnapped; it happens all over this country! I just can't bear to think that sir would do something like that, even if madam was desperate for a daughter.'

Harpreet was stunned. He expected Preeti to be suspicious if he asked too many questions, yet here she was telling him everything, confirming what the team thought had happened.

'What do you want me to do, Preeti?' Harpreet asked.

'If this girl has parents that are still alive and looking for her, don't you think they would want to see her again? Will you help me find them?'

'That's a lot to ask,' Harpreet stated, 'let me see what I can do.'

He needed to talk to the team. He wouldn't draw Preeti into this if he didn't need to.

'We need information, documents, etc. I suppose anything like that would be in his office?' Harpreet said.

'No, he has a safe, it's in his wardrobe in the master suite,' Preeti said.

Harpreet needed to be able to trust her, and although she seemed sincere it would need to be discussed before he acted.

'Let me think about it. Do you mind if I go out for a while? I won't be too long, I need to feed Peter's cat.'

'It's OK,' Preeti replied. 'I will have a lie-down, they won't be home for a while.'

'Good, and Preeti, you can trust me, I will do what I can to help.'

'I know,' she replied. Her heart rate always rose when he was around, and she knew what that meant. She was falling in love, or at least that's what she thought it was. She looked into his dark brown eyes – oh what she wouldn't give for him to lean over and kiss her, right this minute.

'I'll see you soon,' Harpreet told her.

Preeti watched the handsome man walk off towards the front door and couldn't help thinking that his trousers were just a little too tight. She blushed – she shouldn't even be looking!

Harpreet called as he left the Naik residence to inform Peter that he was on the way with news. Saira and Vanya had already left, but Peter sent his driver to pick them up straight away.

The team waited anxiously. Harpreet hadn't explained what information he had but he sounded excited, and for him that was unusual.

Peter had been pacing nervously ever since the call and was pouring himself a whisky when he heard the front door close.

All eyes were on Harpreet. He walked to the meeting table and laid his phone down. 'You all need to hear this,' he announced with a smile as he pressed the play button. Ten minutes later the team sat there, speechless.

'How the hell do you do it, man?' asked a stunned Vijay, breaking the silence.

'This is fantastic,' Peter said triumphantly. He walked over to Harpreet and patted him on the back.

'I can't take any credit,' Harpreet started. 'It seems like Preeti, the maid, had wanted to get it off her chest for a long time.'

'Where do we go from here?' Vanya asked.

'That's obvious, we need access to the safe,' said Vijay.

'What time will they be home?' asked Peter.

'Jonathan said they would leave just after midnight, so we have three hours maximum,' Harps replied, checking his watch.

'Kush, how can we get into this safe of his?' Peter asked.

Kush smiled, 'easy.' He was already at his desk, retrieving two items from his top drawer.

'This is for the safe,' he said, handing the first item to Harpreet. 'Most home safes have keycodes. All you have to do is hold this against the keypad and it should open within a few seconds, and this one is to use if you happen to find a phone. You won't have time to come here and go back again, so you need to get the info off the phone while you are there,' he said as he handed it to Harpreet.

'How does it work?' Harpreet asked.

'If you find a phone or even a hard drive, place it on the top like so.' Kush demonstrated with his own cell phone. 'Once it's in position, make sure the light comes on at the front here, then this baby will connect automatically and download every bit of information on it. If you need me just call.'

Harpreet was impressed. 'Should I tell the maid about us?' he asked.

'No,' Peter said abruptly. 'Let her help us, she doesn't need to know what's going on. Besides, we have no idea how trustworthy she is at the moment.'

'Harps, if you have the time, take pictures of every document you find, no matter what it is, they will come straight to my screen,' added Kush.

Harpreet made for the door.

'Good luck,' Peter called out.

As the elevator descended to the car park, Harpreet was thinking over what Peter had said about the maid being trustworthy. Why would she give up the information without being pressed for it? he thought. He had grown to like Preeti; in fact, you could even say that he was attracted to her – she was beautiful, smart and funny too. Harpreet shook his head. He needed to focus on the job to the exclusion of everything else, for now.

When he returned, Preeti's mood had changed. Having realised what she had said, the maid was now regretting being so free with such personal information that could get her in big trouble. Harpreet needed to act fast, he didn't want Preeti changing her mind. She was standing at the bottom of the stairs, in a yellow sari, her midriff exposed to reveal smooth unmarked mahogany brown skin.

'Are you ok?' he asked.

'I don't know,' she said, clasping and unclasping her hands.

'I don't want to lose my job. What if sir finds out? This is a bad idea; I should never have told you...' She looked close to tears now.

'Hey, hey, calm down, you can trust me, I said I will help you and I will.'

On impulse, Harpreet stepped forward and took Preeti in his arms. Much to his surprise, Preeti returned his embrace.

'Just hold me,' she said. Her breasts were pressed firmly against his chest. He could feel her heart racing – shit, he thought, as he felt himself getting aroused. That hadn't happened since the last time he was intimate with his wife.

He tried to break away, but she wouldn't let go. Preeti felt Harpreet's manhood pressing against the bottom of her stomach, just above her groin. She was confused. Having never even kissed a man or had a boyfriend, she had no idea what to do. The embrace had moved on from just being friendly; they were obviously attracted to each other.

Harpreet wanted her, but this was not the time. She pulled her head away from his shoulder and looked him in the eyes. Harpreet could resist no longer, and taking her face in his hands, he kissed her passionately.

Preeti wanted him to take her right there and then. Her inexperienced body seemed to have its own agenda and she jumped up and wrapped her legs around him.

Harpreet's member was now pressing against her through her dress and panties. She was soaking wet, and her breasts felt tight and ached to be touched. Harpreet tried pulling away again; he needed to focus on the job and time was running out. Preeti felt his movement but there was no way she was letting him go, not after he had made her feel like this. She let her legs fall to the ground and, leading him away from the stairs, she grabbed his belt to undo it.

'This isn't right,' Harpreet insisted.

Preeti was thirty-two years old and had never been touched, and now she was going to get what she wanted, what her body, which was out of control now, was telling her she needed. Nothing was going to stop her.

'Take me, now, *please,*' she demanded.

Harpreet pulled his trousers down and threw his jacket off. Preeti slipped out of her sari and let it fall to the ground. Harpreet stared at the maid's perfect body. He could see that her pert rounded breasts with their erect chestnut brown nipples were swollen with desire. He reached out and touched them, first with his fingers and then with his tongue. Preeti groaned deeply. She had already climaxed twice and had never felt as good in her entire life.

Harpreet gently bent her over the kitchen counter. He knew they didn't have time to find her bedroom and make love; this lady wanted to be satisfied and he hadn't felt such burning desire in a long time. He took out his hard penis and guided it into her, holding her plump buttocks as he entered slowly, feeling the resistance of her virginity. Preeti let out a scream, a combination of joy and pain, as her hymen broke and she felt her whole body explode.

The whole thing lasted no more than ten minutes. They quickly recovered their clothes and got dressed.

'Thank you,' Preeti said as she kissed Harpreet gently on the lips.

He smiled. He had no idea what to say; he was reeling from a powerful climax, but he knew they needed to get down to business before the family returned.

He kissed her tenderly and asked, 'where is the safe?'

'Follow me,' she said as she made her way up the stairs. Harpreet watched as her hips swayed from side to side – she is so hot, he thought. He realised she had been a virgin and he longed to make love to her unhurriedly.

Preeti opened the wardrobe door where her employer's safe was; thankfully her nerves seemed to have disappeared now.

'Here,' she said pointing to the safe door.

Harpreet pulled the small rectangular box out of his pocket and placed it against the keypad. They heard a beep, then the sound of metal sliding as the door unbolted.

Preeti looked at Harpreet in shock.

'I didn't think it would work either!' he laughed.

There wasn't much in the small safe, just a couple of folders containing some plans but underneath them was a Motorola flip phone, which looked well out of date now. Harpreet photographed everything and did what he had been told to do with the phone. The light came on as he placed it into position. He had taken a picture of the safe before touching anything so he could put it all back exactly as they had found it.

Preeti had calmed since their encounter but still felt exhilarated by Harpreet's presence and her involvement in what they were doing. She walked him down the stairs to the elevator; it was ten past ten and he wanted to get back to Peter's before he had to pick the family up.

'What now?' Preeti asked as she reached for his hand.

'We will talk,' he replied.

Harpreet held out his free hand, 'pass me your phone.' He put his number in and handed it back.

'What now with all this, I meant?' she asked again.

'Well, I'll need to find out what's on that phone. You say you've never seen him use it before and it's quite old so it could be from around that time. I'll let you know as soon as I hear anything, but not here, OK? I will be back later with the family, please try to act normal.'

Their eyes met and held as they remembered what they had done on the kitchen counter.

'Yes, I had better clean up,' Preeti added, blushing.

'See you soon,' he said and gave her another kiss.

Preeti was stunned; she had no idea what had come over her earlier. She walked back to the kitchen, dizzy with happiness.

Harpreet got stuck in traffic on the way back; a truck had lost its load of plumbing pipes after cornering too fast and the surrounding routes were jammed up.

Running out of time, he walked into the office area and laid the two machines on Kush's desk.

'That's everything that was in there,' he said.

'Cool,' replied Kush grabbing the larger of the two machines. The photos of the documents that Harpreet had taken and uploaded to his system had no relevance to anything they were interested in. 'Give me a few minutes,' he added, 'and we can see what was on this phone of his.'

Kush plugged the data extraction unit into his PC and walked off to make a coffee. By the time he got back to his desk, the program had only retrieved some deleted calls and text records.

'So, we have two numbers. The first one, we have a message that says *"I have it"* and two calls, the last one being on the twenty-sixth of December, 2008.'

There was a collective gasp – that date was a few days before Rose's kidnap.

'The second, two calls and an incoming message containing a picture, the last call being around three p.m. on the twenty-ninth of December.'

'The day it happened,' Vanya stated.

'Open the picture,' Peter said, his jaw set.

Kush clicked on the small photograph to enlarge it and as it appeared full size, everyone saw a picture of two children with their bicycles.

'That's Rose,' was all Peter could manage before his voice broke with tears.

Danny leaned in closer. 'Wait, that's me,' he said. 'This was taken just before Rose disappeared.'

'I know it was a long time ago, Danny, but have you any idea who took it?' asked Vijay.

Danny closed his eyes tight. 'Yes,' he said. 'I have lived every minute of that day over and over to find something out of the ordinary and there was one thing that I never really mentioned, it didn't seem important at the time.'

'Danny, are you telling us that you know who took that photograph?' demanded Peter.

'You're not going to like this, I am so sorry. It meant so little at the time, I didn't even think of telling anybody. Oh God, this is all my fault, she could have been found years ago.' He picked up a chair and flung it against the wall.

'Danny, tell me who took the picture right fucking now!' Peter shouted. His hands were clenched, and he was showing his teeth like a dog about to attack.

'Hey, come on, we all need to calm down. Let the man talk,' Saira said.

Danny took a deep breath. 'It was Uncle Jack.'

'Wait, Peter's brother Jack?' questioned Rahul. He was the one that had investigated the brother at the beginning of their mission, just in case, and had come up with nothing, apart from the fact that nobody knew where he had been for the last few years.

Peter stood staring at Danny. 'Tell me exactly what happened, and don't miss anything out.'

'Well, Rose and I were washing our bicycles; she was so obsessed about keeping it clean, she would hose it off at the slightest sign of dust. You guys were all inside and Uncle Jack came over with a camera.'

Peter was astonished, he didn't believe what he was hearing. 'Go on,' he said, his voice low.

'He told us to smile and then he took a photograph, that photograph,' he said pointing to the screen.

'And then?' Peter prompted.

'Well, he just walked off.'

'Did he say anything?'

'He mentioned a family album, *"that will go in the family album"* – or something along those lines.'

'I'm sorry, Peter, it was Rose's uncle. It was Christmas, maybe he wanted to take the photo because he had not been there for Rose's birthday. We were innocent kids, how could I, we, have known what he was up to?' Danny sounded close to tears.

'Oh my God,' exclaimed Saira.

Peter was silent, trying to take it all in. He felt lost. He wished that his wife was there to guide him through this, she would know how to react.

'I swear it's the truth, Peter,' Danny insisted.

Peter took a few deep breaths to compose himself.

'I believe you, Danny, it's ok, I just can't understand how he could do it, to his own niece.'

The whole team were waiting for Peter's outburst. This was too big to just let slide, and they all expected another chair to go flying across the room.

'I am going to put a bullet in that motherfucker's head myself,' Peter said calmly.

Harpreet looked at him. He had seen that look many a time. This was a man who was serious.

'Peter, this murdering business, it's not good for us to be involved in,' Rahul said. He hadn't been happy about their previous conversation about killing, but seeing the look in his employer's eyes now, frightened the life out of him.

'My own brother sold his niece for twenty pieces of silver on the day we found out that her mother was dying. He took her away from us and bold as brass came over and asked if there was anything that he could do to help! The motherfucker!'

Peter's voice got louder with every word. The team looked at each other and at Harpreet, who knew this would happen when his boss found out who was responsible. He had seen many revenge attacks in his career; they rarely ended well, because you needed to be of a very strong character to avoid depression, even suicide, trying to live with the guilt of taking a life.

But Peter would be just fine handling it, Harpreet thought. He knew that was the only route that would lead to any kind of closure for him.

'Let's take a few minutes for Peter to process this and then we can decide what our next move is. We have the number that sent the message and, hey, you never know, we may still be able to track the owner,' Kush said. He could feel the tension in the room and decided it was an appropriate time for a break.

Vijay opened a new bottle of whisky and poured a drop into each of the cups being held out by everyone except Harpreet and Vanya. They stood in silence, waiting for Peter to speak. Kush had dragged the pinboard over to the group and added two pieces of paper, one blank and the other with the phone numbers on.

'Right, what do we have now?' Peter asked the group.

'We know that of these two, one is dead and the other is still at large.' Vijay pointed to the mugshots of the kidnappers, 'we have your brother...' Peter flashed a disapproving look at Vijay.

'Sorry, we have Jack, whose whereabouts we still don't know, although we haven't really tried looking for him as yet, and these two phone numbers. The first is the one that sent the message. This is our key player, could it belong to Jack?'

Peter considered this for a moment.

'No, he's not smart enough to organise this, it must have gone through a third party.'

'OK, so this number belongs to a middleman, a fixer,' Saira added.

'Someone with connections here and in Goa,' announced Vanya.

'And there is the other number of someone who may or may not be connected, although I would say that if this phone was used solely for one purpose, then whomever this number belongs to must also be involved somehow,' Kush announced.

'So, we have three people to find – Maalik, Jack and Vikram – and we haven't the first idea where to start,' said Peter.

'Can we get a photograph of Jack? That would help,' Rahul said tentatively.

'OK, I'll sort that out. I'll need to visit Goa; I could do with a break from this place, anyway,' Peter told them.

'Good idea, Peter,' Harpreet said, 'take some time out, we will hold the fort here.'

'Let's all get some sleep, it's late now. Everybody come back in the morning and you can take a fresh look at things, I will be gone by then.'

'Do you want me to travel with you?' asked Harpreet.

'Thanks, I will be OK, I will take Mack with me. Besides which, I want you here with the Naiks.' Peter turned to the rest of the team, 'we need to find out who those numbers belong to –

please have some news for me on my return, guys, I'm counting on you.'

They all signalled that they would do all they could. Grabbing their bags, the team left, glad to be getting home before midnight.

Peter, Harpreet and Danny sat down at the meeting table.

'Harpreet, I want to thank you, you have brought us a vital clue today, well done.' Peter shook the man's hand.

Harpreet had seen Peter growing more desperate as the days passed without news, but now, now it looked like a weight had been lifted from his shoulders.

'Danny, I understand why you never said anything before, you trusted him, we all did.'

'Do you have any idea why he would have done such a thing, Peter?' Harpreet asked.

Peter drew a deep breath; his brother's betrayal had cut him deeply.

'Money, he owed money to some bad people. He was a gambler. I reckon he sold his niece for a gambling debt.'

'Oh man,' exclaimed Harpreet.

'Were you serious about what you wanted to do to him, Peter?' asked Danny.

'Deadly serious, young man.'

'Good,' Danny replied.

Harpreet received a text message; it was his cue to pick up the Naik family. 'Got to go,' he said. 'See you guys soon, take care in Goa, Peter.'

Chapter Forty-Four
Nariman Point, Mumbai, 7:18 p.m., 13th March

'You did what?' Vikram shouted.

'I'm sorry, I didn't know what to do, he'd been acting strangely for the past week, saying that the girl on the billboards is the one that we took from Goa all those years ago,' Maalik answered.

'What girl, what billboards?' asked a confused Vikram.

Malik produced a folded-up advertisement from his back pocket that he had cut out from a magazine. He passed it to the man who had been his boss since he and Sunil had moved to Mumbai from Goa. Vikram hated loose ends and admitted to himself that he had made a mistake not killing this pair of idiots after delivering the girl in question. He unfolded the page and looked at the young lady's face.

'I barely saw her and that was what, probably ten years ago, how am I supposed to remember her now?'

'Turn the page over,' Maalik demanded.

There was an interview with her – favourite movie stars, music, etc. Vikram's jaw dropped when he read the name 'Angelica Naik'. He remembered the guy who bought the girl, scared little prick he was, and his surname was Naik too.

'How can this cause me any problems?'

'Sunil was going to the police, he said he couldn't live with it any more.'

'Why did you wait so long to tell me?'

'He was on his way to the station when I met him, he wouldn't change his mind. If he had told the cops, all of us would have been spending the rest of our lives in jail. I had no choice but to take care of it. Sunil was my friend but I'm not going to jail for anyone.'

'Get up,' Vikram demanded, 'so you shot your best friend?'

'Yes, boss, to protect you.'

'Don't give me that shit, you fucker – you did it to save yourself.'

'And you,' insisted Maalik, getting to his feet. He had a bloody nose and had taken a few blows to the stomach when Vikram's goons had picked him up.

'Did he tell anybody else about this?' Vikram quizzed, pointing the revolver at Maalik's head.

'I have no idea, please don't kill me, boss, I'll do anything,' he begged.

'I don't want any comeback from this. What you have done to your so-called friend is going to have the cops sniffing all over the place. You need to get rid of her, or I'll get rid of you.'

'Yes boss, with pleasure,' Maalik replied, managing a smile.

Chapter Forty-Five
Naik residence, 6:18 p.m., 14th March

Harpreet and Angelica were training nearly every day; she had learned a lot and was loving every minute of it. There was a large area on the mezzanine that they had turned into a temporary studio. Jonathan had purchased some crash mats, weights, punch and kick pads, and a top-of-the-range punching bag hung from the concrete ceiling in the middle of the space. Harpreet was pleased to have someone to spar with again, and Angelica had been spending most of her free time there. She could feel herself getting stronger, faster and was gaining confidence daily. Harpreet had decided that today she would start learning how to fall correctly. They would be practising sweep techniques.

Angelica was looking at herself in the mirror, dancing, which made Harpreet smile. Not so long ago he was on the street and felt ignored by the world but now, here he was. He had a fantastic job with a team that he liked and on top of all that he was here with this young lady, who had no idea what her real father was doing, to get her back.

'Come on miss, can we be sensible and focus, please,' Harpreet said, blocking a volley of jabs and crosses as Angelica rushed at him.

'Spoilsport,' she called out, laughing.

'OK, so I'm going to teach you front and back sweeps today, and also how to break your fall correctly, how does that sound?'

'Putting you on the floor sounds good, big man!'

Harpreet shook his head – what had he got himself into, he thought. They stood on the mats, Angelica adopting a boxer's fighting stance.

'Ready?' Harpreet asked.

'Go for it.'

Harpreet dropped to the floor and spinning around one hundred and eighty degrees, extended his rear leg, taking Angelica's legs from under her. She hit the mat hard.

'Now that's not how you want to land,' he laughed.

Angelica brushed herself off and got to her feet. Harpreet went on to show her how she should break her fall in a way that she would not hurt herself. After an hour of sweeps from both legs, Harpreet was confident that they could move to the tiled floor.

'Come on,' he said, as he walked away from the mats.

They moved a few metres to the left.

'I'm ready!' Angelica declared.

Harpreet swept with his right leg, Angelica went down perfectly and within a second, was on her feet again. Harpreet smiled.

'Well done, that was good form.'

Angelica nodded and beckoned him to come again. He did, but this time, Angelica's attention was diverted as she saw a butterfly flying past out of the corner of her eye and she fell off balance. Her right hand was supposed to take the brunt of the weight but as she went down, she flew backwards with her arm underneath her and hit her head with a dull thud on the tiled floor.

'Shit,' Harpreet cried out as he dropped to his knees. Angelica's eyes were shut. She was out cold. Harpreet looked around but there was nobody in sight. Gently he slapped Angelica's cheek – he was supposed to be looking after her, not knocking her unconscious! Thirty seconds later her eyelids twitched and Angelica started to come round, Harpreet breathed a huge sigh of relief.

'Miss, are you OK?'

Angelica opened her eyes and felt the back of her head where an impressive lump was forming.

'I'm good, stop panicking,' she said, as Harpreet helped her to a sitting position.

'I will find your mom; you need to go to hospital to get checked out,' he insisted.

Angelica grabbed his hand as she tried to get to her feet.

'Don't, if my parents find out what happened they will stop all of this, they wouldn't understand.'

Harpreet gave her a stern look. He knew she was right, but on the other hand, her safety was his priority.

'What if something happens to you, I couldn't live with myself,' he exclaimed.

'OK, OK,' she started, 'let's get ice cream and then go to the mall.'

'How is that going to help?' he asked.

'You take me to the hospital, I can get checked out and we don't need to tell anyone, silly!'

'I'm sure it's nothing but I would rather you go, so OK,' Harpreet agreed.

'Pull me up, big man,' she said holding out her hand.

Harpreet waited downstairs while Angelica got changed. Preeti was in the kitchen, cooking; they hadn't been able to get a second alone since their spontaneous tryst.

'Hi, how are you?' he asked. Preeti looked around to check the coast was clear.

'I'm fine, thank you,' she replied shyly.

Harpreet moved closer so as not to have to talk too loudly.

'I really enjoyed… err, you know.'

'Me too,' she said, blushing, 'so, are you ever going to call me?' Harpreet nodded; he had been so busy that by the time he finished work he fell into bed as soon as he got home.

'I promise I will call you tonight, is ten o'clock fine? I'm still working for my employer as well as being here, I'm sorry.'

'I look forward to it,' she replied.

Preeti heard footsteps on the staircase and turned back to the stove.

Angelica appeared. 'Mmm, that smells delicious,' she announced.

'Thank you, are you going out?'

'Yes, Harps is taking me to do a few things, I need a new top for training.'

'Oh, how is that going?' Preeti asked, 'you definitely sound like you are enjoying yourself upstairs.'

'Yes, I'm having a banging time,' Angelica stated, giving Harpreet a cheeky smile.

'Come on, big man,' she said.

'Why can't you call me by my name?' Harpreet asked, with his hands raised to the heavens.

'See you later, big man,' Preeti joked.

Laughing, Angelica made for the elevator. 'Someone has the hots for you…' Angelica dug Harpreet in the ribs, raising her eyebrows up and down for effect.

'Really?' he asked.

'You like her too, don't you?' she said, prodding him in the chest with a finger.

The doors opened. 'Saved by the bell,' Harpreet said, heading for the Mini Cooper.

They spent just over an hour in the hospital. The doctor wasn't too keen to see a patient who would only give limited information, but he took her in and did a few tests.

'You should be fine, you have some bruising which will be tender for a week or so. Take painkillers for tonight but if you start getting headaches after tomorrow you will need to come back, OK?' he said.

They made a quick trip to the mall for appearances' sake, where Angelica bought a couple of crop tops and a pair of leggings. On the way back Harpreet turned to Angelica.

'I am really sorry, I thought you were ready for today,' he said.

'Oh, I am ready, I just lost concentration, it's my own fault. You heard what the doctor said, I'll be fine. We can continue tomorrow.'

'OK,' Harpreet replied, 'but we'll be careful with that though.' He pointed to her head.

'I want to practise my kicks.'

'Done, we can work on the bag tomorrow!'

***

Peter decided that he would only stay in Goa for two days; he wanted to get back to work ASAP. He had visited Carmen, who was doing well. She was coping, with the help of Juanita, Danny's mom, who had been staying with her a few nights a week. They really enjoyed each other's company and their mutual interest in sewing had seen them start a small enterprise making purses and bags. They'd even been to various local markets to sell their products. They didn't make much money from their new venture but they both did it for the fun of it. Peter had visited Maria's grave, and Mack helped him while he spent the afternoon cleaning it, which was something he didn't want to pay to have done. Mack was sorting through the pictures of Jack; there weren't many of him as an adult, but he picked out two that should suffice. Peter had asked around and Jack seemed to have disappeared in the early part of 2009.

Peter's phone rang. 'Hello?'

'Peter, sorry to bother you.' It was Carmen.

'No trouble, is everything OK?'

'I'm fine, it's just that seeing you today jogged my memory. Do you remember the letter that Vic left for you? I just wondered, if I'm not being too nosey, about asking what it said?'

'Oh, I don't know, I forgot to open it, I've been so busy what with work and everything else.'

'Oh, OK.' Carmen sounded disappointed

'Thanks for reminding me though, I will let you know when I get home.'

'OK, take care Peter, and good luck with the search.' Peter hung up the call.

How could he have forgotten the letter? He had put it in a drawer, meaning to read it, but it must have slipped his mind. He dialled Mack.

'Can you see if we can bring the flight forward please, Mack? We need to get going now if we can.'

Mack made a call to check. Peter didn't fly commercial any more, he had enough money to charter a private jet whenever he wanted to, it was quicker and more efficient. Hell, he had enough money to buy his own plane. Mack had even suggested it but Peter didn't think it was right for him.

'We can leave whenever you like, Peter, it's ready for us now.'

'Very good, and Mack, thanks for helping me today, it means a lot.'

'Boss, it was my pleasure. All the things you've told me about Maria, I only wish I'd met her.'

'She would have liked you,' Peter replied with a wink. 'Come on, let's get out of here.'

***

The team had been hard at work for the last two days. Vijay needed to pay a hefty sum to one of his friends at the Indian equivalent of the NSA to track the phone records of the two numbers. One belonged to Derek Jacoby, who was now dead. The other belonged to a crime boss called Vikram Chatterjee. It was still in use and had been tracked to an address in Mumbai.

This guy was seriously bad news, and Kush was nervous about telling Peter. He really didn't want his employer getting mixed up in mafia business.

'What do you think he'll do?' Kush asked Harpreet as he returned from making a call upstairs.

A smiling Harpreet shrugged his shoulders. 'He wants to see this through to the end.'

'But ...' Kush was cut off by Harpreet.

'Listen, Peter has assured me that he wants to find all of the people involved and make them pay.'

He opened his suit jacket to reveal the Glock nestled tight against his side. 'I will make sure that no harm comes to him, so stop worrying.'

'And you're fine with killing them?' asked Saira.

'That's what I've done for as long as I can remember. I killed bad guys for the government – now, same bad guys, different employer,' Harpreet replied.

Peter and Mack arrived, Mack laden down with their luggage and the extra things they had picked up from Peter's home in Goa. Peter looked over the group, smiled, said a quick 'hi' and made straight for his living quarters; he needed to find the letter from Victor.

'Everything OK?' asked Rahul.

'Yes,' answered Mack, 'the boss says that he forgot to check something. Anyway, I'm off home now, I will see you all tomorrow.'

Mack left, and the group awaited their employer patiently. Five minutes later, Peter appeared holding a creased white envelope.

'What's that?' asked Harpreet.

'I have no idea,' Peter said, 'but it may well have something to do with the case. My father-in-law Victor left it for me when he died; I put it away and forgot to open it when I came back from Goa after his funeral.'

Peter picked up a knife from the table and slid it along the length of the letter, reached inside and pulled out a single sheet of paper. He read the few handwritten words.

'Well, what does it say?' asked Vanya, the suspense too much for her.

Peter handed her the piece of paper; his face was white.

'Looks like we have confirmation of Jack's involvement,' Vanya announced and read what was written.

'JACK,' on one line, and underneath, *'look into him Peter, he has something to do with Rose's disappearance, I'm sorry I couldn't tell you face to face, I thought you would never believe me – find her Peter, I love you son.'*

Vanya looked at the date on the envelope. 'He must have written this a month before he died.'

'Yes,' Peter said, 'well that's it, if Victor had him worked out then this letter confirms what we already knew.'

Vijay, Harpreet and Saira suggested that the other members of the team go home for some rest while they filled Peter in on the progress they had made.

'What do you want to do now?' asked Harpreet.

'We confront Vikram,' replied Peter.

'Is that wise?' Vijay asked, concerned that they were about to poke a hornets' nest. 'What are we going to do, kill him in cold blood?'

'You've done your part of the job, the rest is up to me.' Harpreet's eyes were cold, showing no emotion.

'Fine,' Vijay shrugged. He could see there was no point in arguing.

'We have the address, we can pay him a visit tomorrow,' Peter suggested.

'No, no, no, Peter, we need time to plan. If we rush into this, things will turn sour. Besides, *you* are going nowhere near him; *I* shall be doing this alone.'

'But...'

'This is my area of expertise, and you joining me would only jeopardise both our safeties. You are not coming and that is final.'

'What do you expect me to do, Harpreet? This... *thing* took my little girl from me!'

'And that's exactly why you can't be there, you're too emotionally involved.'

'Of *course* I'm emotionally involved, she's my fucking daughter!' Peter stopped short. 'I'm sorry, I just wanted to be the one to do it – you know, finish him off.'

'This isn't a movie where the good guy kills the bad guy, and everything turns out fine Peter. You hired me to protect you and your daughter, and I will *not* be taking you with me. If you don't agree to that then I'm afraid I will have to leave your employment.' Harpreet stared at Peter.

'Look, let's all go to bed, tomorrow is another day, we can begin planning a proper assault on the man then, one that I can execute with precision and where nobody else gets hurt,' Harpreet said, his tone more conciliatory.

'He's right, Peter. Harpreet knows what he is doing and if you want to go along for the ride and get injured or worse, then where does that leave Rose? All this would have been for nothing,' Vijay said.

Peter sighed. 'OK, I will leave it to you brother, goodnight!' Peter went to his room, watched the men saying goodbye out on the street, then went back to the office and took a photograph of the address that Vijay had left on his desk.

Chapter Forty-Six
Naik residence, 7:42 a.m., 16th March

Angelica woke suddenly, unable to breathe. She felt like a heavy weight was crushing her; her pillow and mattress were soaked in sweat. There was a disgusting taste in her mouth and her head was throbbing.

Somebody was knocking at her door.

'Yes?' she croaked.

Preeti poked her head inside. 'I heard you screaming, is everything OK, sweetie?'

'What, me, screaming?' Angelica looked confused.

'You must have been having a nightmare.' Preeti crossed to her bedside and stroked her damp forehead.

'Can I get you anything – tea, coffee, warm milk?' the maid asked.

'Just some warm milk, please Preeti, and some painkillers, my head is killing me.'

'Maybe you should have a shower and I'll change your bedding.' Preeti had noticed the dark sweat stain on Angelica's pillow. Strange, she thought, she had never known Angelica to have nightmares before.

'Thanks, Preeti, you're an angel.'

The maid laughed, 'no, you are. Hop in the shower, I'll be back soon,' she replied as she left the room.

Angelica turned the shower on and let the water warm up. She threw her soaked pyjamas onto the floor and stepped under the soothing stream.

She stood there for a while, trying to wash away the night before. Suddenly, she got goosebumps all over. The taste! 'Ewww,' she muttered and lifted her head to let the water pour into her gaping mouth, swished it around then spat it out. As she raised her head and closed her eyes, a smiling face with decayed teeth, stained red, appeared behind her eyelids. She gasped. The smell – it was almost real and utterly disgusting.

Angelica squirted a large blob of lemon-scented body wash into her hand and started rubbing it into her face, but all she could smell was rotten fish. She scrubbed her whole body twice and after drying, brushed her teeth three times but still couldn't rid herself of the stench.

When she finally left the bathroom, Preeti was already in her room replacing the sheets.

'How do you feel now?' she asked.

'I don't know, I think I had a bad dream, but it felt real, almost like a memory.'

'A recent memory or from the past?' the maid asked.

'I can't tell, it was just a face, the feeling of being crushed and a hand over my mouth, and a God-awful rank smell. I can still smell it, ewww.'

'It was just a nightmare. Have you watched any horror movies lately?'

'No.'

'You want some food? I can make you puris, they always make you feel better.'

'OK,' Angelica said, swallowing hard; she could almost taste the foul smell now.

'Good, come to the kitchen when you're dressed.'

Preeti left the room. On her way to make Angelica's breakfast, one thing the girl had said ran over and over in her mind; *'hand over my mouth'* – that sounded more like a memory to her. Should she keep this to herself or tell Harpreet?

Angelica sat on the bed; she couldn't get the image of that face out of her mind, or the smell from her nostrils. If this is a memory then what the hell happened to me? she asked herself. She had always thought that if her memory came back it would surely involve the car crash.

Preeti made her the milk and puris as promised.

'Are you going to tell your mother and father about your nightmare?'

'No, I don't think so,' Angelica replied.

'You're up early,' Jonathan called out from the mezzanine.

Angelica looked at Preeti. 'Yeah, I wanted to get some extra training in this morning,' Angelica lied.

***

In Peter's apartment, it had been decided that Vijay and Saira would stake out the warehouse that Vikram was linked to; they had finally received a ten-year-old police mugshot to go on and needed visual confirmation before they could move forward with their plan.

The pair left the apartment, armed with all the surveillance equipment they needed and a flask full of coffee for the six hours they would be spending in the car together.

'Peter,' Harpreet called out as he entered the apartment. 'I think you need to hear this. The maid, Preeti, told me something about Rose this morning.'

'Aren't you supposed to be at work?' Peter asked.

'I left for an early lunch, said I needed to run some errands for you.'

'Go on, what do you have?'

'First, I need to tell you something that happened the other day... Rose banged her head when we were training, and she was knocked out,' Harpreet said.

'What?' Peter shouted, 'is she OK?'

'She's fine. I took her to the hospital to get checked. She didn't want to tell the family, so nobody knows about it.'

'Oh, OK. Please try and be careful, Harpreet, you're supposed to be looking after her, not throwing her around.'

'I know, I'm sorry, it's just that something happened this morning.'

'And?'

'I was talking to Preeti and she said that Ange..., sorry, Rose, had some kind of nightmare last night. She mentioned a man's face and a hand over her mouth.'

'Is that it?' Peter asked.

'Yes,' Harpreet replied. Why hadn't his employer realised the enormity of what he had just said?

'Jesus,' exclaimed Rahul, 'it wasn't a nightmare, it was a memory. Don't you get it, Peter? She gets concussed and now this! It has to be a memory – the face, the hand over her mouth to stop her from screaming. Her memory is returning!'

Peter staggered and almost fell onto the chair behind him. What had started as an accident seemed to be turning out to be a blessing in disguise.

'Shit, you're right, it must be! My God, Harpreet, you're a genius, an idiot but a bloody genius!'

'Well, I certainly didn't mean to hurt her, Peter, I can assure you.'

'I know that, man!' Peter replied.

'Let's not get too ahead of ourselves,' Vanya added, removing her headphones. She had grown used to the team now and, although she still wore them, they were turned down low so she could hear what was said in the office.

'I did a lot of reading on this subject when we first found out and yes, it may be a memory, it certainly sounds like her brain has subconsciously started to recall an important event, but it's no guarantee that she will start to remember her past life.'

'But it's a start, right?' Peter asked.

'Oh yes – sometimes all the brain needs is a nudge in the right direction, hence the expression, to jog one's memory.' Vanya smiled.

Peter smiled back. All he could think about now was Rose being able to remember him. Could it happen? Did he dare to hope?

Chapter Forty-Seven
Peter's apartment, 8:47 p.m., 19th March

The team were standing in front of the pinboard staring at two photographs. The first was a mugshot from the police, the second the clearest picture that Saira had managed to take of the man at the warehouse.

'So, are we all agreed?' Peter asked.

There was a resounding 'yes' from the team. They had found Vikram, the man who orchestrated the kidnapping, and they knew where he was. Over the last three days, Vijay and Saira had seen him go in and out of the address on several occasions, normally accompanied by only one other man.

'The guy is definitely armed,' Vijay said, pinning up a photograph of the man they assumed to be one of Vikram's henchmen.

'They usually arrive at around six to six-thirty and leave by eight. The street is not too busy, so I suggest that this would be the best place to catch him,' Saira added.

'Cameras?' Harpreet asked.

'Two facing the entrance and one on the side door,' Vijay confirmed.

'No problem, we can jam them with this.' Kush pulled a device out of the bottom drawer of his desk.

'This guy came straight out of a Bond movie, no?' joked Vanya.

'And what about building plans?' asked Harps. He wanted as much information as he could get before deciding what he would do.

'Here,' said Rahul as he laid a sheet of paper on the desk in front of them, 'it's the only thing I could find. It's fifteen years old, so we have no idea what alterations there might have been in that time.'

'OK, well at least it gives me an idea of the place,' Harpreet added. He rarely trusted any info that was provided to him by a third party; it was always best to be ready for the unexpected.

'When are we... I mean you going to do this?' Peter asked Harpreet.

Harpreet gave Peter a speculative look.

'Give me a couple of days. I want to check the place out for myself. I may even sneak in there beforehand when it's empty, I don't know yet.'

'A couple of days?' Peter said impatiently.

Harpreet gave his boss another look that said it all.

'Of course, patience, in your own time,' Peter held his hands up.

The next day Kush answered a call from Saira; she and Vijay had decided to keep watching the warehouse and they had just hit the jackpot.

'Yo, what's up?' he asked.

'Maalik has just turned up,' Saira announced.

'Say *what*?' Kush shouted, getting the rest of the team's attention, 'hold on, putting you on speaker.'

Rahul gave Kush a questioning look.

'It's Maalik, he's turned up at the warehouse!'

Rahul, Vanya and Peter were at Kush's desk in an instant.

'We're all here!' Peter announced.

'OK, so Vikram opened up just before six and Maalik entered the building a few minutes ago.'

This was better than they could have hoped for. They had both of their known suspects in one place.

'What do you want us to do, boss? Saira asked.

'You need to follow Maalik when he leaves. Don't lose him, no matter what, we may not get another chance with this one. I want to know where the bastard is staying!' Peter told them.

'OK, will keep you updated,' she replied and hung up.

'Yes,' Kush cried out and high-fived Rahul. '*Now* we're getting somewhere.'

Peter tried to call Harpreet, but he wasn't answering. This was driving him crazy; he wanted to go straight there and get the pair of them right now.

'OK everyone, take it easy,' Vanya said trying to calm the mood. 'Let's hope that Vijay and Saira get an address for our guy, then we can go from there. Harpreet isn't here so we can't do anything at the moment.'

Peter dialled Harpreet, but again no answer. 'Aaarrghh,' he cried out in frustration.

'Hey, come on, remember what Harps told us,' Vanya said.

***

In the warehouse, Vikram was looking annoyed.

'Well?' he asked.

'I'm trying, boss. But she never leaves the place alone. They have this bodyguard now too, a Sikh guy, tough-looking bastard,' Maalik replied.

'So, what are you saying, you can't do the job I have given you?'

'Boss, I need more time. I'll get her when she's alone, I promise.'

Vikram thought for a moment. This whole situation was making him nervous now; he would get rid of this idiot when he had completed his task. That would leave Jonathan as the last loose connection, who would surely spill his guts if the police even looked at him sideways; he would need to go too.

Rasheed and Avinash had been involved. He knew he could trust Rasheed; they went way back, and Avinash was his right-hand man and totally loyal.

'I will give you until Tuesday, that's two days Maalik. If you haven't managed it by then...' On cue Avinash picked up the gun that was lying on the desk and pointed it at Maalik, 'you understand?' Vikram continued.

'Yes, boss!' Maalik almost ran for the door.

'Rasheed made a mistake getting those two idiots involved,' Avinash announced.

'Too fucking late now,' replied Vikram, 'I will have to tidy this mess up myself.'

***

Saira tapped Vijay on the arm. 'He's leaving,' she said. Vijay started the engine. As they watched, Maalik walked around the corner. They started to follow. Maalik hopped onto his scooter and took off at speed.

'He's in a hurry,' Vijay noticed, as he put his foot down to keep up with their target.

In fact, Maalik had spotted two people in a car on the opposite side of the street when he left – he knew they were watching him.

'Fuck that,' he said as he twisted the throttle on the Honda, 'he's going to have me killed. I knew it, the bastard!' 'This guy is spooked,' said Saira. 'Do you think he spotted us?'

'I hope not.' Vijay swerved to avoid a pedestrian.

They had been using a different rental vehicle every day and kept a low profile on the stakeout.

'He's turning left,' Saira called out, 'headed for the bike bridge. If he makes it there, we're going to lose him – *come on Vijay.*'

'I know, I know, I'm doing my best.'

'You need to take him out, it's the only way to stop him!' Saira shouted.

'Fuck it,' Vijay shouted as he swerved around the car in front of them. The pair were running out of time. Vijay had his foot flat to the floor and the road ahead was clear. Saira was starting to regret being involved now. If they crashed it was going to hurt, a lot.

'Nearly there, just a few more feet,' she shouted.

The rear of the scooter was so close, all they had to do was nudge the wheel and he would be going nowhere. They could see the bridge in the distance, it was specially designed for two-wheeled vehicles only. The car bridge was over two hundred metres away.

'Fuck!' Vijay screamed as he hit the brakes and swerved wildly to the left; they were on two wheels now and close to rolling. Vijay shimmied the car back onto all four wheels and screeched to a halt. The driver of the truck that pulled out of the side road without looking was honking at them.

They watched as Maalik escaped over the bridge and into a melee of vehicles beyond.

'Bastard!' Vijay screamed, slamming his hands onto the steering wheel.

They wouldn't catch him now, that was for sure.

'You OK?' Vijay asked.

'Just a bit of shock, that's all. I think I saw my life flash before me.' Saira gave a weak laugh.

'Yes, it was close.'

'What are we going to tell the boss?' Saira asked.

'We'll have to tell him the truth.'

'He's going to be pissed,' she declared.

'He's not the only one,' Vijay replied. 'Come on, let's go and face the music, I need a stiff drink after that.'

'Me too!' Saira said.

Back at base, Saira and Vijay told their story and apologised to the team. Peter looked disheartened; he wanted this guy so badly, but he knew they had no chance of chasing a scooter.

'How did he know he was being followed?' asked Vanya.

'We did everything by the book. He came out in a hurry – maybe something happened inside?' Vijay replied.

'Don't worry,' said Peter, 'although you should have backed off. I know I said not to lose him, but putting yourselves in danger wasn't what I was talking about, and he obviously knows he's being watched.'

'At least we know he's alive and connected to Vikram,' Kush said as Saira and Vijay looked crestfallen.

'What time will Harpreet be back?' asked Rahul.

'I messaged him, but still no reply.' As he spoke, Peter's phone rang.

'Ah, talk of the devil,' Peter announced as he answered the call. 'We found Maalik, come as soon as you can,' Peter said and hung up.

He didn't want Harpreet discussing their business at the Naiks' home.

Harpreet made his excuses and left as soon as he could. He had missed the messages that Peter sent due to Angelica's extended training session; she was even tiring him out now!

***

'Right then, here's what's going to happen,' said Harpreet, after listening to what had gone on earlier.

'This could go one of two ways. If Maalik was spooked by you guys outside, then he would have informed Vikram and we will have missed the opportunity to get the pair of them.'

He looked around at the disappointed faces of his team.

'However, if he left in a hurry, it may have been because of something that happened inside.'

'I thought that,' Saira said.

'He did look anxious, even before we started tailing him,' agreed Vijay.

'The main thing is that you two are OK,' Rahul announced.

'We need to go now!' Peter snapped.

Harpreet turned to him. 'Peter, if Vikram has been alerted, what if he's waiting for us? What if he's called on more of his thugs? I don't want to go strolling into a kill box with my eyes closed. I'm good Peter, I'm exceptionally good, but I'm not superman. I'm not bulletproof!'

Everyone agreed with Harpreet, even Peter.

'So what do you suggest?' he asked.

'We wait.'

'I agree,' said Vijay, 'we need to scout the place tomorrow and see if anything has changed. If Vikram turns up, it's likely he was the one that made Maalik shoot off like that.'

'Vijay is right,' said Harpreet. 'We need to put someone else in tomorrow, though. Rahul, are you feeling up for a spot of reconnaissance?'

'I'll join him,' suggested Vanya. She was fired up from the exciting story and wanted a piece of the action herself.

Harpreet looked at Peter, who shrugged. 'It's up to you,' Peter said.

'OK, you two go tomorrow. Different car, different spot and whatever you do, you are not to interact with anybody. If you get busted then you leave immediately, do you understand?' Harpreet said sternly.

'Cool,' Rahul said nodding at Vanya, who smiled back at her new partner.

Harpreet looked at Peter long and hard. 'If Vikram is there tomorrow then I will go in before he leaves.'

Peter smiled. Finally, time for action, he thought.

Chapter Forty-Eight
Naik residence, 5:37 a.m., 21st March

Preeti had been sitting by Angelica's bedside for almost an hour. The girl was tossing, turning and groaning as though she was in pain. Stationing herself in the room after she was sure her employers were sleeping, Preeti would watch over Angelica until she was needed. Having loved the girl like her own child since the day she arrived at the Naik home, Preeti couldn't bear seeing Angelica suffer this way. What they thought was just a one-off had turned out to be a nightly occurrence.

Preeti had covered for Angelica and helped by being there to comfort her when she woke up. Angelica had described things that just didn't make sense – the man holding her face and crushing her, being in the back of a truck, different men carrying her; she was either having the worst kind of nightmares or the girl was describing something that had actually happened to her before she arrived. Preeti had a terrible feeling it was the latter.

In the darkness, Angelica suddenly sat upright, scaring Preeti half to death. 'Hey, it's OK, I'm here,' she said as she picked up the small towel that she had been using to mop the poor girl's brow.

'It's that man, I can't get him out of my mind, I can smell him, even taste him, it's disgusting!' Angelica burst into tears and held out her arms.

Preeti hugged her.

'Don't cry, my love, I am here for you, I always will be.'

'This is real, it has happened to me, I am sure of it!' Angelica said after she had calmed down. 'Tell me what happened and how I arrived here. Why did I go so long not being able to remember anything?'

Preeti told her all that she knew.

'I'm going to ask father.'

'No, you can't do that, promise you won't ask him,' Preeti begged.

'Trust me, just give it some time. I swear to you I will find the answers you are looking for,' the maid said.

'If my memory is returning then why don't I remember being in a car crash? That's odd, don't you think?'

Angelica was close to panicking now. Preeti rocked her back and forward like a baby.

'Listen very carefully, my poor girl. You cannot talk to anyone about this – you need to trust me, I beg you. The time will come when you find out, but it is not now.'

Angelica slumped back against the headboard. 'OK, Preeti, I won't say a word,' she said.

Chapter Forty-Nine
Outside Vikram's warehouse,
6:38 p.m., 21st March

'Yes!' Rahul whispered, as he saw Vikram and his heavy arrive at the warehouse.

Vanya pulled off her headphones. 'What do you think? They seem normal to you?' she asked.

Rahul shrugged. 'I mean, yeah, I suppose so.'

The two men unlocked the shutter to the entrance without looking overly vigilant.

'I'll call base,' Rahul said. 'Let's just keep a close eye out to see if anyone else enters, because if half a dozen guys turn up then we know we've been found out.'

Kush answered on the first ring.

Peter was anxiously waiting for news.

As he hung up the call Kush said, 'no worries boss, it seems that all is OK; they suggest that we wait for an hour or so, just to make sure they are alone.'

'Good idea,' Peter said.

'Shall I message Harps?' Kush suggested.

'No, I'll do it, I'm going out for a while.'

'Where are you off to Peter, don't you want to be here for this?' Vijay asked.

'I just have a few things to take care of. I will call Harpreet on the way downstairs.'

'OK, you're the boss,' he shrugged.

Half an hour had passed and there was no movement from the warehouse, apart from Vikram's man going to the store and returning with a large bottle of water.

Vanya shot upright from her slouched position and whipped off her headphones. 'OMG,' she shouted and slapped her hand over her mouth.

A stunned Rahul was also staring at the man now walking towards the warehouse entrance. 'What the fuck is he doing here?'

'This is not good,' Vanya replied, 'this is so not good, where the hell is Harps?'

Rahul pulled his phone out of his pocket and hit redial.

'Yo, anything to report?' Kush asked.

'What the hell is Peter doing here?' Rahul shouted

'What?' Kush said, 'what do you mean?'

'Both of us have just watched Peter walk through the warehouse door, it's definitely him,' Rahul replied, 'what shall we do?'

'Er, er, wait, just wait, stay there, don't move and let me know the minute you see anything else; I'm calling Harps on another line as we speak.'

Harpreet answered straight away. He had kept his phone on during today's training session with Angelica. They had finished and were warming down when he heard it ringing.

'Kush?' he said.

'We have a big problem; we need you right now, man. The guys on stakeout duty have just seen Peter walk into the warehouse.'

Harpreet nearly dropped his phone; how could Peter be so stupid?

'OK, I'm leaving now! Who else is there?'

'Just Vikram and his heavy – and now Peter.'

'I'm on my way. Tell Rahul and Vanya to stay put and let me know if anyone else joins the party.'

He hung up. Angelica overheard some of what he had said.

'Everything OK?' she asked.

'No, yes. Listen, I have to go – I will see you tomorrow.'

Harpreet grabbed his suit, ran downstairs and made for the front door. He was wearing sweatpants, training shoes and a T-shirt. His gun was hidden, wrapped inside his suit jacket.

'Bye,' called Preeti.

Harpreet didn't hear her. He was focused on saving his boss. He knew that the man had walked into a world of trouble and really would be incredibly lucky to still be alive by the time he arrived. He slammed the car into gear and was at the gates before the guard could open them. He was around twenty minutes away from where he needed to be.

'Why didn't he listen to me?' he shouted, as he held his hand on the horn.

'What's going on? Jonathan asked Preeti; he had just got home and seen Harpreet speeding past him.

'I don't know, but he left in a hurry,' she replied.

'He had to do something for his other boss, I suppose,' Angelica added, as she came downstairs.

Danny left work straight away after getting the call from Kush, who demanded all hands on deck at the office.

'Harpreet's ETA?' Vijay asked.

'Fifteen minutes,' Kush answered. He had fitted trackers to all the hire vehicles that they were using, just in case.

'Come on Harps,' Saira said, 'you *have to* save him.' They all felt so useless, not being able to do anything.

***

Peter stood just inside the open doorway for a couple of minutes, trying to muster up the courage to confront the man who had been behind his daughter's kidnapping. He had collected the extra Glock 19 that he kept for himself in his bedroom before leaving the apartment. He knew he was stupid, turning up here alone, but his patience had simply run out. He was sweating profusely, there was no air conditioning in the place, and it stank of stale booze. Peter took a deep breath and walked into the open expanse of the warehouse holding the gun in front of him.

Rahul's phone rang. 'What's happening?' Harpreet asked.

'No change, just hurry up and get here.'

'What do you think I'm doing?' Harpreet shouted, his hand sounding the horn continuously.

'I'll go in!' Rahul offered.

'**You stay right there**!' Harpreet thundered. 'I don't need to be saving anyone else today, I will be ten minutes.' Harpreet cut the call, dropping the phone on the passenger seat just in time to avoid a collision.

His heart beating faster, Peter saw a lone figure sitting at a desk in an office in the far-left corner of the warehouse.

There were a few stacks of boxes and drums, and a table with four chairs, covered in empty takeaway food containers. Peter walked as quietly as he could manage towards the open door. The man inside was facing him but focused on reading something; he was wearing a suit and looked to be around forty-five years old. Peter kicked an empty soda bottle that was lying on the floor, which made a dull thud as it hit a concrete post. The man looked up.

Peter swiftly closed the ten-metre gap between himself and the door.

'Don't move,' Peter ordered, hoping he sounded braver than he felt.

'Can I help you?' asked the man.

'Are you Vikram?'

'Yes, but surely you don't need the gun. Put it down and let's talk.' Sweat was visible on the man's forehead and upper lip.

Peter entered the office. 'You kidnapped my fucking daughter,' he said softly, his right hand holding the Glock at Vikram's head.

'Kidnapped?' the man squeaked, 'that's a very serious allegation.'

Peter was trembling. All he wanted to do was pull the trigger and end this guy's life, but there were things he needed to know first.

'You are going to answer my questions, or I will put a bullet in your head,' he shouted.

'Oh, I don't think so,' Vikram answered, as his eyes, which had been locked on Peter's, moved slightly to the left of him. Peter realised what was going to happen just as the butt of a gun hit the back of his head.

Harpreet was two minutes away now, but some road construction had brought traffic to a halt. He pulled into a parking space at the side of the road, grabbed his gun and leapt out of the car. Within seconds he was sprinting full speed along the pavement towards the warehouse.

'He's out of the car,' Kush called as he saw the blue flashing circle on his screen stop moving.

'He'll be there in no time,' Saira assured them. Vijay called Rahul.

'Can you see Harpreet yet?'

'No, nobody in or out – oh hold on, wait, here he is, he just came running round the corner!'

Peter came round to find himself on the floor, face down with his hands bound behind his back.

The man who'd hit him was now holding a gun to his head.

'So, it's *your* daughter that the Naik guy wanted, eh?' Vikram started. 'What the fuck are you doing here and who the hell do you think you are, pointing a fucking gun at me?' He kicked Peter hard in the side. Peter screamed in agony as his ribs broke with a loud crack.

'You came here alone? Why?'

'You bastard, you took my little girl away from me!'

Vikram motioned for Avinash to lift Peter to his knees.

'It was business, just another transaction,' Vikram shrugged, smiling. 'So now I need to get rid of another body and clean up more mess!'

Vikram took a step closer. Peter could almost see down the barrel of the gun.

Peter tensed as he heard a deafening noise ring out – *bang! bang!* I'm still alive, he thought. He could feel no pain.

'No!' Vanya cried out, hearing the two gunshots. She grappled with the car door, throwing it open. Rahul leaned over her and slammed it shut.

'We can't help,' he said, holding her hands.

Peter watched the small hole on Vikram's forehead trickle blood, the surprise in his eyes fading to a death stare. The gun fell from his hand and he slumped to the floor, the smell of his bowels emptying filling the space. Avinash also fell, landing behind him.

Peter was disoriented. He had no idea what had just happened. He felt something tugging at his wrists and then his hands were freed as the cable tie that bound them was cut.

'Woah, woah, woah, there's someone else going in,' Rahul shouted as he saw another man approach the entrance.

'Hold on, is that *Jack*?' Vanya said.

'I don't know, can't be sure,' replied Rahul.

'Peter, that was an extremely stupid thing to do,' Harpreet said stepping into his employer's view.

Peter let out a shuddering sigh of relief as he heard his friend and saviour's voice.

Harpreet's phone rang; he answered the call.

'There's someone else inside,' Rahul informed him. Harpreet spun round ninety degrees to face the door, raising his gun.

'Wait!' said Rahul, 'no, he's run off – is everything ok in there? It's time to get out **now**!'

Jack was running some errands for Vikram, nothing serious, just small-time stuff. He'd frozen to the spot when, through the office doorway, he saw a man on his knees. Was it his brother? It couldn't be, he thought. There was a huge Sikh guy holding a gun and one or two bodies on the floor. Jack wasn't going to stick around to find out what was happening.

Peter was now on his feet. Harpreet checked the man that he hit in the chest for a pulse; he was dead.

'Neither of these guys will be answering your questions now, will they?' Harpreet said sarcastically, picking up the two shell casings.

'Let's go, we need to get out of here,' he said.

'Where are you going?' Peter asked as Harpreet ran to the other side of the office.

He came back a few seconds later with a black box. 'It's the CCTV hard drive.'

Peter nodded. He was in way over his head and was so glad he had people around him that knew what they were doing. He had been reckless and could see that Harpreet was angry. He was also in agony with his ribs.

Rahul spotted the two coming out of the warehouse and started the car.

'What the hell happened?' Vanya asked as the pair sat down on the back seats, Peter crying out in pain as he did so.

'Drive us to the hospital,' Harpreet demanded. 'Peter needs to be checked, he has some broken ribs and we need to make sure his lungs are not punctured.'

Harpreet turned to his employer. 'Peter, if you **EVER** pull anything like that again, I swear I will shoot you myself. You were seconds away from decorating that office with your brains.'

Peter frowned. 'I'm sorry, Harpreet. You saved my life again.'

'Well, it's my job, what did you expect me to do?' Harpreet could not meet his boss's eyes. He sat staring out of the window, muscles tensing in his neck, his lips a thin line.

***

Jonathan ate his dinner alone. Angelica had already eaten; she was famished after her training session and Elizabeth was busy working in her office upstairs. After Preeti disappeared to do some laundry, Angelica's curiosity got the better of her.

'Dad?' she said.

'Yes, dear?'

'What do you know about my real parents?'

Jonathan's heart skipped a beat.

'What, why do you ask?'

'I've been having dreams that feel like memories.'

'That's good,' he replied cautiously, his mind racing. He didn't know what to do now, this was not supposed to happen.

'I've been remembering things, dreadful things, but nothing about a car crash. There was no car crash, was there?' she said softly, looking deep into her father's eyes.

Jonathan was caught off guard. 'Come on now baby, you must be having nightmares, what is all this silly talk? I think you've been doing too much training with Harpreet; it's over-stimulating you.'

'Tell me the truth, what really happened to my parents?' Angelica demanded.

Jonathan was panicking now. 'I only know what the adoption agency told me. You were in a car crash, and your parents died in the accident.'

Angelica could tell he was lying.

'Then why do I keep seeing a man's face, feeling a hand covering my mouth?' Her voice was raised now.

Jonathan needed to stop this.

'I, err...,' he stammered.

Angelica was standing over him; she didn't believe a word he was saying.

'Tell me the truth – **now**!' she screamed.

'Darling, calm down, please... I don't...'

Angelica kicked over the stool she'd been sitting on, grabbed her hoody top and headed for the door; she was still dressed in her training gear.

'Where do you think you're going?' Jonathan shouted after her.

'Out! And don't try to stop me!'

'You're not allowed out alone,' Jonathan said as the door slammed.

'Do you two mind? I'm trying to work,' Elizabeth called out as she walked down the stairs. She had heard the commotion from her office.

'Angelica wanted to go out on her own, I told her not to but...,' Jonathan said helplessly.

'Where's Harpreet?' she demanded.

'He left in a hurry earlier.'

'Well, what are you waiting for? Call him and get him here now!' Elizabeth was furious – how had Jonathan let their daughter out alone?

After Peter had been checked over at the hospital and his chest bound to protect his ribs, he, along with Harpreet, Rahul and Vanya, arrived back at the apartment, joined by Danny. All of them had let their boss know how angry they were at what he had done, and Vanya had gone as far as to slap him on the face.

'It's OK, let's all calm down people. He's here and he's safe,' Harpreet stated, holding his hands up.

'I'm sorry, boss,' Vanya said.

'Hey, I deserved that,' Peter said rubbing his cheek.

'So, I suppose now's a good time to tell you who turned up and then ran away after Harps went in?'

'Who was it?' asked Peter.

'Vanya thinks it was Jack, but I'm not so sure, although I'm not the one with the photographic memory,' Vijay said.

'My brother?' Peter questioned, 'what was he doing there?'

'No idea, he arrived a minute after the shots were fired; he must have seen you and run off.'

'So, he was working for Vikram,' added Vijay.

'With these two dead, we're short on leads. We need to find him; I think there are a few blanks in our story that he could fill in,' Saira told them.

'Yes...,' began Harpreet but he was cut off by his phone ringing. 'It's Jonathan,' he exclaimed, 'what does he want?' Harpreet raised his hand. 'Shh, everybody. Hello?'

Harpreet let the guy talk for a few seconds then said, 'I'll be there right away.'

'What now?' asked Vijay.

'It's Rose, she's stormed out alone, after some sort of row.'

'I'll come with you,' Peter said.

Harpreet fixed Peter with a cold stare.

'You stay right where you are, Peter. I mean it! Don't even think about fucking me around again; besides, you need to rest and let those ribs heal. Danny, come with me. The rest of you, do **not** let Peter leave this apartment – lock the door, tie him to a chair, I don't care what you do, just do not let him leave,' he demanded, as the pair raced for the door.

'Can this day get any worse?' asked Saira. 'I need a drink,' she said as she walked to where they kept the whisky.

'Count me in,' agreed Vanya, for the first time in her life.

***

Angelica had raced through the lobby and out into the dark street and kept running, with no idea where she was going. She just wanted to get away from the apartment.

In her haste, she hadn't noticed the stranger sitting on a motorbike opposite the building.

'Bingo,' Maalik said to himself. He started the engine and followed her. He needed to finish this job to get Vikram off his back; maybe after this he would disappear to somewhere new. Maalik didn't like being threatened. This was going to be more pleasure than work – the girl was older now, and very attractive.

Harpreet was driving while Danny checked his phone for possible places Rose could be heading for.

'She's slowly been getting her memory back,' Harpreet announced.

'What? Really?' Danny was shocked. 'What has she told you? What does she remember, does she remember me?'

'I don't know what or who, only that ever since she banged her head ...'

'*You* banged her head!' Danny corrected.

'Yes, alright, alright! Ever since that happened, she's been having some memory recall, mostly in her sleep.'

'How do you know?'

'She and the maid are close, and the maid has been telling me what's been going on,' Harpreet said.

'What about that coffee shop that she went to before?' Danny asked. 'It doesn't seem like there's anywhere else close by for her to go.'

'Yes, that will be a start. I'll drive to the apartment block first, then we can make our way from there. You take the car and I'll go on foot.'

Angelica had indeed decided to go to the coffee shop but found it closed. 'Shit,' she stamped her foot.

Angelica looked left and right. The road was empty and the streetlights dim. Out of breath and dejected, she turned to make her way home. She wanted to see her mom, who would take her to a friend's house for the night, if she asked her to.

She noticed a man on a motorbike who was around fifty metres away in the direction that she was heading but Angelica paid him no attention; she had other things on her mind.

Outside the Naik apartment block, Harpreet jumped from the driver's seat and Danny replaced him.

'Check the side streets, I'll head straight there. Let me know if you see her.'

Now Angelica felt a frisson of fear run up her spine. She could tell the guy on the motorbike was watching her and she avoided eye contact.

She made fists with her hands, kept her head down and carried on, just as Harpreet had taught her. He had also shown her how to use her peripheral vision to watch people without attracting attention. Using this technique, Angelica saw the motorcycle drive past her and come to a halt on the same side of the street. There was nobody else around; by now, Angelica was sure that the guy was following her. She thought about turning round but decided to carry on; her place was closer than anywhere else she could get to. The man got off the bike and her body stiffened with fear.

She looked up and was astonished to see the face that had been haunting her every night for the past week staring back at her.

'Hello again,' said Maalik.

Angelica froze – the face, the teeth, the stench! This man had laid his hands on her before! She wanted to run but was glued to the spot. She tried to scream but could not draw a breath.

'I wanted you the last time we met but I was told not to touch,' Maalik announced, licking his lips before spitting some paan out across the pavement. 'But now,' he looked around, 'now there's nobody here to stop me!' He licked his lips again and the stench of his breath assaulted her nostrils.

Angelica wanted to throw up. It was his disgusting body that had crushed her all those years ago.

'I'm going to enjoy this,' he said as he looked her up and down.

Angelica fought for breath and managed a lungful. Before she could let out a scream, Maalik had slipped behind her and covered her face once again with the same dirty stinking hand. He dragged her into an alleyway. Angelica wanted to fight, to lash out, but the memory of what happened before made her acquiesce. She was giving up; not her mind, but her body.

Maalik slammed her against a large container, pushing her face against the top of it. She could hear him undoing his belt, his breathing heavier now, the stench making her want to vomit.

Maalik had already pushed his pants down and after groping her breasts, made for Angelica's leggings. She felt his hand on her waist trying to slip his fingers inside the waistband but they were tight, and he was having trouble. Angelica felt his left hand grab the inside of her leggings and panties.

This is it, she thought. In went the other hand. She had never even kissed a boy and now she was going to be raped by this disgusting creature?

'No fucking way!' Angelica spun round slamming her left elbow into his nose, which immediately burst open. 'Don't you **EVER** touch again me with those disgusting fucking hands,' she screamed at her attacker.

Maalik stumbled back then lunged at her throat; he needed to get rid of her one way or the other. But Angelica, now feeling in control, used a move that Harpreet had taught her. Putting her hands together she slipped them through his as hard as she could, breaking his grip. He let go and fell back.

Angelica lifted her right leg and landed a front kick straight into his chest. He catapulted backwards, tripping on a brick. Angelica heard a sickening crunch as a rusty steel rebar protruding from the unfinished concrete wall pushed its way through the back of his head and out of his left eye socket.

Harpreet had been down the street when he heard the commotion and was at the end of the alleyway as the man died instantaneously.

'Angelica?' he called.

Angelica didn't turn around; she was wiping at her face with her sleeve.

'It's me, Harpreet,' he called out.

Still nothing.

Harpreet started towards her. She turned to face him and in a voice as cold as ice, said, 'I think he's dead.'

'He wanted to rape me; I couldn't let that happen.' She sounded almost conversational.

'It's OK,' Harpreet replied. 'Come on, let's get you out of here.'

Harpreet was fishing in Maalik's pockets for his phone when Danny pulled up. Angelica turned when she heard the car, still stunned. She automatically started off towards the vehicle. Harpreet followed her.

'Rose?' Danny called. Angelica ignored him.

'Danny?' she asked. It was dark, but she could just make out the young man's handsome features. 'What on earth are you doing here?'

'Angelica,' he corrected. 'Get in, we need to go.'

They sped off and stopped about half a mile away to decide what to do.

'Danny, why are you here?' Angelica asked.

'It's a long story,' he replied.

'Who was that guy?' Danny asked Harpreet, but Angelica answered for him.

'He was trying to rape me. I kicked him, and he died,' she said in the same conversational tone.

'You have blood all over your top,' Harpreet told her.

'We can't take her home,' Danny insisted. 'She will never be able to explain this,' he said, pointing to the blood splatter that covered her chest.

Maalik's eye had popped straight out and had hit Angelica on the breast with a liberal amount of brain and blood.

'You want answers, don't you?' Harpreet asked Angelica.

'Wait, what do you know, what's going on? Can somebody please tell me what the fuck is going on right now?' she shouted.

'We're taking her back to base, we have to,' Harpreet told Danny.

'We can't do that,' Danny insisted. 'Peter will kill us, literally.'

'Who is Peter?' Angelica asked. 'Please, please just tell me what is going on.' She was crying now.

'The girl needs to know the truth; we are taking her back with us Danny – look at her.'

'OK,' Danny agreed.

On the way back Harpreet texted Jonathan to tell him that Angelica was safe, and she wanted to stay the night at a girlfriend's house. Angelica then messaged her friend to ask her to cover for her.

'It's going to be OK, you're safe now, we will look after you,' Harpreet assured Angelica. 'Oh, and that front kick – wow!' he laughed.

Angelica wiped her eyes. 'I killed him,' she said.

'He deserved it, it's been a long time coming; you'll find out why soon enough,' said Harpreet.

Danny sat in silence; he finally had his best friend back, although she didn't know it yet.

Chapter Fifty
Peter's apartment, 9:28 p.m., 21st March

The team were gathered at the meeting table; no one had heard from Harpreet and Danny since they'd left to look for Rose. Peter was gingerly making himself a coffee when the front door opened. Kush was the first to spot the young lady walking in behind the imposing figures of Harpreet and Danny.

The trio stopped, with Angelica in the middle.

'Say whaaat?' Kush said, his mouth open.

'Well, this is going to be an awfully long night,' added Saira.

The others just gawped at the girl, who was a clear six inches shorter than her companions, her blood-stained top detracting in no way from her beauty. Across the room, Peter dropped the cup of freshly made coffee he was holding.

Nobody knew what to say; they looked from Angelica to Peter and then back to the girl. Angelica spotted Peter and, recognising him, started backing away towards the door.

'Why is that weirdo here? He has been following me too?' Peter said nothing, he couldn't; this wasn't the plan, but then again tonight had turned out rather differently for all of them. Harpreet tried to calm Angelica, who had now edged away from him, turning towards the door.

'Hey,' he called out, 'you trust me, don't you?'

She stopped; if this was a trap, she was seriously outnumbered. She spotted two women, which gave her a bit of comfort.

Angelica turned to face her friend and nodded. They hadn't known each other for long but she knew that Harpreet was a good man. 'What is happening, why am I here?' she pleaded.

Vanya got up and approached her; she hoped someone closer to her age would help reassure her.

'Hey, I'm Vanya, I don't like hugs or crowded places,' she stated, taking Angelica by the hand. The team chuckled nervously.

'You're safe here; this has all been for you,' she said as she swept her arm around the room.

'Can somebody get this girl a cup of tea, please – and maybe a clean shirt?' she demanded as she ushered Angelica to a room off the corridor to change.

Saira jumped up to make the girl some sweet tea and Peter raced into his quarters to find a shirt.

Twenty minutes later, Vanya and Saira had helped Angelica shower and clean herself up. She was now wearing one of Peter's oversized shirts that he used for lazing around, and Saira's spare set of trackpants.

'Why did you bring her here?' Peter asked Harpreet, wincing in pain as he spoke.

'She was being attacked when we found her; well, she was about to be attacked and would have been, if she hadn't killed Maalik first,' he replied.

'Killed Maalik? Lord Jesus Christ,' Peter cried out clutching his ribs. It was almost too much for him to take in.

'She wanted to know the truth, Peter; it's only fair that we explain everything, and after what's happened today I don't think there will ever be a better time for it.'

'Yes...' Peter didn't continue because the three ladies had finished and were making their way to the table where the rest were waiting. They sat down and Vanya started off by introducing everybody.

'Well, you know Saira and me. And that's Vijay over there, we call him old man.'

Vijay rolled his eyes and smiled.

'This is Rahul, and over here we have Kush, the brains of the outfit. You know Danny and Harpreet, and last but not least this is... Peter, our boss.'

Angelica took a few sips of her tea, still eying Peter suspiciously.

'Can I tell the story?' Kush asked, his hand in the air like a schoolkid who knew the answer to a question.

'Peter, what about you?' offered Harpreet.

'I... I... can't,' he stammered. He wasn't prepared, had no idea where to start and was completely stunned by his daughter's presence, and still in considerable pain.

'OK, let the sensible old man get the ball rolling,' Vijay said as he stood up and made his way round the table to join his employer for support.

'Here goes. You may wonder what we are all doing here and who we all are?'

Angelica nodded.

'First, let me ask you what you know, if you don't mind.' Angelica looked confused.

'Sorry, let me make myself clear. You lost your memory and we have been informed that you have started to remember certain things, am I correct?'

She nodded again.

'Now look carefully around the room at each of us and let me know if there is anyone here that you recognise.'

Angelica got up and made a concerted effort to study each of their faces.

'I don't know, maybe, it was mostly the guy in the alley, the dead guy, am I going to get into trouble for that? He attacked me, I didn't mean to kill him.'

'No young lady, you have absolutely nothing to worry about, I promise you that,' Peter insisted. 'Let me try something if I may,' he suggested as he hobbled into his quarters to fetch something.

'You are at the agency, right?' she said to Danny. He nodded.

'And you are our security guard?' she told Harpreet. 'Yes miss,' he replied.

'Who are the rest?'

Peter cut her off as he approached the table holding a photograph. 'Maybe this will help,' he said softly.

Angelica took the picture and studied it closely for a minute or two, looking from it to Peter and back.

'Is that you?' she asked him.

'Yes,' Peter said.

'And that's me?' she asked pointing at the little girl in the photo.

'Yes.'

'Then who is that?' she asked of the third person in the picture.

She looked from Danny to the picture and back several times. He looked different, but she could tell it was him. Angelica started to cry as the penny finally dropped.

'Are you my father?' she asked Peter, who was already in tears.

'Yes darling, I am your father, I've been all over India looking for you.'

Angelica stood up and walked slowly towards Peter, the photograph in her left hand.

'It's OK if you don't remember me just yet, but...'

She didn't let him finish his sentence. Dropping the picture, she threw her arms around him.

'Ouch!' Peter said, and Rose stepped back.

'I had a little accident earlier and broke a couple of ribs,' Peter explained, but he gathered his girl to him on the side that hurt least, and she sobbed into his jacket.

'I've missed you so much, Rose,' was all he managed to say. Their embrace lasted well over a minute. Vanya was being comforted by Vijay, who was in tears himself. Saira, Rahul and Harpreet looked like they could all do with a box of tissues too.

Kush turned to Rahul. 'Looks like our job is done?'

Angelica broke the embrace and bent down to retrieve the picture. Holding it she walked over to Danny. 'So are you my brother?' she asked.

Danny laughed, trying hard to hold back the lump in his throat. 'No, Rose, I was your best friend, I lived two houses away from you.'

'D'you still want the job?' she asked, smiling and holding her arms open.

'Yes, yes I do, if you'll have me,' he said, as she embraced him.

Peter was mesmerised. Harpreet went over to join him. 'Well how about that?' he said smiling.

'Today is a good day, Harpreet. Thank you, my brother, thank you for bringing her home,' Peter replied.

'My pleasure,' Harpreet said with a wink.

'What did you call me?' Angelica asked Danny

'When?'

'Just now, what did you call me?'

'Oh, Rose, that's your name.'

'My name is Rose? Hmm, I like it,' she smiled.

'Rose Angel Rosario,' Peter added.

'OMG, this is like the happiest ending ever,' Vanya declared.

Peter poured them all a drink and the team spent the next hour chit-chatting, Rose sitting with Danny.

'We still have a few things to take care of, Peter,' Harpreet reminded him.

'We can worry about that in the morning, let's just enjoy tonight, eh?'

'Yes, boss. Well, if you don't need me, I'm pretty tired and could do with a good shower and a few hours' sleep.'

'I will always be in your debt, Harpreet, what you have done for me, for Rose...'

'Hey,' Harpreet said as he shook Peter's hand gently to spare him further pain from his ribs. 'The smile on your face, that is enough for me. You have found your daughter and that has made me a happy man.'

'Anything that you want, anything, it's yours, no matter what the cost,' Peter insisted.

'Just your friendship, brother. Take some of the painkillers they gave you at the hospital and I'll see you in the morning, OK?'

Rose spotted Harpreet making his way to the door. 'Wait,' she called out to him.

Harpreet stopped and turned. As she reached him, Rose looked him in the eyes. 'Thanks, big man,' she said and kissed him on the cheek

'Goodnight, Rose,' he replied and left for home. It was over a year since he had taken a life and the two he took that day were probably the most justifiable. The team left shortly after to give Peter and his daughter some space.

'Danny, you can stay here if you like,' Peter told the young man.

'If you don't mind?' he replied.

'Of course.'

'Dad,' Rose said. It felt strange calling another man that, but something inside was telling her it was the right thing to do.

'Yes Rose?' he said.

'What about mom?'

'She... she passed away not long after you went missing,' Peter said sadly.

'Oh.'

'It's a long story. I can tell you tomorrow, but you have a grandmother back in Goa who I know would love to see you. We have a few things to take care of here first, but we can visit after that, if you like?'

'That would be nice,' she replied, 'can I take another shower?'

Peter poured two whiskies for Danny and himself.

'We found her,' Danny said.

'We did son, we did.' Peter was getting drowsy now, as the painkillers kicked in.

'So, what about the guys? What's going to happen to this place?'

'I don't know yet. I want to go home for a while.'

'That's a good idea, maybe being in Goa will help Rose regain her memory.'

'I hope so,' Peter said.

Rose stood under the hot running water. She could still feel the hands of her attacker on her, but the smell, the taste in her mouth, seemed to have disappeared now. She had so many questions to ask but didn't know where to start. The one thing she did know was that she felt safe now.

Chapter Fifty-One
Naik residence, 7:30 a.m., 22nd March

Elizabeth and Jonathan were lying in bed. He had hardly slept from worrying, not so much about his daughter but about what was going to happen when she came back.

'What happened yesterday?' Elizabeth asked.

Jonathan's web of lies was unravelling and he had no idea how long he could keep the truth from his wife.

'Oh, she wanted to go out and got mad at me when I wouldn't let her, that's all. She will come back today and apologise, just you wait,' he said.

'We're lucky to have Harpreet around, he's a good man, and you know, I think Preeti has a thing for him,' Elizabeth replied, appearing to be mollified.

'Really?' was all Jonathan managed. Staff relationships were the last thing on his mind but at least he seemed to have put Elizabeth off the scent, for now.

Preeti was in her room; she had just finished a call from Harpreet. He hadn't told her much but said he would explain later that day. She was smart enough to know the connection between what had happened yesterday and the things Angelica had been remembering. She was not sure she could work for such a family and was packing some of her things, just in case.

***

Saira brought the team pastries for breakfast and was the last to arrive at Peter's apartment. Rose had slept right through the night and was looking ten times better than the day before.

Peter had explained the story to her, as best he could, over the last hour and a half, and they had already drunk three cups of coffee each. The aching from his ribs was under control with the painkillers and he felt surprisingly good.

'So, my other dad had someone kidnap me, is that what you are telling me?' she asked.

'Yes,' Peter replied.

'And you think he bought a drug off some other guy to erase my memory?'

'Yes, and everybody here has had one job – to find you.'

'And the kidnappers,' Vijay added.

It sounded like the plot of a movie. Peter didn't want to tell Rose about her Uncle Jack; he had already decided that Harpreet would deal with him quietly. Brother or not, he didn't care, there was only one thing to do to a man like that. Harpreet had been hesitant at first but agreed to it nonetheless.

Rose looked around. 'All this for me?' she asked.

'Yes,' they answered in unison.

'Where do we go from here?' asked Vijay.

Harpreet stood up and said, 'I have a small matter left to clear up. I need to talk to Jonathan.' He glanced at Rose.

'Don't mind me,' Rose said quietly. She felt a strange mixture of emotions; anger was one, but Jonathan had always been kind to her, had loved her and she had loved him too.

'Shall we go now? No time like the present,' Harpreet asked.

'Yes,' Peter said, taking Rose by the hand.

***

The private elevator doors opened into the apartment. A shocked Elizabeth and Jonathan greeted them.

Preeti saw them and took the hint from Harpreet's subtle gesture to get out of the way. She decided to finish packing; this would be her last day working for the Naik family.

'Angelica, are you ok?' Elizabeth asked as the trio approached the kitchen where the Naiks were standing.

'Peter? What are you doing here?' Jonathan asked.

Rose stepped out in front of the two men that were with her. She turned to Peter and lifted her right hand.

'This is Peter Rosario, my father, and my name is Rose,' she told them, fighting back tears of anger and pain.

'Jonathan, what is she talking about?' Elizabeth was obviously genuinely confused.

'Jon!' she shouted. 'Wake up man!'

Jonathan was frozen to the spot and the blood had drained from his face.

'Let me explain, if your husband can't,' Peter said as he stepped up to Rose and put his arm around her shoulder.

'This man, if you can call him that,' Peter started, pointing at the still stunned Jonathan, 'stole my daughter from us a few days before her mother passed, eight years ago.'

'Jonathan, what the fuck?' Elizabeth was mad now. She slapped him hard across the cheek. 'What have you done, you idiot?'

'I did it all for you,' he replied, finally joining them again.

'I assume he didn't tell you this?' Peter asked.

'Is this true, Jonathan?' she demanded, pushing her husband against the kitchen counter. He offered no resistance.

Peter said, 'I should kill you for what you did to my family. Do you know how many lives you have ruined?'

Jonathan didn't speak, neither did he try to defend himself. Peter wanted to shake the man, but his ribs held him back.

'I will destroy you,' he said.

'Angelica, I'm so sorry, I just wanted you to be happy,' Jonathan whimpered.

'She *was* happy,' Peter shouted, 'Rose was happy with her family.'

Elizabeth hugged Rose to her; the girl knew that she had nothing to do with the kidnapping and Elizabeth knew some part of her daughter would hurt for Jonathan.

'Goodbye,' Rose said and kissed her mother on the cheek.

'Peter, I think that's enough, we should go now,' said Harpreet.

Peter, Harpreet and Rose made for the front door, leaving Elizabeth crying and Jonathan defeated. Preeti was waiting in the corridor with her suitcase. She didn't want to face the Naiks to say goodbye, her priority was the girl.

Harpreet was beside her now. He took her hand and said, 'come on, let's get out of here.'

In the elevator, Peter had calmed down.

'This is my real dad,' Rose announced to Preeti.

'And you, who are you?' Peter asked.

'I am Preeti, I am... was the maid for the Naik family.'

'Nice to meet you, Preeti.'

'She's been my best friend for like, ever,' Rose said.

'So, I guess you are part of the family now too?' Peter asked her.

'If you wish, sir,' she replied.

'You have looked after my daughter like your own and comforted her when she needed it. Call me Peter, please.' The elevator doors opened with a ping and the four of them got into the waiting car.

'Everything OK?' asked the driver.

'Everything is fine,' answered Peter, looking around at his extended family, noticing Harpreet and Preeti were holding hands.

Upstairs, Jonathan stood opposite his wife. 'I am so sorry my love,' he offered, as he tried to put his arms around her.

Elizabeth pulled away and stood up. 'Don't fucking touch me. I would have forgiven anything Jon, anything, even cheating, but this? You kidnapped a little girl and took her away from her family, how could you do that?' she asked, as tears welled up in her eyes.

'Darling, I did it for you, you wanted a daughter so much…'

'Don't you **dare**!' Elizabeth shouted. 'I'm leaving. This is over!' she hissed, as she made her way upstairs, shaking with rage.

Jonathan walked over to the drinks cabinet and poured himself a large whisky. He downed it in one and sat on the sofa with his head in his hands. He was still there ten minutes later when he heard the elevator doors close. He poured himself another and took the bottle out onto the terrace. It was hot and humid, he felt like he couldn't breathe; he was lost. Only a couple of days ago his life had been perfect and now he was alone. He downed the second drink and tried calling Elijah. He wanted to talk to him so much, but his son didn't answer.

Jonathan threw the empty glass against the wall, put his phone on the table and stepped over the balustrade onto the twelve-inch-wide concrete ledge on the other side. He lifted the bottle to his mouth and gulped the rest down. He heard the sound of his son returning his call as he stepped off the ledge. He hit the ground, twenty-two floors below, his head exploded across the street.

Chapter Fifty-Two
Peter's apartment, 1:23 p.m., 22nd March

Kush had ordered far too much food. Peter, Rose and the others returned to find the place looking like a pizza restaurant.

Rose said to Peter, 'I want Preeti to stay with me.'

'Of course, she's one of us now.'

'Peter,' Vijay beckoned, 'I know where Jack is. He's panicked and is making mistakes; he's been asking questions all over the place, here's the address.' Vijay handed Peter a piece of paper.

Peter caught Harpreet's eye and waved him over.

'You know what to do,' Peter said as he gave him the note.

'Is he alone?' asked Harpreet

'Yes, from what we know.'

Harpreet scanned the address and slipped it into his pocket. 'I'll be back soon,' he said.

'Watch yourself,' Peter advised.

'Don't I always?'

Rose watched Harpreet leave.

'Where is he going?' she asked.

'He just has a little business to attend to, it won't take long,' Peter assured his daughter. 'Are you full yet?' he asked, pointing at the stack of boxes on the table.

'I'm stuffed,' Rose said and kissed him on the cheek.

Harpreet reached the address, a run-down apartment block. He got out of the car and made for the building, Glock in hand. The door marked 4B was gloss black and had two locks. Harpreet put his ear to it and heard what he thought was a TV or radio. He knocked three times – no answer.

Jack was inside; an acquaintance had let him hide out there and he was not expecting any visitors. Seeing his brother in his dead boss's office yesterday had freaked him out. He received a call earlier telling him that Vikram had been murdered. The Mumbai underworld was awash with rumours of the shooting. He had no idea what was going on but wanted to get as far away as he could. He was cramming the few clothes he owned into a holdall as the door came crashing in.

The Sikh man from the warehouse had a gun pointed at his head. 'Jack?' Harpreet asked.

'Who wants to know?' Jack replied, his mouth dry. The only exit that didn't include jumping out of a window to a thirty-foot drop was through the man standing in front of him. 'Somebody wants to talk to you,' Harpreet informed him, as he pulled his phone out of his pocket. 'Sit,' he said and dialled Peter's number.

'Hello?' Peter answered.

Harpreet handed the shaking man his phone, gun still pointed at his forehead.

'Who is this, what do you want from me?' Jack demanded.

'It's Peter,' the voice answered.

'Peter, brother, who is this guy with the gun? Tell him to let me go, I've done nothing wrong!' Jack squealed.

'Oh, you know what you've done Jack, you know exactly what you've done.'

Jack gulped; he could see that it was pointless lying now.

'I'm sorry,' he insisted. 'Rasheed forced me to do it, he was going to kill me, Peter.' Jack was begging now, snot running from his nose, his body shaking uncontrollably.

Peter gestured for Rose to join him and passed the phone to her.

'Who is it?' she asked.

'Just tell him who you are, darling.'

'Hi, it's Rose here.'

Jack's jaw literally dropped to the ground as two bullets tore through the side of his face leaving it a mangled wreck. Harpreet grabbed the phone, stuffed his gun into his belt, picked up the two shell casings and headed for the car without looking back.

'Who was that, and were those gunshots?' Rose asked. Peter placed his phone on the table.

'That,' he started, 'that piece of shit was the reason that we have spent so long apart.'

That was enough information for her, she didn't need to know any more.

'So that's where Harps disappeared to?'

'Yes,' Peter said.

'I see,' Rose said, as she took another slice of pizza. She suddenly felt hungry again.

A couple of hours later, Vanya and Vijay poured glasses of champagne for everybody. The mood was triumphant; the team had worked tirelessly and they were overjoyed to finally see their efforts come to fruition.

Everybody stood, glasses in hand, waiting for Peter to finish what he was doing on his laptop.

'I guess you won't be needing us any more then, boss?' Rahul asked as he joined them.

Before he could reply, every one of the team's phones beeped simultaneously. Vijay opened his to check a message that he had received. It was a series of numbers and an amount of money; at the bottom, the words THANK YOU.

'I thought you were kidding,' he said, dropping his phone in disbelief.

'To us!' Peter raised his glass, grimacing in pain, 'for helping me find Rose, I thank you all from the bottom of my heart.'

'To us,' they all toasted.

Rahul checked his cell phone. 'Fuck, ...sorry.'

Peter laughed. 'As you will all see you now have the details to accounts that contain two million US dollars each. My daughter is the most precious thing in my life and compared to her, money means nothing.

'To Peter,' shouted Kush.

'Rose and I will be leaving for Goa in the morning. Harpreet, I will still require your services if you are interested?'

'Who else is going to look after you?' Harpreet joked.

'Preeti, Rose would like you to stay with us. Take your time to decide, you and Harpreet can stay here while we are away.'

'Thank you, sir,' she replied, embarrassed. She had replaced Peter's bandages earlier that morning and liked the gentle and kind man a lot.

'Peter, please,' he replied.

'Thank you, Peter,' she corrected.

'Danny, you have work to do at the agency, I was thinking maybe you could open a Goa office,' Peter said with a wink. Danny nodded.

'Mack, you are not going anywhere, I will definitely need you to keep organising my life for me.'

Mack slammed his hand on the table. 'Damn, I wanted to take a vacation.' He grinned.

'Maybe next year,' Peter insisted, making everyone laugh.

'And the rest of you – Rahul, Saira, Vijay, Vanya and Kush – your work here is done. You make a fantastic team, I am proud of you.'

'What am I supposed to do now, boss?' Kush asked.

'Hey, we could always start our own detective agency!' Vanya suggested.

Saira rolled her eyes. 'We'll see,' she said, 'first I need one whole week in bed.'

'Can I say something?' Rose asked timidly. 'Thank you, all of you, for everything you have done for dad and me.'

The team raised their glasses again.

'Who would have thought that creepy old man from the coffee shop would turn out to be your father, eh?' Peter said, laughing and wincing from the pain at the same time.

'You'll never let me forget that, will you?' Rose replied, blushing.

'What about you, Rose?' Vanya asked. 'What will you do, you are a famous model after all. Will you continue with your career?'

'I have no idea; I think I'd just like to find out who Rose is for now.'

Harpreet approached Peter and whispered in his ear, 'Jack named this guy, Rasheed; do you want me to deal with him?'

Peter thought for a while. 'No, I think we can leave it there, don't you?'

'As you wish. There is going to be a lot of heat around here, there will be repercussions for what we have done, Peter. You should stay away from Mumbai for a few months, just to be on the safe side,' Harpreet said.

'That's exactly what I intend to do; in fact, I may not even come back. I miss home, and this place, well there are too many murders for a start.'

Harpreet laughed.

'I meant what I said about this place. You and Preeti can stay here for as long as you like; relax, and enjoy yourselves,' Peter suggested.

'To be totally honest Peter, I will be more of a target than you. I think we will join you in Goa, I'm sure Preeti could do with a vacation. It will make a change for her to be waited on.'

'Mack,' Peter called. 'Book us a plane for tomorrow lunchtime, and a suite at the Leela for the lovebirds here,' Peter said pointing to Harpreet and Preeti.

'Yes, boss' Mack replied.

Chapter Fifty-Three
The Alvares household, 3:17 p.m., 23rd March

Mack dropped Peter and Rose off around the corner from her grandmother's house. Harpreet and Preeti had carried on to the Leela Hotel, joined by Mack, who was to wait there in his own room until he was needed, so he still got some sort of vacation.

As they approached the garden, Carmen's roses were in bloom, and you could smell them from several houses away.

'How do you feel?' Peter asked.

Rose turned to him. 'I'm nervous,' she replied.

They reached the gate and entered the garden. Rose stopped halfway down the path. Looking around she took a deep lungful of air.

'Remember this place?' her father asked.

'I don't know,' she replied. 'I feel like I have been here before; the smell, the birdsong, that tree.' She was pointing to the mango tree in the middle of the lawn.

'You spent many a day sitting underneath it,' Peter told her.

The metal security gate to the house opened, and an old lady stepped onto the veranda. She was frailer than when she had last seen her granddaughter but was still able to tend her garden and go to the shops; sprightly would have been a good word to describe her.

Carmen stepped down onto the path. Her eyes were not as good as they used to be and she wanted to get closer. She could tell that it was Peter but had no idea who he was with. Peter and Rose walked on to meet her.

'Carmen.'

'Hello Peter, this is unexpected, you brought a frie...' She stopped dead in her tracks. 'It can't be,' she whispered, studying the girl's face.

'Guess who I found?' Peter asked.

Carmen shut her eyes and opened them after a few seconds to make sure it wasn't a dream.

'My God, it is her!' Carmen held out her arms for a hug and Rose stepped into it, wrapping her arms around her grandmother. They both burst into tears. Looking over Rose's shoulder, Carmen mouthed the words 'thank you' to Peter.

'Are you hungry?' Carmen asked, taking Rose by the hand, and leading her up the stairs, 'I'll make your favourite, tea and puris.'

Peter laughed. 'We have a lot of catching up to do,' he said.

Rose and Peter spent two days with Carmen, who loved the company and having someone to fuss over. Being in Goa seemed to be helping Rose recover her memories and she had not mentioned her life in Mumbai even once during their time there.

On the afternoon of the second day of their stay, Peter got a car to pick them up and take them to where Maria was buried. He had left something important with Carmen and was waiting for the right time to give it to Rose. They stood at the foot of the grave. The headstone that Peter had made for her was a simple one; she wouldn't have wanted him wasting money on anything extravagant.

'You see who I brought today, darling?' Peter asked. 'Rose is home. I didn't break my promise; it took a while, but I did it. Isn't she beautiful?'

'Hey mom,' Rose said, laying her hand on the granite slab.

They had brought a few of Maria's favourite blooms from Carmen's garden. Rose put them in the steel vase and poured in some water from the bottle that she had brought along.

'It must have been so hard for her,' Rose said.

Peter and Carmen had explained everything that had happened directly after her disappearance.

'Your mother was a strong woman, she never showed how much she was suffering. Hey, this is for you,' Peter said, pulling out the letter from his jacket pocket.

When he thought about the time of her death it still hurt far too much.

'What's this?' Rose asked.

'It's from your mother. She wrote it a couple of days before she passed away.'

Tears were already welling up in Rose's eyes as she sat on the grass and carefully opened it.

To My *Beautiful Rose*,

My darling, you disappeared before I got the chance to say goodbye. So here I am, saying goodbye. Your father promised that he would find you and considering that you are reading this letter, it looks like he did just that!

First, I want to apologise for keeping my illness a secret from you, I didn't want to burden your beautiful soul, you were always so happy.

I am writing this as I slip away, I only have days left, your father is a mess and God only knows how he will cope. I am tired, I sleep a lot and can't get out of bed now, all I have are memories. I think about you all the time, hoping you are alive and safe. I have no idea what happened that day, I just wish I had been there for you when you needed me most. You made my life worth living and I shall treasure every day that I got to spend with you. I miss your smile, your energy, your love for life. Your father is a good man, please take care of him; he will be useless without me (haha).

You will always be my beautiful Rose. Whenever you look up to the heavens, please remember that I can see you, so don't forget to smile.

I love you from now until eternity.

Mom.

She handed it back to her father to read and looked up at the sky.

'Love you too, mom,' she said, smiling.

Epilogue

Rasheed's gambling den, Panjim, 6:08 p.m., 23rd March

Harpreet's boot took one kick to cave in the door of the small industrial unit. A shocked Rasheed looked up. He was with a half-naked girl, her legs splayed in front of him. She looked to be no more than twelve years old.

'Knock knock,' Harpreet said, as he walked over to the man.

Rasheed was struggling to pull up his jeans when he felt Harpreet's gloved fist shatter his nose and the man's arm snake around his neck in a chokehold.

'Go outside and wait for us,' he said to the girl, who had already put her T-shirt back on and was cowering against the wall, tears streaming down her face.

As the girl left, Rasheed realised that he couldn't move; the powerful man was far too strong for him. He could only watch helplessly as his masked accomplice plunged a six-inch blade into his groin area. His screams of agony became a gurgle as the knife slit his throat.

'You will never, ever touch another child, you disgusting piece of shit,' Preeti spat into the man's face.

His life slipping away, the last words that Rasheed heard were, 'this is for my friend, Rose.'

Harpreet let the lifeless body collapse to the floor. 'It's over now,' he said.

'Thanks, I needed that,' Preeti replied, as she followed him to the waiting car with Mack behind the wheel.

Preeti took the trembling girl by the hand and, with a reassuring smile helped her into the car, 'come with us,' she said, 'you are safe now.'

Lightning Source UK Ltd.
Milton Keynes UK
UKHW021840100122
396936UK00003B/366